Gnight, Sara /
Night, Heck

GNIGHT, SARA / 'NIGHT, HECK

Copyright © 2024 Justine Castellon and Mike Dee

Paperback ISBN: ISBN: 979-8-9883810-7-5 / ASIN: ASIN: B0D2NYCQZJ
Ebook ISBN: ISBN: 979-8-9883810-6-8 / ASIN: ASIN: B0D2NYCQZJ

Printed in 2024

Published in the United States of America

By Brandbureau Consulting LLC
Cheyenne, WY 82001

Spotify Reading Playlist

For every Sara and Heck navigating the wild seas of adventure and discovery, this book is dedicated to you.

PART ONE

"Sara, listen to me. You're young, and that means you have the privilege to make mistakes. That's the beauty of youth. And you have all the time in the world to correct them. You'll never know if something will work unless you take the risk. Give it a shot."

- Heck

1

SARA EMILY MILLER

(Sara)

The morning sun sliced through the vertical blinds of my cubicle, casting long and narrow shadows that danced over piles of unfinished reports and strewn Post-It notes across the pale blue surface of my desk. I stared at the sterile glow of my computer screen, the cursor blinking back at me with an almost mocking rhythm, mirroring the relentless ticking of the clock on the office wall.

Grasping my Ralph's Coffee mug, a $49 splurge from 5th Avenue that celebrated landing my first job, I stood up and looked outside. The coffee was still hot. The sun kissed the skyscrapers with a warm, golden glow. There was an unmistakable shift in the air. Ahh, the tail end of summer as the city was poised on the cusp of autumn — my favorite time of the year. A season of transformation.

Below the 26th floor where I was standing, New York City was bursting with life, pulsating with unstoppable energy. It was a vibrant tapestry of sounds and colors, yet here I was, trapped within the sterile confines of my work called 'agency life.' My dreams of a grand life had condensed into an impersonal grey cubicle — a far cry from the exciting world I once imagined for myself. In this world of marketing and advertising, brimming with the potential for color and creativity, one question echoed through the monotonous grey landscape of uniform cubicles: why? The scene was as puzzling as it was stifling, a stark contrast to the kaleidoscope of imagination that should be at play.

Each cubicle stood like a sentinel of conformity, an unwelcome symbol in a field where innovation should reign supreme. For the love of Pete, this place should be a canvas of inspiration, not a graveyard of grey! This confined space is where creativity, ideas, and fun go to die. Dead inside —like coffins for the living or pretending to be living.

Yet, at Milliford & Associates, efficiency reigned supreme over creativity. The firm's heartbeat thrummed to the rhythm of billable hours, each tick echoing louder as the day neared its end. Their ethos was simple: the more hours accounted for, the better the day had been.

This relentless pursuit of productivity was mirrored in the design of their workspace. Instead of a kaleidoscope of unique and inspiring spaces, they opted for uniformity. Each desk, chair, and corner was meticulously crafted, streamlining work processes like cogs perfectly aligned in a grand clockwork. The spaces were devoid of personal touches or creative flare, but they hummed with an almost tangible energy of efficiency.

The dreams I'd nurtured within the warm cocoon of university faded into the mundane reality of life as a 24-year-old copywriter. This was my sad reality. Here we go again, always complaining about something for nothing.

"Hey, Sara. Stop sulking, will you?" Andi's voice — sharp and always unexpected — sliced through my daydream. The resident rebel of the accounts department, she had a knack for turning our shared coffee breaks into existential deep dives, her words often echoing my own silent musings.

"Trust me, I'd rather be anywhere but this soulless pit," I snapped, bracing myself against the glass wall. My head found rest against one of the cold, metallic beams. In a complex pattern of a jigsaw puzzle, these beams served as steadfast guardians, holding the panes of glass in their intricate embrace. The chill from the metal seeped through, sparking a shiver that danced down my spine. I turned to face her, her features mirroring my own sense of stifling discontent. We were both victims of an age-old paradox — we embodied the tragicomic dichotomy between youthful optimism and the harsh realities of adulthood.

Andi and I belonged to that restless generation caught in the crossfire between expectation and reality. The twenty-something crowd who had stepped out of the university gates, diplomas in hand and dreams in our hearts, only to confront the stark, unromantic truth of adulting. Armed with a unique voice — funny, subversive and unflinching — we stood ready.

"Noticing the greener grass outside of this fence?" she probed, her gaze fixed on the world beyond our glass cage. Her words hung heavy in the air, painting pictures of a future we could only dream about. She didn't turn to look at me as she continued her dramatic monologue, her voice laced with a potent mix of cynicism and longing.

"We were told that our future was a blank canvas, ours to paint in any color we desired," she mused, her voice barely above a whisper. "They fed us tales of limitless possibilities, of dreams just waiting to be chased. 'Follow your dreams,' they said, as if it were the simplest thing. But they never told us how relentless the chase could be, did they?"

My dream was as vivid as the ink on a well-loved page: a 2-bedroom haven in Manhattan, awash with sunlight and the aroma of brewing coffee. It was a realm where I could delve into the world of literature, crafting stories that danced off my fingertips, unfettered by the shackles of uninspiring assignments or the humdrum rhythm of the nine-to-five.

"I know we're explorers in a strange land, Andi," I ventured, trying to sound hopeful, "but we've made it to New York City. That's 20% of the dream fulfilled, isn't it?" My optimism felt forced and fell flat.

Andi, adrift in her own thoughts, clung to her coffee mug as if it were her sole lifeline in this vast ocean of disillusionment. The steam from her coffee gently stirred her pixie bangs, painting an ethereal halo around her. I found myself studying her, a mirror to my own restless spirit. Our generation was a riddle wrapped in an enigma — packed with questions, teetering on the edge of dissatisfaction. Were we simply ungrateful?

"I know," I began, my voice a murmur in the stillness. "We were promised a world brimming with opportunities, a chance to forge our own paths. Instead, we found ourselves caught in a relentless rat race, chasing after elusive deadlines and fleeting promotions." Andi didn't turn to face me, her gaze held captive by the monoliths that towered across us, their silhouettes stark against the sky.

"Regrettably, our lives haven't unfolded like the cinematic masterpiece we once dreamt of," I continued, a wistful note creeping into my tone. "We're missing the montages of triumphant victories, the stirring background scores to accompany our struggles, the romantic screenwriters scripting our paths towards guaranteed happy endings."

Life, I realized, was not a meticulously edited movie. It was a tapestry of scenes, each more real and raw than the last, stitched together in a pattern that often made sense only in retrospect. Each day was a snapshot, a moment frozen in time.

We had once been eager students, eyes sparkling with dreams and hearts pounding with ambition. We took on student loans, studied tirelessly until our bones ached, denied ourselves simple pleasures, and endured to reach this point. Yet, where I stand now, the view was not quite as breathtaking as I'd envisioned. It was not a desolate wasteland, but far from the glamorous life our hard work promised us.

"Maybe fortune will smile upon us someday," Andi murmured, her gaze anchored to some distant point. "For now, our lives are not tragedies. They're just... ordinary."

God, we sounded like silly, dreamy children.

"Ordinary, yes," I echoed, bitterness lacing my words. "Burdened with crippling debt. The relentless bills. The monstrous rent... especially in Manhattan!"

New York City, the city that never sleeps, the city of dreams, or so it seemed on glossy paper. But let me tell you, living in the gentrified neighborhoods of NY freaking C was far from the dream it was painted to be. The rent, oh, the rent… it devoured your paychecks whole. Right now, that dream remained just that… a dream.

The city has come far from its gritty *Taxi Driver* days. Yes, it was cleaner, brighter, more welcoming now. But with progress comes cost. Everything was pricier now, from a cup of coffee to each square foot of living space. Try finding a job that comfortably covers your rent, basic necessities, bill payments, and all the other things they say you need for a fulfilled life. It was like searching for a needle in a haystack. A very expensive haystack of gentrification.

The taste of disappointment was bitter on my tongue, a stark contrast to the sweet dreams of success I had once savored. But beneath the layers of disillusionment, I could still feel the faint pulse of the dreamer within me. The girl who yearned to spin stories from her soul, see her name etched on the cover of a book, and touch lives through the magic of her words.

"Two years, and nothing is happening," I murmured, my words echoing through the silent room like a sad refrain. Two long years since I had stepped out of NYU, my eyes sparkling with anticipation, my heart brimming with hope. I was a newly minted writer then, brimming with endless possibilities, ready to set the world alight with the power of my prose. I have a lifetime of words and stories yet to be unleashed. I used to shout 'Watch out, world!' at the top of my lungs… but not anymore.

Reality, as I've come to learn, had a cruel sense of humor. The chaotic circus where I work replaced the grand stage I had envisioned. Mocking my lofty dreams and aspirations. Instead of penning captivating stories in manuscripts, I was caught writing bold headlines for consumer products, a whirlwind of mundane tasks, and endless, senseless paperwork. My optimism, once as boundless as the ocean, was slipping away like grains of sand escaping through tightly clenched fists.

Andi's voice sliced through my thoughts, her words pulling me back to reality. "You know, Sara,' she began, her tone tinged with a challenge. "At least your work closely aligns with your original aspirations. Sure, creating taglines is a far cry from penning a novel, but you're still in the business of storytelling, but to help market products. Nothing wrong with that."

I nodded, acknowledging her point. "Yes, these things I do, like using words to paint pictures, evoke emotions that drive consumers to purchase," I conceded. "But there's a part of me that can't shake off the feeling that these words are essentially deceptive words, designed to make things seem better than they truly are," I said.

My confession hung in the air, an admission of my struggle with the art of curation. The task was often about selecting words that bore little relevance to the actual product, but were instead artfully constructed to capture a potential buyer's attention, to lure them into the illusion we had created. It was a dance on a tightrope, balancing truth and fiction in the pursuit of commerce.

As I cradled my coffee mug, the warmth seeping into my palms stirred me from my daydream. I looked at my hands and couldn't help but notice the stark contrast with Andi's manicured ones. My fingers, with chipped nails, while they were clean, were a less refined version of Andi's pink polish. Why couldn't I emulate Joan Harris from *Mad Men*? Despite working in the high-pressure environment of an advertising agency, she always appeared impeccably dressed, her makeup flawless, and her fingernails perfectly manicured. Why does reality seem so distant from our dreams? Then there was Andi. Even with her eccentric fashion sense, she somehow managed to outshine me. Once again, here I was, easily distracted. One moment, I was completely immersed in a thought, and the next, my attention was hijacked by something else entirely. Shaking off these wandering thoughts, I turned my focus back to Andi.

"Funny thing," I began, a hint of humor dancing in my eyes, "in a world fraught with rampant misogyny, I found myself inexplicably drawn to the world of Don Draper from *Mad Men*."

"But, Sara," Andi cut in before I could finish, "you are more Peggy Olson than anyone else."

I chuckled at her interruption, our shared understanding painting a comfortable pause between us. "True, Peggy's journey resonated deeply within me," I admitted, a thoughtful pause hanging in the air. "Yet it was Draper's captivating allure that was nothing short of enchanting. His presentations, a mesmerizing spectacle, held an uncanny ability to unveil the sheer genius behind the creative team's ideas in front of the executives — a quality that sparked a hunger within me. This magnetic charm and the spellbinding brilliance it unfurled was something I yearned to emulate," I confessed, my voice a soft whisper against the hum of our surroundings.

A playful smile tugged at the corners of Andi's mouth as she leaned back, her gaze holding mine. "Hold on there, Sara. Draper is me. Remember? I'm the one from client account management." Her words, a gentle reminder of our roles, punctuated our conversation with a sense of camaraderie and shared ambition.

I couldn't tell Andi how I yearned to craft something equally captivating for my book — a tangible extension of my soul. This was not an ordinary product languishing on a dusty shelf. No, this was a progeny of my thoughts, sculpted from the labyrinthine depths of my intellect. It could never be just another drab composition lost in mediocrity. It demanded significance. It yearned for impact — just like Don Draper's riveting pitches.

But if all I managed was to produce meaningless fluff, what did that say about me? Was I truly ready to write, or was I just unwilling to confront the possibility that I might be a mediocre writer? Was I even a writer at all?

The harsh truth hit me as I stood there, trapped in my thoughts. Life had become a constant battle against the ordinary, a struggle to keep the flame of creativity alive amidst the downpour of routine. But I was determined to fight back, to wrestle my dreams from the clutches of this grey cubicle. I yearned to paint the world with my words, to breathe life into characters, and to create stories that would echo in the hearts of readers long after they had turned the final page. I wanted to create characters that felt like they lived in lives and worlds that were complex but relatable. And I knew then that no amount of reality's cruel humor could ever extinguish the fire within me.

That was the root cause of my relentless struggle against a life of normalcy. I strongly rejected the idea of being ordinary, regarding it as the ultimate act of self-cruelty. I harbored a constant longing to live a life less conventional, less ordinary, because in my mind, that was what truly living meant. How could I be expected to pen extraordinary plots if I didn't allow myself the freedom to lead an equally extraordinary life?

I sighed, pulling myself back to reality. There was work to be done. The world wouldn't stop for my existential crisis. I needed to dive back into the sea of tasks that awaited me. I couldn't help but dream of the day my words would finally set the world ablaze. Until then, I would continue fighting, one word at a time... on cardboard boxes of cereal.

"Hey, you two!" Alexi's voice sliced through the humdrum of our office chatter, like a lighthouse beacon piercing the foggy night. His words snapped me back into the stark reality of our fluorescent-lit workspace. "Did you hear the latest scandalous whisperings from the HR department?" he asked, his voice dropping to a conspiratorial whisper.

Alexi was the flamboyant heartthrob from the art department. His statuesque build, captivating green eyes, and rugged good looks were the stuff of office legends. Yet, he was as gay as a rainbow, his vibrant personality adding an extra dash of color to our otherwise monotonous days. He was our confidante, our partner in crime at office parties, willingly playing the role of our straight beau when needed.

"What?" Andi's eyes sparkled with the thrill of juicy gossip, a trait that made her and Alexi fast friends.

"Greg and Iver were caught getting a little too familiar in the bathroom," he whispered, his eyes gleaming with mischief.

"When you mentioned they seemed 'a little too familiar'," Andi questioned, her fingers sketching air quotes as she echoed Alexi's words, the anticipation in her voice unmistakable. "Are you implying they were tangled in a clandestine tryst within the confines of the restroom? Who discovered them?" The question hung in the air, ripe with intrigue and the thrill of scandalous adventure. Her eyes sparkled with the excitement of the unfolding drama, her words painting a vivid picture that was both audacious and fascinating.

Alexi's eyes sparkled deviously as he revealed his latest gossip haul. "Yes, caught in the act, so to speak, like smooching in bare backs... and buttocks!" Alexi's mischievous eyes twinkled with his current rumor find. "And it wasn't just anyone who discovered them, it was Gina, the new head of HR! They were literally caught with their pants down!"

Caught off guard, I couldn't contain my surprise. "Hold on... Iver is gay?" I blurted out, my surprise echoing through the room.

Laughter reverberated off the walls as Andi and Alexi erupted into fits of giggles, filling the room with a contagious energy. Even I started to giggle through my confusion.

"Oh, Sara. You didn't know?" Andi managed to gasp out between her bouts of laughter, her eyes twinkling with amusement.

Alexi, still chuckling, shot me a look of feigned shock, as if I had just revealed that I believed the Earth was flat. The twinkle in his eye seemed to say, "Welcome to the real world, Sara."

"I really have no idea. I'm as clueless as a sailor in a desert," I confessed, my words tumbling out in a rush of surprise. "So, what's gonna happen now?"

"HR is set to unleash a memo into the wild," Alexi explained, his voice tinged with a hint of melodrama. "A form for us to sign, a pledge to unveil any romantic entanglements within these corporate walls."

"That's a storm I can weather," I declared, an air of confidence wrapping around my words like a well-worn cloak.

Before either could volley back a response, a sudden flurry of activity rippled through the corridor. The arrival of one of the high-ranking executives was like a shark sighting in calm waters, sending our little congregation scattering for cover. Andi and Alexi retreated to their cubicles, disappearing behind the paperwork fortress, shielding them from prying eyes.

I sank back into my own coffin. My fingers danced over the keys of my computer in a well-rehearsed symphony of pretense — the art of appearing busy.

The office was a swirling vortex of kinetic energy, a storm of activity that swept everyone up in its relentless pace. Young and wide-eyed interns darted around like sparrows in a gale, their faces reflecting a chaotic cocktail of fear and exhilaration. Phones echoed with the never-ending noise of ringing, printers coughed out reams of paper like mechanical dragons, and the ever-present hum of coffee machines provided a rhythmic undertone to the symphony of heated conversations that filled the air.

Zero words, and a few minutes later, the screen was still blank. Slipping my Air Pods into my ears, I found myself lost in the familiar rhythm of scrolling through my iPhone. My Instagram feed, a vibrant tapestry of daily musings and city explorations, had been dormant for weeks. I used to relish in capturing fleeting moments —the soulful performance of a subway musician, the evocative vibrancy of street art — anything that struck a chord within me. But lately, those chords seemed muted, their resonance lost.

My fingers danced across my Spotify playlists, a motley collection reflecting the broad spectrum of my musical tastes. There were days when classical symphonies sang to my soul, but lately, my playlists echoed with melancholy melodies. They felt like haunting lullabies serenading my subdued spirit. Selecting "Not For All The Love In The World" by The Thrills, I set it on a loop, letting the mournful notes weave their magic around me. These were my saviors. 'The' bands. The Strokes, The Thrills, The Vines, The Shins, The Kooks, The National.

I reached into the bottom drawer of my desk, pulling out a worn notebook, its pages filled with scribbled thoughts and half-formed ideas. Seeing it stirred something within me, a spark of hope that refused to be snuffed out. I yearned for the freedom to bring my personal laptop to work, to escape the confines of my sterile cubicle. I envisioned a more vibrant workspace with colorful beanbags instead of drab computer chairs. I could see myself nestled in one of those beanbags, lost in the world of my nearly 50,000-word work in progress.

Despite the stark contrast between my reality and my dreams, I clung fiercely to my aspirations. I was entangled in the harsh threads of reality, yet I held on tightly to the flimsy strands of my dream. My story was still a blank canvas, waiting to be painted with words. The journey ahead was daunting, but I knew I had the power to chart its course. No matter how tumultuous the waves were, I was determined to steer my ship toward the beckoning horizon of my dreams.

Suddenly, a voice sliced through the chaos, sharp and precise as an icicle — the cold voice of death. "Sara, do you have the Nature's Way Tomato Sauce pitch material?"

I turned, my heart sinking at the sight of my boss, Kelly, looming at the entrance of my cubicle like a storm cloud. Her icy blue eyes were locked onto me, her lips pursed into a thin, disapproving line. Dressed in a tailored suit over a light blue silk blouse, she looked more like a Wall Street trader than someone from advertising. I had privately nicknamed her 'The Ice Queen' for her uncanny ability to freeze the warmth out of any conversation. There were other name candidates. Among them Iron Bitch, Graceless Slave Driver, Kelly Dreadful, and my favorite one, Kell Me Now. I forced a smile onto my lips, feeling it stretch awkwardly under the weight of her icy gaze.

"Just putting the finishing touches on it, Kelly," I managed to say, maintaining a steady tone despite the rapid pounding of my heart. Had she caught me with my personal notes at work? I knew her gigantic, thick glasses could see from a mile away.

Her gaze swept over me, a silent critique of my ensemble for the day. The apple-green and white striped shirt with its pristine buttons, tucked neatly into a short white skirt, and balanced by the playful touch of yellow wedge sandals, were all under her scrutiny. Once she had taken stock, she dropped the bombshell. "Could you perhaps dress in something more sophisticated tomorrow? We have a pitch with the new head of marketing at Gold Standard Bank in Manhattan." Perhaps if they paid better, I could get better threads, too. But she was right, I do have to stop dressing like I was going to writing class.

"Absolutely," I said, my hands instinctively smoothing down my skirt as if to iron out any perceived imperfections.

She responded with a curt nod, her gaze never wavering, before spinning on her heel and striding away like a queen leaving her court. I released a breath I hadn't realized I'd been holding. My heart pounded a frantic tattoo against my ribs, a reminder of the constant battle for survival in this corporate concrete jungle.

Just then, one of the interns, a young man with glasses too big for his face, approached my cubicle, clutching a stack of papers. "Sara," he began timidly, "where do I put these?"

"Top drawer on your left," I said, pointing towards the filing cabinet. He gave me a grateful smile and scurried away.

I sighed, my gaze returning to the slivers of sunlight dancing across my desk. My thoughts drifted towards Tribeca Trickle, the quaint coffee shop I had discovered last week, my secret haven. It was a place where I could flee the chaos and immerse myself in the world of my book. There, I was more than just Sara, the junior copywriter; I was Sara, the author.

My fingers found their way to the keyboard, beginning to type out the pitch material for Nature's Way Tomato Sauce. But as the keys clicked under my fingers, my thoughts were already weaving a story, a story that was waiting to be told.

Shitty sauce for your shitty pasta for your shitty family. No, too mean. I did not mean to take out my own boredom on an imaginary shitty family.

Made with real tomato, tastes like non-biodegradable waste. Ha ha! This will make me lose my job in seconds.

The secret sauce of the top-notch moms. Too generic.

Quick cook best liked by the tasteless…

This is going to be a long day. I need to switch from Pete to Don to Peggy mode.

2

HECTOR ALEXANDER ARCHIBALD IV

(Heck)

Today reminded me of when I was 7 years old, as I was summoned into my father's office — a consequence of schoolyard brawls. I found myself nervously perched on the edge of a chair that probably cost more than my entire year's salary. Ah, my old man's office, it was like walking into the belly of the capitalist beast. You could practically smell the money in the air, like a heavy cologne that sticks to your clothes long after you've left. And the place, oh boy, it was like stepping onto the cover of *Interior Design For The Obscenely Wealthy*. Leather and mahogany dominated the space, big ol' desk that screamed 'I'm important,' and shelves stacked with fancy books that I bet my last dollar he had never cracked open.

He got art from the masters. Like that famous oil painting by Degas, the 'Young Spartans Exercising'. Securely hung right behind his desk. Big canvas in oil painting, about 40 by 60 inches. It depicted two groups of kids — four girls and five boys. Looked like the girls were teasing the boys or something. Girls on the left, boys on the right, and there was this other group in the back, just watching. Odd thing was, they were all dressed up while the kids in front were all naked or half-naked.

Over the years, my father had stuff done by all sorts of big-name artists. They were all there, lined up, looking all high and mighty on his walls, just to rub it in the faces of some poor souls who visit. Like, 'Look at all the stuff I got you'll never have.' And those windows, man. Stretching from floor to ceiling, giving you a bird's eye view of Manhattan's concrete jungle.

Then there was the door. A hulking beast of iron shipped from some ancient fortress in Israel. Felt like it got stories soaked into it, ya know? Perhaps, tales of slaves in torment and cruel masters, living their never-ending nightmare. The whole place was designed to intimidate and impress. It was all a big show.

I was dressed in my usual worn-out jeans and faded grey T-shirt. I felt like a splotch of graffiti on an otherwise pristine canvas. In a coffee shop, my appearance wouldn't seem out of place, but in this office, I looked destitute. I resembled Ed Sheeran's 'Ghost of Christmas Yet To Come', had he not written the somewhat corny ass 'Thinking Out Loud' and instead, well... bombed. Yeah, yeah I know. Jonah Hill said it first. Odd choice for an analogy, I know. Don't even listen to that ginger.

Across from me, my old man, Hector Alexander Archibald III, sat like a king on his throne. He was the closest thing to a king I know. A Tywinn Lannister. He's like... German efficiency and precision in human form. Just lives and breathes it. Whatever genetic lottery doled out those traits, I didn't win them. Not in my biological deck of cards, I suppose. His pinstripe suit was as crisp as a new dollar bill, his silver hair combed back just right. He had his way of looking at me with those piercing blue eyes, eyes that we shared, scrutinizing every little detail.

I gotta admit, I kinda dig the pinstripe suit. But if that were up to me, I'd have 'em custom-made to fit artsy me. Instead of pairing them with the conventional white silk shirt and pricey necktie, I'd opt for a more casual grey T-shirt. And the stripes? They'd spell out 'fuck off' if you looked closely through a magnifying glass.

Suddenly, my father broke the silence. He was leaning back in his chair, all casual-like, throwing around words like they were pocket change. "Son," he began, his voice as smooth and rich as the 30-year-old scotch he loved, "What are you planning to do with your life?" He did not fuck around. No pleasantries or small talk. Cut right ahead to the point.

Art, that was my thing. I was fixing up old pieces, breathing life back into them. That was where I felt alive. So, trying to keep my tone respectful, I shot back, "Dad, I'm into art restoration. It's my life. Just like making bank is yours."

"You should have left your childish ways when you were a child." His response hit me like a sucker punch. He looked at his watch, a Patek Philippe Grandmaster Chime, which fetched $32 million at an auction in 2019, making it one of the most expensive watches ever sold. There was a ruthless history behind that. He didn't need it. Christ, he didn't even like it. He threw in a bid anyway. Just to fuck with somebody, y'know? Now, who was it again? Another bidder? Or the old owner himself who wanted to get it back? Can't quite recall. But here's the kicker: he owns it now. All his. Price didn't matter at all. Yeah, a lot of zeros on that price tag. A lot of sweat and blood. He now felt he was in a position where he could acquire anything or anyone, be it you or your company, without so much as batting an eyelash. He knew how to fuck up commas. His throat bobbed up and down like he was swallowing rocks. He was trying to say something, but the words weren't coming. Just the ticking of the watch, loud in the quiet.

We were just a few feet apart, but it felt like miles. Mountains of unsaid things piled high between us. There was always my father's personal Rushmore when it came to me. Those things you feel all the time... but for him, they were always disappointment, resentment, frustration, and indifference. He cleared his throat again, a rough sound like sandpaper against wood. I watched him, waiting.

The tension was thick, filling up the room, pressing against me. I could almost taste it, bitter and sharp, like stale coffee. It was always like this with him. A chess game where neither of us knew the rules.

I sat there, my hands clenched into fists, my heart pounding. But why? Was I scared? Angry? I didn't even know anymore. I was toughing it out. Pretending to be a killer. All I knew was the gnawing feeling in my gut, the need to prove myself and show him I was worth more than he thought.

Suddenly, he said, "When will you ditch your dead-end job and start picking up the family business? You know, the one you'll be running someday, and by running, I clearly mean not leading it to its demise."

I knew this road we were headed down all too well. It was well-trodden, riddled with potholes, and always led to an argument. I knew he found it difficult to call what I do a job.

"Dad, let's not do this again," I pleaded. "I'll step in when I feel ready. I'll get there. That's a promise."

"You are an Archibald. Act like one. Don't be stupid enough to waste that." The old man rocked back in his chair, turned his gaze to the window, and fell silent. He knew where this kind of talk would lead — a disaster my mom had been begging us to avoid. He was the antithesis of that whole savior complex thing. Got a bit more of a 'fuck you' vibe to him. If they ever bothered to put that in books, he'd be the prime example, no doubt. His mug shot would be plastered right on the cover.

Yeah, I was one of those silver-spoon brats from New York City. Born with a platinum credit card in my mouth, or so they say. Just another rich kid, right? Raised by nannies and housekeepers, not parents. I didn't give a flying fuck about him or his opinions. The only reason I was here was because ignoring his summons would lead to an even protracted discussion.

Well, not quite. See, I was supposed to be the golden boy, the heir apparent to the big business empire. Old money shit. But honestly? Screw that. The whole idea made me want to puke.

I mean, why should I follow their rules? Why should I play their game? That was not me. That was never me. I'd do it, but I'm pretty sure I'd shoot my head off soon, too. All this money, all this power — it was a joke. A sick, twisted joke.

So, what did I do? I rebelled. Yeah, you heard me. I turned my back on the family business and went for art. Art, man! Art with its colors, textures, emotions — tangible, meaningful stuff, not just numbers on a screen. They called me a troubled child. Distracted. But I was anything but distracted. I was focused. Focused on something real. Besides, you can say I left maybe around $50B on the table. That $50B, though, never left the table.

Love? Ha! Don't make me laugh. My relationship with Sophie... well, it was complicated. We were like two beautiful statues, cold and perfect. We looked good together, sure. But love? Nah. Love was more than just a pretty face and a nice body. But at this point, who cares about feelings? I didn't even know what it was like to need someone. To really, truly want. We looked good on paper. Or at least to my mom, we did.

So, yeah. That was me. Heck. The rich kid who didn't want to be rich. The heir who didn't want to inherit. The lover who didn't know how to love. Just trying to figure out this crazy, messed-up life.

My father interrupted my thoughts. "Your engagement, Heck," he began, his voice smooth and calculated, like he was discussing stocks and not his son's future. "Have you discussed the prenuptial agreement with Sophie?"

Ah, did I mention we were engaged? Sophie. Top-tier eye candy. Her parents, upper-crust New Yorkers, new money, were already planning the wedding, while my mind was still lost in the world of paint and canvas.

"Prenup," I echoed, rolling the word around my tongue, feeling its odd weight. The concept sounded like it was borne out of a settlement proceeding, more at home in the sterile environment of a lawyer's office, a lovechild of cold, hard cash and battered love. Talk about stripping the romance out of wedding plans. His eyes betrayed a flicker of concern. It wasn't about the money, really. It was about legacy. The Archibald legacy that I had zero interest in carrying forward.

"Yeah, Dad," I finally managed, pasting on a smile. "I'll talk to her."

"No, Heck. Let our lawyers take care of it. Let them talk to her," the old man was at it again.

"Dad, I don't need a lawyer or lawyers to talk to her," I said. It came out sharper than I intended. The room felt small all of a sudden.

"Son, you don't understand. It's not about what you want," he replied, his voice like gravel under a tire. "It's about what you might need."

He was looking at me, but he wasn't seeing me. He was seeing dollar signs and legal papers and a future he couldn't predict. And it irritated me, this view he had of me. Like I was just another one of his investments.

I could feel my temples throbbing. A headache was coming on. Or maybe it was just the sound of my patience wearing thin. Perhaps that was the intended effect of this room. To an extent, I understood his need for the prenup — it was not for my protection alone. What was left unsaid was its role in safeguarding the family's interests. His interests. What belonged to the family, both now and in the future, stayed in the family. Like the money and everything that came with it was a heirloom.

"Sophie isn't after my money," I said, trying to keep my voice steady. But it trembled just a little. I knew it was a lie. My money was part of what made me attractive to Sophie, or any woman, to be more precise. Her family was once wealthy, but recent years had been unkind to them. I was pretty certain that my father was aware of this. If my dad suddenly woke up to find his money ended with Sophie's dad, he'd probably kill me himself.

He sighed, leaning back in his chair, that watch of his ticking away like a time bomb. "Heck, it's not about Sophie. It's about protecting yourself."

"Protecting myself from what?" My voice echoed in the room. The silence that followed was deafening.

Before he could answer, the door opened, and there was Mildred, his personal secretary. "Apologies, Mr. Archibald and Heck," she said, eyeballing me and my father.

"What is it, Mildred?" he asked, his tone frosty.

"It's the people from Milliford's," she went on. "You wanted to meet them yourself about the corporate PR plan." Mildred's a looker, no doubt about it. Probably in her early forties. Pulls in a paycheck that could rival our company's top brass. But hey, nobody's questioning it, not even my mother. There were talks that she got a lavish apartment in Park Avenue and London, courtesy of my father.

"Let them wait," he tossed out, just like that. "Get Raul and his CorpComm crew on the horn," he tacked on quickly. Mildred nodded and pulled the door shut behind her.

He looked at me again. There was something in his eyes then, a flicker of something. Regret? Understanding? I couldn't tell. All I knew was that I was standing on a cliff, teetering between the world as I knew it and a future unknown. And all the while, the ticking of that damn watch.

"This is something I can handle, Dad. Just let me do it," I pleaded.

His nod was curt, satisfied. And just like that, we were done. No 'how are you', no 'love you, son'. But then again, that was us. Hug? He was more likely to combust instantaneously. *Get the fuck out of here.* That was Archibalds for you. We were not much for sentimentality. It was always about business. No fucking around.

Stepping out of the office, I nearly smacked into someone. Probably one of those about to meet with my father. What was she doing loitering in the hallway, anyway? I gave her the once-over and caught a pair of hazel peepers glaring back at me. On any other day, I might've shot her a grin. But today? Nah. Got my own shit to deal with.

I couldn't help but ponder the path I wanted to take—the one where I wasn't Hector Alexander Archibald IV, but simply Heck, the wannabe artist. For now, though, I was stuck here, teetering between the world of finance and art, between Hector Archibald III and Sophie, between who I was and who everyone expected me to be.

———————

Stepped out, and there it was. Amith, the valet, had my ride purring —
a reborn '67 Mustang Fastback. Quick thing about this beauty. It's like
the one Tom Cruise flaunted in *Vanilla Sky*. Not the dream sequence set
of wheels, but we'll circle back to that. Pretty obvious, I'm a fan.
Scratch that, more like obsessed. Cameron Crowe's genius. Easily in
my top 5 GOATs… greatest of all time. That movie just did something
to me.

I caught the Crowe bug kinda late, around 2011, with his *Pearl Jam
Twenty* docu. Blew my mind. Had to binge everything Crowe after
that. Turns out, the guy wasn't just about docu's. He's possibly the
coolest writer-director I've come across… ahh, arguably one of the
most fascinating writer-directors I've encountered, particularly during
that period. Crowe has a unique ability to write eloquently about
movies, music, and perspectives, especially on love and relationships,
managing to be romantic without being sappy. His connections ran
deep in the music world. Not only was he married to rocker Nancy
Wilson, but he also spent time with musicians and was a music critic
who mingled with bands before they they hit big. Who was this man?
He was all about that grunge vibe before it was even a thing. And *Pearl
Jam*? They popped up in *Singles,* still rocking their *Mookie Blaylock*
name.

His first big movie, *Say Anything*, is like the ultimate love story. *Fast
Times at Ridgemont High*? Comedy gold. *Almost Famous*, though, that's a
whole other level of amazing. Forever thankful to that film for
introducing me to "Tiny Dancer." His writing? Always hits right in the
feels – so genuine, straight from the heart. When he and Nancy Wilson
split, hit me hard. Like, if the guy who wrote *Say Anything* couldn't
make that work, what chance do the rest of us have?

So, diving back into *Vanilla Sky*. That soundtrack? Like your first taste of wine. Confusing at first, but then you're hooked. Todd Rundgren pops up again, just like in *Almost Famous*. Crowe's got this soft spot for him - makes sense, been chatting him up since his Rolling Stone kiddo days. And those tunes from Sigur Ros, Radiohead, Jeff Buckley's big hit? Epic.

Crowe went all out this time, messing with our heads. If you missed *Abre Los Ojos*, the original, you were in for a ride. This remake? Killed it. Felt like Crowe hit some sort of god mode. And Tom Cruise playing David Aames? Saw a bit of myself in him, David. Not totally, but bits and pieces. Guy had it all, thanks to dad's fortune. More about playing boss than actually being one.

Kinda hit close to home. The whole rich kid vibe, making decisions with, well, not the smartest part of our anatomy... Felt that. Aames got dubbed Citizen Dildo by the board, and honestly? Kinda deserved it. All about chasing fun. And with Cameron Diaz's Julianna as his so-called fuck buddy — though they made her out to be a bit much. Even her song, kinda cool but also kinda creepy. He snagged all his toys from auctions. So, when he leans towards the less flashy, more genuine Sophia played by Penelope Cruz? Totally get it.

Then, before it all goes dark, those two cars. That first one, in what turns out to be a dream (wasn't half the movie a dream?), that legendary Ferrari 250 GTO.

So, here's the scoop: there are supposedly only two of those beauties in the whole wide world, and chances were slim to none that I'd stumbled upon one. Turns out, it was a replica. A vintage blue '76 Datsun 280Z. Not too shabby, right? Around the globe, folks dig it. Heard it affectionately dubbed the "Fauxrrari." Got me thinking, why not give it a whirl? Rebuild one myself. Now, don't get me wrong. Wasn't exactly a car nut. Still ain't. Well, maybe just a tad. For some, it's all about *The Fast and The Furious* vibes. For me? It was this. Funny enough, think they both hit the scene around the same time. But here's the deal — wanted something that was all me, built from scratch. And so I did.

Stumbled upon the exact model out in Buffalo, NY. A blue '76 Datsun 280Z. My dad's mechanic, bless him, took me under his wing. Through his car-lover connections, he spotted it. Wasn't even up for grabs. We made an offer out of the blue. Turned out, the seller was this guy, disowned his kid over something or other, left the car to gather dust. There it was, sitting unloved in some collector's garage. Saw my chance. I was just 15, but managed to sweet-talk my dad into fronting me the cash. Dragged it back home, to our empty garage, much to my folks' confusion. Mom even tried to get me a brand-new ride for my sixteenth. Hard pass. Something about bringing the old back to life just clicked with me. This car? Lit the fuse on my art restoration journey. My first real project. How long did it take? Who knows. Wasn't racing against the clock. But when it was all said and done, slapping on a Ferrari logo just didn't sit right. Felt off. Wanted no part in playing pretend. Loved it for what it was. No labels needed.

Not long after, got my hands on another piece from *Vanilla Sky*. This time, a '67 Mustang Fastback. And this baby was the real deal. Not pristine by any stretch when we found her, but she had potential. The previous owner, a widow, her husband was the car buff. Now it was just her. Made my move. I got the car, rebuilt it with all genuine parts, had to bring it back to its original glorious state, unlike the previous one. There was no changing what it was.

My venture into being David Aames? Nailed it. Well, almost. Just missing that dramatic car crash makeover.

Didn't usually take her for a spin around the city, but today? Figure I'd give Wall Street a show, kill some time. Sun's still hanging high and, hell, ain't like I got anywhere else to be.

Cruisin' down Wall Street in this toy is easy like driving on a Sunday mornin'. Got that low hum of power beneath me, purring like a well-fed cat. Ain't nothing quite like it. See, it was all about the ride — the way the leather seat fitted just right, how the wheel felt in my grip, the wind whistlin' past the open window. It ain't just about getting from point A to B. Nah, it's about the journey, man.

As I rolled down the asphalt, I passed by the titans of industry – NYSE,

Goldman Sachs, J.P. Morgan. Steel and glass monsters reaching for the sky, all business during the day, but now? They're just shadows against the setting sun.

And there was Trinity Church, standing proud among 'em all. Old gal's seen more history than any of us ever will. I tilt my head back and tried to catch the last rays of the day dancing off her steeple.

I cruised past Federal Hall, where old George took the oath. Think he'd ever imagine a guy like me, in a car like this, rolling past his old stomping grounds? The sun's dipping low now, painting the city in gold. Traffic's thinning out, leaving me and the GTO to own the streets. No rush, no destination, just me, the car, and the fading light.

Yeah, this is living.

When I reached Manhattan, I parked the car in MoMa. I made the choice not to head home. Not yet. The thought of Sophie and her incessant wedding chatter was too much to bear. Nah, I couldn't face it. Didn't have time or energy for that. I needed some time to think, some alone time. Some room to breathe. Do you know how folks do that Pomodoro thing, right? Some go for a stroll, some stretch their legs, and others find their zen to clear the ol' noggin. A reset button. Me? Oh, I'm all about jotting things down or, let's say, doodling thoughts onto paper, any which way they tumble out. Got a little notebook I carry around, which fits snugly in my back pocket. I mean, I'll scribble on pretty much anything... napkins, receipts, even a tissue if I'm desperate. I didn't care enough to keep them anyway. But this notebook is my go-to.

I got a whole pile of these things, filled with my brain junk. Don't really keep tabs on 'em. What mattered was getting it all out of my skull. Expression, man. Seemed oddball to most. I haven't met another guy who does the same, but hey, each to their own, right?

Now seemed like a good time for a mental dump. You just gotta scout out a quiet spot first. A walk seemed like a solid plan, a chance to shake the cobwebs loose. So, there I was, wandering down 2nd Avenue with no real direction in mind. Then I spotted it. A tiny coffee shop tucked away, the Tribeca Trickle—one of those blink-and-you-miss-it joints. But if you were lucky enough to catch it, you knew instantly it was already a vibe from the outside. A hideaway from the world. I hope the coffee was as promising as the exterior.

3

COFFEE AND BRINNER

(Sara)

Life, I've learned, is a series of unexpected encounters. Mine was no different. I was still trying to carve out my niche in the bustling city. My life was the epitome of ordinary. It was mundane, but not anything to complain about. I was in alpha city, after all. But as they say, even the most ordinary lives can take extraordinary turns. My own hit like a curveball in a game I wasn't even aware I was in.

Like any other ordinary day, I was cozied up in the corner of this charming, slightly worn café. Tribeca Trickle was the kind of place where everyone knew your name, and the baristas' smiles were as warm as the lattes they served. The intoxicating aroma of freshly ground coffee beans blended with the comforting sizzle of bacon and pancakes, creating a symphony of scents that felt like a warm hug on a cold day. Tonight, the café was busy. Hunter College students were hogging tables. Considering how quiet and intense they were while reading their books and scribbling notes, it must have been a hell week.

This was a small place tucked away between E 76th and 2nd Avenue, a hidden gem mainly known to students and faculty. The interior was a harmonious blend of rustic and modern aesthetics. Exposed brick walls, painted a soft cream, provided a beautiful contrast to the dark mahogany tables scattered around the room. Each table was adorned with a small vase holding a single fresh flower, adding a touch of color.

A long, cushioned bench lined one wall, filled with an assortment of colorful throw pillows. The opposite wall boasted a large chalkboard menu written in whimsical, looping cursive. The counter was a masterpiece in itself, made from reclaimed wood and topped with polished granite.

Behind the counter, baristas moved with practiced ease, their faces lit by the warm glow of pendant lights hanging from the ceiling. Shelves lined with an assortment of teas, coffee beans, and pastries were visible within the glass tabletop cabinets along the counters, promising a treat for every palate.

The atmosphere was welcoming and calm, a stark contrast to the energetic city just outside its windows. Soft indie music played in the background, punctuated by the occasional clink of coffee cups and the low hum of conversation. This café was more than just a place to grab a quick coffee; it was a sanctuary for those seeking respite from the busy university life. In my case, a corporate slave secretly trying to carve her mark in this world.

Just as I was about to take a sip from my steaming cup of coffee, life decided to toss a plot twist in my mundane story.

A good-looking guy — a complete stranger — walked up to me. His stride was confident yet unassuming, like someone who was comfortable in his own skin. He paused by my table, his gaze warm like a cozy fire on a winter night. He appeared as though he was born into a privileged minority, the aesthetically blessed individuals, yet he was consciously striving to present himself as grounded and humble.

"Is this extra seat taken?" He asked. His voice was casual, almost calm, as he gestured towards the vacant seat across me. "Do you mind if I sit?"

"Go ahead," I nodded.

There was an easy charm about him that was hard to ignore. "Just so we're not strangers, I'm Heck," he said, extending a hand. His grin was infectious and could light up even the gloomiest days. And just like that, my ordinary day took an extraordinary turn. Little did I know that this simple encounter would change the course of my life in ways I could never have imagined.

Now, let's get one thing straight. This was not a typical episode in my life. I was a creature of routine, a stickler for habit. My daily schedule was as predictable as the sunrise: wake up, plunge into the whirlpool of work where I craft catchy taglines for ad campaigns, and then retreat to my sanctuary here in this café, my mind brimming with dreams of penning the next great American novel. The last thing on my agenda was having my solitude interrupted by a ruggedly handsome stranger. But then again, who am I to argue with the universe's plan?

This cutie, who introduced himself as Heck, towered over me at approximately six feet and two inches. His stature exuded an undeniable charm that was impossible to ignore. His hair was a wild mess of waves, suggesting he had just rolled out of bed, while his stubble hinted at a shave long overdue. Typical for a man who was unconcerned with societal norms. His outfit, worn-out jeans and a snug grey T-shirt that clung to him just right — the kind of guy who doesn't obsess over his wardrobe; anything comfortable and non-contradicting works for him.

While he was clad in a pair of worn-out jeans and a plain T-shirt, what caught my eye was the stunning timepiece adorning his right wrist. I was ashamed of how superficial I seemed, but I wasn't normally the type of girl who judged people by their possessions. And I still wasn't judging. This beauty was impossible to ignore; it demanded attention and appreciation. I didn't care about watches or jewelry. I probably even noticed that it was a Rolex much later. What caught my eye was that bright, light blue face, excuse me, dial that you didn't see so often.

It seemed so youthfully playful in color yet royally elegant. You could wear it with ripped jeans or a formal suit with a tie with a matching color. You could have had a heavily tattooed wrist with its right smack in the middle, but it still wouldn't look out of place. Was it a custom piece? A curious choice for today's guy. Not a Daytona, Yachtmaster or

Submariner. Not even a sports watch. It even seemed smaller than most. God, what am I turning into? Was it even important? And even stranger was that it seemed eerily familiar.

So, who could be audacious enough to pair such a rare and pricy watch with a pair of distressed jeans? As intriguing as the watch was, what truly captivated me were his eyes. Hidden behind black-rimmed glasses were the most mesmerizing blue eyes that held an irresistible charm. He was a far cry from Matt, my impeccably dressed, clean-shaven boyfriend.

My gaze remained fixated on his wrist, a sense of familiarity washing over me. I had worn something similar once, not mine, but a loaner. Heck's eyebrows shot up in surprise as he noticed my intense stare.

"That watch..." I commented absentmindedly, "It's a 1978 Rolex."

His face flushed slightly, and he smiled sheepishly. "Yes...?" He responded, his statement sounding more like a question than an answer.

"I've been fortunate enough to wear an identical piece for a brief fifteen minutes when I escorted a client to a luxury watch press conference," I elaborated, trying to contain my excitement. The watch was a masterpiece, its mesmerizing allure outshining every other timepiece I'd ever seen. It was a subtle display of wealth; it didn't scream 'expensive,' but to those acquainted with the elite world of horology, it was a statement. I knew little about watches, but I knew this one was stunning.

"In case you're wondering where I stole this from..." Heck's voice trailed off to a near whisper.

"An elderly lady you charmed into bequeathing her wealth to you?" I teased, playing along with his narrative.

"How did you know?" He looked at his wrist. "This belonged to her late husband who stole it from someone else," he finished, flashing a mischievous grin. We both erupted into laughter.

"I don't want to appear overly fascinated, bordering on gold-digger, but that watch is truly a sight to behold. It was a thing of beauty, albeit briefly adorning my wrist. I returned it as soon as I could, unable to bear the responsibility of such a valuable item. Clumsy as I am, I would have inevitably scratched it. I didn't have the insurance to cover that," I explained, realizing I was oversharing again.

"I can't really afford this. It was a gift from my mother when I turned 21," he admitted shyly.

"There's a 1966 date code stamped on the folding clasp," I blurted out.

He chuckled at my observation, giving me a look that was equal parts amused and bewildered. But then, he flashed me the most beautiful smile, revealing a set of perfectly straight, white teeth.

There was something about Heck's appeal that drew me in. However, I couldn't place my finger on it yet. Was it the smile, laid-back tone, easy-going confidence, or the street-grunge outfit he was wearing? It was like a breath of fresh air, a stark contrast to the polished, tailored men I usually found myself surrounded by at work or in Matt's social circle, I might add, who seemed like Patrick Bateman wannabe Philistines types right now. And that glint of mischief dancing in his blue eyes piqued my curiosity.

"I'm sorry. I'm Sara," I finally said, gesturing towards the empty seat. Enthralled by his presence, it had slipped my mind that he was still standing right in front of me trying to introduce himself properly. I didn't take Heck's hand — no formal handshakes, no customary pleasantries exchanged. Not even a simple 'hi' — just an unspoken acknowledgment of each other's presence in that moment.

"Brinner, huh?" His gaze shifted playfully towards my plate, a smirk tugging at the corners of his mouth.

"A what?" I asked, pausing mid-bite.

"Breakfast food for dinner... brinner," he explained, his eyes twinkling with amusement as they landed on my plate piled high with fluffy pancakes drenched in golden syrup and topped with banana slices.

"Ahh, I adore everything breakfast. It's simple, uncomplicated, serves a purpose — to satiate your hunger," I responded, meticulously cutting my pancakes into neat triangles and allowing them to bathe in the sweet syrup.

"I'm partial to bacon and eggs for dinner. Toast crisped just right, eggs slightly charred around the edges," he shared an air of melancholy surrounding his words. "Uncomplicated, too, I guess," his smile was endearing, perfectly showcasing his pearly whites. *Who is this Lothario?*

One of the few things I first noticed was his military-grade shoulders. Without thinking, I blurted out, "Do you frequent the gym, Heck?" As soon as the words left my lips, I wished I could reel them back in. Making personal comments on someone's body already?!

He shook his head, chuckling lightly, "Nah, in fact, I loathe it," he confessed. The way he said 'no' was cute. "Treadmills are the worst… too monotonous. How about you?"

"An occasional yoga class, which, when I say occasional, it's more like practically never," I admitted, joining him in laughter.

"So what brings you here, aside from wolfing breakfast food at dinner time, alone, with a pen and notebook? Aren't you too young to spend Friday evening in a café?"

"I'm attempting to write something. Not quite sure what it is yet. Home tends to get a bit crowded," I confessed.

"Living with parents?" he asked, his tone casual yet curious.

"Boyfriend," I responded, suddenly acutely aware of the personal nature of our conversation.

"Ahh. I see," was all he said. His order arrived — a double shot of espresso and a half-cup of soya milk. As I watched Heck expertly pour the espresso into the soya cup, I took a moment to really look at him. He had that hipster vibe: lean, probably from a dairy-free diet. Maybe even vegan. But he liked bacon, though. Yes, that vibe sans the eclectic,

32

unconventional fashion sense and the tousled man bun.

"So, what do you do for a living, Heck?" I asked, leaning back in my chair and curling my hands around my warm coffee mug. The café was beginning to quiet down, the once loud chatter and clatter of cutlery now a gentle murmur.

Heck looked at me, a playful smirk gracing his lips. "I'm an art restorer. I breathe life back into old masterpieces, help them reclaim their former glory."

I found myself staring at him, my eyebrows arching in surprise. I didn't see that coming. "Wow, that's like... incredibly unique. And fascinating."

His laughter echoed around us, a rich, hearty sound that seemed to envelop our little corner of the café. "Well, it's not as glamorous as it sounds. There's a lot of dust and chipped paint. But it's rewarding in its own way." Then he turned his attention back to me. "And you? Let me guess, a budding writer?"

I found myself laughing. Again. I realized I had laughed more tonight than I usually do. I hope he doesn't notice I was giggling too much. "Not quite there yet, but I'm trying. Maybe someday. For now, I need something that pays the bills, so I work as a copywriter."

"I'll let you in on a little secret," he offered, pulling out a small, leather-bound notebook from his back pocket. He untied the string holding it closed and revealed pages filled with scribbled notes and poems. I scanned them, fascinated. It didn't even strike me as odd that he casually carried around a notebook filled with poetry. Could he be here to write?

"Wow, you have something here. I couldn't tell what yet. But something. Have you ever considered getting these published?" I asked, genuinely impressed. I looked at him again, finding myself met with his cool blue eyes that seemed to penetrate the depths of my soul.

"I'm not sure if they're good enough," he confessed with a modest smile.

"Write the story, take out all the good lines, and see if it still works..." Before I could finish, he interrupted me.

"You're quoting Hemingway to me," he said, his smile widening.

"I am. See? You know your stuff." I responded, feeling a sense of camaraderie building between us.

"Sometimes, I feel like I'm Gil Pender from *Midnight in Paris*. That character seemed to have hijacked my dream job," he confessed, a wistful note evident in his voice.

"Ah, so you're a Woody Allen fan," I responded, delighting in the last bit of my banana and pancake combo.

As we let the soothing warmth of our coffee seep into our bones, we stumbled upon shared interests. It turned out that we were both ardent fans of the movie *Midnight in Paris*. I saw it when I was 10. It was one of the first films that started my fantasies of being a writer. It changed things for me. My own aspirations could be divided by before and after *Paris*. I always found myself finishing the movie regardless of what part I got on cable television, and each time, I learned something new about it. I was delighted to find someone who liked this movie, too. Heck and I saw ourselves with Gil Pender, 'whose life is pending between two women, two cities, and two times,' according to some reviews.

We found ourselves immersed in a lively discussion about the enchantment of walking in the rain, the captivating allure of bygone eras, and the undeniable charm of Paris under the midnight sky. Heck had a remarkable knack for describing scenes in such vivid detail that they sprung to life. His words painted images as vibrant as any artist's canvas.

"Did you ever find Gil neurotic?" I asked.

"Sure, Woody is neurotic and made a more likable and charming version of himself. It's what I love about Gil." He replied, his fingers tracing the contours of the mug. *What might having those fingers tracing*

34

paths on my skin feel like? With a mental shake, I shrugged off that thought as quickly as a character in a plot-twisting mystery novel might discard a red herring. I hope he didn't notice me watching his hand so closely.

The air was thick with excitement as I studied Heck. There was an undeniable pull between us, a magnetic force that seemed to stir the very atoms in the room. His eyes, such an intense shade of blue they could have been plucked from a summer sky, were locked onto mine. They held a depth that was both compelling and terrifying, like diving into an unknown ocean.

I could feel the heat creeping up my cheeks, a telltale blush coloring my face. It was as if his gaze had the power to seep under my skin, igniting a fire I hadn't known existed. An electric current of attraction pulsed between us, crackling with an energy that was impossible to ignore.

"I went blind when I watched it for the first time — I didn't read any reviews. So every time a literary icon appeared, I was in awe!" I confessed, my voice resonating with the thrill of past memories.

"The beauty is precisely in that surprise," he responded, punctuating his words with a playful wink that spoke volumes.

A giggle bubbled up from my chest in response, escaping my lips before I could stop it. It was a nervous laughter, an attempt to mask the whirlwind of emotions surging through me. Laughter, they say, was the best disguise, and in that moment, I hoped it was true.

What about him made my heart pound so wildly in my chest? Was it his allure, the raw masculinity that radiated from him, or was it something deeper, something that touched the core of who I was?

As I sat under the spell of his cerulean gaze, I realized that this wasn't just about physical attraction. Heck was uncharted territory, a thrilling adventure waiting to be explored. And I was drawn by the promise of discovery and the allure of the unknown.

Heck and I were having a wonderful time talking about films and TV series we both like. We shared an adoration for the characters Joel and Clementine from *Eternal Sunshine of the Spotless Mind*, as well as Bobby Axelrod from *Billions*.

Heck suddenly posed a question: "Would you ever consider erasing a memory, just to forget someone who consistently brings you pain?"

"Do you mean like what Clementine did in *Eternal Sunshine of the Spotless Mind*?" I queried in response. "I might consider it. Sometimes, it's better to let go of memories entirely if they only serve as a constant reminder of pain."

"I always thought Joel was somewhat of a coward for his decision," he mused. "I'd prefer to endure the pain if it means I can also remember the good times."

"I'm not certain where I stand," I admitted. "My capacity for enduring pain has always been somewhat limited."

Following our exchange, a silence fell between us. He idly toyed with the remnants of his now cold coffee, while I found my gaze fixated on my own empty cup.

I stole a surreptitious glance at Heck's face. His presence resonated within me like a melody I had known all my life, hinting at a connection that seemed to run far deeper than our initial meeting. I caught his gaze, intense and probing as if he were an archaeologist and I, a fascinating artifact awaiting discovery.

We were explorers charting a forgotten territory — the art of old-school conversation. Each word we exchanged was a step deeper into an adventure that promised thrilling twists and turns. Our interaction was actually an authentic human connection, stripped bare of technological crutches.

This was not just another conversation; it was a journey into the heart of connection, an exploration of the shared human experience, and a rediscovery of the lost art of conversation. And in that moment, I knew this was an adventure I wanted to embark upon.

Before we knew it, the café was preparing to shut its doors for the night. The server named Lily (written on her pinned nametag) approached our table. Her expression was apologetic. "I'm sorry, guys, but we're closing up."

Caught off guard, Heck and I rose from our seats. Our deep, fulfilling conversation was abruptly cut short. As we exchanged our goodnights, I felt an unexpected twinge of disappointment. Our dialogue had been so stimulating, so full of zest.

"It's been a pleasure. Gnight, Sara," he murmured, his voice barely above a whisper.

"'Night, Heck," I echoed.

But as I moved away, I couldn't help but feel a sense of warmth enveloping me. Tonight, I didn't write a single word, but it didn't matter. The joy of having spent the evening discussing my passions, sparked by a chance encounter with a stranger on a Friday night in my favorite café, was exhilarating. There was something quite beautiful about finding such a profound connection with an absolute stranger. In a city as densely populated as New York, the ratio of oddballs and jerks often seems to outnumber the sane ones. But tonight, I had found that rare gem. A person of substance amidst the chaos. My mind felt invigorated, possibly even inspired. It was a sensation I had long thought lost to me. I was enthralled.

4

PANTIES AND NAZIS

(Heck)

"What was that?" I asked myself. *"Definitely not something you see every day,"*

It was a soft night, the wind messing up my hair as I strolled down these well-trodden streets. But who cares about that right now? My mind was abuzz, full of echoes from our chat. I couldn't shake the image of Sara. I found myself marveling at her extraordinary beauty. Her long, wavy hair was a rich shade of brown that seemed to drink in the sunlight. It was cut shorter at the front to frame her face, adding a touch of softness to her features. Those locks just casually tumbled over one shoulder, a rogue strand falling on her face as she dug into those pancakes.

Her eyes were a stunning hazel, fanned with long lashes and well-groomed eyebrows. There was an intensity in her gaze that felt almost piercing, as though she could look straight into your soul. Those eyes, though. Big, doe-eyed, hazel ones that seemed to be... what? Searching for something in me? It was a gaze that held a certain honesty, a transparency that was both disarming and captivating.

She stood taller than most women I had encountered, easily measuring around 5 feet 7 inches. Her figure hinted at the lean, toned physique of a swimmer, though it was modestly concealed beneath her jeans and floral blouse.

What struck me most about Sara was her natural beauty. She wore no makeup, not even a hint of glossy lipstick, and her nails were unpolished. Yet, she radiated an allure that was raw, unadulterated, and completely her own. Her appearance felt as though it belonged to a different time, distinct from today's hyper-filtered and manipulated image of the Kylie Jenner era. It was entirely different. Untouched, whatever imperfections there might have been, I didn't see them. Her beauty wasn't crafted or manufactured, but rather a reflection of who she was — genuine, refreshing, and absolutely magnetic.

She was... interesting. Yeah, that was the word. It was not 'interesting' like an old dusty book or a scratched record. Nah. She was interesting, like a catchy tune that gets stuck in your head, like a poem that keeps you tossing and turning at night. She had something to say all the time, and that was something I would listen to all day if she let me. Safe to say, I was in awe of her. I was in complete awe.

"What's your game, Heck?" I muttered to myself, words hanging in the cool air. "You got a girl waiting for you. Why fuck up a good thing?" *Because I am me, and it's what I do. Typical Heck.*

I kicked at some fallen leaves scattered on the sidewalk. Summer was packing up, its lively buzz making room for fall's quiet contemplation. God, why does this feel like Smiths' "God Knows I'm Miserable Now" song? Miserable, pathetic motherfucker. But Sara... she felt like a splash of summer sunshine in the fading light, warm and glowing. She was a distraction. A good one.

"Everybody finds a crush... you get attracted to someone from time to time," I reminded myself. Especially suckers like me. You know, most times, a crush was just... surface-level stuff, right? All about the looks and the outside. But this? This felt different, man. Deeper somehow. Like there was this rare connection, a bond that went beyond the superficial. It's wild, isn't it?

"She's just a stranger. At least share something more than a movie to make the distraction worth its while," I reasoned, trying to shake off the lingering thoughts. Just a stranger I bumped into on a Friday night at some café. But as I huffed up the stairs to my apartment, her laughter ringing in my ears, I knew she was a stranger I wouldn't forget anytime soon.

Unlocking the door, I stepped into my sanctuary, the room that knew my secrets. The air was still, heavy with the scent of my girl Sophie. I could see her through the open door of our bedroom, sprawled on the bed, a mess of golden hair and alabaster skin, lustrous under the dim light.

I stepped out quietly onto the balcony. Flicking open my Zippo, the metallic sound rang out in the quiet night, marking the start of my five-minute ritual. See? A single cigarette stick usually took me five minutes — three if it was an extraordinarily stressful day. As I drew in a deep puff, I watched the city below. It was a chaotic symphony of lights and sounds, a jumbled mess that somehow soothed me. The wail of ambulances and distant chatter all faded into the background as I lost myself in thoughts of tomorrow's tasks.

This week had been particularly draining. Balancing work, running errands, and visiting my old man... the latter being the most emotionally taxing of all. On top of this, there was Sophie, who had been engrossed in our wedding plans while also managing her fitness and wellness routines. Additionally, there were the regular shopping trips and the seemingly endless list of tasks that come with planning a wedding... these weren't as simple as writing a check. All these activities had become a part of our shared routine.

As someone with deep affection for writing, I've consistently favored retaining these plans in the confines of my mind. Somehow, putting them onto paper or a phone screen seemed to elevate their significance to an uncomfortable level. Weren't they supposed to be important? I found myself constantly pushing the thought of the wedding to the back burner of my mind.

I suspect this is a common sentiment among many grooms-to-be. It's usually the bride and her entourage who tackle these tasks with enthusiasm. Meanwhile, we men often find ourselves eagerly awaiting the bachelor parties and the wedding day itself. The day arrives with a hangover and the lingering scent of last night's sex, marking the end of an era for play. After all, the night before was the last one for such freedom.

I slipped back in the apartment and slumped onto the new loveseat, or whatever the hell they call this. The backrest was far too soft for my liking. Oh, how I longed for my lumpy, worn-out couch, its familiar grooves that perfectly accommodated my body's contours. Another cigarette found its way between my fingers, the burn of the smoke a welcome distraction. I watched Sophie, the rise and fall of her chest, the way her eyelashes fluttered against her cheek. She slept like an angel, innocent and pure, a stark contrast to the wild creature she became when we were tangled in the sheets.

She was wearing nothing but her white panties and a yellow tank top, clothing that left little to the imagination. Sophie and I were both 28. She was a fitness enthusiast, hitting the gym five days a week and filling the rest with yoga, pilates, and biking. Her body was proof of her dedication – lithe yet strong. Her skin was fair and smooth. Her blond hair fell perfectly around her face, thick and voluminous. She could easily pass for a college student, and sometimes, I couldn't help but think of Elisha Cuthbert in the film *The Girl Next Door*, sans the porn star part.

Her body was a masterpiece, with curves and lines that would put any artist to shame. It was a body that stirred something within me, a primal desire that I couldn't quite shake off. But it was more than that, wasn't it?

Her face was peaceful, untouched by the harsh reality of our world. The face that I've traced with my fingers, a face that I've kissed more times than I could count.

The vibe I was catching right now? It was miles away from being all innocent and caring. There was not an ounce of sweet tenderness in what I've got planned at this moment. This was desire, pure and unadulterated. A hunger gnawed at my insides, a thirst that she quenched. She was like a drug, intoxicating and addictive, and I was a man lost in her haze. This right here? It was lust, man. Screaming out, begging to be noticed.

41

My gaze lingered on her, taking in the sight of her. I let the smoke curl around me, fill my lungs, and numb the ache. What was it about her that drew me in? Was it her beauty? Her body? Or was it simply the way she made me feel?

I sat there, lost in my thoughts, the silence deafening. Do you ever feel that? Like a gnawing longing, a yearning so fierce it's almost savage. It was not even about someone specific, man. It was just... there. A fevered infatuation, a wild fervor. Like your heart is on fire, and you don't even know why.

The smoke from my cigarette danced in the air, a silent witness to my introspection. I was not in love with her, but god, do I desire her. And as I watched her sleep, I couldn't help but wonder if that was enough.

The city lights flickered and danced across the satin sheets, where she lay sprawled out in peaceful slumber. She was a creature of comfort, always tangled in the soft fabric, even on the warmest nights. Yet, the intrusion of my presence didn't rouse her. Her sleep was deep and tranquil, much like the calm surface of a still lake.

I admired her flawless features as I gently brushed a strand of hair from her face. She stirred slightly as I peeled the satin sheets, revealing her long legs. Her skin, bathed in the soft glow of the bedside lamp, was proof of her meticulous self-care routines. I could still catch the faint scent of her expensive lotion, a blend of vanilla and jasmine that lingered in the air long after she applied it. It was intoxicating, just like her.

I stubbed the life out of the stick, dead and obtusely angled in that open coffin of an ashtray. Tried to keep the hard scent of smoke and nicotine of my hand away from her sense of smell but still within the realm of opening the opportunity of intimacy. As I reached out, my fingers ghosted over her left calf. The touch was feather-light, almost reverential. Her skin was smooth, cool to the touch, yet radiating a warmth that drew me in. My hand moved higher, tracing the curve of her firm thighs. There was something incredibly satisfying about the way my hand could barely span half her thigh, a silent acknowledgment of her dedication to fitness.

She had always known how much I appreciated her body... the feel of her skin, the sight of her barely covered. She knew I liked it when she slept with barely anything on. And tonight was no exception.

This gentle exploration stirred her from her dreams. Her eyelids fluttered open, revealing the familiar glint of anticipation in her soft blue eyes. A knowing smile played on her lips, a silent welcome into her world of intimacy. Invitingly, she parted her legs just enough for my hand to slip between them.

"Ohh, Heck," she whispered, with her eyes gently shut, as she seductively bit her lower lip.

This was a dance we've perfected over time. We were in tune with each other, aware of our desires, and comfortable in our shared silence. This was our symphony, our connection, our story unfolding in the quiet hours of the night.

As my fingers explored her more intimate areas, she guided me. She took my hand and allowed me to feel her wetness. Fingertips traced her, a mix of reverence and desire. My index and middle fingers danced on her while my thumb circled that particular spot, her pleasure nub that drove her crazy. Her approval echoed around the room, a soft moan swallowed by the night.

She arched her back, head tilted backward, surrendering herself to the sensations. Her body gravitated towards mine, an invisible force pulling us closer. The fabric of her top gave way under my eager hands, revealing her breasts — perfect in their symmetry, bathed in soft moonlight. Her nipples hardened beneath my touch.

I paid homage to each one. Lips trailed kisses, and tongue swirled around sensitive peaks. As I tasted her, my hand continued its exploration, a single finger sliding into her slick warmth. Her response was instinctual, her left leg lifted involuntarily, a silent plea.

"Heck, I want more," she cried. These were the signs I knew she was ready... her ragged breaths and flushed skin. I took the next step. I discarded her panties and my own clothes followed suit in a hurried frenzy. And then, I was there, hovering above her, the anticipation thick in the air. A moment frozen in time before I joined her in our intimate dance.

We moved together, lost in our own world of shared pleasure. Her eyes met mine, a look of contentment and relaxation that tightened slightly with each thrust. After a while, she signaled for a change, and she rode me, her body fully exposed in the dim light.

The sight of her, the feel of her, it was intoxicating. Her movements slowed as she reached her climax, and I took over, driving into her until we both found our release. We lay there afterward, bodies intertwined, the scent of sex filling the room. It was an end to another day, another chapter in our story. No usual cuddling and exchanging of romantic moments.

I stood from the bed. I lit up another cigarette, the smoke curling lazily around my fingers. Sophie, all tangled hair and sleep-heavy eyes, stretched cat-like. The sheets whispered secrets as they shifted, a sigh of cotton against the skin.

Our bedroom was a mishmash of us. A valuable old painting — *The Girl of Guernsey* — from an anonymous artist hung above our bed... not something from the old money that flowed through my veins. The painting was passed on from one generation to another until it got to me. It was a portrait of a woman probably in her twenties in oil, inherited from a lineage I only half understood.

Rumor had it that this woman was my great-grandfather's first love, someone he met in Guernsey when he was working at the maintenance of local defenses under the Royal Guernsey Light Infantry. Sophie hated it, but this painting and I had withstood years together. She quit bugging me about it when I made up a story about its provenance that it was made by a Dutch painter, looted by the Nazis, and somehow ended up in a Brooklyn apartment 80 years later. It was a bullshit story, but it shut her up.

As I watched the smoke twist and twirl, I let my gaze drift to that painting. *'Why'd he let you go?'* I asked the silent portrait. It stirred thoughts of narratives and history, of a time when my great-grandfather, a seemingly unfeeling German man, found himself embroiled in the recruitment of many Guernsey people in the Allied cause during the first world war. "Someday, I'm going to find the place where you and my great-grandfather met and fell in love," I whispered, a promise hanging heavy in the air.

His name was Heinrich Aleksander Achenbach, a name we buried, a constant reminder of where we came from. He wasn't what you'd call a hero, but he wasn't a villain either. He was just a man caught in the gears of a machine that chewed up humanity and spat out horror.

So, here was the thing. My family? Nothing special. Sure, if you were an outsider peering in, we'd seem like some fairy-tale, high-society types. But don't let the bling and the glitz fool ya. Underneath all that? Cold, hard cash. And a never-ending thirst for more.

Oh, the tales of my great-granddad. Those were our go-to bedtime stories when we were knee-high. Picture this: he hightailed it from Germany just as the storm clouds of war started to gather. His roots? Berlin — the throbbing heart of Jewish life at that time.

Germany. It was like a powder keg waiting to blow. The air was filled with an intense surge of patriotism after the sting of World War I. Power-hungry folks, ravenous for change, began to stir the pot. My great-granddad had the foresight. He saw what was coming down the pike.

And before the bigwigs had their ducks in a row, he was aboard a steamboat, America-bound. Once he set foot in the land of the free, Heinrich morphed into Hector — Hector Alexander Archibald, to be precise.

But unlike most immigrants, he wasn't broke. He'd been a banker back home, had sold all his stuff, stashed the cash, and made the move. Once he hit the States, he found himself in the thick of finance. He had this knack for making money work, not just his but other people's, too. And investing? Oh, he had a nose for that. Always knew where to drop a dime. It was like he could smell a good deal from a mile off. With war on the horizon, he pumped funds into military supplies. Didn't matter who they were supplying. All he cared about was the bottom line. By 45, he owned his own bank. The Gold Standard Bank, the first branch in the heart of New York City. A few years later, he set up offshore banking. Filthy rich, that was what he was. Had a long run as a banker, married a fellow immigrant, and had two sons, one of them my grandad.

Grandad, like his old man, had a head for numbers. Expanded the bank across the East Coast. The big plan? The next generation would take the West Coast, then go global. High expectations, right? Grandad married a Broadway actress and had three kids: two boys and one girl. The eldest? That was my dad. Followed in the family's footsteps. Became a big-shot fund manager.

And then there was me. Fourth-gen immigrant brat with a globe-trotting upbringing, mainly in Europe. Future heir to the family fortune. You might say I'm the one the universe chose to be born into this family, destined to one day captain our financial ship. And everyone was looking at me like I was gonna be the one to blow it all. Not that I was reckless with cash. I've got expensive tastes, sure, but they were minimal. And these days? I wanted very little. Sick of the high life, the obscene wealth. It ain't me anymore.

I exhaled, the smoke a ghost of my thoughts. My gaze returned to Sophie, her body a landscape I knew by heart. I thought of the first Hector, of the legacy he left me. The old money, the painting, the guilt. It was all part of me, like a DNA strand that twisted through generations.

I existed because of his choices and his actions. But I wasn't him. I was Heck.

These days, it was all about the art for me. I worked in restoration, preservation, and longevity of arts. But what really got me going was the creation. Diving into the nitty-gritty of an artwork, separating the flaws from the intent. The artist's life — the struggles, the insights, the raw emotion turned tangible — that was what I lived for. Van Gogh slicing off his ear, Jim Morrison drinking himself into oblivion, and Richard Linklater using his Euro trip as inspiration for a movie trilogy. That stuff. The art, man, that was the core of it all. To hell with the critics. I knew a true artist when I saw one. And a phony, too.

Being a hack? Heck the Hack. My worst nightmare. That was probably why I never tried to be an artist myself. I knew my limits. I could appreciate the master, but I'll never be one. And that was cool with me. Even without being an artist, I wanted to be part of the scene. On the sidelines, maybe, but still in the game.

I had no idea how I went from panties to Nazis. Man, my thoughts were all over the place, bouncing around like a pinball. One minute I was thinking about lacy undies and the next, I was somehow on Nazis. Freakin' Nazis! Must be some kinda mental hiccup, my brain veering off onto random tangents. Were the drugs from my youth finally catching up with my brain cells? Who knew where they'd dart to next?

Right now, though, it was all about Sophie. She was wearing those white lace numbers I was so fond of, the ones that made her look all innocent and stuff. But then, outta nowhere, Sara popped into my head. What was she up to right now, I wondered. Is she tangled up with her boyfriend in the same way I was with Sophie?

"Get a grip, Heck!" I scolded myself. *"You barely know the girl. Plus, you're in bed with your own girl."*

I went back to bed, took a long drag from my smoke, and let the harsh taste fill my lungs before I blew it out slowly. As I closed my eyes, the last image that flashed across my mind was a pair of hazel doe-eyes. Sara's eyes. Yeah, this was gonna be one hell of a night.

5

I LOVE YOU SUNDAY SUNSET

(Heck)

"Hey Heck, if anyone's got the magic touch for piecing things back together, it's gotta be you," Zaldy, my apprentice, said. We hit it off right from the get-go, him and me. This cool cat hailed from India and landed on New York's doorstep a few moons ago, hunting for a gig. Tess, my old friend, brought him into my life, a favor she called it, after adopting him during her Bombay escapades. Zaldy, he's a real Zen dude. Teaches yoga on the side, too. Right now, though, we were both up to our elbows in the innards of some ancient relic.

"Man, I swear, in another life, I was one of the guardians of these ol' treasures," I mused, my fingers danced over an ancient piece of pottery, dusting off years of history. It was set to feature in our upcoming exhibit, a collection of golden jewels, pottery, artifacts, and sculptures — all under this roof, my art gallery.

Before this, I was an art restorer... basically an artist. Who'd have thought that this gallery I opened five years back would become a home for new artists, a haven for antique collectors? My little corner of heaven, Entre Nous — 'between only the two of us' in French — tucked away in the concrete jungle of the Lower East Side. Nestled between a charming old bookstore and a family-run deli, it's the perfect blend of old-world charm and modern magic. Living in NYC, you're spoiled for choice when it comes to art. It was not just about world-famous museums like The Met, MoMA, the Guggenheim, or the Whitney. The city was bursting at the seams with galleries, each championing artists at every stage of their journey.

Step inside Entre Nous and you will be stepping into another world. A world brimming with artistic wonders and historical treasures. The walls pulsed with color, texture, stories. Art from every era, every corner of the globe, all restored to their original glory by yours truly.

The air in here had a unique scent. A cocktail of oil paints, aged wood, and a hint of dust. It was intoxicating. It was making you feel like you were part of something bigger, something timeless.

How did I become an art agent? I'd like to think of myself as the guy who breathes new life into these pieces. But hey, a guy's gotta make a living, right? So, when I wasn't breathing life back into some ancient artifact, I was hosting exhibitions, showcasing these gems to folks who appreciate 'em as much as I do.

Unlike my old man, who was big on ownership, property, all that jazz. Me? Not so much. I ain't no communist, but the idea of 'owning' art? Nah, not for me. I don't think art can be owned. Rent it, sure. Got a blank wall? Slap a painting on it. Bask in the joy it brings. Revel in the message that it spoke to you. But own it? Nah, it outlives 'ya. You were just a chapter in its story. A footnote in its history. A tick on the price tag. If anything, it owned you. You were just one of the suckers who paid for it thinking that you owned it.

Take that piece hanging by my door, for instance. A black stallion tamed by a slave. Painted for Henry VI, then hung up in some Duke's manor. Ended up in a Swiss chalet owned by a Nazi, then snagged at auction by a tech billionaire. And now, here with me. I was cool with being part of that motley crew. Just another name on a list that'll keep growing long after I'm gone.

"You ever get tired, Heck? Ever feel like it's all becoming a bit too... mundane?" Zaldy cut into my thoughts while tidying up brushes next to me. I shot him a sideways glance, a grin playing on my lips. His man bun made me chuckle. Not every guy can pull that off.

The joint was as quiet as a Sunday mornin', even though it was Monday. The hushed whispers of paintbrushes from nearby rooms, the silent ballet between canvas and color. The New York City clamor – it was out there, but in here, it was a different planet. A place where time took a smoke break, allowed you to marinate in the silence.

The room basked in this gentle, forgiving light. It tenderly stroked the artifacts, each shadow holding a secret, each gleam narrating a tale. The air was heavy with history and hushed whispers, with a hint of coffee wafting from the café next door. My workbench was a wild mess of tools and trinkets, lost pieces yearning for their homes. The artifact – it was a thing of beauty, a maze of intricate patterns and delicate details. Time had etched its autograph on it, like wrinkles on an old man's face. Each chip, each crack, a testament to its voyage.

So, here I was with Zaldy two days after meeting Sara. We were surrounded by an unknown artist's forgotten masterpiece: a weird gig, no doubt. But the fact of just being in my gallery every single day was enough compensation for me. Of course, I couldn't tell my old man about that sentiment. I'd probably be here every day just to kill time anyway. But there was something about pumping fresh life into these ancient art pieces. Removing the discoloration and bringing back the original colors as their creators intended. They've got tales to tell, y'know? Tales that've been around longer than you and me. People eventually see lines or wrinkles, paintings go from yellowish to a shade of brownish. Without the proper care, these paintings would be in different colors in 30 to 40 years. Who knew? Those Da Vinci's have some details in them that have been obscured by settled elements by now, and that was the reason why they say we've never unlocked the secrets behind all of them.

This thing I was doing wasn't exactly a money-spinner. But hey, it wasn't about the greenbacks for me. Who needs it, right? I mean, for me, cash was like a bad case of the clap... a venereal disease. Nobody really needed that kind of trouble. I was one of the lucky ones, born with what you call generational wealth. I was just looking for something that lit my fire and made me feel alive. This gig didn't exactly have me rolling in dough, but it got that spark, that thing I needed. I've seen the inside of a punishing and limiting cubicle, and

I'd choose this over that any day of the week. No contest. I'd rather kill myself than read contracts and paperwork. I prefer that you give me literature — and more time to go with it.

"Hey, Heck, Tess mentioned you're engaged. Thanks for telling, bro. I thought we were buds. How did you know she's the one?" Zaldy interrupted my thought. He was like a kid with a bottomless pit of questions.

"Honestly? No clue. One night, you're hammered, you pop the question, and she jumps right at you. Next morning, you wake up, and boom, you're engaged," we both burst into laughter.

I glanced at the old-timey clock hanging on the wall, its hands moving slowly as molasses. I shook my head, a half-smile tugging at my lips. I couldn't help but think about that café girl. Sara. If she were still on my mind by clock-out time, that wouldn't be good at all. I wondered if our paths would cross again. This was me giving in to my self-destructive tendencies.

"Hey, Heck, you're gazing at that ancient clock again, ain't ya? Wearing that goofy grin, too," Zaldy pointed out, his voice layered with a teasing lilt. "Bet my last buck there's a lady involved, and it ain't Sophie."

"Z, you've got a knack for sniffing out secrets, but swear on your man bun, don't let Tess catch a whiff of this," I shot back, a playful warning lacing my tone.

"Heck, man, if Tess gets wind of this, she'll hound you till kingdom come, demanding every juicy detail," he chuckled, his laughter echoing around the artifact-laden room.

"So, where are you meeting this mystery girl?" Zaldy inquired, passing me a worn-out brush. His curious eyes sparkled with intrigue, a stark contrast to the ancient artifacts surrounding us.

"Already thinking about going back to that café. Coffee's subpar, but we know I'm not there for that," I said.

We spent the rest of the day lost in a whirl of colors and brushstrokes, time slipping through my fingers unnoticed. Today's work felt better than yesterday's. I was guessing I knew exactly why. When the clock chimed six, I shrugged into my jacket, heart thumping a little louder than usual. It was time. I could've called it a day earlier and gone straight to that place, but it was too obvious and exciting.

The sun was beginning to set as I stepped out onto the bustling streets. The city was transitioning from day to night, and my evening commute from the Lower to the Upper East Side was about to begin.

I made my way towards the subway station, merging with the sea of New Yorkers leaving their workplaces. The aroma of street food filled the air, the mouth-watering smell of one-dollar pizza, blending with the faint scent of the city after a long day.

Descending into the subway station, I swiped my MetroCard and joined the mass of commuters on the platform. The atmosphere was a mix of exhaustion and anticipation. Overhead, the speakers crackled with the occasional announcement, adding to the symphony of the city's heartbeat.

With a familiar rumble and screech, the subway car arrived. The doors slid open, revealing a cross-section of the city. Business suits shared space with artists, students, and tourists, all co-existing in this shared moment of transit.

The train jerked forward, and we were off. The rhythmic clatter of wheels on tracks became a soothing background noise, accompanying the soft hum of conversations and the rustle of evening newspapers.

Outside the window, the city flashed by in a blur of lights and shadows. Each station we passed offered a fleeting glimpse into another corner of this vast, diverse city.

As we sliced through Manhattan, I watched the neighborhoods transition. The vibrant, eclectic charm of the Lower East Side gradually merged into the refined, elegant streets of the Upper East Side. It was a fascinating study in contrasts.

Finally, the train slowed, and the familiar robotic voice announced my stop. I stepped out onto the platform. Then I made my way to that café, that snug little nook of the world.

———————

Bingo! There she was. Just as I had been hoping for all day. Same spot as before, scribbling away in her notebook, nibbling on her brinner. Bacon and eggs this time, paired with a side of roasted cherry tomatoes. Yesterday, I wanted to be a pancake. Today, I wanted to be bacon. First time I wanted to be a swine. Lucky bastard! Should I break her concentration with her writing? Maybe if I do, she'll write me into her story. Or maybe, just maybe, I was already a character in her narrative, living and breathing between the lines and curves of her handwriting.

I ruffled my hair and smoothened my black tee as best as I could with my fidgety hands. Drew in a deep breath and let it out slowly. Here it was, another shot at a chat with Sara. *Do not fuck this up*, I told myself. *What the fuck was I doing?* Just another laid-back night at the café, right? Perfectly innocent. But my pounding heart begged to differ.

"I thought I'd find you here," I said. She looked up at me. Her eyes lightened. This time, she was decked out in a white blouse and jeans tucked into brown knee boots. She cleaned up well. Better than the last time. Was it for me, though? Her smile's so wide, it could light up the whole damn café. I think it did.

"Heck! Good to see you again," she greeted, her voice a welcome melody. Warm and eager. I noticed her eyes weren't the usual shade of brown, somehow lighter. Is it hazel? Her teeth were straight as a picket fence. I imagined her with braces as a kid. Cute.

I noticed a smudge of tomato sauce on her lip like an abstract painting,

53

kinda adorable, messy vibe.

"Hey, Sara..." I waved my hand around my face, the universal sign for 'you got something there.'

She swiped at her face with a finger but kept missing the mark. "Did I get it?" She was cute, like watching a kitten chase its tail.

"Nah, it's just a smidge to the right," I guided her.

I gestured for her to wipe it off. She couldn't locate it, so I reached across the table. My thumb brushed against her skin, soft as a feather. Cool as mint. But the jolt! Man, it was like I'd stuck my finger in a socket.

She smiled, a little awkward-like, and it cranked her cuteness level up a notch. Touching her delicate skin was like touching a live wire. A mental note was made. I don't think I will ever forget this. First time touching her face. She didn't even flinch. That's gotta be a good sign, right?

"Thanks," she muttered shyly. I slid into the chair across from her. I signaled the waitress, who already knew my order by heart.

"So what's on your agenda today," I asked as if I wasn't thinking of her the whole day, "apart from devouring your brinner?"

"Trying to wrangle my story outline. Words are playing hard to get today, so I thought I'd stick to outlining," she said, snapping her notebook shut. "What brings you here?"

Her question caught me off guard; my mind was scrambling for a suitable answer. But I decided to play it straight with her. "I was actually hoping to run into you here," I confessed.

Her gaze flickered to her plate, then back to me. "Oh, is that a good thing or a bad thing?" she asked. Man, I sure hope she doesn't think I was just twiddling my thumbs, killing time.

"That depends on how you see me. Do I look like some nutjob fresh out of the loony bin?" I retorted.

"I sure hope you're not Dahmer or Manson," she quipped.

"Don't worry 'bout that. I left my aviator glasses and black van at home. You're safe," I said, flashing her a grin that was all kinds of Dahmer-spooky.

She burst into laughter. It was a hearty laugh. Not too demure or loud. My God, she looked even more beautiful. Her laughter made me adore her all the more; it was as infectious as it was disarming. Was this what feeling God's smile upon you was like? #Blessed. Just making her do more than smile was a thrill in itself. I had never felt funnier or more charming. Perhaps she was just boosting my ego, but it felt incredible nonetheless. But man, I wouldn't mind hearing her waves of laughter for the rest of my days.

That night, we dissected my poem. It was the first time anybody other than me had seen it, and she gave it serious thought. It was strange how at ease I felt to have someone read my words, previously exclusive to me. I've always thought about judgment, but not right now. I didn't care at all. I handed it over to her and, with a red pen pulled from her pouch — which, by the way, was stuffed to the brim with markers and pens of all colors — she began.

She turned to the page I had been working on the past few days. With her soft voice, she started reading it out loud.

I Love You, Sunday Sunset

Oh, sweet Sunday sunset, love of mine,
A gentle whisper in the twilight's chime.
Your amber hues kiss the day goodbye,
As we bid adieu with a contented sigh.

You are the pause before the week's new song,
The quiet moment when shadows grow long.
A soft surrender to the night's embrace,
As Monday's promise begins its chase.

No more the echo of familial laughter,
Now anticipations of what comes after.
The nights, the days that are wholly ours,
Unseen, untouched by the sun's final hours.

We yearn for the freedom that darkness brings,
Underneath the moon and its silver wings.
For when Sunday's sun dips low and bows,
Begins a tale that the silent night allows.

Gone are the elders' watchful eyes,
In the cloak of night, our secret lies.
A world that spins for us alone,
A love as wild as the wind has blown.

So here we stand at the edge of light,
Hand in hand, ready for the night.
With every Sunday sunset, my heart takes flight,
To the promise of days bathed in our own delight.

So, I love you, Sunday sunset, end of the week,
You're the prelude to the adventure we seek
With you, the mundane quietly recedes,
And in its place, our own story proceeds.

"'I Love You, Sunday Sunset' is sad yet beautiful. It's as if you're trying to escape some sort of routine. What comes after Sunday?" she said.

"After Sunday sunset come the days outside of the usual grind. Days when you can just be yourself. No one is breathing down your neck, telling you what to do. I don't know, something like that." I laughed at my own rambling. Did she think I was crazy or at least unhappy? Could she tell?

"I get you. I like my post-Sundays to be all about me," she echoed.

My espresso arrived, along with a side of soya. I closed my eyes and took a deep breath. I was all about that aroma, y'know? As I poured the dark brew into my mug of soya, I caught Sara eyeing my cup like she was witnessing some sort of ritual.

"You seem to be quite into that," she observed. I hope my hand didn't shake while stirring. At least not while the caffeine's not yet in my system, aggravating my own nervousness.

"Fancy a sip?" I passed the mug her way. She took me up on it. A surprise. Most girls worry about smudging their lipstick. Others like to leave a lipstick mark on the guy's cup, indicating that she's into you. But then I noticed she wasn't wearing any.

"That's good," she declared, passing the mug back to me.

She was flipping through my notes now. "I think you need to flesh this out a bit," she suggested. "Show, don't tell."

"So you hit me with another Hemingway," I chuckled.

"Yes, I am," she retorted, leaning closer to scope my notes. She smelled sweet. Not perfume-sweet. It was her shampoo. Lavender mixed with her natural scent. As she leaned over to get the sugar jar, a button on her blouse popped open. I got a quick peek at her lacy white bra and a fleeting glimpse of the fullness of her breast, which the cup couldn't conceal before she quickly buttoned it back up.

Man, talk about a power surge. A glimpse of her skin, and I was buzzing like a neon sign. This ain't your garden-variety thrill. Nah, this was something else. Never felt this kind of spark before, not by just looking at a hint of breast. Nope, not with anyone. Not even Sophie.

Did Sara take extra time and effort to choose that piece? I think she did. She came prepared. That white lacy piece was something you wear on a date to impress. *My God*, I mused silently. *Is she playing with me? 'Cause if that was the case, it was working like a charm.* I was teetering on the edge, just a breath away from reaching out for her hand and pulling her close. I was not unhinged, though. We were not at that stage yet. Wishful thinking, perhaps, but no dice. Yet, I felt my self-restraint wavering. All I wanted was to be near her right then. You didn't flaunt that kind of lingerie unless you were aiming for some attention. That was promising, right?

Our conversation and discussion came quickly and naturally, only to pause for coffee sips, which were still warm even after we finished the poem. Suddenly, the café music shifted gears, and one of my favorite songs filled the air, adding a whole new layer of mood to our little corner of the world.

"What's that song?" She asked, her eyes drilling into me with an intensity that could almost be felt.

"That?" I leaned toward her like I was sharing a secret. That made Sara lean in closer to me. The music swam around us, a melodic tide pulling her in. She didn't fight it. "It's 'Transatlanticism' by Death Cab for Cutie. "

I mean, how do you explain a band like that? It was like trying to describe the taste of water. But I gave it a shot anyway.

"The song? It's about... distance or something. But not just that. Connection, too." She was nodding, soaking up every word, wanting to understand what I saw in this song that made my eyes light up.

"Just listen," I urged, my fingers tapping out the rhythm on the table, "especially to the last part. The melody... the arrangement... it's thick with emotion. It's like an emotional sucker punch."

So we sat there, lost in the music, humming along to the hauntingly beautiful tune. I could see Sara felt something stir within her, a connection to the song she hadn't expected.

"Do you feel it?" I asked, my voice barely above a whisper.

"I do," she admitted. "I really do."

And I couldn't help but think, wasn't it crazy how a song can do that? How it could make you feel seen, understood, and be part of something bigger. And I looked at Sara, and I knew she got it. She really got it.

The night rolled on, filled with easy conversation and fits of laughter. We even held hands at times — hers are soft, her long fingers without a trace of nail polish. I couldn't remember the last time I held somebody else's hand and felt this way. I was tempted to lift her hand to my lips, but it was too soon. The strangest thing was she didn't pull away.

And that was when it hit me! Tonight was Saturday. Date night. I've got a dinner date with my girl! My phone has been on DnD mode. When I finally checked it, I was greeted by a barrage of unread messages. I knew I was in for it.

"Guess I gotta hit the road, boyfriend duties and all," I announced.

She grinned at me. "Okay. 'Night, Heck."

"Gnight, Sara," I replied.

And with that, I exited the coffee shop.

———

Rushing towards Saga, I was mentally kicking my own ass. Forgot about date night. What the fuck, Heck? You were always late. Sure, a little late, no big deal. But a whole hour? Lucky if you still have a table. Lucky if Sophie doesn't rip you a new one.

An hour late. And still 15 minutes away from Pine Street. Hail a cab. Cut that 15 down to 10, maybe less. Threw some extra cash at the driver to step on it.

Finally, I stepped into Saga, rushed to the 63rd floor of the Art Deco building and there she was. Sophie in a theatrically lit bar near the terrace with an unending skyline and a view across a wide stretch of the East River to Brooklyn. Looking like a million bucks. All dolled up.

"Where the fuck were you?" Pissed as hell. "We've had this reservation for weeks, Heck!"

"I'm sorry, babe, I completely spaced." I could see her trying to stay mad. But I could sense she was melting, just a little. Because she knew me. Knew I was screwed up. But also knew I'd make it up to her. Somehow.

Naturally, our table was gone. The maître d' had shuffled Sophie off to the bar, since they don't seat incomplete parties. So here we were, stuck with bar bites, these fancy-looking nibbles that cost an arm and a leg. And booze, of course. But the hostess was a peach, promised us the next two-top that opened up. Looked like it was going to be one of those long nights.

I needed a drink, something strong to take the edge off. A double shot of whisky. One for ruining this dinner and one for leaving Sara so abruptly. Ah, the perfect antidote to neutralize the disaster of today, served neat. The waiter shot me a knowing glance, his eyes silently acknowledging that I was grappling with a rough day.

The Saga, a relatively new establishment that opened its doors two years ago, is always bustling with activity, making it challenging to secure a reservation. Their culinary approach is deeply rooted in European techniques, yet it draws inspiration from eclectic sources. This includes the flavors from our childhood memories, our travel experiences, and the rich diversity of cuisine available in New York City.

There was a cool breeze blowing in from the open windows. Felt good. Calming. Just what I needed right now.

6

MATT & THE BEASTIE BOYS

_____

(Sara)

The city lights twinkled, a constellation in the urban night, as my Uber wove through the intricate maze of the Upper East Side. I found myself cocooned in the backseat, my thoughts moving back and forth between Heck in the café and Matt back home. My heart still pulsed to the rhythm of Heck's poem, "I Love You, Sunday Sunset." It was almost surreal. The depth of connection I felt with someone through mere words was uncanny. I had chanced upon a poet — a rare fusion of beauty and yearning encapsulated in their verses. An anomaly, especially among men of this era. Or was it? Maybe I needed to broaden my perspective beyond the men I currently knew. None of them embodied such a characteristic. Had I been fraternizing with the wrong crowd? Was I entrenched in the *Succession* circle when I should be drifting among the *Midnight in Paris* set? But where does one find such guys? Paris, perhaps?

There must be a catch, a concealed imperfection within this poetic soul. It was only a matter of time before it would surface. Engaged? Could that be perceived as a flaw? He hadn't made any untoward moves or advances, so perhaps that didn't quite qualify as a fault. I was hinting at a more grave kind of wrong — a level of wrong that bordered on the psychopathic. Or the deceptive schemer, the con-artist level of wrong. Or even the chilling spectrum of serial-killer wrong.

With each traffic light we passed, my thoughts turned like pages of a book, each filled with the memory of our second meeting at the café. The way Heck's blue eyes, hidden behind that pair of black-rimmed glasses, sparkled with secret mirth, the warmth in his voice, the jolt that shot through me every time his fingers brushed against mine — it was all so vivid, so real. Tonight, he didn't hide the fact that he intentionally went to the café hoping to see me. That was a good sign — as long as he's not Bundy. Remember, Bundy was a charmer too... No, Heck will never be a Bundy.

Our encounter today was uncanny, to put it mildly. It was an unexpected, peculiar twist in the ordinary, like stumbling upon a rare gem in a mundane coffee shop. The idea that such serendipitous encounters actually happened outside of wishful and naive rom-coms was mind-boggling. And Heck — he was a character straight out of a book, a refreshing deviation from the typical. He embodied the prototype of the ideal millennial male.

I've grown accustomed to the cynical belief that everyone unknown was potentially a jerk or a creep. Particularly men who struck up conversations with women in clubs and bars. Predators often lurked in such places, preying on unsuspecting victims. Their modus operandi was simple: get the girl's number, make her laugh, wine and dine her, lure her into their web, discard her, and then move on to the next. If you were not cautious, you fell victim to their game in a single night. Having spent a considerable amount of time in NYC, I've grown to harbor certain suspicions.

I've always been mindful of who I allowed into my personal space. Especially those smooth talkers — the skilled ones who possessed an almost magical ability to speak eloquently. They tried to find common ground in the most unlikely scenarios — the coffee shop guys. Those masters of seduction were the menace, lurking in every corner. I'd like to believe these types might even harbor darker intentions.

But Heck was different. He didn't fit the mold of the typical creep. There was an authenticity about him, a warmth that was disarming. His words didn't feel rehearsed or manipulative but sincere and genuine. Does he appear too perfect? Too well-suited for me?

The memory of our conversation lingered, a haunting melody that echoed in the silence. His laughter, his insightful comments, the way his eyes lit up when he spoke about his passions — these were not the traits of a pick-up artist but of a man who wore his heart on his sleeve. As I replayed our encounter, I couldn't help but smile. It was strange, yes, but also thrilling. It was an adventure, a departure from the mundane.

But amid the excitement, a sliver of doubt lurked. Was Heck truly different, or was he just a better actor than the rest? Only time would reveal the truth. For now, all I had were memories of a strange encounter and the hope that not all coffee shop guys were creeps.

The contrast between coffee shop guys and club guys was as stark as day and night, both literally and figuratively. In the dimly lit corners of a club, intentions were unambiguous — it was a hunting ground for fleeting connections, where the end goal was often a sexual encounter. The club environment was engineered for this purpose — the thumping music, the intoxicating buzz, the uninhibited dancing with friends or strangers. It was a realm where confidence was artificially boosted by liquor, conversations were drowned by the deafening beats, and everything was superficially glamorous. You spent hours getting dolled up not for a heart-to-heart, but for the thrill of the chase. A few shared glances, interesting quips, and drinks later, you've reached the 80% mark in the club's conversation quota.

Yet, in the bright, calm ambiance of a coffee shop, the game changed dramatically. Here, the focus sharpened, the noise dimmed, and conversations are less bullshit as opposed to ones done in a bar or club. Coffee shops are social arenas, too. They were sanctuaries for those seeking solitude to work, study, read, write, or simply enjoy their coffee in peace. Antisocial stuff. It also means that if somebody strikes up a conversation here, it should not be something that is mundane, bland or inconsequential. It needed to be something worth the disturbance of somebody's peace. Besides, there were too few conversations happening here. If you strike out, no exchange of numbers, no name, and even worse, everybody in the café heard it and saw it happen. And with the non existent frequency that it happens, everyone will remember it and you. Take note, too, that everybody here is sober. You are now a marked man. Marked loser. Might as well have yourself banished. Go find another establishment where not everybody knows you striked out.

Only the pros navigate the coffee shop terrain skillfully, and Heck, he seemed like a pro. Was this a calculated move on his part? Had he dug up my love for *Midnight in Paris?* Not many people I know share my enthusiasm for Woody Allen, especially at our age. Maybe I posted on my Instagram, I couldn't remember. Heck's knowledge of my interests was uncanny. His perfection raised red flags — perfect looks, perfect talk, perfect manners. An artist, a writer who frequented coffee shops to write? And the cute way he came up with 'brinner'? A poet as well? It seemed I might have stumbled upon someone who could be Brandon Boyd's spiritual youngest brother.

For all I knew, he could've been a Walter White in disguise. Was this some set-up? Was my friend and former neighbor Hope Williams trying to match me with one of her showbiz writer-actor friends? Had she fed him information about me? She never liked Matt. I had made it clear to her that Matt and I were fine. Sure, I might have vented about some minor issues, but nothing that warranted a break-up. Matt and I shared an apartment, a life. What was this bizarre twist in my otherwise predictable life? The questions swirled in my mind, each one adding to the intrigue and uncertainty of this unexpected encounter.

On the flip side, there's Matt — he was beginning to mirror the chilling precision of Patrick Bateman from the 2000 film *American Psycho*, portrayed by Christian Bale. Again, I found myself inexplicably drawn to the dark allure of serial killers. Was this my type? My ideal carriage suddenly seemed to be an unmarked, inconspicuous white van.

Matt's days unfurled with the exactitude of a Swiss clockwork—awake at 5 a.m., followed by a rigorous workout session. Each morning was marked by a painstakingly thorough dermabrasion routine. By the time most people were rubbing the sleep out of their eyes, Matt had already plowed through more than half his daily itinerary.

His commitment to skincare and physical fitness was awe-inspiring, so much so that it cast a shadow over my own, and I was the woman in this equation. His brisk daily walk to work, he claimed, was an additional sprinkle of cardio. It wouldn't shock me if he meticulously logged each step, insisting on landing his foot on the same spots every day. Was this a sign of obsessive-compulsive disorder or just an extreme form of meticulousness?

Not that I was complaining, mind you. The results of his regimen were undeniable. He was leaner, more energized, radiating a vitality that wasn't there when we first met. But his infatuation with routine can be stifling. Sometimes, I felt like an unwelcome interruption when I coaxed him out of his rigid schedule, and he didn't hide his annoyance well.

Our date nights have become another cog in his well-oiled machine of life. Fridays — because those were the days when he permitted himself the luxury of staying up late. The next day, he just shifted his routine a few hours later. We always ended up at the same spot, a restaurant we used to love. But after a year of weekly visits, the charm has worn off, much like the previous place before it was replaced in the rotation.

I've become a part of his routine, a checkbox to tick off in his daily list. There was a bitter taste of resentment growing within me, a feeling I'd never voiced aloud. The predictability, the monotony — it had become a cage. I yearned for spontaneity, for the thrill of unpredictability, for an adventure that broke the shackles of routine.

The fascinating encounters with Heck brought a taste of that longing. And I found myself craving for more.

The way I looked forward to seeing Heck again was an adventure in itself, a thrilling ride that sent waves of excitement coursing through my veins. The world outside the car window seemed to mirror my inner turmoil, the vibrant cityscape an indication of the untamed joy that bubbled within me.

The memory of Heck and our unexpected encounter cast a warm glow over the familiar surroundings. The city lights outside seemed to twinkle with newfound excitement, their rhythmic dance a reflection of the anticipation that pulsed within me. Everything appeared to be nicer and more pleasant. It became challenging to uncover any sense of dread or gloom anywhere.

"Miss, we're right here." My thoughts were interrupted by the Uber driver as the car pulled up to my apartment building on 89th Street.

"Oh, thank you, and good night," I said.

Stepping out of the car, a sense of familiarity washed over me. The Sung's floral shop, Veronica's Bloom, nestled at the foot of the building, was a beacon of tranquility amidst the urban chaos. I breathed in the heady fragrance of fresh flowers, their scent a soothing balm to my racing heart. The walk from the street to the elevator ride going to my floor was a quiet interlude where I could gather my thoughts and steady my emotions. The sight of the father-daughter duo meticulously arranging the blooms late at night was a comforting constant, a symbol of the enduring beauty of life.

"There you are, Sara! How's work? Have you written some stories today?" Charlie Sung excitedly asked me. His white hair and beard and that wide smile reminded me of Miyagi in the 80's *Karate Kid* movie.

"Howdy, Charlie! Not much today, I have so much work, and I met with someone who wrote great poetry," I replied.

Charlie's eyes twinkled. "Good, you're meeting more interesting ones."

"Hey, wanna come over for *Queer Eye* marathon?" Veronica asked while busily arranging the pink roses in the tin can. She was around my age, and we constantly watched TV series together. Veronica and I were totally opposite physically. She's a petite Asian with long straight hair. Oddly enough, we found ourselves attracted to these good-looking gay men. Could this be what being gender fluid entails? I knew Veronica missed our neighbor Hope, who now lived in the Upper East Side with her superstar boyfriend Richard Collins.

"Rain check?" I asked. "Matt is already home, I guess," I pouted.

"Alrighty," she said, "see you when I see you!"

"See you when I see you," I shouted back as I got into the elevator going to the 7th floor.

The familiar strains of Beastie Boys seeped through the door to the apartment I shared with Matt even before I could extract my keys from the lock. It was unmistakably Matt's anthem. Born and raised in Jersey, his heart had always been set on the pulsating rhythm of New York City. And what could be more quintessentially NYC than Beastie Boys?

He often spoke of their local roots with a sparkle in his eyes, conveniently overlooking the fact that this particular album was largely created in Los Angeles. One of the band members had relocated there to chase an acting career, collaborating with the Dust Brothers. This geographical shift had undeniably altered their music's sound, making his 'local' argument somewhat moot. Regardless, it was still a fantastic album. I knew this because my dad's youngest brother, Uncle Ted, the family's self-proclaimed 'cool and hip' member had introduced me to them during my Christina Aguilera phase. "Egg Man" was playing. Good choice.

Unlocking the door, I was greeted by the familiar sights and sounds of our modest home. The single bedroom, the tiny kitchen-dining area, and the small living room — every nook and cranny held a piece of our shared story, or the lack of it. Everything was impeccably tidy, just the way Matt liked it. He must have gotten home early and taken the time to clean up.

The hallway was dimly lit, its shadows only pierced by the warm glow emanating from the living room. Matt must be in his Peloton sanctuary. And sure enough, there he was, a vision of determination and perspiration. I found myself hesitating, unsure if I wanted to plant a kiss on his sweat-glistened cheek.

"You're home late, babe," he greeted me, his voice devoid of any trace of suspicion. He knew I'd gone out to write.

"Sorry, I lost track of time again. Did we have plans?" I queried, my heart pounding slightly.

"No, but we could've gone out," he responded, his words laced with a hint of disappointment. But Matt was never one for spontaneity. His only plan was to adhere to his rigorous exercise schedule, a ritual he'd kept for countless months. His plan was for himself, not us.

"I'll be done in a bit," he assured me, indicating that he'd been at it for at least an hour already.

"Take your time," I responded, my thoughts drifting back to the coffee shop and the enigmatic Heck, a stark contrast to the predictable rhythm of life with Matt.

I walked into the tiny living room. The apartment's crowning glory was the balcony, my private haven in the heart of the city. From here, I could watch the world go by, my thoughts free to float amidst the sea of lights and sounds. The city's pulse was my lullaby, its rhythm a constant reminder of the endless possibilities that lay before me.

As I leaned over the railing, the cool breeze kissing my face, I couldn't help but smile. Heck's words echoed in my mind, their melody interwoven with the symphony of the city.

My gaze returned to Matt. At 27, he was already a seasoned player in the corporate rodeo, a veritable cowboy of the trading floor. His pedigree screamed financial analyst, armed with a Series 7, a CFA, and an alphabet soup of other certifications. I don't even understand them, but the way he explained it to me, these are the gold standard in selling securities, or whatever those mean. Yet, Matt lacked the stereotypical temperament of an analyst. Those who pored over financial sheets, scrutinized mergers and acquisitions, then whispered buying and selling advice into brokers' ears like oracle predictions.

Analysts read economic triggers and benchmarks with the same fervor that some devote to holy scriptures. Some danced with graphs, candle bars, and trends, spinning their predictions into existence. But not Matt. He preferred to keep his ear to the ground, to listen rather than shout in speculation. He dismissed the hype, choosing instead to walk the path of fundamentals. In him, I saw shades of a young Michael Burry, the famous hedge fund manager who made a killing in the market when the housing crash hit in 2008.

When the Gamestop fiasco unfolded, Matt watched with growing unease as the underdogs triumphed against the establishment. They were sticking it to the man, but Matt found himself siding with the man. Perhaps, deep down, he envisioned himself becoming 'the man'. And watching him climb the corporate ladder, I had no doubt he'll reach that pinnacle by 40.

Two years ago, choosing Matt felt safe, even logical. He was older by a couple of years, a beacon of adulthood when I was just stepping out of the cocoon of college at 21. He was already a part of the working world, a suave figure who swept me off my feet. He introduced me to fine dining, always impeccably dressed in a suit, branded shit, while I was still finding my footing, a student living off parental support, comfortable but not affluent.

This finance whiz took me to restaurants and bars far beyond my reach, showering me with gifts I'd never asked for. Pastries brought to your table by cart, fine wine, places with a coat room, and bathrooms without lines. He had been snatched up straight out of college, armed with a signing bonus and a lucrative salary. His success was undeniable.

Our relationship took a romantic turn when he surprised me with a weekend getaway to Montauk for my birthday. Just the two of us in a quaint house by the shore, surrounded by nothing but convenience stores and a lone gift shop.

We filled our days with ocean swims and our nights with beer and steak, perfectly grilled by Matt's skilled hands. Under the influence of alcohol and the mesmerizing blanket of stars, we dared each other to skinny dip — a challenge he accepted readily after I took the plunge first.

Later, as we lounged on the porch, we wove dreams of our future under the starlit canopy. Matt's vision was a picture of a suburban idyll — kids running around in a garden, a beautiful house, a perfect family. But where did that leave me, just venturing into life on my own? As we lay in bed later, the scene felt eerily reminiscent of Joel and Clementine in the film *Eternal Sunshine of the Spotless Mind*. I should have seen the threatening implications, but one was blind when one was distracted, and I have to admit, I was distracted then. The parallels of our lives with Joel and Clementine were uncanny, and the uncertainty of our future hung heavy in the air. Like our own version of eternal sunshine.

I found myself lost in the memory of the intense conversation I'd had with Heck about Joel and Clementine, and their desperate wish to erase all recollections of each other. The depth of Heck's emotions was clear as day; he yearned to clutch onto every fragment of his memories, even the painful ones, just as long as they painted a picture of the person he cherished deeply. His sentiments ran so deep, they were almost tangible.

I couldn't relate to such profound emotions. Perhaps I hadn't yet experienced love in such an overwhelming capacity. Could he have? The thought lingered in my mind, creating ripples of doubt and curiosity. But, deciding it was better left unanswered, I shrugged off these thoughts and made my way to the bedroom.

"Matt, I'm heading to the shower. Are we going out tonight?" I asked. I don't think we're going out tonight. None of our friends called to hang out. My friends knew I was planning to write. At least, that's what I told them in our Telegram group. Not much writing happened, but it was worth it. Heck distracted me. Not that I was complaining. That beautiful and interesting guy was worth it. Not a minute was wasted, as far as I was concerned.

"Go ahead," he shouted back as I was already on the way to the bathroom. "And, no, babe. We're staying home tonight."

When I emerged from the bathroom with my hair still wet, the dinner table was already set. He had cooked dinner for us —a DIY date at home. I pretended to enjoy it even if I had already had my brinner. *He made the effort. Don't be ungrateful*, I reminded myself.

"How many pages have you written?" he asked while biting into the salmon steak.

To be fair, he was very supportive in that way. Or maybe he liked it because he knew writing was my own thing, thus I had to do it alone, thus leaving him to his alone time, thus more exercise or quiet time. I didn't want to begrudge him for that. He was nice enough tonight— at least he tries. At least he had reached that point where, after some thought and minimal attempts, he almost succeeded.

"Got a couple of chapters," I lied. "And you?"

"Same old trade this, trade that. The war in Ukraine was causing inflation to accelerate and further causing the market to shrink, or lag," he explained. Our discussions ended there. I have to admit I wasn't interested in any of it. I found the whole idea summarized as buy low, sell high and basically soulless.

After I put the dishes into the washer, Matt asked me to watch an episode of *Suits* on Netflix. I'd rather see *Billions* because I think the screenwriting there was so much sharper. I liked Axelrod more than Mike or even Harvey. But actually, I'd like to see *Midnight in Paris* right now. Just to see if Heck was right about the things he said. But Matt liked *Suits*. Which was weird, because considering he was a stock trader, he would have been into *Billions* more. I knew he had a crush on Meghan Markle. I joined him since it was his only time to enjoy television. He'd be in bed by 11 usually. He took care of his health so much. Since I was late tonight, there'd be no sex in the cards, which was fine with me. I wasn't in the mood anyway .

Sex with Matt was satisfactory, even thrilling at times — yet there remained room for improvement. Not that I found myself in a state of constant complaint. The early days of our physical exploration held more allure, much like the initial charm of a new restaurant before its novelty wears off. There were instances when our encounters felt rather monotonous, yet they blossomed into something more captivating whenever we opened up about our desires. It was like attending an Alcoholics Anonymous meeting, a strict reminder to maintain sobriety. However, these improvements were fleeting, and we'd soon find ourselves reverting back to our old routines. We both played our part in this dance of regression. We were both complicit in that. God, we sounded like we'd been married for decades. Was I not too young to harbor such thoughts? Or perhaps, was monotony creeping into my heart? Life is a series of peaks and valleys, and at this moment, I found myself traversing the valley.

But I was wrong. I was nestled in bed, clad in shorts and a white tank top, my eyes tracing the lines of a book. Matt entered the room, his body still humming from his workout. He was restless, pacing around the room before finally settling on the edge of the bed.

"DTF?" he asked. Another *down to fuck* night. Sigh. His voice was casual but tinged with eagerness. He could have been mistaken for a character from *Jersey Shore*, his playful demeanor masking his true intentions.

"Hmmm..." I responded with a non-committal eyebrow raise, my book acting as a shield, hiding my amused smile.

In response, he slowly pulled off his shirt, revealing his chiseled physique, still glistening from his workout. He had a habit of showcasing his body post-exercise, seemingly aware of its effect on me, just like a potent aphrodisiac. Perhaps I had encouraged this behavior, signaling appreciation for the care he took of his body. The truth, however? I detested it. Don't get me wrong — I enjoy the intimacy of sweat at the climax of passion, but not before sex. But, it was too late to express my disdain, so I smiled and responded as he expected, by drawing back the blanket to reveal my parted legs. A silent invitation, reluctant on my part, lingered heavily in the air between us.

Without another word, he was on top of me, his lips eagerly seeking mine. Our bodies ignited instantly. As his hands explored my body, my mind couldn't help but wander back to Heck. The thought of him added a layer of complexity to our usual routine. Our bodies met in a familiar dance. The rhythm held no surprises, but the memory of Heck added an unexpected undercurrent of excitement. It was an odd sensation, like reading a thrilling novel while sitting in your favorite, worn-out armchair. There was nothing sexual about my encounter with Heck, at least not yet. But his presence in my mind right now had stirred something within me, adding a dash of intrigue to an otherwise ordinary day.

As Matt and I lost ourselves in each other, our bodies moved in sync, each thrust amplifying the connection between us. His touch was familiar yet exhilarating, a comforting anchor in the sea of my thoughts. In the midst of our passion, we found ourselves in a new position. I was on my back, my right leg resting on his shoulder as he knelt beside me.

"Matt, I want you rough," I encouraged him to go harder, to push the boundaries of our routine.

"Get on four, Sara." Matt commanded as pulled himself from me.

I turned around and went on my knees, my elbows on the bed as he positioned himself behind me. This was unfamiliar territory for us, and the novelty added an edge to our intimacy. His pace quickened, his hands roaming freely over my body. This was more fucking than making love.

The intensity of the moment was too much for him, and he reached his climax before me. As I lay there, catching my breath, I couldn't help but reflect on our relationship. There were countless nights when I had to stare at the ceiling during or after sexual intercourse. I had to fake my orgasms to avoid hurting his ego. We were at the stage when we were comfortable, predictable even. But maybe, just maybe, there was room for a little adventure.

Then, as if summoned by my wandering thoughts, the image of Heck's piercing blue eyes invaded my consciousness once again. They held a promise of uncharted territory, a tantalizing hint of the unknown. There was an inherent thrill in them. These eyes did not see things as other people saw them. They offered a unique perspective that found deeper beauty, even in the most boring things — something I was not used to. As the silence of the night enveloped us, I found myself whispering into the darkness, a clandestine message carried on the wings of the night, "See you soon, Heck."

With that secret confession hanging in the air, I allowed myself to surrender to the soothing pull of sleep, my last conscious thought hopeful anticipation of what tomorrow might bring.

7

DREAM OF PARIS

———

(Sara)

Tossing and turning, I found myself trapped in an insomniac's ballet, while Matt snored away, oblivious to my internal turmoil. It was 3 in the morning. I had woken up in the dead of night with a dream of Heck. The evening's events replayed in my mind like a movie on a loop. Heck and I were at the café, our easy banter, the way we clicked. It all felt so... right. Just the thought of him made my heart beat faster, as confirmed by my reliable Apple Watch.

I remembered how he held my hand mid-debate, his grip firm yet gentle. An unexpected electricity surged through me. I trembled when he reached over to wipe that stray smudge of tomato sauce from my lip. What was that sensation? Was that fluttering in my stomach? Why did his touch ignite a spark I hadn't felt in so long? Whatever it was, I hoped he hadn't noticed. I wrestled with these questions deep into the night — rather, morning — and sleep eluded me. It's going to be a rough day.

The promise of sleep tugged at my heavy eyelids, reminding me of the mere three hours I had before work required my attention. Easing myself out of the warm embrace of the bed, I ventured into the dimly lit room in search of clothing to shield my naked body from the cool air.

Clothes were strewn about like fallen leaves, an indication of the whirlwind sex that had swept here earlier. A triumphant smile tugged at my lips as I spotted my shirt and panties lying innocently near my petite dresser. Slipping them on, I padded through the quiet apartment, cradling my laptop in my arms, and headed towards the sanctuary of my kitchen.

With the comforting hum of the fridge as my companion, I resolved to write. Booting up Spotify, my fingers danced across the keyboard, summoning the familiar notes of Death Cab for Cutie. A fleeting thought of Heck's music taste crossed my mind. Perhaps I should've asked for his Spotify account, but we had this unspoken agreement to steer clear of personal inquiries. His full name, his address, even his social media presence were mysteries yet to be unraveled.

He didn't strike me as a social media enthusiast, but his undeniable passion for music suggested he might have a Spotify account. I found myself typing 'Heck' into the search bar, only to be greeted by a sea of Hecks. Frustration nipping at my patience, I surrendered my search, opting to immerse myself in the band's melodious symphony instead. Plugging my Air Pods in, I let the soothing rhythm of "Marching Bands of Manhattan" wash over me.

As I began to write, my fingers flying over the keys, I realized the male protagonist taking shape was an uncanny reflection of Heck. His laugh, the way he'd casually brush his hair with his fingers, his mannerisms — they had all found their way into my narrative. A warm smile bloomed on my face as I allowed my emotions to bleed into the words.

When the first rays of dawn pierced through the veil of darkness, I'd crafted more than 7,000 words. As I shut my laptop with a satisfied sigh, I began my morning routine, hoping tonight would bring another encounter with Heck.

As I returned to the bedroom, Matt had already disappeared into the shower, the hum of running water signaling his morning rituals. I busied myself with smoothing out the creases in our bed, the act almost therapeutic in its simplicity. Emerging from the bathroom, Matt was a picture of corporate finesse, his crisp white shirt and black pants a stark contrast to Heck's laid-back style.

The shower was a welcome wake-up call, droplets of water cascading down my skin, washing away remnants of sleep. The morning brought with it a sense of eagerness. Dressing more carefully than usual, I slipped into my black sleeveless dress, its flowing skirt dancing around my knees. I attempted to apply makeup, but something held me back. Why should I dress up for Heck? He should see me as I truly am — no frills, no pretense — just Sara. I put my makeup back into the cosmetic box.

Once I deemed myself presentable, I gathered my bag, joining Matt who waited patiently in the living room. We shared a silent farewell, our paths diverging as we locked the door behind us.

As the elevator doors slid open, I was greeted by Charlie, cradling an armful of fresh pink roses. "Good morning, Matt! And you, my dear Sara," he crooned, rolling my name off his tongue with an extra dash of charm.

"Good morning, Charlie! Those are truly beautiful," I replied, smiling at his flowery embrace.

"Just like you," he retorted with a wink. Matt, however, remained aloof, barely acknowledging Charlie's greetings. As we spilled onto the street, Matt veered right, while I turned left, drawn by the familiar allure of Dunkin' at the corner. Armed with my coffee and muffin, I navigated the busy streets towards the subway, breakfast in hand and anticipation in my heart. The disparity between Matt's and my morning routines was strikingly obvious. And Charlie? Oh, he'd catch on. No missing it.

Work passed in a blur, my thoughts consumed by the prospect of seeing Heck again. I finished Kelly's pitch material. Worked with creatives for some pending ad campaigns. As the day drew to a close, I made my way to our favorite café, heart pounding. And there he was. Heck, in his usual attire — grey T-shirt and jeans, looking as casual and charming as ever.

Seeing him there, I felt a wave of relief wash over me. A sense of homecoming. It felt like I've been waiting for this moment for too long. But along with it came a pang of guilt. Was I being unfair to Matt? This seemed harmless; only two people in the world knew this was happening — three if you include Lily, our usual barista. But, I will not worry about that now. We'll cross that bridge when we get there. If we even get there. The chances of it happening were quite slim. I pushed the thought aside. Right now, all I wanted to do was lose myself in the depth of Heck's blue eyes and the warmth of his smile. I wanted to see where this goes.

"Ah, there you are," I greeted him, my eyes lighting up. Our table was a cozy breakfast decked with two plates. One was generously piled with fluffy pancakes and fresh berries, the other brimming with crispy bacon strips, toast slathered with jam, and sunny-side-up eggs. Typically, I disliked it when others make choices for me, or act prematurely on my behalf, but this time, I didn't mind.

In his casual charm, Heck said, "I ordered the usual, so take your pick." He smelled intriguingly of cologne and cigarettes. Usually, I detested cigarettes, but somehow, on Heck, it was an intoxicating mix. I didn't mind. With his relaxed demeanor, I probably would have let him get away with more.

"Can we just pick and mix from both?" I asked, already eyeing the pancakes.

He chuckled, a warm sound that echoed around our little bubble. "Of course. But I'd love to see those perfect triangle slices you make out of the pancakes," he replied, pushing the pancake plate toward me.

"Don't you find it weird," I mused, my knife sawing through a stack of pancakes, "how we've been dining on identical meals since we've met?" My eyes remained fixed on the task at hand, unfazed by his presence.

"Actually, I'm finding it rather enjoyable," he responded with an air of nonchalance. His gaze shifted, landing on an object nestled beside my bag. "You brought a book today."

"Ah, yes," I paused, extracting the well-worn tome from beneath my bag. It was dog-eared and vibrant with highlights and annotations. Placing it on the table, I declared, *"The Guernsey Literary and Potato Peel Pie Society* by Mary Ann Shaffer and Annie Barrows... an all-time favorite light read of mine."

"That's quite the tongue twister," he chuckled, reaching over to inspect the book.

"I know," I laughed in agreement, "Most people, including the publisher named Sidney in the novel, share that sentiment. But it's a gem. Go ahead, leaf through the pages," I suggested, gesturing towards the book.

Heck turned it over to the back cover and read aloud what was written there. "The protagonist is a writer named Juliet Ashton who receives correspondence from a stranger—a founding member of the Guernsey Literary and Potato Peel Pie Society. Set against the backdrop of 1946 on the island of Guernsey during German occupation, Juliet finds herself drawn into a captivating tale of the island and its extraordinary society."

With a thoughtful glance at him, I added, "You know, you'd make an excellent narrator," while deftly spearing a strawberry with my fork and cutting a slice of pancake.

In response, he gifted me with a boyish grin. He opened his mouth as if to say something, but then seemed to rethink his words.

"I'm actually acquainted with Guernsey, the island. I have a painting of a woman from there... in my bedroom," Heck paused, chuckling at my arched eyebrows. "It belonged to my great-grandfather. He met a woman from the island, and ever since, I've felt this unique connection to her and the place. Perhaps one day, I'll trace their roots and uncover their love story."

"That's fascinating, Heck," I said, genuinely impressed. Each meeting with him unfolded like a chapter in a book, revealing layers of his character that I hadn't seen before.

"It's something, isn't it?" He mused, thumbing through the pages.

"Ah, yeah. I love the fact that it's written entirely in letters... real correspondence. It evokes a longing for simpler times when everything felt more personal," I said wistfully.

"I know, Sara."

As we sat across from each other in the dimly lit café, the ambiance felt almost cinematic, just like a scene straight out of a film. I thought about us, our meetings that were no longer accidental. "One more chance encounter here, and we're practically just like Jesse and Celine, though in a café rather than meeting on a train," I mused aloud, the corners of my mouth lifting into a smile.

"*Before Sunrise*," he responded promptly, his voice carrying a hint of excitement.

Surprised, I leaned forward, my interest piqued. "You've seen that film, too?" I asked, excitement bubbling within me.

His eyebrows arched playfully as he corrected me, "You mean films?" He paused, then continued, "I have a particular fondness for *Before Sunset*. It captures the essence of life without the reckless abandon of youth."

Sadness crept over me as I thought back to the first film. "*Before Sunrise* has its own kind of magic, though. It's about allowing yourself to be foolish, to embrace the recklessness of youth," I said, my gaze drifting to a random carving on the wooden table beneath my fingers. "I've always dreamed of experiencing something like that — meeting someone on a train and deciding to spend an entire day together to do crazy things, just on a whim."

He seemed puzzled, almost frustrated, as he pondered the characters' actions. "I don't get it. They did almost everything a couple would do — shared adventures, opened up about their lives, and even had sex twice in a park. But it baffles me... they never bothered with the basics, like exchanging full names or phone numbers," he remarked, his tone laced with a blend of annoyance and bemusement.

"You're missing the whole point, Heck," I countered, locking eyes with him. "Both of them just want to experience an uncomplicated relationship... sort of something you remember when you grow old. That's the beauty of it — an uncomplicated bond, that one moment of adventure in a lifetime."

He nodded thoughtfully, then added, "Yet, they seemed to reconsider their stance at the last moment."

"Their decision to meet again after six months was fraught with tension," I admitted softly. "The uncertainty must have been agonizing for Jesse, especially when Celine didn't show up."

His expression turned serious, yet there was a glimmer of something else — hope, perhaps. "I wouldn't shy away from taking a chance, not unlike what I did today by hoping to see you again," he confessed.

Laughter escaped me, light and carefree. "First off, I'm not going to sleep with you in Central Park," I joked, then grew more serious. "And we won't exchange numbers or full names."

He chuckled at that, the sound warm in the quiet café. "So, we'll leave it to fate? If one of us happens to be here?"

"Yes! That's what makes it magical, Heck."

A comfortable silence fell between us, filled with unspoken possibilities. "We'll talk until we run out of things to say," he proposed, his voice soft yet determined.

"That could take quite a while... Did you know Ethan Hawke and Julie Delpy contributed to the screenplays for the second and third films?" I shared, eager to continue our connection through shared interests.

"I did," he replied, his tone tinged with a hint of sadness. "But *Before Midnight* struck a different chord with me — it felt somewhat depressing."

"It's more grounded in reality, dealing with the complexities of midlife," I mused. "I'm not sure I'm ready to confront that level of conflict just yet."

That night, Heck and I journeyed through conversations that spanned across our Spotify playlists, favorite books, and unforgettable movies. Then, Heck threw a curveball. "If you could reboot your life, do one thing differently, what would it be?"

His question caught me off guard. I looked down at my food, avoiding his gaze. He gently tilted my chin upwards, forcing me to look into his eyes. His touch was soft, yet firm. I cleared my throat. "I would pack my bags, leave New York, and move to Paris. Live in an attic because I can't afford to stay in a hotel like Gil Pender in *Midnight in Paris*. Write in sidewalk cafés. Find my own Gertrude Stein. Just me, alone in that beautiful city."

His eyes sparkled with curiosity. "Why don't you? You're young and talented. You don't need much right now, except for pen and paper to do your thing. Go out, see the world," he encouraged.

"It's not as simple as that, Heck. My life is... complicated," I admitted.

"Then uncomplicate it, Sara, while it's still a choice," he said, not breaking eye contact.

I decided to return his question. "What about you?"

He sighed, a shadow crossing his face. "I don't know. I just put a ring on my girl's finger a few months ago. Am I ready? I honestly don't know." My heart sank at his confession. He was engaged! On the other hand, he didn't exactly hide his own uncertainty.

"Do you love her enough to marry her?" I asked, hoping for an answer I wanted to hear, not one that would shatter me.

"I think so. Maybe." His gaze shifted past my shoulder, as if trying to find an answer in the distance.

His eyes, a momentary mirror of confusion, shifted their focus back onto me, the topic of conversation swerving with liveliness. "Sara, seriously, pursue your dreams. Paris isn't a world away. You'll find a sense of belonging, settled in those Parisian cafés, crafting stories during the day. And when night falls, watch as they morph into lively pubs, brimming with laughter and more fun!"

"You seem to hold an intimate knowledge of Paris," I observed, curiosity piquing.

"It's a favored vacation destination in my family," he replied, his tone devoid of any sentiment.

"And what about the rain?" I probed further.

"Ah, you'll find Paris transforms on rainy days," he said, his eyes twinkling with a hint of nostalgia. "The city becomes a magical wonderland. The raindrops tap-dancing on cobblestone streets, the gleaming wet rooftops reflecting the diffused glow of the city lights, the scent of petrichor mingling with the aroma of freshly baked croissants - it's enchanting. Even the Eiffel Tower seems to stand taller, piercing the rain clouds, a beacon of hope in the soft grey skyline."

As he painted this vivid image, I could almost hear the rhythm of the rain against the window panes, feel the cool mist against my skin. It felt like an adventure waiting to unfold, a chapter begging to be written. His words had breathed life into Paris, and suddenly, my dream didn't seem too far away.

"You know, Heck, it's only just dawned on me that *Midnight in Paris* isn't really a romance. I mean, does Gil truly love Adrianna? He might be fond of her, sure, but love?" I mused, my fingers tracing the contours of the cup in my hands as if it were a sculptor's masterpiece.

"No, his heart belongs to Paris and the art of writing. He's even prepared to forsake his thriving Hollywood screenwriting career, you know, the one that lines his pockets quite nicely," Heck countered, reaching across to ensnare my hand in a playful bout of thumb wrestling, a game we'd devised for moments of deep discussion like these.

"Would you do it, Heck?" I asked, curiosity piquing.

"Do what exactly? Abandon a lucrative job to chase a dream?" His brow furrowed in thought. "Perhaps, but my situation differs from Gil's."

He paused our thumb wrestling match to hold my hands gently yet firmly. "So, are you afraid to relinquish a job that ensures financial stability to pursue a venture with an uncertain outcome?" he probed further.

"I am, Heck," I admitted, meeting his gaze. His smile offered reassurance in its simple existence.

"Sara, listen to me. You're young, and that means you have the privilege to make mistakes. That's the beauty of youth. And you have all the time in the world to correct them. You'll never know if something will work unless you take the risk. Give it a shot," he said.

That's what I love about Heck. He always knew the right words to soothe my doubts, to pacify my fears and sweep away my worries, enabling me to press forward.

Throughout our exchange, an unspoken agreement hung in the air between us. Neither of us reached for the comforting distraction of our phones. Instead, we were content to simply exist within the confines of this shared moment, reveling in the unfiltered connection that a face-to-face conversation offers.

The café around us hummed with life as the aroma of freshly ground coffee beans swirled through the air, intertwining with the faint scent of worn leather from the booth we occupied. The low murmur of nearby conversations served as a gentle soundtrack, punctuating the pauses in our own dialogue and filling the room with a symphony of human connection.

As the evening slipped away, our conversation began to wind down, our words growing sparse but no less significant. The impending conclusion of our night together hung over us like an uninvited guest, casting an inescapable shadow.

Finally, it was time to step out into the cool night air. We emerged from the warm cocoon of the café, trading its comforting embrace for the crisp chill of the night. As we stood at the door, almost under the soft glow of the streetlights, I turned to him, my heart heavy with a mix of satisfaction and longing.

"'Night, Heck," I said, my voice barely above a whisper, as if speaking any louder would shatter the delicate bubble of our shared experience.

Heck, with his hands nonchalantly tucked into his jeans pockets and his eyes reflecting the moonlight which was now peeking through the tall buildings, mirrored my sentiment. "Gnight, Sara," he replied softly, his voice carrying a hint of reluctance, echoing the unspoken wish that the night could have stretched on just a little bit longer.

In that moment, under the glow of the café lights, our goodbye felt less like an end and more like a pause — an ellipsis rather than a period, looking forward to more shared moments and conversations yet to unfold.

8

FINALLY, SUNSET.

(Heck)

The last thing I wanted was for that day to end. My brain was still buzzing.

Sunday. Me and my girl, lunch with her fam. So there we were, me and Sophie, pulling up to the Sullivans' place in Queens. It was one of those homes that just screamed 'curated.' Like every brick, every blade of grass, had been placed with purpose. And, man, their backyard. It was like a piece of Eden right in the middle of the city. The day was bright, too bright for someone nursing a semi-hungover.

Peter Sullivan, Sophie's old man, was standing there, a glass of wine in hand, looking like he'd stepped straight out of a Ralph Lauren Fall ad. The afternoon sun dappled through the leaves overhead, casting a golden glow on everything. It felt like walking into a painting, only this one had a soundtrack of distant city sounds and the occasional bird call.

"Good to see you, Heck," Peter greeted warmly, his voice as smooth and rich as the Merlot he held out towards me. I took the glass, indulging in a sip of the fine wine. Internally, I found myself longing for the refreshing simplicity of a chilled beer. However, I knew better than to expect such a beverage in the Sullivan household. Beers were

85

considered crude, beneath their refined palate. The Sullivans had a predilection for presenting their best side, particularly during my visits.

Sophie, the youngest Sullivan, threw her arms around her old man and planted kisses on both his cheeks.

"Missed your baby girl, Daddy?" she asked, all smiles and sparkling eyes.

"Always!" He responded with a hearty chuckle. At 55, Peter was still in prime shape, remarkably fit, proof of a life dedicated to physical wellness. The entire Sullivan clan were fitness enthusiasts. Health buffs who had nothing else to do whenever the markets were closed. Peter's salt-and-pepper hair added a touch of maturity and sophistication to his appearance.

The aroma wafting from the kitchen lured me in. Jennifer, Sophie's mom, was directing the housekeeper and cook. Her face lit up when she saw me. "My dear Heck! How are you?" She kissed both my cheeks. The Sullivans were all about making me happy. After all, they saw me as their ticket to saving their shaky business empire. Good luck with that.

Jennifer, just like Sophie, was slim and looked a decade younger, thanks to expensive skincare, sauna sessions... and maybe a nip and tuck here and there.

Peter cornered me back to the garden, the 'talk' looming in the air. And, as expected, he brought up the prenup.

I sighed internally. I knew this was coming. Why couldn't we just chill, enjoy the wine, and the pretty garden?

"Yeah, Peter," I replied, straining to keep my voice steady. "It's a family thing, you know? We all do it."

Peter shook his head, his gaze serious. "Heck, you don't need to do this. You and Sophie..."

I tuned him out. Irritation bubbled within me, but more than that, I was exhausted. Tired of defending myself, my family, our ways. I could feel his scrutinizing gaze on me. He was probing, trying to figure out how to get his way. That was the stark difference between him and my old man. This man needed to devise a plan to get things done. He was a worker and a thinker. Undeniably brilliant in his own way, but he had to work for it. My father, on the other hand, did not share these traits. He simply acted on his impulses. He didn't have to think things through. With the boatloads of cash he paid on retainers, he left it to his lawyers to manage any fallout or even deal with the consequences. Such were the privileges of wealth. Peter wanted that, but he wasn't getting it from me.

"Peter," I cut him off, my tone sharper than I had intended. "This isn't up to me. And as far as my family is concerned, this isn't up for discussion. It's completely non-negotiable."

"All I want is a fair deal for my daughter, Heck. She's the finest match you could hope for and would be a stellar addition to your lineage. A veritable trophy wife for you," Peter pressed on, clinging to his dwindling hope of overturning the prenuptial agreement. As someone who was willing to do anything to further in life, he got my respect. However, as a father, his actions today, were utterly disgraceful.

"Reconsideration isn't on the cards, Peter. Even my mother signed a prenup when she married my father. Sophie will not be an exception," I asserted.

Peter heaved a deep sigh, a reluctant admission of defeat. However, he was quick to rebound, steering the conversation towards another pecuniary matter. "Heck, I have a business proposal that might interest you or your father. Would it be possible to arrange a meeting?" Damn. Incredible! This man didn't miss a beat. He wouldn't let any opportunity pass him by.

"I'll see what I can do," I responded, eager to bring the uncomfortable discussion to a close. But I knew that broaching the subject of business with the Sullivans to my father would result to a resounding 'no', quicker than a bullet train.

Just like that, the beautiful backyard lost its charm. The wine lost its smoothness. And me? I was just a guy, trapped between the woman I was about to marry and the crumbling empire she was desperate to save. Damn, adulting's complicated.

The lunch, however, was top-notch. The Sullivans certainly knew how to host an impressive spread. Jennifer's outdone herself, no surprise there. The table? A masterpiece. Like, if Michelangelo did food instead of ceilings. First up, there was this chicken like it had been marinated overnight. Herbs clinging to it like they were hanging on for dear life. Juiciness overload. Flavor explosion. Then, there was the roast potatoes. Golden, crispy on the outside, soft as clouds inside. Salt and rosemary doing a tango on my taste buds. Couldn't help but go back for more.

Oh, and couldn't forget the greens. Steamed to perfection. Bright, vibrant. Tossed in this light dressing that's got a hint of garlic, a whisper of mustard. Made eating your veggies feel like a treat, not a chore. Now, the wine. Peter brought out this red. Bold, but not too in-your-face. It was like it was made to marry with the chicken. Sips between bites and conversation. I was listening, nodding along, totally engrossed.

Dessert's on the horizon, but I was already content. Full, but in that perfect way. Where you were satisfied, but you could maybe, just maybe, find room for a little something sweet.

Jennifer caught my eye, with a knowing smile. "How's the food, Heck?" she asked.

I could only grin, words kind of failing me. "It's... amazing. Really. My compliments, Jennifer. This is truly exquisite," I acknowledged. I wasn't lying. She knew her way around her kitchen.

"I'm delighted you're enjoying it, Heck. I've been telling Sophie she should start learning some culinary basics," Jennifer remarked, casting a pointed look at her daughter.

"Mom, that's hardly necessary. Heck and I will hire a full-time housekeeper and a cook post-wedding," Sophie retorted, rolling her eyes at her mother's traditional views. Expectations.

"But, darling, there's something special about doing it yourself. After all, the best way to a man's heart is through his stomach," Jennifer gently chided her daughter.

"Your mother has a point, Sophie. Look at how well she's taken care of me over the years," Peter chimed in.

The scene unfolding before me resembled a sitcom, complete with rehearsed lines and familial dynamics, with me as the sole audience member. This reminded me of *Everybody Loves Raymond* crossed with *The Royals*. The entire act was beginning to grate on my nerves. All I craved at this juncture was the comforting ritual of a post-meal smoke. However, the Sullivan family had a strict rule: no smoking within the confines of their home. Seeing that was an odd experience. Felt like the future was tapping on my shoulder. Whispering, "Heads up." Showing me this sneak peek. Married life, huh? All its twists and turns, the what-ifs lurking around corners. "Strap in, buddy. Ain't gonna be just smooth roads ahead." Saw my future flash before me... but nah, too boxed in. More like me, forcibly domesticated, tamed or kinda pushed into playing house in a house I might not want to be in.

I went back to the backyard. I was supposed to be enjoying this day with my future in-laws. But I was elsewhere, y'know? My mind was wandering, drifting back to Sara. Brinner at the café, week after week. So many words spilled across those tables, never running dry. It was also never about nothing. Man, I wanted to be back there. If time travel wasn't just sci-fi nonsense, you bet I'd be zapping back to that moment on repeat. Just soaking it all in, again and again, not changing a damn thing. Maybe stretch it out a bit. And here I am, wandering off down memory lane... again.

I got a wink from my girl. A reminder of where I was supposed to be. What I was supposed to feel. This lunch was taking longer than usual. Or was it only in my head? I have to squash this thing brewing for Sara. I couldn't let it grow.

End this madness, Heck, I told myself. Might be too late, fucker. This is your life now. Deal with it.

But every time I tried, it was like halting a river with your bare hands. Impossible. And, damn, do I love watching that Sunday sun dip below the horizon. It was finally sunset. A new day coming, like Stone Temple Pilots' Scott Weiland song, "Days of the Week". Finally.

———

Monday rolled around. Work was a blur. I was there, but not really, you know? Like autopilot or something. My head was off in its own world, somewhere, just itching to hit the café, see Sara...

Work, just a fuzzy backdrop to the eagerness to see her. The minute hand finally hit six, and I was outta there, like a bolt of lightning slicing through the sky, making tracks for our café. That cozy little corner in the city that felt like home to me.

Our usual spot, that corner table with a view of the bustling street was waiting, empty. I dropped into the chair, its familiarity wrapping around me like a warm hug. Lily, our barista and part-time matchmaker, caught my eye. She gave me a smile that said, "I gotcha," before spinning around to whip up our usual. Brinner. A crazy idea born from late-night chats and shared grins.

Lily came back, the smell of bacon and pancakes wafting off the plate, my double espresso with soy milk steaming gently beside it. "She's not here yet?" she asked, a note of surprise in her voice.

"Work stuff, probably," I shrugged, trying to sound cool about it.

"Enjoy your meal," Lily winked, leaving me to my thoughts and my notes. Last night, inspired by Sara, I'd turned into some kinda poet. I shook off the sudden feeling of being exposed, plugged in my AirPods, and hit play on "Last Nite"' by The Strokes. Each song in the playlist was a tribute to Sara, her hazel doe-eyes, and the strange fluttering in my chest. It was a fun one. Even silly and kinda goofy.

Every now and then, my gaze would dart to the door, hoping to see Sara walk in. But she didn't. Her usual punctuality had taken a hit today. Probably work, I told myself again, trying to ignore the unease creeping in. As I sipped on my now-cold coffee, I watched the early exit of autumn outside the window. Winter was coming.

Three months of these café meetings, and all we knew about each other was what we shared here. Past? Who knows? Future? Who cares. It was all noise. But the here and now? We knew what we had and felt complete. That was golden rule. Felt like we got the whole world figured out. Just knowing the other's there, breathing the same air. Living in the moment. That's the ticket. Or, at least, it used to be.

The clock ticked past 9 p.m. No Sara. I began to worry. The empty chair across from me felt like a taunt. Hours passed, and still no Sara. We never swapped digits, addresses, or even last names. Kinda felt like we were tryin' to go old school. Like those before us, with no fancy social media accounts or nothin'. Not even a dang email. It has always been just Heck and Sara, lost in our own little world within the café. Damn that stupid unspoken rule. I realized I didn't know anything about her outside of these four walls.

I was worried, but what could I do? She was a ghost outside of the café…

Midnight. I have to call it a night. A sick feeling lodged itself in my stomach. Had I scared her off? Did it get weird? I hope not. I got up, pulled on my coat, and stepped out into the chilly night. As I left the café, I found myself whispering into the empty street, "Gnight, Sara."

9

CHASE YOUR DREAM. FLY TO PARIS.

(Sara)

The harsh glare of the office lights dimmed behind me, giving way to creeping shadows that seemed eager to pull me back into the monotonous humdrum of work. But tonight promised a different rhythm — an intoxicating blend of anticipation and mystery. My sanctuary, the café, awaited me. And with it, the intriguing, elusive Heck. It wasn't a date, just a regular meeting — or so I told myself as I smoothed my crisp, cotton-white T-shirt underneath my fitted navy blue blazer.

A smile played on my lips, a feeling of eagerness bubbling within me. It was a sensation I hadn't felt in a while; this thrill of meeting someone was new. Just as I was about to step out of my cubicle, surrendering to the promise of the night, my phone rang.

It was Matt. His voice, normally steady, rang out like a gavel's strike in a quiet courtroom. "I hope you're on your way home. I've already ordered our dinner," he commanded. His words felt like chains, pulling me back from the tantalizing brink of freedom.

"Matt, I need to write tonight in my usual place," I protested. My mind scrambled for excuses, but they fell flat against his unyielding resolve. Heck was waiting, but I had no means to reach him. The decision loomed over me, heavy like rain-laden clouds threatening to rupture.

Eventually, I chose the path of least resistance — a quick dinner with Matt, then a stealthy escape to the café. I hoped that the night would still hold some of its magic when I finally got there.

The moment I stepped through our front door, a tidal wave of sensory overload swept over me. The strong aroma of soy sauce and stir-fried vegetables swirled in the air, wrapping around me like an unwelcome shroud. My gaze settled on the Chinese takeout containers littered across our dining table, their greasy contents in unruly heaps.

A pang of disappointment tugged at my heartstrings. This was not how I envisioned my evening. Eating out of these impersonal boxes was one of my pet peeves, a quirk Matt knew all too well. Yet, here we were, drowning in a sea of cardboard and MSG.

"Matt," I began, my voice barely above a whisper, as I poked aimlessly at the tangled nest of noodles with my chopsticks. "You know how much I detest eating out of these boxes."

His reaction was a mere shrug, a nonchalant dismissal that felt like a slap. His eyes never left his food, an invisible barrier of unspoken tension erected itself between us.

Feeling the weight of the silence, I decided to venture into forbidden territory. Paris — a topic Matt hated. It was a gamble, a desperate attempt to pry open the oyster of our conversation and find a pearl within.

"Can we go to Paris?" I asked, my voice laced with a cocktail of longing and nervousness. The question hung in the air, waiting to spark a wildfire of repressed conflicts. "I think… I want to go to Paris."

His eyes narrowed, irritation creasing his forehead. It was a disruption, an unwanted noise in his meticulously planned symphony of life.

"I'm going alone if you won't come," I asserted, my voice a thin veneer of calm over a sea of turmoil.

His response was swift and unyielding. "No." The word hung in the air between us, sharp and cold as a whip's crack.

I tried to reason with him, to make him understand the urgency that was clawing at my soul. "Matt, it has been ages since I've had a break. I need this trip for my writing," I pleaded, hoping to find a shred of empathy in his steely gaze.

But he simply put down his chopsticks, their clatter against the ceramic plate a jarring punctuation to his next words. "That dream of writing is a waste of your time, Sara," he said, his eyes locked onto mine across the table. "We both know you will never be a writer. Why don't you just focus on your job? Who knows, you may even get promoted someday."

His words ignited a spark within me, a simmering anger that threatened to erupt. "How dare you, Matt! This is my dream, and I won't let you belittle it," I retorted, my voice wavering on the edge of breaking. I felt the familiar sting of tears threatening to spill, but I held them back. I didn't want him to see me crumble, not now.

"The fuck, Sara! I can't handle any more of your drama!"

Hearing those words, I was taken aback. My fight was about more than a mere holiday; it was a crusade for my dreams, my ambitions, my essence. "This isn't just about Paris, Matt! It's about the freedom to chase my passion, to write, to weave stories out of thin air. It's about proving I am more than this, and more importantly to myself, that I'm more than just an office drone, destined for promotions and pay hikes. I'm a writer, a creator of worlds, and I won't let anyone, not even you, tell me otherwise!"

Our conversation swiftly escalated into a heated argument when Matt retorted, "Do you think you're good? That you're going to make it as one of those writers who could publish their work? You aren't, Sara. You're not extraordinary. You can't even decide for yourself. I really have to tell you what to do with your life."

I couldn't believe I was hearing these harsh words hurled like lethal daggers in the enveloping darkness. Each painful word, whether they're true or not was like inflicting a wound deeper than the last.

I stood up from the table, ready to flee from the battlefield, but he clutched my arm. He spun me around and seized my face with excessive force. I felt his fingers pressing into my bones.

His hold on me grew even firmer, his eyes ablaze with an infernal fire I had never seen before. "Fuck, Sara! I refuse to be dismissed like this," he spat out, each word dripping with venomous intent. Then, without warning, he forcefully pushed me away. My inherent clumsiness failed me and I found myself staggering towards the wall. The world spun around me as I collided with the hard surface, a sharp pain radiating from my cheek in intense waves.

"Don't you dare walk out on me like that, ever again!" His voice rang out, bitter and chilling, reverberating in the hollow silence. He showed no concern for my wellbeing, focusing solely on his bruised ego. It was clear that Matt's pride mattered more to him than anything else.

There was no hint of remorse in his words, only a venomous sting that pierced my heart. Retreating to the sanctuary of the bedroom, I slammed the door behind me, the sound echoing my inner turmoil. Alone in the dim light, sobs wracked my body, tears soaking the pillowcase in a silent testament to my pain. It was then that I knew it was over. Something inside me died. I didn't know what it was. I knew I was ready to sever it. This time I knew for sure.

The moonlight, usually a soothing balm, now cast an eerie glow on my solitude, transforming the room into a stage for my unraveling. I could taste the saltiness of my tears, feel the burning imprint of his fingers on my cheek, and hear the echo of Matt's harsh words. It was a mix of pain and regret, playing out in the hushed stillness of the night.

A deep sorrow washed over me, not just for the argument, but for myself — for the girl who once yearned for adventure and instead found herself confined within a cage of hurtful words and painful actions. The taste of my dreams turned bitter, and the echoes of my aspirations were drowned by the harshness of our conflict. I lay there, swallowed by the night, a captive of my own heart's longing for freedom and the harsh reality of my situation.

―――――――

Awakening to the savage throb of a splitting headache, I squinted at the digital clock on the bedside table. It was 8 a.m. Matt had already left for work, his side of the bed untouched, proof of the tumultuous events of last night. He had chosen the couch, leaving me alone with my thoughts. My tardiness for work was the least of my concerns.

Dragging myself to the bathroom, I confronted my reflection in the mirror. The girl who stared back at me was a stranger, her eyes shadowed with sadness and ringed with a bruise that bloomed like a sinister flower across her upper left cheek. A solemn promise hung in the heavy silence: never again would I let a man mar me this way. With one last, lingering look at the unfamiliar face in the mirror, I stepped into the shower.

The icy water was a balm, soothing the raw ache that clung to my skin. Once dry, I carefully selected my outfit for the day — not just clothes, but a shield against the world. Applying makeup with meticulous care, I painted over the bruise. No one should see it. I didn't need anyone's pity.

The day passed in a blur, hours slipping away unnoticed amidst the mundane humdrum of work. My AirPods firmly lodged in my ears served as an unspoken 'Do Not Disturb' sign, warding off any potential conversation. Even Kelly, my usually inquisitive boss, maintained a respectful distance. As soon as the clock struck 6 p.m., I rose from my cubicle, eager to escape before prying eyes noticed my hasty retreat, and sought solace in my sanctuary.

―――――――

The night was a frozen montage, the bits and pieces of autumn's rain turning the air into an icy chill. There was something about the rain that always got me. It was like nature's own playlist, a symphony of pitter-patter against the pavement, a melody that spoke directly to my soul. Last night, it played on a relentless loop, a torrential downpour that echoed the storm brewing inside me. I missed our usual spot at the café. I had to deal with Matt and our 'complications.'

Today, the sky wept again, a steady drizzle that had been going on since dawn. Armed with my trusty umbrella and clad in my long green coat over a powder blue T-shirt and jeans, I braved the gloomy weather. Each step towards the café felt like a step towards clarity, a chance to untangle the knot of emotions within me.

The moment I pushed open the café door, the aroma of freshly brewed coffee wrapped around me like an old friend. Ah, the scent of possibility! I scanned the room, my heart skipping a beat as my gaze landed on our spot. And there he was — Heck. His smile was like the sun peeking through storm clouds, a ray of warmth in the cold drizzle outside.

"Hey, stranger," he greeted, the corners of his eyes crinkling with his smile. I couldn't help but return it, my worries momentarily forgotten.

"Hey yourself," I replied, shaking off my coat and settling into the seat across from him. Our little corner of the world felt right again. The rain outside might have been relentless, but inside the café, with Heck's comforting presence, I found my safe harbor.

Just like usual, we didn't ask how our days were. He didn't ask why I didn't show up last night. We simply went to where we left off, talking about anything.

"Hey, Heck, tell me, are there other things that you love to do apart from art restoring and writing poetry?" I asked, eager to hear his voice

97

and distract myself from my messed-up life.

He glanced outside the window, searching his memories. Then, turning his attention back to me, he gently placed his hand on the table and softly circled his thumbs over mine. "I restored a car from scratch when I was 15," he said with a smile.

"Really?" I couldn't hide my excitement as I longed to learn more about the younger Heck.

"Yes. Have you ever watched Cameron Crowe's *Vanilla Sky*? It stars Tom Cruise," he inquired.

"The most quotable quotes film I've ever seen" I blurted out, quoting a line from the movie.

"Aren't you curious about my nickname?" he teased.

"I don't have to ask, Citizen Dildo," I retorted, playing along as we quoted dialogues from the movie during our conversation.

"That film is one of my favorites," he admitted, smiling warmly. "It's such a mind-blowing experience. I saw it in the theater when they brought it back for a special screening after many years. Stepping outside into the vast, bright blue sky afterward, I was stunned and overwhelmed. The film's only flaw was casting Jason Lee as an intellectual who couldn't pronounce 'intellectual' correctly. It completely blew me away. I went in blind, having seen everything else Crowe had done up to that point, and it was nothing like any of them. Note that he directed *Jerry Maguire* and two other films before, then *Almost Famous*. Conceptually, it was a giant leap."

"I fell in love with the soundtrack, Heck!" I exclaimed excitedly.

"Who hasn't? Radiohead, Todd Rundgren," he replied, then began to hum "Can We Still Be Friends?"—my favorite song from the list. I let him continue until he became aware of himself and chuckled.

"I love Jeff Buckly's 'Last Goodbye'! It's totally epic!"

"It's not just the soundtracks you love, Sara, but the storyline, and the yeah the quotable quotes, too," he observed, his intense gaze nearly making me melt. "I can't blame you. Those stayed with me," he paused, looking at our hands.

We fell silent. Then, he asked, "He lost her when he got in that car, right?"

"Seriously?" I asked, finally making the connection between the movie and his passion for restoration. "That must have been the start of 'Heck the Restorer!'"

"Possibly. It took me years, but it was all worth it. I'll tell you more about it, or better yet, maybe I'll show you..." His voice trailed off, perhaps hesitant to make a promise. Our relationship is still at the stage where we're on a first-name basis, without much personal background shared.

Once again, we were silent, lost in our thoughts. The topic of car restoration was completely forgotten.

The warmth of Heck's gaze returned to me, his blue eyes as deep and mysterious as the night sky, softly illuminated by the overhead lamps. They held a familiarity, a sense of belonging that made this corner of the café feel like home. Months of shared laughter and dreams had gradually transformed our friendship into something more, something I couldn't quite put into words. A longing stirred within me, a yearning to feel his lips on mine, to melt into his embrace, to find solace in his arms from the relentless loneliness.

"Sara?" His voice, soft yet firm, snapped me back to reality.

I managed a smile, pushing my unspoken desires aside. "Do you remember the first time you had sex, Heck?" I asked, a playful grin tugging at my lips as I speared a piece of pancake with my fork. Damn, where did that question come from! I almost choked on my buttered pancake. Were we even at that level of intimacy? My inner voice chided me, *In your dreams, Sara. You wish.*

Heck, unfazed by my sudden question, chuckled warmly. "Ah, sure, my first time? You mean the grand spectacle of high school, complete with the fireworks and the awkward fumbling?" His eyes sparkled with amusement, clearly enjoying the trip down memory lane. "I was a freshman, with a girl five years my senior. She was stunning. I attended a boarding school, and we boys would venture out to meet some English roses," he reminisced, chuckling at the somewhat absurd memory. "We did it in the field concealed behind a massive tree trunk. Oh, man! That's a tale for the ages. How about you, Sara? Did you see your own fireworks show back then?"

"Oh no! Please don't laugh," I responded, wanting to hide my face from embarrassment. "My first time wasn't until halfway through university. He was a teammate from my swim team. Alas, there were no fireworks. Rather pathetically, I was staring at the ceiling the whole time, hoping it would be over instantly," I said. I almost added that I still stared at the ceiling most of the time.

We laughed, our shared stories weaving an invisible thread between us. But then, his laughter faded as he noticed something off about me. His gaze focused on a spot just below my left eye, a spot I had painstakingly concealed with makeup. I should've touched up before I came here but I had been in a rush.

"Hey, what's that, Sara?" he asked, angled his head to get a better look. His voice sounded concerned, alarmed, and urgent all at once.

I turned my face away, hoping to dodge his stare. But Heck was persistent. He gently held my chin, turning my face back towards him. His expression changed when he saw the purplish bruise hidden under my concealer.

His fingers ran through his hair, a sign of distress I had come to recognize. His eyes were stormy, a mix of concern and anger. "Who did this to you, Sara?" he demanded, his voice a harsh whisper. It was the most intense expression I had ever seen on his face. His normally boyish and handsome features were transformed into something far more frightening, a visage ready to commit murder at that very moment.

I tried to avoid his gaze, but the pain in my eyes betrayed me. Tears welled up, then cascaded down my cheeks, blurring my vision as I murmured, "Please, Heck."

Heck let go of my face, his hand falling onto the table with a thud. His fingers curled into a tight fist. He looked at me, his blue eyes filled with sorrow, reflecting the pain I harbored within me. "I'm so sorry, Sara," he uttered, his voice choked with emotion. He was offering an apology for a misdeed he hadn't committed, as if his words could somehow alleviate the agony I was experiencing.

The dam broke, and tears streamed down my face. I had managed to hold it together until now, but Heck's empathy was too much. I sobbed, my body shaking with the weight of my pain. Heck reached across the table, holding my hands in his. We sat there for a while, lost in our shared sorrow, the laughter of our earlier conversation a distant memory.

Heck broke the silence, his voice a soft whisper that barely cut through my sobs. "Promise me something, Sara," he implored.

I sniffled, trying to regain some semblance of control over my emotions. "What is it?" I managed to croak out, my voice raspy and strained. I withdrew my hand from his firm grasp, hastily wiping away my tears with the back of my hand. Heck, ever the gentleman, reached out to gently brush away the remaining tear stains with his thumbs.

"Chase after your dream. Board a flight to Paris, find a home in a quirky attic," he whispered, gently tilting my face so that our eyes met. "Write until your fingers cramp from the exertion, and dance freely under the rain," he urged me further. As I looked into his eyes, they were pools of sadness, reflecting my own torment. I nodded, my heart aching with the earnestness in his words. He released my face, only to seize my hands with a firm grip, a silent vow of unwavering support.

We remained like that, two silent silhouettes in the dimly lit café, seemingly worlds apart yet bound in our shared emotion. It was the deepest connection we had forged in the many months we'd been meeting.

There was an uncanny parallel between the rain outside and the tumult within. As the heavens wept, I found myself yearning for the simplicity of our café meetings, the shared smiles, the comfortable silence, the unspoken bond. But life isn't a straight road; it's a maze of unexpected turns and dead ends.

The café lights flickered, signaling closing time.

"'Night, Heck," I murmured, standing up reluctantly.

"Gnight, Sara," he replied, his voice carrying a hint of sadness. Our goodbyes hung in the air as I stepped out into the night, leaving behind the warmth of the café and the comfort of Heck's presence.

10

FULL LOOP

(Heck)

And so I found myself once more running aimlessly. Central Park. Just me, my winter running shoes, and the 6.03-mile Full Loop that wraps around the whole park like a big ol' hug. On a normal day, it was a favored route among joggers, offering a comprehensive experience of the park's beauty. But not today.

Nah, today, the park resembled a giant scoop of vanilla ice cream, all white and frosty. Winter had rolled in, and trust me, it showed absolutely no regard for my top-of-the-line winter gear. This was hardly the setting I would typically choose for my regular cardiovascular exercise, but I needed a distraction... My anger was reaching boiling point.

I was mad as hell!

As a rule, my runs were more... therapeutic. In springtime and summertime, the park was a riot of life. Imagine a patchwork quilt of greens in the heart of a concrete beast. Birds doing their thing, squirrels running wild, and the city's relentless pulse just a murmur in the backdrop. It was my daily sanity pill... this run. Just me, the rhythm of my breath, and the open road.

But today? It felt more like a punishment. Like I was running away from something, or maybe towards it. As I jogged, my mind wasn't on the icy patches or the biting cold. Nah, my mind was wandering, getting itself tangled up just like those bare branches above. Mad as hell, for reasons I couldn't quite pin down.. Never got this worked up before, not even when stuff got personal.

And her? She's not even my girlfriend, not someone close. For Pete's sake, she's practically a stranger! Don't even know her last name... just Sara. Yet here I was, fury surging within me, pushing my pace faster than usual. 'Cause sometimes, when anger hits, running's all you've got.

Sara. The way she tried to hide that bruise under layers of makeup, like she could conceal the hurt. The anger bubbled up inside me, hot and raw. I could still picture her face, trying to smile through the pain, her eyes not meeting mine.

She didn't deserve that. No one did.

Each stride I took, each breath I drew, fueled the raw fire of my anger. My heart pounded in my chest, not from the exertion, but from the rage. I could feel it, a livewire of emotion coursing through my veins.

Who did this to her? Why? These questions, man, they were buzzing in my brain like some pissed-off hornets. I wanted answers. Hell, I needed answers. But who was I kidding? The answers weren't necessary. It was easy to figure out who did it. I didn't need to know the reason and motive behind it. There wasn't a reason in the world that would have made it okay. But more than all that, no man should lay a hand on her. God, I needed to shield her. Wipe away her pain. Make sure no one ever laid a finger on her again.

Didn't really care about the whys or hows. Everything just kinda turned this angry red for me. Like a big ol' "Danger" sign flashing in my brain. Logic? Tossed it out the window. Didn't matter what went down, what she said, or if she was asking for it. All that mattered was what that guy did. Did he even get it? That he was stealing bits of her spark? She was all about living large, dreaming big. Not afraid to stumble or fall. A girl with guts to pack up, move to Paris, chase her dream of writing. And here's this jerk, trying to snuff out the light that makes Sara, well, Sara.

Now, all I've got bubbling up inside is this rage. This primal urge to smash someone's face in.

I wanted to hurt him. Pummel him into the ground. Mess up that pretty boy's face of his. Shatter every damn bone in his body. At this point, he wasn't even a person to me. Just a thing that deserved to be on the receiving end of a world of pain.

My hand curled into a tight fist, itching to connect with something. To do some damage. These hands were ready to maul and batter. I was gonna fuck that guy up. Bet he'd look like a mix of post-fight Brian Ortega and that jerk neighbor from Goodfellas if I ever ran into him on the street.

He wouldn't know what hit him. All he'd register would be the force of my fist meeting his skull and the scrape of his face against the cold, hard pavement. He'd wake up not knowing where the hell he was or what the hell happened.

My fists clenched and unclenched as I ran, each movement a drumbeat to the tune of my fury. Everything else? Just a blur. The park, that duck pond, all just noise background, screamin' rage in my head. Sara. That was all I could see. That was all I could feel. Anger like a white-hot flame, burnin' me up from the inside.

As I pounded the pavement, feet drumming a relentless beat, breath puffin' out in frosty clouds, I could feel the city yawning and stretching awake around me. It was then, in the frigid morning air, that I made a promise.

A promise to Sara.

A promise to myself.

This ends. Here. Now.

I've got to get this sorted if I'm gonna protect her. No more whispers, no more secrets. We need to meet beyond the confines of that café. I have to know her, really know her... where she lays her head at night, where she punches the clock... all the nitty-gritty details.

I could sense her need for me. But what she didn't know was how much I needed her. Keeping her safe, it wasn't just for her, it was for me, too. It was for my peace of mind, knowing she was safe and under my watchful eye. With me around, not a single strand of hair on her head would be harmed.

No more ducking and dodging, Heck! I reminded myself.

No more running.

11

———

(Sara)

I was sitting in our usual spot, idly spinning my pint of beer on the worn wooden table. It felt different tonight — no pancakes, no coffee, just a quiet night hanging in the air. I was about to drop a bombshell on Heck.

As if on cue, he walked into the café. He embodied hipster charm — a plaid shirt paired with well-worn jeans, his usual 5 o'clock shadow, and those thick-rimmed glasses that made him look like a modern-day Hemingway, if Hemingway was born in the middle of the grunge era. His blue eyes always had this spark, a kind of mischievous twinkle that made you want to know what he was thinking. I was wondering if last night's conversation was still on his mind.

He slid into his usual seat across from me, a look of surprise crossing his face as he noticed the absence of our typical spread. His brow furrowed, a silent question hanging in the air between us. I didn't have to say it. He knew something was up. In response, he signaled our favorite barista, Lily, and asked for whatever I was having.

It only took Lily a couple of seconds then returned to our table. "Here's your pint, Heck," she announced, setting the beer down with a soft thud.

I offered Lily a grateful smile. Heck lifted his pint, taking a generous swig. A frothy mustache clung to his upper lip, and I found myself laughing softly. Reaching out, I brushed it away with my thumb, a tender gesture that felt as natural as breathing. The soft chime of glass meeting wood echoed around us as he set his drink back down.

"So we've graduated from caffeine to beers now. Reverse adulting," he mused, letting out a ripple of laughter exposing a flash of teeth in his wide, infectious grin. Oh, that smile! It was a sight I could easily lose myself in.

Taking a deep breath, I nudged a folded copy of today's *New York Times* towards him. "I took the liberty," I began, my voice shaking slightly, "of sending your poetry to the paper."

Heck's gaze dropped to the paper, then snapped back to me, his eyes wide and brimming with disbelief. "You did what?" he stammered, amazement carved across his face. He pored over the paper, where a quarter of the page was taken by a colored silhouette of a man gazing into the horizon, swallowed by the sunset. Then, there it was — his poem, "I Love You, Sunday Sunset".

"Bylined by 'A Guy Named Heck from the Café,'" he read aloud, a wistful chuckle escaping him. "I love how you named me, Sara."

"You will always be 'The Guy Named Heck' to me," I managed, painting a fragile smile across my face, desperately hiding the pain within. "I'm sorry, I should have asked for your full name for the credit first, but that would mean breaking our rules," I said.

"No, it's fine. In fact, I like it this way."

"I also considered signing it as 'Pender', but then we're both Pender," I laughed. Friends like couples have their own ways of referring to each other, like 'dude', 'buddy', or 'partner'. But for me and Heck, it's always 'Pender' because of our shared fondness for Gil Pender from the film *Midnight in Paris*.

"This is surreal. Who would've thought my random thoughts would find a home on this page?" He looked at me, his gaze intense, as if trying to bridge the chasm that had silently grown between us.

How do I bid farewell to the boy who set my heart racing just a beat faster than usual? His face haunted my mornings, the first thought upon waking. Those blue eyes that kept me restless through countless nights.

"That was beautiful, Heck," I whispered, reaching for his hand. The moment our fingers intertwined, I knew I couldn't let go.

"It was," he agreed, his grip tightening. "I just can't believe it." Behind his joy, a flicker of something else shimmered — perhaps hope or gratitude. No, it was anticipation... he had news, something significant to share. I could feel it; we were at a crossroads. He took a deep breath, squeezing my hand once more. But when he finally spoke, all he said was, "Thank you."

What are you holding back, Heck? Or am I clinging to illusions, yearning for something beyond friendship? Before he could say anything more, I placed my other hand over his. "I'm moving to Paris, Heck," I announced, my voice barely above a whisper. "Next week. Without Matt."

Just like that. No cushioning of the blow, no sugarcoating. It was delivered as a stark announcement, sharp and clear like a surgeon's incision. There was no space left for the pain to seep in, no moment to absorb the shock. I yearned for it to be swift, for the end to come as abruptly as the words had spilled out.

The air between us grew heavy, laden with unspoken words. Our hands lingered together, as the realization of our impending separation settled like a cold shadow upon our hearts. The silence that followed was deafening. Heck looked at me, his expression a kaleidoscope of emotions — surprise, confusion, and something else I couldn't quite put my finger on. Was it... loss?

He let go of my hand momentarily. And I watched him, his fingers raked through his hair in a way that spoke volumes. It was a familiar gesture, one that screamed *'Heck's in deep thought.'* He took my hand again. His grip tightened just a bit. Our conversation had stirred up a whirlwind of emotions, and this was his way of staying grounded.

When he finally found his voice, it was soft, like the rustle of leaves in the wind. "Paris, huh?" He asked, a half-smile playing on his lips, reminiscent of the Cheshire cat from our favorite book, *Alice in Wonderland*. He had done this grin many times before, but not with these sad eyes. "I'm glad you're finally chasing that dream, Sara. I am absolutely happy for you. Hard to say I'm thrilled, but I am." Then, as if struck by a sudden thought, he added, "Oh, you'll send me those postcard-perfect photos of you, dancing in the Parisian rain, right?"

I squeezed his hand, my smile tinged with a hint of bitterness. "I don't think I should, Heck. I complicated your life. We have something special, but I am painfully aware that you love her, more than anything in this world. I'm just an interruption to your regularly scheduled program."

"An interlude," he added.

Heck sat in silence, his eyes becoming a mirror for the tumultuous thoughts storming within him. His gaze locked onto our intertwined hands, a quiet recognition of the truth embedded in my words.

"You're being unfair, Sara," he murmured, his voice barely more than a whisper against the hum of the coffee shop.

"Whoever promised that life would be fair?" I retorted, my words more bitter than I intended.

The silence that followed was deafening, each tick of the clock echoing like a scream in the quiet space between us. I found myself unexpectedly vulnerable, questioning my own actions. I had allowed my guard to slip, revealing the depths of my feelings in a moment of unguarded honesty. Had I just confessed my love to Heck? Was it the impending end of our café dates, or whatever this undefined relationship was, that prompted me to lower my defenses and reveal my true feelings? Yet, his reaction was neither one of surprise nor of evident excitement. It was as if he had anticipated this moment, yet the lack of enthusiasm suggested that the revelation didn't elicit the response I had hoped for.

"It's funny," Heck finally broke the silence, "we've been seeing each other for months, connecting on such a deep emotional level. We've shared so many parts of ourselves, yet... the basics remain a mystery. I don't even know your full name, your number, or where you live."

"And that, Heck," I replied, my voice wavering as I fought to suppress the tears threatening to spill over, "will remain just as it is. For now. Maybe someday."

Another moment of silence stretched out between us, punctuated only by the soft clink of coffee cups and the distant murmur of conversation. Finally, Heck asked, "So, we have a few days left of coffee dates?"

The question hung in the air, a heartbreaking reminder of the ticking clock, the end of our story looming on the horizon. The sense of adventure and hope that once colored our meetings had been replaced by a melancholy introspection, a painful awareness of the inevitable goodbye.

"Heck, this is our farewell. I don't think I could bear another heart-wrenching goodbye," I confessed, my voice barely a whisper. Heck nodded, understanding painted deeply across his face. And just like that, I knew that Heck, with his eclectic style and soulful eyes, truly understood. Despite the riot of emotions undoubtedly churning within him, he was there for me, standing beside me as he always had. His silent support was my anchor in these stormy seas. And that meant the world to me.

We sat in comfortable silence, our unspoken words weaving an intricate tapestry of shared understanding. He didn't say much. Between news of his poem being published in the *New York Times* no less and my own surprise of unexpected farewell, I could imagine the swirl of emotions engulfing him mirrored my own. A cocktail of confusion and perhaps even relief. The silence felt like a warm blanket on a cold night — soothing and reassuring. Our thumbs playfully wrestled, creating a rhythm that was uniquely ours, a secret symphony composed of our shared moments and memories. In the midst of the bustling coffee shop, we existed in our own little world. A world that was about to shift on its axis, forever changed by our impending parting. The weight of our goodbye hung in the air, a sad reminder of the fleeting nature of time.

I had never envisioned our farewell to unfold this way. Words felt heavy and elusive, too inadequate to encapsulate the whirlwind of emotions swirling within us. Oh, how I yearned for Heck to declare his desire to journey with me, to hear him say he needed me as much as I did him. How I wished we could spread our wings and take the flight to Paris together. But reality was a harsh mistress and such dreams were mere illusions. The daily ritual of seeing him, yet knowing he would never truly be mine, was a torment too great to bear. Love, in its rawest form, was an exquisite pain.

Lily's voice broke our bubble, "We're closing early today," she announced, her words cutting through the thick atmosphere like a knife. "It's the anniversary celebration of the café's foundation, a private party intended for staff members only. The announcement was made last week," she explained, gesturing towards the unassuming advertisement standee that stood sentinel by the counter.

"Of course, Lily. My heartiest congratulations, and may your evening be filled with joy," I managed to say.

And so, it had arrived — the agonizing farewell. I turned my gaze once more upon Heck, those captivating blue orbs reflecting back at me. I would miss the comfort of those eyes watching over me. I extended my hand, letting my fingers trace a gentle path across the contour of his jawline.

The moment had come. "Thank you for everything, Heck," I murmured, rising from my chair. As I began gathering my belongings, Heck mirrored my actions. He reached into his pocket and pulled out a couple of bills, laying them gently on the table as though offering a tribute to the memories we had created in this space.

Together, we walked towards the exit, each footstep echoing our shared reluctance, resonating against the hardwood floors and reverberating in the hollow chambers of our hearts. Our goodbye wasn't marked by grand gestures or passionate declarations, but by the solemn silence that spoke volumes more than words ever could. Each step took us closer to the door, closer to the end of us, the final chapter in our bittersweet symphony.

"So, this is it," I said, fighting back the tears threatening to spill over.

"It's our very first and, sadly, the last time to be physically together outside this door," he said. Heck closed the distance between us, tilting my chin up towards him. I closed my eyes, bracing myself for what was to come.

"Open your eyes, Sara," he said softly. When I did, he traced his thumb across my lips, a tender touch that spoke a thousand words. "I'm going to miss you, Pender," he admitted. With that, he kissed me. I had every reason to resist, but I wanted it, too. Maybe even needed it. If this were closure, I'd take what I could. He kissed me not as how lovers would. His was soft and gentle, bordering on innocence and sadness, long enough to remember them forever. It was a proper goodbye.

"I know. 'Night, Heck," I replied, my voice barely audible.

"Gnight, Sara." His whisper was warm against my ear as he pulled me into his arms one last time. And then, just like that, he let me go. He turned his back and walked away, leaving me standing there, alone.

I took one last look at him, a silhouette against the dim street lights, and whispered into the night, "Bye, Heck."

****

PART TWO

"You have your choices. Do what makes you happy. You can always discover yourself without losing who you are in the process."

- Sara

12

FAREWELL, PENDER

(Heck)

What's next, Heck?

That question was a broken record in my head. The punishing cold New York air had a bite to it, like it was trying to chew me up and spit me out. I'd just left the café, Sara's goodbye ringing in my ears like some twisted love song on repeat. Man, it felt like a gut punch.

Trudging down the snow-kissed streets of the Upper East Side, my heart was heavy, like it had been dipped in lead. The city was all hushed up, whispering secrets to itself. Snowflakes pirouetted down from the heavens, each one unique, each one as cold as my heart felt right now.

My boots crunched on the fresh white blanket, leaving a trail of my loneliness behind. I was hugging my jacket tighter, like it was gonna shield me from more than just the biting chill. It was freezing, man. The kinda cold that seeped into your bones, made you feel hollow. Streetlights cast long shadows, painting everything with an eerie glow. Winter got the city in its icy grip, yet there was an undeniable beauty in its grasp. It was as if the city had been captured in a black and white photograph: stark and haunting, yet undeniably captivating.

I found myself a part of this picture, a living element within the still life. The beauty was tinged with gloom, the stillness echoing with stories untold. It was as if the heavens themselves had chosen me to be a pawn in this grand display, a showcase of the quiet resilience of a city under winter's spell. Tonight, I was no mere observer. I was part of the artistry, a character in the narrative being woven by the frost-kissed night.

I shoved my still shaking hands deeper into my pockets, shrinking from the world. The silence around me was loud, filled with thoughts I'd rather not think, questions I didn't wanna answer. The cold was nothing compared to the frost creeping up inside me.

Damn! I should've said more when she told me she was leaving New York. I should have revealed my intentions of taking our relationship beyond the confines of our usual café. I should have done more when I kissed her. Felt how she responded, I knew if I'd held on a little longer... But no, I let her go. Too unsure, too damn confused. My mind was a jumbled mess. Info overload. Way too soon. I mean, did I care if my rhymes ever got printed? Nah, not really. But then Sara... she went and made it happen. And you'd think I'd be stoked or something? But nah, not even close. I just didn't give a damn anymore.

She used the whole thing like some sort of smokescreen, hiding the real bombshell that was about to drop. I had this gut feeling that she planned it all, messed with my head on purpose. It was as if she had delivered a one-two punch; first a dose of seemingly good news, swiftly followed by a devastating blow. BAM! A sucker punch straight to the gut. Simple but damn effective, enough to knock anyone off their feet. Fuck it, Sara!

Why couldn't I hate her? Because I always knew that, in the end, I would choose her happiness over my own. Because this feeling, this wild emotion, was more than just a simple liking her. And it scared the shit out of me to admit it. My hands won't stop shaking. I was all over the place, man. Couldn't tell if it was her bombshells doing a number on me or her just up and leaving. She'd spun my head right round, a real mind fuck. That kind of thing? Doesn't happen often. Like, almost never. And that's precisely why I was stuck in this mess, not knowing how to handle it

I kicked at the snow piled up around my boots. "Damn it, Sara! You got a lotta nerve doing this to me!" I hollered, not giving two hoots if anyone heard. Felt like I was gonna burst from the inside out. Part of me wanted to hate her, really hate her, for throwing me in this mess. But did she do anything wrong, really?

Nah, she didn't know. She didn't do anything to hurt me. She didn't know I love her. Fuck! I was in love with her! She didn't know I'd been carrying this torch for her all along. I didn't even realize it had come to this. Shit! I'd been head over heels for her this whole damn time. I could feel this cold realization creeping up on me, chilling me to the bone.

My hands won't stop shaking. Maybe it was the cold? Nah, who am I kidding?

I kept walking, lost in a maze of thoughts until I didn't even know where I was. I lit up a cigarette, the nicotine calming my frayed nerves. Sophie would nag about the smell, but I couldn't go home just yet. How was I supposed to act normal around her after all this? It was all just too damn fucking weird... and sick! I needed something to knock me out cold. Something to end my brain processing all this information and feelings, at least for now.

I pulled my collar up, burying my face deeper into my green scarf. Each breath I took was sharp, stinging my lungs. It was just another winter night in New York, but for me, it felt like the longest walk I've ever taken.

Sara's news hit me pretty hard. No. It devastated me. I needed to regroup and find a little bit of clarity that I was in desperate need of right now. I needed a drink. Something stronger than a beer. There was a pub just around the corner of 3rd Street, but I didn't want to run into anybody familiar. I was in no mood to talk. Agony mixed with sadness has always been a terrible combination for me. This usually takes days to subside.

How I can be so cowardly? I finally bumped into this crazy beautiful, downright charming girl who seemed to dig me. I mean, she must've, right? Why else would she throw her time and attention my way? Yeah, we clicked, no doubt about it. I hung onto every word she said, even the mad ones. And get this, she seemed to get a kick out of my babble, too. She always had something interesting up her sleeve. Couldn't remember when I last fell head over heels like this. Not even for Sophie.

She was a dream, understating it really. Things felt right between us, despite the messiness. But she stuck with that douche… grade-A jerk! And this pathetic me was on the brink of tying the knot. Life's a twisted game, ain't it?

But man, was she a sight for sore eyes. Sexy as hell without even trying. I don't think I ever caught her with a lick of makeup on… except that time she hid that nasty bruise. Her face was smooth without any trace of powder. Her lips were naturally moist. And that white lace bra… I couldn't shake that image from my head for days. Damn, that was something else.

We had something… me and her. Not some fleeting curiosity, but a real, soul-deep connection. You don't stumble upon that every day. Man, some folks go their whole lives without it. But us? We had that spark.

It was like the thrill of a new romance, only it felt like it could stick around forever. Our time together could've been straight outta movie. Nah, not those dime-a-dozen Netflix flicks. I'm talkin' timeless classics. The kinda stories that nudge couples from just 'seeing each other' to 'actually dating', or even further. Stories that make people believe in love. That was exactly what it felt like.

We swapped stories, shared experiences. She made me laugh, made me feel at ease. And that was the kicker, wasn't it? What was this thing called? Ahh, emotional intimacy… more powerful than mind-blowing sex. I was sharing moments like that with her. Or at least I thought. It sure did for me. She stirred up emotions in me I thought were reserved for Sophie. I was changed by her, transformed into someone smoother, more articulate, a bit of a poet even. It felt silly sharing those things with anyone else. But not with Sara… with her, it just felt right.

I loved how she looked at me, made me feel like I mattered. She didn't see my flaws, she saw something different. She saw promise, potential. Whatever I said, she understood, just as I meant it. I hadn't connected like that with anyone, not in a long while. That, my friend, was compatibility, and I reckon she saw it, too. It was damn near impossible to deny.

So, we held hands. Might've been nothing to her, but it sure as hell wasn't to me. That ain't normal. Sophie or any of our friends would've lost their minds if they found out. Hope Sara didn't peg me as some playboy, not that I give a damn. Didn't know where all this was headed, only that something good was brewing. . . until she ended it tonight. Fuck!

Never saw it coming, that night being our last. Yeah, told her, "Hit up Paris, chase that dream." But damn, was hoping she'd mull it over a bit. Take her time, you know? Not just... bam, gone. Like, seriously, Sara, you had to take my word for gospel? Why, though? Am I the guy you let call the shots on your life map?

Gotta hand it to her, that was ice cold. Left me in a tailspin. Can't be mad at Sara though, can I? What's my excuse? Had to tell her I was happy for her, even if it was a lie. She needed to hear it, and it took guts to say it. The least I could do was offer her some comfort while she was dealing with her own mess. Stone cold Sara, pulling a fast one on me.

I kissed her, right outside the café. Not just a peck, a proper kiss. A couple blocks down from where I lived with my soon-to-be wife, and I didn't give a hoot. Wasn't about being reckless... maybe I wanted to get caught. Maybe that was my out. But why was I looking for an out? Sara was leaving, and I wasn't on her guest list. Couldn't bear to look at that café again. It'll only bring back memories of Sara. Her gorgeous face. It was too much. I couldn't go through this again.

I stopped at my apartment shared with Sophie. I paused, staring up at the darkened windows, only a flicker of light probably from the television screen.

I looked up at the night sky, feeling infinitely small beneath it. A whisper slipped from my lips, carried away by the cool night breeze.

"Stay... " I murmured to no one, a plea to the universe, a confession to the empty street. But the city just hummed on, oblivious, and I was just another lonely soul swallowed up in its midnight serenade.

I trudged down the sidewalk. Damn, why hadn't I told her? Why hadn't I asked her to stay? We had something, didn't we? Something more than shared smiles and stolen glances over lukewarm coffees? I hated myself a bit for that... for not having the guts.

Finally mustered up the nerve to head home. I fumbled at my key and went inside. There she was, Sophie, sprawled on the couch, binging on *Emily in Paris*. Bloody Paris again. What's the deal with women and Paris? Did they get a thing for revolutions?

She's been glued to this show for a week. I haven't managed to sit through one episode. Not that I'm not interested. Just had too much on my mind this week. Our apartment was all hushed and dim. Got this weak yellow glow from the table lamp. The TV's light was painting the room in shifting colors. Everything's neat and tidy. She had already had her dinner. Sipping wine, eyes on the screen. She looked good, lounging in her shirt and panties. Still a knockout without even trying.

I cracked open a beer and slid onto the couch next to her. Warm cushion, like she'd been planted here for hours.

"How was your day, babe?" she asked.

"Just fine. Same old, same old. Went out for a drink with the gang," I replied. Trusty ol' Sophie... didn't even bother to ask who or where. Inside me, I'm screaming, *'Today was the worst day of my life.'* Might've lost the love of my life today. The irony was almost funny. Playing it cool like any other night, but inside, I was falling apart. Felt like *Dante's Inferno* was playing out in my head. So raw, I might break down at the slightest touch.

I forced myself to look at the screen and pretended I was interested in what she was watching. Gotta thank Emily in Paris for saving me from a conversation I wasn't ready to have. My beer tasted good. Wished

Sara was there with me, sharing a brew. Not to dull the day's sting, just to enjoy each other's presence. Wished Sara would be there next time I hit up that café. But I knew those days were gone. Back to reality, huh?

By the time the episode wrapped up, I was feeling that warm, fuzzy buzz. Sophie looked content, though I couldn't really share in her satisfaction. She was eyeing me, her foot tracing a lazy path up and down my leg.

"Hecky, I want to fuck." She said it like she was declaring it. Not like asking for it. More like demanding it.

Just what I needed. Her leg, long and inviting, bent enticingly as she traced a path from my thigh to my groin. She seemed to relish the effect she was having on me, and I couldn't deny she was succeeding. The booze was dulling my senses, but paradoxically, everything felt sharper.

"This kitty could use a rub," I shot back, smirking. I leaned in, no words needed, and kissed her the way she liked. But while my lips were on hers, I was somewhere else, with someone else. I kissed her with a fervor borrowed from another. I moved from her lips to her ear, down her neck, over her collarbone. Her soft moans were all the approval I needed.

"I've missed this, Heck," she breathed out, voice shaky. It was the sex she missed, not me. As I explored her neck with my lips, my left hand cradled her head, while my right ventured under her panties. I could feel her heat, knew she was getting worked up. My left hand tightened in her hair, tilting her head back, baring her neck to me. I knew how much she loved this. Her eyes squeezed shut as I lavished attention on her neck, now flushed.

I slid her panties aside, revealing her glistening arousal. My fingers danced around that sweet spot, the tiny nub that drove her wild whenever I traced a circle around it.

"I want more, Heck…" Her blue eyes bore into mine, pleading, before squeezing shut again.

My grip on her hair tightened, anchoring her to me. My fingers slipped lower, spreading her wetness. I felt her buttocks and thighs twitch at my touch. With a swift movement, I stripped her of her underwear. Her eyes were ablaze when they met mine again.

Standing up from the couch, I shed my clothes one by one… pants, shirt, boxers. She traced her fingers along my torso as I undressed. Then, I was back on top of her, right there on the couch. Her thighs were hitched up, knees bent, legs resting against my backside. She was opening herself to me, her toes curling, pointing away. Our kisses grew more heated as I moved within her, and damn, she felt good. Pounding into her until my back ached, my abs strained. My arm twitched, shoulder spasmed. Sweat prickled on my skin, Sophie's body gleaming in the dim light.

She took charge, she helped me roll over, and straddled me, guiding me inside her. Her top came off, leaving her completely bare. Grinding against me, forward and backward. My right hand gripped her ass while my left explored her breast. It was a sight to behold. Our moans filled the room, intertwining as she rode me. We locked eyes, and I hoped she couldn't tell I was thinking of Sara. This dance continued until we both found release together.

Post-coital clarity hit me like a truck. All the booze had been fucked out of my system, leaving me wired, sober. Cracked open another beer, stepped out onto the balcony, lit a smoke. There I was, mind drifting back to Sara, that accidental slip of a button revealing her white bra. This is madness! I just had sex with my fiancée.

Why did it feel like I had just cheated on Sara? Why did I feel like I'd just betrayed her and not Sophie? Was it guilt or regret that weighed heavily on my conscience?

The question gnawed at me, a relentless beast that refused to be silenced. My mind refusing to stay tethered to the present moment. Instead, it wandered off, drawn by the haunting allure of Sara.

I knew I loved Sophie, didn't I ? But why had I allowed a ghost of another woman to intrude upon our sacred space? Casting a pall over what should have been a moment of shared bliss.

I sighed, the sound barely audible over the rhythmic hum of the city outside. The guilt was a bitter pill to swallow, its taste lingering despite my attempts to wash it down. Had I made a mistake? Or was this just another cruel trick played by the heart, forever yearning for what it couldn't have?

As the night deepened, I found no answers, only more questions. I felt like I was drifting, lost in a sea of confusion and guilt. And for the life of me, I didn't know how to swim back to shore.

I should move on... get on with life, right? Work, Sophie, all the usual shit. Do everything expected of me. Try to forget Sara.

But not quite there yet. Her memory wasn't fading anytime soon. Haven't even stalked her online, I just couldn't. I want to give her space.

In the days that followed, I was often caught in deep thought by Sophie, by colleagues. Like something was eating at me. Ain't gonna spill, though. No one needed to know. Would tell Sara, if she were here. But if she were, I wouldn't be in this mess, would I?

Sophie was probably thinking it was cold feet for the wedding. No one knew for sure. Exactly how I wanted it. This was me, stuck-in-the-café moments. Didn't happen to me usually. It was the exes who pine, not me. Been told I've got this unattainable vibe or some shit. Now I got it. Sara was the one who was unattainable this time around. Screw you, Heck! This was all fantasy. Real life's with Sophie, smoking hot Sophie. Got it good, you lucky bastard. Just think of all the things she let you do to her. She worships you, dotes on you, loves you. A smirk tugged at my lips, thinking about this ridiculous dilemma. Still, I didn't have a clue what to do next.

13

(Sara)

The vibrant, pulsating energy of JFK airport came alive under the early morning haze as I stepped out of the taxi. Its lights twinkled like stars caught in a hazy dream. The symphony of bustling travelers swirled around me — some darting with hurried determination, others sauntering leisurely, their faces lit up in eager anticipation. Each soul embarked on a unique journey, each story diverging on different paths. But mine was unique. I was bound for Paris, the city of light and love, on a quest to discover myself and pursue my dream of being a writer.

With a deep breath, I wrestled with my bulky suitcase, coaxing it towards the check-in counter. Its wheels protested against the cold tiled floor, their rhythmic clatter echoing the frantic drumming of my heart. I found myself contemplating whether I should need to get one of those multidirectional luggage. Perhaps, I should be more like them, with no predetermined path, simply rolling wherever the uneven terrain leads me. Or maybe I was already more like these luggage than I cared to admit, emotionally packed and rolling uncontrollably downhill. As my luggage slipped from my grasp, swallowed by the conveyor belt, a wave of finality swept over me. There was no turning back now.

The familiar threads of my past were unraveling, leaving in their wake an uncharted path that held no space for regrets.

Navigating through the complicated expanse toward the passenger counter, I hand over my passport and ticket to the scrutinizing gaze of the ground crew. My eyes danced over the sea of faces around me, each a mirror reflecting a spectrum of emotions — the electric spark of excitement, the subtle tremor of anxiety, the introspective calm of deep thought. I couldn't help but wonder if any of them mirrored my own confusion, if they too were fleeing from the ghosts of their past, seeking solace in the embrace of an unfamiliar future.

The echo of my recent past still echoed within me. It had been mere days since I broke up with   Matt. The breakup wasn't just messy — it was soul-shattering. The memory of the night he struck me, intentional or not, turned our shared apartment into a prison from which I had to escape. But to where? To my mom or my sisters? I don't want them to see me like this. In desperation, I reached out to my friend and former neighbor, Hope Williams. She answered after just two rings.

"Oh my gosh, Sara! I've missed your voice!" she exclaimed, her words a lifeline in my moment of despair. Her concern was all it took for my resolve to crumble, and I began to sob. "Hey, what's wrong?" she asked, her voice filled with worry.

"I... I need a place to crash for a few nights," I managed to choke out between sobs.

"Of course. Richard is filming in Toronto right now. Where are you? I can have the twin goons, Shen and Arthur, pick you up," she offered, referring to her bodyguards with a fondness that belied their intimidating titles.

"No need, Hope. I can take an Uber to your place," I replied, trying to maintain a semblance of still being in control.

"I'll prepare your room," she assured me, her voice warm and inviting.

Upon arriving at Hope's Upper East Side penthouse, my composure completely unraveled. I spent the entire night crying, enveloped in a grief I couldn't articulate. Hope stayed with me in the guest room, offering silent support without pressing for details. She simply held me as I poured out the ordeal with Matt. I chose to leave Heck out of the conversation for now; my heart wasn't ready to untangle those threads. As dawn broke and my tears finally ceased, Hope persuaded me to take the first step toward my dream.

"Look at the silver lining, Sara. There's nothing left for you here. Your future might be in Paris. You'll love it there," she said. "Did you know I wrote the first draft of my novel in Paris when Richard took me there for the first time? Our hotel room overlooked the Eiffel Tower, and just imagine me, penning those beautiful love scenes."

"How I wish it were that easy, Hope. Yes, I have savings, but it isn't enough to start my life over in one of the most expensive cities in the world," I argued.

"Money shouldn't stand in the way of what you want in life. You're young and talented. You can find a job there. I've accumulated miles from my travels with Richard. They're unused, especially now that Dad won't allow me to fly commercial. I can use them for you," she offered.

"That's incredibly generous of you. But, I don't think I could impose any further. Staying here for a few nights is already enough trouble for you," I said, grasping her hand.

"Firstly, I couldn't use them and they will expire soon. Secondly, this isn't trouble at all. I'm so glad to have you here. I needed company. It gets lonely when Richard isn't around."

That first night with Hope, we talked more about Paris and writing. We planned the next steps and, with a gentle determination, she helped me book a one-way ticket to Paris using her airline miles.

I left work early the next day, determined to collect my belongings. With only two suitcases to my name, I knew I could only take my clothes, even though almost half of the furniture and knick-knacks were mine. But truthfully, I had no desire for them. As I hastily removed my clothes from their hangers, Matt burst into the bedroom, catching me mid-action as I packed my belongings into the suitcases strewn across the floor.

"What the hell are you doing, Sara?" he demanded, yanking clothes from the suitcase and tossing them back into the closet. "Look, I really am sorry for raising my hand. You know I'm not like that at all."

I hurriedly resumed packing. This was just the beginning of a very short and meaningless apology. We've been in this situation several times before. We argue. Sometimes, it escalated to physical confrontations, then he apologized and if I was lucky, he threw in some gifts. But this wasn't Paris anymore. We were way past that stage.

"Can you please stop that? Let's talk," he said as I continued to ignore him.

I kept on folding and tucking my clothes in the suitcase. Facing him, I declared firmly, "I'm leaving, Matt."

"This is ridiculous, Sara! Just because I didn't support your Paris dream? I thought your Paris plans were foolish... yes, they are! And, you're going to pack up and leave... just like that? What the fuck?" He grabbed my right arm forcefully.

I shook him off. "Don't you dare touch me again, Matt! I'm not afraid to call 911," I warned, my eyes darting to the phone beside my luggage.

"What the fuck did you just say?" His face flushed with anger, his body tensed as if to strike, but the resolve in my gaze made him reconsider. He knew I was serious. "You know what? Go to Paris, go see for yourself what a miserable life aspiring writers have. You'll come crawling back! See if you can last a week as a penniless tourist! Do you think you can make it in Paris? To write and publish?" He kicked the pillow scattered on the floor with his frustration. "I didn't know I was fucking the next Proust right here," his laugh was scornful, almost sinister.

"No, Matt. That's not the plan right now. But I will, eventually. For now, I need to distance myself from all of this," I gestured around the room, unable to stop the tears streaming down my face. "I want to rebuild my life. I can't do that here… and I can't do that with you."

"Look, if you need some space, maybe that's something we both need. I could check into a hotel for a couple of days. You can have the house to yourself," he offered, his tone softening as he grasped the gravity of our situation.

"No, Matt. I'm done. We are done. Our love faded long ago. We've just been too preoccupied to notice," I said, wiping away tears as I continued to pack.

"Come on, Sara! This is stupid and you're being childish. You can't just throw away the years we've invested in this relationship. You have a great job; why complicate things with dreams of writing? You can't just pack up and leave."

"Matt, I said I'm done! It's not just about my dream. I'm not happy anymore. And neither are you. There's someone out there who will love you more than I ever could." My gaze lingered on him one last time. I used to adore this man; he was everything to me. Where did we go wrong?

"Is there someone else, Sara?" he asked, suspicion creeping into his voice.

"No, Matt," I lied, Heck's image flashing through my mind. My heart ached as I realized the truth — I loved him. And yet, I barely knew him. How was that even possible? I pushed those thoughts aside. This wasn't about him at all. This was me leaving. I focused on Matt, who seemed lost in thought, likely calculating his next move. I hoped that this was the last chance I'd have to do this. Closing the last suitcase, I cleared my throat. "Feel free to do whatever you want with our things. I need to travel light," I said, my words carrying a double meaning as I prepared to start anew.

"Where will you stay? I know you can't afford to rent another place," Matt said, his voice laced with a mix of concern and disbelief.

"Not any of your business anymore, Matt," I replied, a hint of jest in my tone, attempting to inject a lightness into the heavy atmosphere.

"I see..." His response was curt, carrying an undercurrent of resignation.

I grasped both suitcases firmly, avoiding any further eye contact or farewell exchanges with Matt, and left the room. Shen and Arthur were there in the corridor, ready to escort me back to Hope's penthouse. They quickly took my bags. Strangely, there was no pang of sorrow or regret despite the years we had shared. Instead, I felt an overwhelming sense of relief, as if I were embarking on a flight to freedom. We descended to the ground floor in the elevator, and upon reaching it, Veronica was there waiting for me. She enveloped me in a tight embrace.

"Take care. Chase your dreams, Sara," she whispered, her voice thick with emotion. "I'm going to miss you."

"I'll miss you, too. But this isn't goodbye. We'll see each other again," I assured her, clinging to her a moment longer before finally releasing her. With a determined stride, I headed towards the black SUV where Shen and Arthur awaited. Casting one last, silent farewell to the building that had been my home for so many years, I stepped into the vehicle.

The entire experience of cutting ties and announcing my impulsive decision to move to Paris seemed surreal, as though I were merely a spectator in my own life drama. The image of Matt's stunned face, his eyes clouded with hurt, remained imprinted in my mind. The support from Hope and Veronica was overwhelming; I hoped to one day repay their kindness.

Despite embarking on this journey, a part of me remained uncertain, questioning my decision. Yet, escaping the constraints of my relationship with Matt, which had become a stifling burden, was essential.

The buzz of my thoughts was punctuated by the rhythmic tapping of keys, pulling me back into the present.

"Miss Sara Emily Miller?" The question floated towards me from a ground crew member, a new one this time — a vibrant young woman whose name tag read 'Reese'. Her infectious smile radiated warmth, cutting through the impersonal atmosphere of the airport. A total opposite of the first one with a scrutinizing gaze.

"Yes," I responded, my voice barely more than a whisper, a small smile playing on my lips. As Reese busied herself with the computer in front of her, I caught sight of my reflection in the sleek surface of the counter. My chocolate brown hair, usually tamed into submission, chose today of all days to cascade over my shoulders in wild waves.

I took in the sight of my olive-green pants, hugging the contours of my legs, and my sunny yellow chiffon shirt that peeked out from beneath an oversized white cardigan. I had never seen myself as strikingly beautiful — my eyes, though large and framed by naturally long lashes, were of a forgettable hazel hue. And my body, while not the stuff of magazine covers, was athletic from years of disciplined swimming during my NYU days. Standing at 5'7", I was often the tallest among my friends, a fact that I wore like a badge of honor.

"Would you prefer a window seat or aisle?" Reese's voice broke through my self-reflection, bringing me back to the task at hand.

"Window, please," I said, the words tumbling out almost instinctively. I wanted to watch as I left my old life behind, to see the city shrink into nothingness as I soared towards my new beginning.

Reese smiled at me, her eyes sparkling with an unspoken understanding, as she handed over my freshly printed boarding pass. "Have a wonderful trip, Sara," she said, her well-wishes wrapping around me like a comforting shawl.

"Thank you," I replied, my voice steadier now. As I turned to leave, I clutched the boarding pass tightly, its edges pressing reassuringly against my palm.

As I settled into the threadbare airport chair, a sense of solitude wrapped itself around me. It was an intense isolation, the kind that reveals itself only when you're stripped of familiarity. At this moment, I felt unsure of how to navigate this new world. I was alone. Truly alone. And I couldn't remember the last time I had been. It was like the first day of college — except now, the entire world was my campus and consequences were my sole instructors. I found myself wondering about the intensity of Hell Week.

The idea of Paris had been a wild spark in my mind, a spontaneous decision ignited by a desperate yearning for change. Was it because of Heck? The enigmatic guy I met nightly at our shared sanctuary, Tribeca Trickle. No, 'dating' wasn't the term for it. We shared time and space, nothing more. Beyond the confines of the café, our real worlds didn't intersect. To me, he was just Heck, his full name remaining an elusive mystery despite months of shared company. And to him, I was simply Sara.

Heck was a canvas of attractive contradictions — tall yet unassuming, charming but aloof. His hair, a tousled mess of waves, suggested a man who had just sprung from slumber. His lived-in jeans and perennially grey T-shirt hinted at a man who treasured comfort over aesthetics. His black-rimmed glasses were the finishing touch to his effortlessly casual look.

Heck was instrumental in my journey towards self-realization, nudged me toward standing my ground, and encouraged my dormant dream of writing. Our shared moments often played out like scenes from *Midnight in Paris*, complete with Gil Pender's whimsical charm. The memory of our single, fleeting kiss still tingled on my lips, a lingering ghost of what could have been.

As much as I wished for his comforting presence, I was navigating this journey alone. The truth was I was stepping into the unknown, armed with nothing but blind faith. Did I need travel insurance? The thought hadn't even crossed my mind. But it was irrelevant now. The lure of a new beginning had me booking the earliest flight out, leaving no room for second thoughts — a lesson Heck had drilled into me. *'Don't overthink, Sara. Just do it,'* he would often say.

"Am I being childish, Heck?" I found myself whispering into the void, my gaze lost in the endless stretch of runway, half-expecting him to materialize and offer words of wisdom. "Is this immaturity?" I questioned again, my voice barely a murmur. But with a shrug, I pushed the doubts away. This was my journey, my story to write. And every good story needs a dash of impulsiveness.

"Heck, if this was what being childish felt like, then so be it. I wasn't thinking about thriving. Just surviving. Just being. As what you keep on telling me," I whispered to myself. It seemed so easy for him to tell me to go and find myself, yet he couldn't bring himself to do the same. He was bound by his own commitments. He recognized that I, too, had my own obligations to deal with. But unlike his, mine were workable. I still had an opportunity, a small window of time. Matt was the only one who couldn't see that. He saw my decision as madness or a symptom of having a meltdown. But everyone else supported me. Hope. Veronica. Andi. Alexi. And of course, Heck.

Whatever the price of this newfound freedom, I was willing to pay it. It wasn't about conquering the world or reaching new heights. Not yet. For now, it was about finding my footing in this shifting landscape of self-discovery. I planned to chalk up everything to experience, while that option still lay open before me. I'm aware that as age advances, such opportunities tend to become more costly, or so I've been led to believe. As Heck would say every so often, *'It's about just being, Sara.'*

Clutched in my trembling hand, the boarding pass felt like a lifeline. My fingertips traced the embossed letters spelling out 'Paris.' A smile twisted at the corners of my mouth, its bitter sweetness tinged with a cocktail of anticipation and nervousness. This wasn't a dream anymore. It was as real as the pulsing beat of my heart, as tangible as the chill seeping through the airport windows.

The overhead speaker crackled to life, its voice echoing across the cavernous expanse of the airport. "All passengers to Charles de Gaulle, please proceed to the boarding area." The words hung in the air, a clarion call ushering me towards the next chapter of my life.

With a final glance at the retreating panorama of the airport, I stepped onto the tube that led me to the aircraft. I was seated at the window side. I put my carry all that contained my laptop and my notes under the seat in front of me. This seven-hour flight to will give me time to write.

Finally, I was seated. I adjusted my seatbelt, my fingers trembling slightly as they brushed against the cool metal. The hum of the plane's engines was a steady, mechanical heartbeat pulsating beneath the passengers' hushed whispers and rustling movements around me.

As I leaned back in the cushioned economy seat, my gaze wandered to the small oval window. The horizon was painted with twilight hues, the sun dipping behind the clouds like a shy artist hiding behind his masterpiece. The sheer expanse of the sky was overwhelming, a vast canvas filled with shades of pink and gold that seemed to mirror my confusion.

Leaving the familiar confines of my life behind was akin to stepping off the edge of a cliff, only to realize I had wings. Untested wings, yes, yet they yearned for the thrill of the open skies.

I would miss my friends. My mother's comforting presence in the harsh reality of the world. But above all, I would miss Heck — and our little corner in the café, his smile as intoxicating as the aroma of freshly brewed coffee.

"Here's to freedom, Heck," I murmured, raising an invisible toast to the man whose mere presence had set off a symphony within my heart, a rhythm that danced to the tune of love and longing.

My heart pounded against my ribs, a wild drum resonating with the rhythm of my silent goodbye. Paris awaited, an unwritten chapter in my book of life, filled with mystery, allure, and the compelling promise of self-discovery. Yet, as the plane soared higher, part of me remained rooted to the ground, anchored by the ties of affection and memories I had left behind.

The roar of the engines was now a lullaby, lulling me into a world of dreams and possibilities. As the plane pierced through the clouds, I felt myself surrender to the journey. My heart trembled with the thrill of the unknown.

My lips moved, a barely audible whisper lost amidst the constant drone of the aircraft. "Find your way to him," I breathed into the air, my words a secret prayer carried away by the invisible currents: a message, a plea, a promise meant for Heck. But before all that, I needed to find myself first. He wasn't some quick fix for my messed up world. I got to find my peace with myself before anything else.

I put on my AirPods and opened the playlist that Heck and I worked on together. I played "Transatlanticism" by Death Cab for Cutie, one of the songs Heck loaned to me, and the first song we heard together in the café. Ben Gibbard's singing was like the actual sound of longing and wanting. Too earnest and vulnerable, I felt each and every bit of sadness of his line that time. I looked at the lights of the city were beginning to twinkle in the distance, their glow a comforting reminder of the life I was leaving behind. As the plane climbed higher, I pressed my forehead against the cool window, whispering a farewell into the night.

"'Night, Heck."

The words were a soft sigh, a silent prayer carried away by the winds of change. And with that, I soared into the unknown, ready to embrace the adventure that awaited me in the City of Lights.

14

BE HAPPY, SARA. I WILL FIND YOU.

(Heck)

"She's outta the picture, Heck." I muttered to myself, my voice barely a whisper in the quiet twilight. I was perched on one of the bar stools in my balcony, one foot rested on the iron rail, a cig hanging from my lips. The smoke curled up in small clouds, disappearing into the sky, just like Sara did.

The sound of Red Hot Chili Peppers' "Dosed" echoed softly from my vintage turntable, one of the few remnants of a past life that survived Sophie's interior design massacre two years back. That song, man, was a gateway to memories, a time machine back to days with Sara. It was one of our tunes. At least for me, it was our song.

Below me, New York sprawled out like a living, breathing entity. The city was all neon lights and honking horns, a vibrant symphony of life that never stopped, never slept. But despite the chaos below, up here, it was just me, my thoughts, and the ghost of a girl.

I watched the city, its heartbeat pulsating in the form of twinkling lights that were about to creep into the shadows of twilight. But my mind? Nah, it was far from here. It was wandering down memory lane, lost in a maze of 'what ifs' and 'if onlys'. Sure, I was here in body, but my head? I was with Sara, reliving moments that were now just fragments of a broken past.

In those solitary, quiet moments, her hazel eyes and broad smile would pop up in my thoughts. Like she was nudging me, making sure I didn't forget her.

But she had already left this city, this jungle of dreams and despair. She packed her life and memories into cardboard boxes labeled 'past'. My gaze turned toward the sky. Was the horizon just a smear of oranges, or was it gold and purple, like God got drunk and spilled his paint? In the sky, I was seeing Sara's face.

I liked her. No, scratch that. It was more than like. I thought I loved her, but a part of me was in denial. But I do like her. I still couldn't get over the fact that the girl I fell for wasn't feeling the same. Perhaps I was drawn to her. Magnetized. Like flourine to electrons. Whatever this thing was called, it was a tricky business. It sneaked up on you, wrapped you in its warm cocoon until you were too far gone. And, man, I was way past the point of no return. As a soon-to-be married man, I was in dangerous territory.

I was still missing her… our thing at the café. The way she'd laugh at my lame jokes, the way her eyes would light up when she talked about Paris. Hell, I even missed the way she nagged me to kick the smoking habit… Nah, not nag, more like a gentle nudge.

"I need you alive, Pender.," she'd say. "What am I gonna do with nights like these if you up and die from lung cancer 'cause you won't quit smoking?" She'd usually toss that line my way, then she'd reach out with her open palm, asking for my pack of smokes. She was right, I knew it. Only real reason to kick a habit. Never saw it that way 'til she said it. No one else could've gotten through to me, not like that.

I couldn't stand it when girlfriends – Sophie included – would bitch about my smoking. Didn't like or even let anyone boss me around. Maybe it annoyed me that other people were telling me what to do. But Sara? It was different. When she'd give me those big hazel eyes and pouty lips as she murmured 'please', man, I was just drawn in by her charm. Handed over the pack without a second thought.

"But you ain't here, are ya, Sara? So I'm just gonna burn through this pack 'til my lungs scream," I muttered under my breath. I took another drag from my cig, letting the burn fill my lungs, hoping for it to smother the ache in my heart. Or at least calm my nerves. But even as the city buzzed below and the music played on, my world was filled with nothing but silence. The kind of silence that screamed louder than words. The kind of silence that came after a storm, when the wind had died down, and all that was left was the wreckage.

"C'mon, Heck," I sighed, flicking the burnt-out cig off the balcony, watching as it spiraled down into the abyss below. "She's gone. She's not coming back."

I lit another one, took one drag of that cigarette and watched the smoke curl up into the twilight. I whispered into the wind, hoping my words would find their way to Sara. "Be happy, Sara. I will find you. I promise you that." My voice barely rumbled against the city's symphony, carrying with it a wish, a prayer, a goodbye.

As I watched the sun dip below the skyline, my heart was heavy, but there was also a strange sense of peace. I was letting her go, setting her free. I encouraged it. Hell, I'd been the one pushing for it. I'd nudged her towards self-discovery, helped her see she had choices to make, and they were hers and hers alone. She didn't need to let anyone else call the shots. It would've been a damn shame if she'd stayed on that path, particularly if her primary consideration was that jerkoff Matt, who was riveting as a dose of Valium.

"Gnight, Sara."

What have I done? I encouraged her to leave and find herself, only to watch her slip away from my grasp. Because that's what you do when you love someone, right? You let them fly.

15

BIENVENUE À PARIS

(Sara)

Sixty days. Just like that, they'd sped by in a blur and vanished. Today was my writing day — a 'no-work-kind' of day — finally a day free from the shackles of work. I was seated at a corner table with my laptop, cocooned by the gentle hum of a quaint Parisian café. My heart mirrored the skies outside: cloudy and a bit melancholy. The air was thick with the aroma of freshly brewed coffee, mingling with the sweet scent of pastries still warm from the oven.

It was springtime in Paris, and the city was alive and blooming. People strolled past the café, their laughter and chatter just a distant murmur that barely pierced my bubble of solitude. Parisian cafés were a world apart from those in New York, where tables and chairs huddled together in twos or fours, and sometimes a long bar played host to a line of stools. Here, in the heart of Paris, outdoor cafés boasted snug tables and chairs, with additional seats lined up, all facing the streets — a theater set for the art of people-watching. I found myself captivated, my concentration wavering from the writing task at hand, as I too became an observer of life's play unfolding on the streets. Every corner seemed to have its own story to tell.

Couples strolled, hands interlaced, their smiles outshining even the sun as it peeked coyly from behind the clouds. Children, their hearts filled with joy, chased pigeons across the cobblestone streets, their laughter echoing through the air like the most beautiful music. Striking individuals paraded around in their captivating spring attire, a riot of color and style. On a good day, it's a patchwork of all things magic. To be underdressed here, well, that could be seen as a fashion faux pas of the highest order. But, hey, Paris is a symphony of high fashion, culture, and history.

Bicycles whizzed by, their riders navigating the narrow alleyways with practiced ease. The contrast between New York's athletic-gear-clad riders and these Parisians was stark. Here, women in flowing dresses and men in navy suits and audacious pink pants or pinstriped suits took to the streets. It was as if they'd stepped right out of the glossy pages of a high-end fashion magazine. Bikes were everywhere, like poetry in motion.

It was a ballet of sorts, these Parisians, each engrossed in their own world yet part of this beautiful, ever-changing tapestry that was Paris in the full bloom of spring. It was a different life. It seemed so simple without losing its sophistication.

Inside the café, the clink of cups and the low murmur of conversations created a comforting backdrop. I cradled my coffee, the warmth seeping into my palms, a stark contrast to the chill creeping into my heart.

I watched as a petal lazily detached itself from a nearby cherry blossom tree, floating gracefully onto the table in front of me. It was a sad reminder of the fleeting nature of everything — beauty, love, happiness.

Then, I remembered the moment I stepped onto Parisian soil for the first time. My heart fluttered as if it was woven from pure adrenaline and unadulterated excitement. My new home was a modest flat nestled along Rue Delambre in the 14th, a stone's throw away from the verdant expanse of Luxembourg Park.

As I unlocked the door and stepped into my sanctuary in the city, I was greeted by a space that was small, yet so full of life — almost intimate, with a bedroom that barely had space for more than a single bed and a tiny desk by the window. It was a comforting sight after a long day. The sheets, though not new, were clean and inviting.

Its charm lay in its simplicity, in the way the sunlight slanted through the lace curtains every morning and danced on the polished wooden floors. The first thing that caught my eye was the window pane, its paint peeling slightly from years of weathering. It offered a view of the busy street below, a tableau of Parisian life that never failed to captivate me. Beauty and character were both inspiration and distraction in this place.

It didn't boast a view of the Eiffel Tower, but every time I peered out, I was greeted by the sight of cobblestone streets humming with life and the faint aroma of freshly baked bread wafting from the nearby boulangerie. On sunny days, the light streamed through the window, casting a warm glow on the worn-out carpet beneath. Its faded patterns tell a tale of many a footfall, of countless stories lived within these four walls.

To the right, tucked into a corner, was the kitchen — so small that I could reach the cabinets, stove, and sink without taking more than a step or two. It was cramped, yes, but it was also where I prepared meals that nourished both body and soul.

The dining area was hardly a separate room, just a small table accompanied by a mismatched chair, squeezed into the remaining space. It was a setup that was perfect for two, making every meal an intimate affair. The worn wooden surface of the table, scarred with cuts and burns, bore witness to countless meals shared, conversations had, and memories created.

Yes, it was small. Yes, it was old. It bore the marks of age and held countless stories within its walls. I fondly likened it to a more modest and unassuming version of Julie Delpy's apartment in the film *Before Sunset*. And yes, there was no working elevator, making every trip upstairs a mini workout. But this cozy apartment, with all its quirks and imperfections, was more than just a place to live. It was a testament to my life in Paris, a space that reflects who I am, and a home that I wouldn't trade for anything else.

Every morning, fruit stands would spring up like mushrooms after rain, their wares spilling over with vibrant colors and tantalizing scents. Apples gleamed like rubies, oranges radiated a sun-kissed glow, and strawberries blushed passionately. At both ends of the street, cozy sidewalk cafés stood like sentinels, their tables perpetually filled with locals nursing cups of coffee and tourists poring over maps. At night, these cafés were miraculously turned into pubs.

I was lucky to find this charming place posted on Spot A Home website while I was still in New York. With a series of Zoom meetings with my landlady Juliette Moreau, a petite woman with a hearty laugh and twinkling eyes, who made sure I had everything I needed including pots and pans so I won't have to buy them. The first few days, she brought food while I was busy making my small flat a decent home.

My first brush with the enigmatic neighbor Antoine Dubois was nothing short of unexpected — it unfolded in the narrow, time-worn hallway that connected our apartments. He looked like a man who had seen four decades of harsh life, yet his spirit was undeniably youthful. His words were sparse, but his welcoming smile spoke volumes, instantly melting away the unfamiliarity.

"Are you *la nouvelle* Juliette talks about?" he asked. His unruly salt-and-pepper hair and crooked teeth made him look even older than his years. Antoine's English was fragmented, each sentence a charming mosaic of mispronounced words and grammatical slip-ups.

In return, I tried to respond in my rudimentary French, stumbling over the elusive pronunciations and tricky conjugations. "Yes, I am the new girl in Apartment 5C. *Oui, je suis la nouvelle fille de l'appartement 5C.*"

"Welcome. *Bienvenue à Paris*," he said and extended his hand to me.

I took his hand and replied, "*Merci.*"

Our conversations were a delightful dance of linguistic confusion, but somehow, in that beautiful chaos, we understood each other.

The scent of freshly brewed coffee became a familiar invitation from

Antoine, a ritual that wove its way into the fabric of my new life. Juliette, our cheerful landlady, would often join us. We were bonded by our love for books. Our gatherings, more often than not, mirrored scenes from my favorite novel, *The Guernsey Literary and Potato Peel Pie Society*. We found ourselves slipping into the roles of Amelia, Eben, and Juliet with ease, our lives intertwining and reflecting the characters I cherished so dearly.

Our bond, however, was not merely cemented by our shared appreciation for coffee or our mutual love for literature — the pages of countless books serving as bridges between our souls. No, it was the comforting rhythm of our routine. Often, it meandered around the city and its hidden treasures, painting vivid pictures of cobblestone streets and quaint cafés tucked away in unsuspecting corners. Antoine's tales of Paris, told with a sparkle in his eyes, guided me through the labyrinth of my new environment. They were a compass pointing me toward the magic tucked away in the city's every nook and cranny.

For days, our laughter echoed through the halls, our banter a symphony of the fellowship and shared understanding, bouncing off the time-worn stone walls. These walls seemed to soak up our joy, becoming silent witnesses to our budding friendship and the magic of literature and the bonds it can forge.

For a while, I found myself utterly entranced by this new life, swept up in a whirlwind of adventure. The memories of Heck and the life I had left behind seemed to fade into the background, like an old photograph losing its color. This was a different world, one where excitement waited around every corner and every day held the promise of a new discovery.

But as the sun dipped below the horizon, surrendering the sky to the stars, memories of him would creep back into my thoughts. The echoes of our conversations in that dimly lit café in New York, the way his laughter would fill the room, the warmth of his hand in mine — they all came rushing back like waves crashing onto the shore. Oddly yet predictably, it was the thought of Heck that persistently lingered, overshadowing the memories of the guy from my most recent breakup.

The nights were a stark contrast to my days, filled with nostalgia and longing. But as I lay in my small bed, staring at the moon through the lace curtains, I realized that perhaps this was what I needed — a place where I could cherish the past while embracing the future. Paris, with its blend of old-world charm and modern vibrancy, felt like the perfect canvas for my new beginning.

My journey down memory lane was halted by a stray ball that darted around my feet. Looking up, I saw an apologetic boy rushing to retrieve the ball from beneath my chair. I offered him a comforting smile and reassured him, "It's okay, no harm done." I knew he likely didn't understand my English, but nonetheless, he returned my smile before dashing back onto the bustling street.

As I sat there, enveloped in the flow of the city, I felt a strange sense of tranquility wash over me. Despite my sadness, there was a unique charm in finding peace amidst the chaos, in being alone within a crowd. After all, this is Paris. Even with the weight of a heavy heart, it was impossible to resist falling in love with this city and its infinite spectrum of emotions. This seemed like a perfect choice to start a new life. While nothing was guaranteed, this was clear: my starting point this time wasn't mired in chaos.

16

DISTRACTION AND COMPLICATION

———

(Heck)

I was lounging on one of those plush couches, taking a leisurely drag from my cigarette. I managed to blow a perfect smoke ring. My God, I was bored out of my mind. Is it even permissible for me to be here? Just weeks ago, Sophie had been incessantly nagging me to accompany her to her first dress fitting. Naturally, I declined, citing the old adage about it being bad luck.

"Come on, Hecky! I don't buy into that superstition. And neither do you," she protested, perching herself on my lap. In one fluid motion, she plucked the cigarette from between my lips and extinguished it in the ashtray. How could anyone resist such a bold move from a beautiful girl?

"Your mother would have a fit, Soph. You know how she is," I pointed out.

"She doesn't need to know. I just want you to see the dress on me before I walk down the aisle," she retorted, her lower lip jutting out in a pout.

"But..." I began, only to be swiftly interrupted.

"Besides, Josh saw Mia in her wedding gown before they got married, and look how well things turned out for them," she argued.

"Josh went to see the gown because Mia called him, panicking that it was damaged and wanted him to pressure the designer... implying more money was needed," I countered, familiar with the storyline and secretly hoping such a scenario wouldn't unfold for me when my time came.

"They're still happily married..." she whispered, leaning in for a seductive kiss. The kind of kiss that unmistakably leads to more intimate encounters. And who was I to refuse?

So, there I was, caught on my day off. Supposed to get my drink on at an unusually early hour. A day meant for unwinding, lounging around, or binge-watching shows at home. Yet, I found myself tagging along with her.

I settled in what they referred to as the lobby, or was it the waiting area? This place was extraordinary. A bridal boutique unlike any other. It felt as though I had stepped into an unfamiliar realm. A whirlwind of tulle, satin, crystals, and lace surrounded me. It was as if dreams had grown weary of the ethereal and had chosen to manifest in fabric instead. This space, meticulously crafted for lovers to immerse themselves in the fantasy of forever. Every detail, from the décor to the furniture, even the seemingly random trinkets, whispered tales of 'happily ever after'.

"Heck! Babe, what d'ya think?" Sophie's voice cut through my daydreams like a hot knife through butter. I was just sittin' there, lost in my own world, basking in the warm morning glow. The sun was peeking through the glass wall, filling up the room with this golden light. Whoever designed this place should be given an award for 'Best Waiting Area for Grooms-To-Be'.

Glad Sophie finally warmed up to this rising designer. She was ticked off, disappointed she couldn't snag a slot with Vivienne Westwood. Kept pestering me to use my family's connections.. But what do I know? Besides, do I look like someone who could pull a string in the fashion world? Sounds like an awful thing to say. So I told her to find someone else and money's no object. Yeah, you might have to splurge ungodly and astronomically amounts on shit like this that lasts only a single day, but it will be worth every penny... you got your peace of mind and your girl wouldn't bug you again.

When Sophie stepped up right into the spotlight, I couldn't help but admire her. Damn, she was stunning in that wedding dress. Her dress... I mean, it was something else. It was like someone took a magic wand and stitched enchantment into every seam. It fit her petite figure like a glove, like it was made for her, and only her.

The dress was this waterfall of lace, tumbling down from her shoulders, pooling around her feet. The bodice was studded with these tiny pearls that caught the sunlight, making her glow. And there was this veil, soft as morning mist, clipped to her hair with a silver comb, just enough to add a dash of mystery.

And the designer got this artist's eye and hands that worked magic. She was all over her, tucking here, pinning there, making the dress fit like a second skin. Every move she made was a testimony to her craft, to the love she put into each dress she created.

"You look... perfect." Words tumbled right out of my mouth before I could stop them. She threw me a kiss, this smile playing on her lips, and turned back to the designer, rattling off instructions for some alterations. Man, I was one lucky guy.

There I was, rooted to the spot, my heart turning somersaults inside my chest. God, she was breathtaking! Her golden hair cascaded past her shoulders, and her sapphire eyes mirrored the joy of the occasion. She was the poster girl for sorority beauty and I was the lucky guy who got to call her my wife soon. But beneath the surface, there was this odd sensation, like I was teetering on the edge of something overwhelming.

Sophie has been the anchor in my stormy seas, my sanctuary in times of chaos, and was about to become my wife. Seeing her in that wedding dress, radiant with happiness, felt right, like everything was falling into place. But at the same time, it was unsettling.

As I stood there, lost in my thoughts, I couldn't help but think about how far we've come, about all the hurdles we've crossed to get here. It's been a crazy ride, full of ups and downs, but we made it. We were here, on the brink of our new beginning, ready to step into our forever. And as I watched Sophie in the mirror, her eyes sparkling with happiness, I knew that this was where I was meant to be. This was my home, my future, my forever… if that even existed.

I was doing pretty well before Sara, my charming café girl. My everyday life was on autopilot. My gallery, pub, my girl, and the odd dive into my writing. It wasn't so bad though. But then came this girl with doe-eyes, brown… or were they hazel? The way her eyes sparkled every time she spotted me stroll into our cozy corner café, or me waiting for her at our spot… it's burned into my brain. Those after-dark chats, scrawling notes, fine-tuning my poems. She was the only one who really got my writing thing.

Now, she was in Paris, probably fumbling in broken French with someone speaking in broken English. Trying to connect with someone who was equally lost in translation. It was just two months ago when she bid me goodbye and it struck me like a bolt of lightning. I had to be supportive. After all, those were her dreams. I couldn't possibly stand in her way. But Sara… she left an indelible mark on me. A secret only known to us, with the other half of that secret scattered somewhere in Paris. Sometimes, I wonder if I could find her online. But what good would that do? The past was the past, and the future… well, the future is standing right in front of me, sparkling with promise and love.

Sara said she was a distraction and a complication. And she wasn't wrong. What she did not know was that I did not care. I wanted it. I wanted her. I was even at the point where I was ready to jump off that cliff if she'd asked me to. Hell, I was ready to pack my bags and join her in Paris, ready to say *'oui'*, ready to be her partner in crime. But she didn't ask. She needed to do this on her own.

See, I could afford to be the fun, carefree backpacking companion. The hefty trust fund tucked safely in my bank account gave me the freedom to work or not. I could leave the gallery to Zaldy or someone else. It had been a hot minute since I last set foot in Europe. Family vacations used to be a regular thing until I hit 19 and decided that vacationing with family was no longer fun. Yeah, it sometimes sucked. I wonder how much Paris has changed since then.

"Babe, let's go," Sophie's voice snapped me back to reality. She changed into a light blue dress that accentuated her features perfectly. She leaned in for a kiss and I responded with equal passion. But as our lips met, I couldn't help but think about that first and last kiss with Sara.

Damn it! *Get a grip, Heck,* I rebuked myself. Sara was at a crossroads, trying to figure out her life, just as I was trying to sort out mine.

"You hungry? We could grab a bite before we head out?" I suggested, hoping to distract myself from the thoughts swirling in my head.

"I know a cozy coffee shop around the corner," she said, her eyes sparkling with excitement. She grabbed my hand and led the way, oblivious to the turmoil brewing inside me.

———

The smell of fresh coffee and the low murmur of conversation washed over me as Sophie and I ambled into the café. Out of all the joints dotting the Upper East Side, she picked the one I'd been steering clear of. But here we were at Tribeca Trickle, back in the same old haunt where Sara and I used to kill time.

I shot a look at our usual nook. A bunch of kids glued to their phone screens had claimed it. The sight was foreign but stung with familiarity.

"Lily," I mumbled, catching her eye. She'd been our regular barista, a silent spectator to mine and Sara's late-night meetings. But today, her grin was muted, swapped with a knowing expression when she spotted Sophie next to me.

I trailed after Sophie towards a spot near the counter, the café's buzz fading into the back. The clink of cups and the hiss from the espresso machine were the only sounds anchoring me to the here and now. Wasn't really in the mood, kept stealing glances at Sophie, wondering if she had a hunch I knew this joint... she was clueless. Typical Sophie, she couldn't care less about working people. She completely ignored how I greeted Lily, too. My slip-up was a giveaway that I frequented this place. Been here loads of times, but never to this part. Feels all out in the open here. Our old corner was more tucked away, just enough off everyone's radar for Sara and me to hold hands on the sly.

"I'll have the hot organic tea, please," Sophie burst out, the minute we settled down, not even sparing Lily a glance. I skimmed the menu in front of me, my fingers hovering over our regular order... pancakes and bacon. Our brinner, as I coined it for Sara. But not today. "Double espresso with soya milk on the side," I managed to spit out.

Sophie was bubbling with excitement about our upcoming wedding. "Heck, I can't wait for you to see the dress I picked for our honeymoon! It's just..." her voice trailed off in my mind. My attention was elsewhere, lost in the ghosts of past memories. The song playing, "Sunshower" by Chris Cornell, that was our jam. Sara's and mine. Felt like a sucker punch, those familiar notes yanking at my heart.

"Heck? You good?" Sophie's voice cut through my trance.

I mustered a half-hearted smile, nodding at her. "Yeah, just... lost in thought... about something."

"Thinking about Dad and the prenup?" She ventured, the question heavy in the air. Her hand found mine across the table and gave it a reassuring squeeze. "It's okay, Heck. Dad's cool with it now. Just wants to chat business with your old man or something."

I looked at her and nodded. I couldn't help but to admire how beautiful she was, with her blue eyes and blond hair. Peter was right, she was a total package and I was God damn lucky to have her by my side. But having Sophie in this very café... the place I shared with Sara, I was beginning to realize how I wanted her to be Sara. And if I followed my heart, I would call off the wedding.

The espresso arrived, hot and bitter. I took a sip, the strong flavor jolting me back to reality. But the taste was different without Sara by my side. Everything was.

17

THE PARISIAN CAFE

(Sara)

The scent of freshly ground coffee beans, accompanied by the rich aroma of baking croissants, wafted through Café Bohème, situated in the heart of Edgar Quinet. I was behind the counter, my hands deftly maneuvering the chrome-plated espresso machine, a symphony of hisses and clinks filling the air. The café was a three-minute walk from my apartment, a charming place that had become my sanctuary, a world away from the frenetic pace of my past life in New York.

The café was abuzz with chatter and the clinking of cutlery against porcelain. Sunlight streamed through the windows, casting long shadows on the tiled floor. Regulars were huddled over their brunch — plates piled high with eggs Benedict, smoked salmon, and warm, buttery pastries. Tourists were scanning Google Maps on their phones over cups of steaming café au lait, their faces lit with anticipation for the day's adventures.

As I set about crafting another espresso, the rhythm of tamping the grounds became a soothing cadence, a dance choreographed in 20-second intervals. The machine hissed its approval as the hot water filtered through the compacted coffee, yielding a rich, caramel-hued crème. As it swirled atop the dark liquid, forming a perfect circle, memories of Heck came rushing back.

We used to have our brinners at this little café tucked away in the heart of New York. Tribeca Trickle, that's the name. We would lose ourselves in our own world, oblivious to the city's constant hum around us. His absence was still a raw wound, but with each passing day, the pain was slowly transforming into a dull ache.

Here, in the heart of Paris, I found a soothing sanctuary in my newfound role at Café Bohème, a quaint haven far removed from the cutthroat world of advertising that once consumed my existence. My days were no longer dictated by deadlines and client demands. Instead, they unfolded leisurely, filled with the fulfillment that came from learning the art of brewing the perfect cup of coffee, pouring velvety milk into a latte with precision, and creating intricate designs on frothy surfaces.

As I surveyed the café, it was pulsating with the infectious energy of couples immersed in their own worlds, reveling in the magic of the moment. A touch of irony tinged my thoughts — I had fled New York to escape the ghost of Heck and his lingering memories, only to find myself here, in the city of love. Yet, every corner, every whispered conversation, every shared laughter resonated with echoes of our nights in that small café together.

Perhaps, deep down, I never truly wanted to erase him from my memory. Maybe, in this café, amidst the clinking cups and the aroma of freshly ground coffee, I was attempting to clutch onto fragments that would keep his essence alive within me. In the end, it wasn't just about running away, but also about holding on to the bittersweet remnants of a love that once was.

My journey at Café Bohème began unexpectedly. One morning soon after I'd settled down in my new tiny apartment, I walked over to this place. As I savored my usual brunch of avocado toast and penned thoughts in my journal, my eyes landed on a poster pinned haphazardly on the corkboard – "'Barista Wanted.' Intriguingly, the advertisement was in English, suggesting they might be looking for an English-speaking barista. Impulsively, I approached the counter, my curiosity piqued.

"Is this job still open?" I asked, pointing at the poster.

The manager, a petite woman named Colette with a pixie cut and sparkling eyes, sized me up before responding. "Are you American?"

I smiled, nodding. "Yes, I am. Are you?"

"Yes," she replied, a soft laugh escaping her lips. "A long time ago." There was a hint of nostalgia in her voice. She carried the grace and wisdom of someone who had lived an interesting life. "I moved here 20 years ago," she added.

"Where are you from, back home?" I found myself asking. The question hung in the air, a touch awkward, as if the roles had suddenly reversed and I was the one conducting the interview.

"I'm from Alabama," she responded, her voice carrying a hint of Southern twang that had somehow survived two decades in Paris. "After graduation, I packed my bags, caught a flight to Paris, and never looked back."

As she turned the tables back on me, her eyes sparkled with curiosity. "Did you just move here?"

"Yes, two weeks ago," I replied, feeling a pang of nostalgia for the city I'd left behind. "I was a copywriter at an advertising firm in Manhattan."

"Planning to stay long?" she asked, her gaze steady on mine.

The question caught me off guard. "Probably. I don't know yet. I hope to work and write my book simultaneously," I confessed, revealing my aspirations for the first time since arriving in Paris. I quickly added, "However, I'm here on a working visa." Thanks to Hope and her father's connections, I managed to obtain it without any trouble. I was aware that securing a working visa in European countries could be complex, a challenge I couldn't have navigated alone.

"Well, you've come to the right place," she said, her lips curling into a smile. "We can offer you 9 euros per hour, plus free meals."

"Really? Thank you, Collette," I exclaimed, the anticipation for this new chapter of my life bubbling within me. "I'm so excited to start working here."

"Can you start tomorrow?" she asked, her tone matter-of-fact.

I nodded, returning her smile. "Yes, I can."

And so, my Parisian adventure began. Each day marked a step further away from my past, a step closer to healing. Café Bohème, with its warm, inviting ambiance, became more than just my workplace — it became my sanctuary. And every cup of coffee I made, every latte I poured, turned into a symbolic toast — to move on, finding joy in the unexpected, and embracing the adventure that lay ahead.

And today, that adventure introduced me to two fellow New Yorkers vacationing in Paris, a delightful reminder of the city I left behind.

"Andrew, for the love of all that is holy, settle on the breakfast platter already. I'm starving!" The edgy plea echoed from a woman about my age, her hair awash in hues of royal purple that danced against her apple green coat over a white T-shirt. She tapped her fingers, each adorned with an intricate splash of artistic nail polish, against the time-worn wooden table. It was a rhythmic protest, a drumbeat of hunger growing louder with each passing second.

Her companion, Andrew, remained engrossed in examining the rest of the menu, oblivious to his friend's mounting impatience. Each passing moment added another layer to this unfolding drama. His eyes scanned the culinary landscape while his forehead creased deeper with the weight of indecision. The world outside might have been rushing by, but in this bubble of anticipation and hunger, time seemed to stretch, making every second feel like an eternity.

I approached their table, my smile warm and welcoming. "Hi, I'm Sara! I'm afraid our breakfast plate is no longer available, but we've got a brunch menu I think you'll absolutely adore."

Andrew, clad in jeans and a pink shirt with rolled-up sleeves, looked up at my intrusion. His eyes widened slightly as he registered my accent. "You're an American?" His own accent had the unmistakable lilt of a New Yorker.

"New York, to be precise," I replied, my heart fluttering with nostalgia at the familiar cadence of his speech.

"No way!" The woman exclaimed, her face lighting up. "We're from New York, too. I'm Tess O'Brien, and this absent-minded fellow is Andrew Davenport." She gestured towards her companion, her eyes sparkling with amusement.

"Pleasure to meet you both. I'm Sara Miller," I responded, the corners of my mouth lifting in a genuine smile. "I highly recommend you try our brunch plate."

With a nod and a grateful smile, Andrew agreed. "Sounds perfect. We'll have two of those and of course, coffee."

Over the next four days, Tess and Andrew became my regulars. We engaged in friendly banter, exchanging stories about New York and my budding writing career while they explored the enchanting streets of Paris. Then, as quickly as they had arrived, they disappeared, returning to the city that never sleeps.

As I stood in the quiet café, the aroma of freshly brewed coffee enveloping me, I couldn't help but wonder about New York. Perhaps, the city is now a more peaceful place, devoid of one discontented individual who was constantly moaning the unfairness of life and how the city failed me. And Heck... his absence left a void no amount of French coffee could fill. His laughter still echoed in my ears, his spirit seemed to dance in the corners of my vision, his presence lingered like a ghostly imprint on my soul. Our shared love for music, our stolen moments wrapped in poetry.

Shouldn't he be happily married by now? Or was he still wandering, like me, caught in the web of what-ifs and could-have-beens? He triggered my own move to this place. The big surprise was that it wasn't even Beastie Boy Matt.

I've thought about Heck a lot but I never acted on anything. I haven't even tried to find him on the internet, I was scared to find something I didn't want to see — afraid of unearthing truths that might shatter my carefully constructed tranquility. The move to Paris was supposed to help uncomplicate my life. But why couldn't I move on? Every day, moving on proved to be an elusive dream. Why did every cobblestone street, every melody whispering through the air, every sip of coffee taste like a question mark? Each day unfurled like a chapter in a novel I was writing, filled with expectation and adventure, yet the protagonist seemed to be stuck, unable to turn the page. Could Paris be the key to unlocking my new beginning, or would it merely serve as a beautiful backdrop to my lingering present? Or perhaps it would be a constant reminder of the guy in the café who encouraged me to chase my dreams in this city.

I shook off those thoughts and reminded myself again that my life is here now, among the aroma of coffee and freshly baked pastries, among new friendships and unexpected encounters. I was even learning French through the music of Edith Piaf. Life was moving on, and so should I.

18

CIGARETTE, SEX AND SARA

(Heck)

Sunday night. Me, sprawled out on the couch in the one place I could still claim as my own. My den. This entire apartment, once a bachelor's fortress adorned with gym equipment strewn about in glorious disarray. No pretentious furniture. Just raw, unadulterated masculinity. Being an Archibald, you see, does come with its fair share of perks. One of them was the luxury of hand-picking a swanky pad in the heart of New York City, the moment you hit 18. And it was not just me, all my cousins, too. So, that birthday? We were all counting down the days. Managed to snag this gem on 5th Avenue when I was just a kid of 19, and never felt the urge to pack up and relocate. This place, it's got character, y'know?

Then came Sophie, two years ago. She swept in with her luggage, her aspirations, and her mother's French interior designer in tow. My rugged haven was transformed into something that bore an uncanny resemblance to a wedding cake, frosted to perfection by a master baker. But this den, this sacred space, remained mine. Untouched and unspoiled.

Got this massive flat-screen mounted on the wall, state-of-the-art stuff. The flicker from the TV cast these long, dancing shadows all around, keeping beat with the drama playing out on screen.

And here we were, the last weekend before I bid adieu to my bachelor days. Just me and my favorite TV series, Billions. It was a wild ride, that one. All about power, money, ego... the works. Everyone was trying to outplay and outthink the other. And in the show where there were no stupid characters, sometimes, you just didn't know where it would take you. Brilliant shit. Watching it felt like looking in a mirror, except with higher stakes and sharper suits... with Axel in his jeans and hoodie sweater.

Tonight? Nothing to write home about. Just your run-of-the-mill Sunday, the calm before the storm that was Monday. The most brutal day of the work week, looming on the horizon. Sunday sunsets, I remembered those. Sara and I had a thing for them. Our little secret code. But now it was just me, my cup of cold coffee, and the ruthless world of Bobby Axelrod of *Billions* playing on my TV.

The coffee cup sat there on the side table, right next to an ashtray that has seen better days... chock-full of stubbed-out smokes. I was on my seventh stick now, letting the smoke dance around the room, not giving a damn about the lingering smell.

I took another drag, the smoke twisting and turning, weaving stories in the air. A peaceful Sunday, just me and my thoughts. No noise, no chaos, just the flickering light from the TV and the soft hum of the city outside.

"Why do we chase what we chase?" I mused aloud to the empty room, the sound of my voice startling in the quiet. "Money, power, love... Was it worth it? The hustle, the grind? A ghost?"

And, Sara...

I let out a chuckle, the sound echoing off the walls. Guess life's just one big game of Billions, huh? I took another puff, the smoke curling around me like a shroud, and for a moment, everything felt strangely right.

Just shy of a week before the big day. The start of the finish line. The beginning of the end. The final solution to all debauchery that bachelorhood has to offer. The last hurrah to all the wild nights and freedom that come with it. Was I having a blast? You bet. Never been one for the boring life. This, all of this, my choice, man.

I've been faithful for the most part, except for a teeny weeny bit interlude that was over too soon and threatened to blow it all apart. Hurricane Sara. If she was one, then I was New Orleans hit by the big one, and left in total ruin. But still, I've been good. Sophie's been good, too. Extraordinarily good, actually. She was excited. She got almost everything she wanted for the day. Everything our high-powered wedding planner could provide. Sophie was beaming. She's also looking her best now. Five days a week in the gym, her ass was staring back at you. She was fine as hell. Life couldn't be better than right now. Or so I thought.

Sinking into my couch, a fresh episode of *Billions* queued up on the screen. The room was humming with that comforting kind of quiet, the kind you only get late at night when the city's finally taken a breather.

I was about to reach for a cigarette when Sophie walked in. She was wearing this powder blue negligee... barely there, if you catch my drift. Make any man shoot his temperature up the roof. You could see her every curve like she had been sketched out by an artist with a thing for the female form. And her teasing smile... it was like she was into a big secret and she was dying to spill.

She was toying with a glass of red, a surefire sign she's got something brewing in that head of hers. Without a word, she plonked herself down next to me. No 'May I?' or 'Do you mind?' She simply reached over, grabbed the remote, and pressed down the volume. Just like that, the room fell silent save for the muted patter of rain against the window.

"Ever had a threesome, Heck?" she asked, her voice cutting through the silence like a hot knife.

"Do you want the honest answer or a lie?" I replied, a smirk playing on my lips.

"Who were they?" she pressed on, ignoring my deflection.

"Some girls I met at a party down in Roosevelt," I said, shrugging nonchalantly. "Don't even remember their names."

"And did you like it?" she asked, her eyes sparkling with curiosity.

"If I did, I'd probably remember their names," I retorted, lit another cigarette, and inhaled deeply. But I did remember. It was Jenny and Candice. But some things, well, they're better left unsaid.

Then, she dropped the bomb.

"I ain't mad, Heck. I knew you weren't a saint when I met you. But I can't tie the knot without getting a taste of the wild side myself."

"You mean... like a threesome?"

"That's the idea."

"And I'm invited, right?" I asked, half-joking.

"Of course, silly."

"Well, I hope it's with another girl 'cause I dunno if I can handle another guy. Not that I've got anything against it, but we might be in for a whole new set of problems if I end up liking it."

She laughed, a full-bodied laugh that filled the room. She had already got this thing figured out, I could tell.

"You remember Zadie, from Beta? We had a few drinks the other night, and she told me I shouldn't get hitched without trying it. Said it's all about exploration, going on a sexual adventure..."

"I'm all ears," I said, grinning like a kid in a candy store. This was starting to sound really interesting.

"She offered to guide us through it."

"I'm in," I said without missing a beat. Ain't needed a guide since I lost my virginity, but what the hell, right?

"You didn't really have a choice, Heck. And look at you, already getting excited," she teased. And you know what? She was right.

Sophie started looking at me in the way she does, all seductive-like, her eyes dancing with mischief in the flickering light. She was there, right next to me, close enough to touch. She was close, so close I could smell her perfume. A hint of vanilla mixed with something spicy. It was intoxicating, almost as much as the look in her eyes.

And then, without breaking eye contact, she reached out and placed her hand on my thigh. Her fingers are long, elegant, French manicured. They traced a path on my skin, leaving a trail of goosebumps in their wake.

No warm-up, no preamble. She just went straight for the kill. Like a reward for my agreement to her proposal, as if she wasn't already a treat. Slid off the couch onto the floor, her hand still on me. She moved it slowly, deliberately, tracing a path upwards until she found what she was looking for.

I could feel the heat of her touch, felt my body responding to her. It was like she got this power over me like she knew exactly what buttons to push.

And all I could do was sit there, dazed and more than a little turned on, as she took control, and I was just along for the ride.

Her hands moved upward gently until she felt my hardened rock inside my shorts. She knew how to turn me on, and it pleased her that she was able to make me hard right now. Without saying a word, in that seductive kneeling position, she unzipped my shorts and pulled them down. She licked her lips wet, and without warning, she put my hardness straight into her mouth. I threw my head back. The TV was still on, but it was nothing more than background noise now, drowned out by the pounding of my heart and the blood rushing in my ears.

Man, she did it expertly, just like the way I wanted. Like I said, life couldn't be better. She took her time and used both her tongue and hands around me. All over me. And I was enjoying it and ready to explode in a few more strokes. Suddenly, she stood and looked straight at me and said, "That's all you're getting tonight. Be ready for more next time."

And that's how she managed to ruin my Sunday night.

I yanked up my shorts, zipped 'em up nice and tight. Lit another cigarette, sucked in a lungful of smoke. Let it out slowly, watching as it swirled around me, filling the room with a hazy cloud.

Closed my eyes then, let myself drift. And there she was. Sara. Her eyes were so big and brown you could lose yourself in 'em. Beautiful, that is what she was. I could see her face as clear as day, even with my eyes shut. That little smile of hers, the one that used to light up the room. The way her nose would scrunch up when she laughed. The dimples in her cheeks. It was all there, imprinted on the back of my eyelids like some sort of a twisted love letter.

I took another drag of my cigarette, let the smoke fill my lungs. Tried to push away the memories. But it was no use. She was there, always there. Like a ghost haunting me.

And I knew then, knew that no amount of cigarettes or booze or late-night regrets could ever erase her from my mind. I opened my eyes, stared at the empty room around me. The silence was deafening, a stark reminder of my solitude. And all I could do was sit there, smoke my cigarette, and remember.

19

PARISIAN ADVENTURE

(Sara)

With an old notebook pressed against my knees, I sat on a weather-worn bench in Luxembourg Park, nestled in the heart of Paris. It was a 15-minute walk from my quaint apartment, a journey that had become as familiar as the back of my hand.

The park had become my refuge, a place where I could sit on the grassy knolls or aged benches, losing myself in the rhythm of the city and the cadence of my thoughts. It was a sanctuary dressed in vibrant hues of nature, adorned with flower beds that spilled over with roses, tulips, and daisies, like an artist's palette gone wild.

Around me, the park hummed with life: children chasing their laughter, lovers whispering sweet nothings beneath the shade of ancient trees, and solitary figures sprawled out on picnic blankets, their noses buried in books. This orchestra of life and love, of solace and serenity, was my muse, my inspiration.

Lost in the mesmerizing dance of my pen over paper, I was abruptly pulled back to reality as a shadow fell across my notebook. Looking up, I found myself locking eyes with a man radiating an effortless elegance. There was an innate charm about him, a magnetic pull that was impossible to resist. His eyes, deep as the ocean, held a hint of warm familiarity that tugged at my curiosity.

"Gabriel Alexander. May I join you?" he offered, his English perfect, his voice a soothing melody that seemed to blend seamlessly with the ambient sounds of the park.

His directness took me by surprise, coaxing a laugh out of me. "Sure, Gabriel," I replied, my words laced with amusement. "But only on one condition, you must promise not to cast a shadow on my notes."

He regarded me with a keen gaze, then his features softened into the warmest of smiles. "Might I inquire if you have a name?" he asked with genuine curiosity.

"Oh, my apologies," I said, hastily setting my notebook and pen aside on my lap. I wiped my hands together, trying to dispel some of the nervous perspiration, before extending my right hand towards him. "I'm Sara Miller."

His chuckle echoed through the air, a rich melody that wove itself effortlessly into the park's symphony. "It's quite fascinating," he mused, "to see a girl alone, her thoughts pouring onto paper. It's refreshingly classic."

I found myself smiling at his observation. "Well, I was introduced to this old-school style of writing by someone," I said, my mind wandering back to Heck and the ever-present leather-bound notebook that was always tucked in his back pocket.

As Gabriel settled onto the bench, I stole a sideways glance, taking in his impressive stature. He was tall and fit, his jeans hugging his waist and accentuating his firm physique. His mint green T-shirt and pristine white designer sneakers were a stark contrast to his ruggedly handsome features. He was the polar opposite of Heck and Matt.

"What are you writing about?" Gabriel asked, his curiosity piqued.

"Nothing particularly interesting. Just a few musings," I replied, folding my notebook and tucking it away. "Are you from around here?"

He nodded, "Just a 10-minute walk from here." He paused, studying me for a moment before asking, "You're an American, aren't you?"

I laughed, "Guilty as charged. A New Yorker, to be precise. I'm relatively new to this beautiful city." As I took in his chic attire, I couldn't help but regret my choice of clothing. My floral summer dress, which ended just above my knees, and my white Onitsuka sneakers with their vibrant red and blue stripes, seemed rather casual compared to his well-put-together look. Not exactly the type of outfit one would choose when unexpectedly encountering a charming man like Gabriel.

"People tend to fall in love with this city," he observed, his gaze wandering over the park. "Once they settle in, they never want to leave."

"I can see why," I agreed, a soft smile playing on my lips. "I'm already one of those people who can't imagine leaving."

What started as a chance encounter quickly evolved into an easy-flowing conversation. Our words danced in the air between us, weaving tales about New York and Paris, writing and dreams, and life's surprising twists and turns. As we delved deeper into our stories, I found myself laughing with a freedom I hadn't felt in weeks. Gabriel's humor, infused with wit and charm, was a soothing antidote to the loneliness that had been my constant companion. His presence, his words, they were a new adventure, an unexpected chapter in the story of my life.

Gabriel was undeniably likable. What was there not to like? He possessed an easy-going personality that made him instantly approachable, coupled with striking good looks that were hard to ignore. Was he a convenient distraction from my past, a way to forget Heck? Since setting foot in Paris, I had deliberately steered clear of the dating scene, feeling a pressing need to allow my heart some much-needed respite. But Gabriel, he was a different story. He was magnetic, impossible to resist. So why hold back? *Heck, you're not here,* I railed silently, my thoughts echoing defiantly within the confines of my mind. *You allowed me to navigate this journey on my own.*

Gabriel's throaty hum pulled me back from the edge of my daydream, "I was wondering," he began tentatively, "if we could exchange numbers?"

"Oh, I'm not much for phones," I confessed, "but you can find me at Café Boheme, just a few blocks from here. My shift typically wraps up around 3 p.m." It was true. I had chosen to live without the constant buzz of a mobile phone and the relentless pull of social media. Besides, Heck and I had managed to navigate our quasi-relationship without sharing any personal details, so why change now?

"I'm familiar with that place," he replied, a hint of intrigue in his voice.

"Excellent! We can share a cup of coffee sometime," I suggested, a hint of eagerness coloring my words.

And thus began my romantic odyssey with Gabriel. He would appear, like clockwork, as my work shift drew to a close. Our dates often found us wandering through museums or browsing the shelves of local bookstores. He didn't possess a natural affinity for literature or art, but I suspected he tolerated these pleasure trips just to please me. And you know what? That wasn't half bad.

———

The moment I stepped into the café, the familiar scent of freshly roasted coffee beans met my senses, pulling me into its welcoming comfort. Slipping into my apricot-hued apron, I savored the softness of its well-worn fabric against my skin.

"A handsome gentleman stopped by earlier with a message for you," Colette announced, her eyes dancing with mischief as she passed me a note folded neatly on canary yellow paper.

"A note from the man I've been seeing recently," I replied as I unfolded it. Gabriel's neat handwriting revealed an invitation for dinner that evening. My heart fluttered like a hummingbird, beating out a rhythm of anticipation. I glanced at my reflection in the café mirror, my smile broadening at the sight of my favorite dress — a summer palette of white and yellow, its hem flirting playfully just above my knees. I was glad I chose to dress up pretty nice today. The dress was a simple design, but it held a captivating charm. The white bodice was adorned with delicate yellow daisies, reminiscent of sun-kissed afternoons. The skirt, a sea of pure white, swayed gently with every movement, enhancing the overall lightness of the ensemble.

"Sara, you're positively glowing," Colette teased, her eyes sparkling with delight. "Nervous about your date?"

"I'm... not sure. Perhaps, I am," I confessed, feeling a warm blush tint my cheeks. It had been a while since I'd experienced the thrill of a real date, the rush of getting to know someone new, the exhilaration of potential romance.

The day whirled by in a blur. So engrossed was I in the dance of customer interactions that thoughts of Gabriel and Heck receded into the background. As the clock struck three, signaling the end of my shift, I slipped off my apron and called out to Colette who was busy in the kitchen. "I'm off, see you tomorrow!"

"Have a wonderful date, Sara!"

I retreated to the tiny bathroom, applying a touch of mascara and a soft peach lipstick. A spritz of my favorite perfume, a floral melody that reminded me of springtime in Paris, completed the transformation.

When Gabriel arrived, he was a vision of relaxed sophistication. His pristine white polo shirt, neatly tucked into well-fitted jeans, gave him an air of effortless elegance. He radiated an aura of cleanliness, of decency. Together, we were like characters plucked from a scene in a romantic film.

"Ready to go?" He asked softly, his hands nonchalantly tucked into his front jeans pockets.

"Absolutely," I replied.

We strolled along the cobblestone streets of Paris, the sun about to set in the horizon, a chill in the air. The restaurant was tucked away in a quiet corner not far from Café Boheme. Its rustic charm and soft candlelight created an intimate atmosphere.

Throughout dinner, Gabriel treated me with a gentle chivalry that was endearing. His eyes held a warmth that made my heart flutter somehow. We savored a rich Bordeaux wine, its complex notes enhancing the flavors of our chosen dishes — a perfectly seared duck breast for him, a delicate trout almondine for me.

After dinner, we resumed our leisurely walk under the starlit Parisian sky. The city, bathed in the soft radiance of the moon, seemed to hold its breath as we moved through its streets. The glow from the street lamps casting a warm, golden hue.

Gabriel gently claimed my hand as we ambled along the streets, his touch a comforting presence against the chill night air. His hold was different — not quite like Heck's, but far superior to Matt's. In an electrifying twist of events, Gabriel deftly cradled my face in his hands, pulling me towards him. His lips met mine in a kiss that was unlike any other I had experienced. There was nothing sweet or gentle about it, not like the one I'd shared with Heck. No, this was something entirely different, something raw and untamed.

His lips were a torrent of sensation, wet and insistent, claiming mine with an intensity that left me breathless. He suckled on my lower lip, his tongue seeking entrance into the warm recesses of my mouth. This was a French kiss, passionate and uninhibited.

I found myself responding to him, my arms instinctively winding around his neck, pulling him closer. Our tongues intertwined in a symphony of desire, each stroke igniting a spark that threatened to consume us both. The world around us blurred into insignificance, our surroundings fading away until all that remained was the intoxicating rhythm of our shared breaths.

We kissed until our lungs begged for air, until the need for oxygen overpowered the heady rush of our passion. And when we finally broke apart, gasping for breath under the stars, I knew that this was what I needed. This wild abandon, this thrilling taste of the unknown. This was the adventure I had been yearning for.

For a moment, I forgot about Heck, his memory fading into the background, replaced by Gabriel who had walked into my life and kissed me passionately.

"Do you want to walk me home?" I asked him. I knew this invitation would lead us to my bedroom. But who cares about what he thinks or what is right or wrong? I needed to ease this loneliness.

He smiled, "I thought you'd never ask!" He stood up and offered his hand as we walked to my place.

As soon as we crossed the threshold of my apartment, Gabriel was a man possessed. In a swift, fluid motion, he pressed me against the wall, his body a solid heat against mine. His lips found mine in a searing kiss, proof of the passion that was simmering between us.

His hands began a tantalizing journey across my body, each touch sending sparks of eagerness skittering across my skin. His right hand deftly hiked up my dress, his fingers tracing an intimate path along my inner thigh. The sensation was electric, a promise of the pleasure that lay ahead.

With a sense of urgency, our clothes were discarded, strewn on the floor like forgotten memories. There was no need for a bed; our passion wouldn't wait. Gabriel took command, his assertiveness a thrilling contrast to his earlier gentleness. Turning me around, I was facing the cold, stark wall, my heartbeat echoing in my ears.

The sound of plastic tearing cut through the heavy silence as Gabriel slipped on his protection. Then, he was there, taking me from behind, standing, our bodies moving in a rhythm. His thrusts were met with my eager response.

I could feel myself spiraling, losing control as wave after wave of pleasure washed over me. Gabriel was good, his movements were both assertive and attentive, exactly what I needed at that moment. I felt him falter, too, his rhythm becoming erratic as he neared his own climax.

Just as the world tilted on its axis, as the pleasure peaked and I tumbled into oblivion, Gabriel pulled out. With practiced ease, he removed his protection and spilled his warmth onto my back. It was a raw, primal moment, proof of our shared passion.

The warmth of Gabriel's body, pressed against mine, created a heady blend of anticipation and excitement in a cozy, intimate bubble. For a heartbeat, we were one, lost in a world that existed only for us. Then, as quickly as our adventure had begun, he stepped back, an unreadable expression etched across his handsome face.

He began to gather his clothes, each movement deliberate, his focus unwavering. The silence between us was thick, charged with the remnants of our shared passion. I stood there, a silent spectator, my heart pounding in my chest as I watched him dress.

Gabriel paused on his way out, turning back to press a lingering kiss against my neck. His lips were warm, a stark contrast to the sudden chill that had settled in the room. "I have to go," he murmured, his voice barely above a whisper. "See you around."

And just like that, he was gone, leaving me alone in the aftermath of our encounter. I began to gather my own clothes as I retreated to the sanctuary of my room. I couldn't help but reflect on what had just happened. My first intimate encounter in Paris, a city that was still foreign to me, had been an adventure as quick and uncomplicated as the man himself.

Yet, despite its brevity, it had left an indelible mark on me. It was a whirlwind of emotion, a dance of desire that was as exciting as it was fleeting. And as I lay there in the quiet of my room, the echoes of our encounter still fresh in my mind, I realized that this was just the beginning of my Parisian adventure. My wanderlust tourist cherry has been popped.

20

SOPHIE & ZADIE

(Heck)

Today is the day. The day Sophie and I have been counting down to, waiting for with bated breath. Me and Sophie, on a date with Zadie. A tryst of sorts, you could say. I managed to slip away from work early, a quick detour to grab a bottle or two of wine from the store. The anticipation was almost tangible. I have to say, the expectation of sex has always been weird. I usually knew if I was getting some later that night, or at least I had an idea. But an actual guarantee that will be a mind-blowing one? How do you prepare for that? Jack off like Stiller did in the 90s film *Something About Mary?* And a threesome at that. Hashtag blessed. Weird but blessed.

Sophie and Zadie, those two mischief-makers, former cheerleaders, and still look like ones, if not better. I could only imagine what they'd been up to in my absence. Probably turning my crib into some kind of playground. Or a red room torture chamber. Who knew? They're probably making out while waiting for me. Sigh.

As I opened the door to my apartment, I was greeted by an entirely transformed space. It's no longer just an apartment; it was a love nest, a honeymoon suite. Candles flickered softly, casting warm, dim light that danced across the room, shadows playing hide and seek. The clutter that usually littered the space was gone, leaving behind an unobstructed view of us... the main event.

The window curtains were wide open, welcoming the majestic skyline that painted an ethereal backdrop. The city lights outside twinkled like distant stars, their soft glow illuminating the room just enough to set the mood. We'll be having sex in the entire house, not just the bedroom. It's definitely going down tonight. Need to bring my A-game. Should have jacked off and did a couple of push-ups.

The sheets? Dark, satin, whispering elegance and seduction. A perfect contrast to bare skin. They were smooth and inviting. The air was filled with a heady mix of scented candles and aromatic oils, creating a sensory symphony.

Pillows? There were fewer, making space on a bed that was usually occupied by two. Now, it waited for three. A full-sized mirror strategically placed against the wall, reflecting the right side of the bed, added another layer of intimacy to our sexcapade.

And the music? Sabrina Claudio's soulful crooning wafted from the Olufsen, her sensual voice setting the tone for the night. It was a soft serenade, a melodic prelude to the symphony we were about to create. Definitely not Sophie's choice. Maybe Zadie's.

My contribution to this carefully crafted atmosphere? A full-bodied wine that was now coursing through my veins, and of course, my own electrifying presence. The stage was set, and the actors were ready. Let the show begin.

"Hey there, handsome." Sophie's voice snapped me out of my thoughts and from astonishment and admiration for their interior masterpiece. I swiveled around, hooking my arms around her petite waist. Damn, she smelled intoxicating. She was rocking this little black number, the fabric clinging to her like a second skin, tracing her curves just right. And her cleavage? A perfect peek-a-boo, teasing and tantalizing.

Suddenly, another set of arms snaked around me from behind. "Hey there, lover boy." That was Zadie alright, her voice a deeper lullaby compared to Sophie. She had donned a dress almost identical to Sophie's, only hers was in white. Her scent? Damn, it was like heaven.

The girls broke away from our tangled embrace, no kisses yet. Instead, they guided me to the cylinder glass stool by the glass wall. Still no kisses. It was torture, pure sweet torture.

"C'mon, Soph. Let's give him a little show," Zadie teased. Her focus was solely on Sophie. She tilted Sophie's face toward her, planting a soft kiss on her lips. She took her time, savoring each second. I could hear Sophie's moan, and then Zadie's. She tugged on Sophie's hair a bit harder, and I saw Sophie wince, but I knew she was soaking up every moment. Zadie was establishing dominance, laying claim. She captured Sophie's mouth in another kiss, all the while locking eyes with me, daring me.

My gaze was fixed, entranced by the sight of my girls. They were lost in their own world, a private spectacle of desire and longing. I was just a spectator, sidelined yet utterly captivated. Both of them were goddesses, bodies sculpted to perfection, thanks to countless hours spent in the gym. Their bodies swayed rhythmically, seductively, to the haunting melody of Claudio's "Unravel Me". It was a dance of passion, a silent promise of pleasure. Inhibitions have long since been abandoned; they were here for the raw, unadulterated thrill of it all. The room was thick with the smell of arousal.

Zadie took the lead, her assertive nature making its presence known. Their lips, glossed and inviting, met then locked in a heated exchange. Zadie's hands cradled Sophie's face, pulling her deeper into the kiss. Sophie responded with equal fervor. It was a sight that was intimately familiar, echoing shared moments between us.

Suddenly, Zadie spun Sophie around to face me, her lips trailing a path of fiery kisses down Sophie's neck and ears. Her gaze never left mine, a challenge gleaming in her eyes. "Look at Heck, Sophie," she commanded.

As Sophie turned to look at me, her normally blue eyes clouded with desire. Zadie fondled her breast over her dress, and Sophie cried when she pinched both nipples. Then she hiked up Sophie's dress, revealing a tantalizing glimpse of black lace. She traced a manicured finger across the lacy panties. Sophie was already wet. Without any ceremony, she dipped her finger inside Sophie.

"Oh, my God, Zade!" Sophie cried out, looking at me. I could see Zadie's finger moving behind the black lace. She suddenly withdrew her finger and placed it on Sophie's lips.

"Taste yourself, Sophie," she whispered. The sight sent a jolt coursing through my veins.

Sophie grabbed Zadie's hand now, her mouth opening wide, those white teeth of hers flashing like a beacon of temptation. Her tongue snaked out, gliding over Zadie's middle finger, tasting herself there. And when she took that finger into her mouth, sucking it with an almost innocent enthusiasm, I nearly lost my cool.

Part of me was itching to join them, to break my spectator status. But another part, a larger part, wanted to stay put, to keep watching this private performance they were putting on... just for me. It was a tug-of-war, a battle between self-restraint and desire. And damn, it was one hell of a show.

"Let's remove your dress for Heck, Sophie," Zadie said as she traced her fingers on her neck and shoulder then unzipped her black dress. Her dress slowly slipped past her breasts down to her small waist it fell on the carpet, leaving her in a matching black lace bra and tiny panties. She was beautiful and sexy, and I was so hard I wanted to take her right then and there. But I knew Zadie wouldn't let me. She was running the show. And just like that, she was peeling off her dress, too, the zipper singing a sweet song of surrender. Underneath, a white thong and a strapless bra. Now they were mirror images but Zadie, with her raven tresses, Sophie a golden blond. A yin-yang of goddesses, a harmony of contrasts. Damn, what a sight!

They flashed their wicked and inviting smiles, before diving back into their make-out session. Me? I began to shed layers of my clothing, one by one. Down to my underwear now, and their eyes were on me. Drinking in the view, appreciating the effect they had. They were pleased, I could tell. And why wouldn't they be? This whole show got me wound up, ready to join the dance.

"Heck, how'd you like me to devour your soon-to-be wife?" Zadie said as she removed Sophie's bra. She grabbed her breasts gently at first, then pinched both her nipples hard without breaking eye contact with me. Sophie leaned on Zadie, both arms were hooked behind her, around Zadie's neck. "Heck? Gentle or rough?" Zadie called my attention again as she pinched Sophie's nipples and sucked her neck, leaving a red mark.

I didn't give a damn care if Sophie was hurting. She existed to be enjoyed. I stood up from the chair and joined them. I grabbed Sophie's hair from the back of her head and tilted her face so she could see me while Zadie continued attacking her breasts. I looked at Zadie and said, "Anything you please, Zadie. You can do anything you want to Sophie. I don't care."

My gaze returned to Sophie and I said, "Right, baby?" Without waiting for her response, I kissed her hard. *Wet*, I thought as I bit her lower lip. Now, Sophie was sandwiched between me and Zadie. My fiancée leaned on Zadie, daring me to watch as she allowed Zadie to play with her breasts and nipples without mercy.

"Sophie, I want to see you play with Zadie's breasts now!" I instructed her. I shifted gear, I was no longer the onlooker. I was now the conductor.

Sophie turned around and unclasped Zadie's bra. Before she could put Zadie's nipples into her mouth, I interrupted her. "I want you to do it gently." Her tongue glided around Zadie's nipple while her other hand played with the breasts. Zadie closed her eyes, enjoying it.

"Heck, touch me, please," she begged.

"Later, Zadie. Later," I replied.

I watched them make out in front of me. Both my girls took my hand and seated me at the edge of the bed. Two naked goddesses at the peak of horniness were ready to devour me. They came for me at the same time but with different targets.

Sophie leaned on me, lips crashing into mine like a damn hurricane. It was a kiss that staked her claim, territory marked with the taste of want and need. Her tongue was doing this dance, in and out of my mouth, stealing my breath away.

And Zadie? She got the rest of me. My torso sprawled on the bed, Sophie's mouth still attached to mine. One of my hands found its way to Sophie's chest, fingers pressing just the way she liked. My other hand cradled her head, pulling her deeper into the kiss.

It was a whirlwind, a sensory overload. But man, what a way to go.

I felt Zadie's tongue and mouth lick my body southward, starting from my chest. She took each nipple in her mouth, wetting them with her tongue. Her tongue was soft and playful, the warmth was ecstasy. She continued licking all the way to my abs, and then went on her knees and teased my manhood with her long hair as she kissed my thighs. Her hand felt my crotch. Resting it just on top of my brief, allowing herself to feel my erection. With my feet still on the carpet, I could feel my legs flex involuntarily from the sensation. It felt so good to be touched by so many hands on different parts of my body. I deepened my kiss with Sophie. I was no longer caressing her breasts, I was mauling them. Then I felt Zadie's tongue as it reached my groin. She pulled down my underwear to my feet and started licking my hard-on. Oh, what a tease as she didn't put it inside her mouth. She knew I was waiting for it. With my frustration, I sucked Sophie's nipple and bit it. I heard her cry in agony. Ecstasy? I don't care. I was only looking out for my own release, which was driving me crazy.

Zadie knew how to give pleasure. She was a total pro. I could feel her wet tongue slithering my entire length. Slowly. My rock twitched and grew another inch. Then like an animal pouncing on its prey, she engulfed it in her warm and wet mouth. It felt amazing!

I broke the kiss with Sophie and turned her head downward to look at Zadie. As if on cue, she looked at Zadie and whispered, "Suck him, Zade. Get him all the way down your throat."

And, without hesitation, she joined her friend. Both of them were now kneeling on the carpet, as if praying to the god called Hard Rock Dick. Both their tongues were playing around my hardness. Both of them were making eye contact with me. Sophie put me in her soft and wet mouth, while Zadie let her tongue slide just below Sophie's mouth. Two tongues were working on me, I was not going to last long. I could feel a hand squeezing me tight and another massaging my thigh. They worked on me pretty hard and never stopped pleasuring me with their mouths. They had total control! I was not going to last long. I could feel my muscles starting to tighten. My breathing became hard and labored. This was how it felt like to be a king being worshiped.

Suddenly, they abandoned me, and Zadie pulled Sophie on top of the bed. I was no longer the king being worshiped. I was back to being their audience of one. It was now Sophie on the altar. She lay on her back with Zadie on her side, kissing her mouth, her hand on Sophie's nipple, kneading, tweaking, pulling. Sophie, who was now completely lost in lust, looked at me with crazed eyes that rolled back as Zadie kissed and sucked her nipple. I kissed and licked her rib cage. I removed her panties, and I saw that she was already wet. I marveled at how beautiful her most intimate self. I kissed that spot between her legs, lingered on it, and teased it, my heaved breathing around her pleasure nub.

"Oh, God, Heck," she cried, and she gripped the back of my head and pushed herself toward my face. She moaned even harder when I deepened my kiss on her wetness and flicked my tongue with a slow thrust. I looked at Zadie, who was feasting on Sophie's neck, nipping and leaving tiny marks until she reached her collarbone. The entire scene turned me on. I lifted my face to see her in pure ecstasy. I inserted a single finger to feel her inside. It was warm and slippery but tight. Zadie looked at me, and we understood each other… we were going to give Sophie her first climax. As I moved my fingers further and touched her G-spot, Zadie sucked her left nipple and pulled the other one. Zadie began to rub herself as she was bringing Sophie to the brink. Sophie worked her hips in unison with my finger and Zadie's nipple kissing. And I could tell it wouldn't be long until she's about to let go. Sophie lifted her hips and exclaimed, "Baby, I'm coming!" I didn't know who she was referring to. Me? Zadie? I did not care at all as I watched her climax then crash.

I was now so hard and begging for a release, and I began to start rubbing my cock to give it pleasure. Zadie saw me and smiled. She pushed me to lie on my back. I was only too glad to comply. She once again put my hard-on in her mouth and then gripped it to make sure I was hard enough for her. Man, I was a hard rock! She got on top of me and slid me into her wetness. She was tight, and it felt so good. She knew what she was doing. Sophie, who had now recovered quickly from her ecstasy, climbed toward the upper part of my body with herself facing Zadie. She didn't want to be left out.

I couldn't remember how we ended the night. I was so tired of pleasuring two girls. Spent. I felt all my energy consumed. We were beside one another when it was over. Sophie was asleep. Drunk and exhausted from all that fucking. Zadie insinuated that she wanted more, but I said to save it for next time. I had a cigarette in bed. Cigarette after sex. Always hits different. But the best drag is always the first post-coital one, and this was it. I was supposed to be in an exhilarated state, but I wasn't. I should've been riding high, but nope, not even close.

Did I enjoy it? Sure, it was hot. But something felt off. Like, what's my deal? Puffing on that cigarette, I couldn't help but notice the room's lingering scent of sex and smoke.

21

ST. PATRICK'S CATHEDRAL

(Heck)

Standing there, right at the altar in St. Patrick's Cathedral, smack in the heart of New York City on Fifth Avenue. This place? Literally a masterpiece, dripping with Gothic Revival vibes. Kicked off in 1858 and swung its doors wide open in 1879. Talking about more than just a church here; it's a slice of history, a cultural icon.

Our wedding? Beautiful didn't even start to cover it. Emotions? Everywhere. The stained glass was doing this thing where it tossed colors all around, turning the pews into a kaleidoscope. Front row, there were my folks. Dad was wearing his classic poker face, while mom was doing her best to shine that proud smile my way. And Andrew, my best man, right by my side, keeping me on this planet. Supposed to be the happiest day, yeah? But, oh boy, there was this guilt, gnawing away inside.

This day was meant to be our big leap… a milestone. And I guess, in a way, it still is. All those nights spent planning down to the last detail, and boom, here we were, D-day. Snagged that Instagram-famous wedding planner. Thought it'd just be a simple transaction. But, credit where credit's due, she dove into every nook and cranny, from invites to chandeliers. Everything was spot-on, exactly how Sophie dreamed. Made you wonder, did she live like this 24/7? Who's up for being with someone who's all about planning every tiny bit? And flowers — who knew there were that many types? Or that many shades of pink and white?

Then the children's choir kicked in with Death Cab For Cutie's "I Will Follow You into the Dark". That song? It was our thing, mine and Sophie's. One of our top tracks. Or maybe, just maybe, Sophie was just playing it up because she knew I was all in on it. That tune, man, it sent me back to simpler, worry-free days. No fretting about what's next. Just some sort of eternal summer until it wasn't.

Most of these bridesmaids and flower girls, yeah, they were pretty much strangers to me. Sophie and her mom picked 'em out. All except for Zadie. Catching sight of her kinda kicked up a storm inside. That night, the one I spent with both Sophie and her, now it was feeling like some kind of betrayal. Like there was this long shadow hanging over today.

And then, there was Sophie, making her big entrance. The church went all dramatic, lights off, just this glow from the doorway framing her like something out of a dream. She was glowing, literally. In that wedding dress? All lace and softness, hugging her perfectly, whispering tales down the aisle. And that smile, man, it could light up the darkest corners. She looked unbelievable. All in, ready to dive into this headfirst.

Her dad, Peter, walking her down the aisle, was a sight. Pure pride. And there I was, soaking up the beauty of the moment but feeling this twist of guilt. Sophie, she deserved everything and more. And here I was, my mind wandering off to someone else.

Then, Sophie was right here beside me, and I was trying, really trying, to ground myself in what we're supposed to have. But it felt like I'm slipping. Thoughts of Sara just sneak in. Why today? Why was I stuck on someone else on what should be the best day of my life?

Locking eyes with Sophie, I was at a crossroads — wanting to bolt yet wishing we could fast-forward through this. The ceremony moved on, my heart's tangled up in joy and regret.

Exchanging vows, I promised Sophie everything. Yet, the guilt lingered, casting a shadow over our day. I knew I needed to face this, but in that moment, looking into Sophie's eyes, I chose to focus on our future. Hoping our love could outshine today's shadows.

The day? Unreal. We laughed, poked fun at ourselves in front of everyone we knew. Gave a speech that got Sophie all teary. My best friend and best man, Andrew? He roasted me, stumbling through a half-drunk monologue he scribbled down five minutes before hitting the stage. The afterparty was lit — a DJ spinning our favorite tracks from the 90s to now. We drank, danced, and dove headfirst into next-level adulthood with the kind of joy only a bit of tipsiness can bring. Saw someone bust out The Worm. That night, made sure Sophie and I celebrated properly. It was... well, it was us, but this time with a wedding gown in the mix. She took the lead, reminders in the form of my shirt's last button yanked a bit too hard. It was good, really good. But as the night wound down, couldn't help but wonder — what was Sara up to? Hope she's okay.

22

THE PIGEON AND THE POODLE

(Sara)

As my work shift dwindled to its final moments, I found myself craving the simple comforts of a homemade pancake and banana — another brinner, as Heck had fondly called it. I prepared my meal with a sense of quiet contentment, the aroma of the pancakes filling the air with a sweetness that felt like home.

With my tray in hand, I made my way outside, drawn by the allure of the setting sun. I chose a table near the street, the city's lifeblood, the perfect vantage point for an evening of introspection and observation.

As I placed my food on the table, the sun began its descent, casting the world in a warm, golden glow. I settled into my corner perch outside Café Boheme, the familiar sound of Parisian life serenading me. The cool touch of my Macbook was a welcome contrast to the warmth around me, its screen lighting up with an expectant glow, mirroring my own eagerness.

I slipped on my headphones, a gateway to my private sanctuary amidst the public throng. The chaotic melody of the world faded into a serene hush as I navigated to my Spotify. A smile tugged at my lips, a silent acknowledgment of Heck. His taste in music had seeped into the fabric of my existence, our love for The National now intertwined with my own identity. As the opening notes of "All The Wine" filled my ears, the world beyond my bubble seemed to pause, the bittersweet symphony resonating with the rhythm of my heart. I hit repeat, the melody becoming my personal soundtrack.

There I was, a solitary figure amidst the bustling crowd, caught in the delicate balance between daylight's last breath and twilight's gentle whisper. The streets of Edgar Quinet came alive before me, a living tapestry of life in all its unpredictability. Cyclists traced their paths through the crowd, their silhouettes etched against the setting sun. Despite the loud sound of my playlist coming from my AirPods, I can still hear the laughter and conversations swirled around me, threads in the intricate weave of Parisian life.

A white poodle, a flurry of meticulously groomed fur, pranced up to a leaking hydrant near the café. With unabashed delight, he rolled on the cool, damp pavement, his pristine coat absorbing the refreshing moisture. His owner's laughter rang out, a joyful witness to the poodle's gleeful disregard for his carefully styled coiffure.

Across the bustling street, a crowd began to gather beneath one of the shop awnings, their attention riveted to an unexpected spectacle. Intrigued, I rose from my seat to gain a better view. A pigeon, seemingly trapped atop the awning, fluttered helplessly, unable to take flight. A cry echoed in French, a plea for animal rescue to intervene.

Moments later, a man emerged from a nearby door, bearing a red ladder like a knight with his lance. He unfolded it with deliberate care, positioning it beside the awning as a makeshift bridge to freedom for the distressed bird. As he gently coaxed the pigeon into his grasp, applause erupted from the onlookers. I joined in, swept up in the collective admiration for this small act of kindness.

Then, as if on cue, a van arrived — likely from the animal rescue service. The bird was handed over to the waiting hands, and with that, whisked away to safety. This everyday scene served as an emotional reminder: humanity's gentle heart beats in every corner of this city.

As I sat on my chair and put my Air Pods back on, the "All The Wine" was still playing on a loop. I began to write, my fingers dancing across the keyboard in rhythm with the city's heartbeat. Each word was a tribute to the world around me, a silent observer capturing the essence of a city that never truly sleeps. I knew I had immortalized a piece of Paris within my words, forever etched in the archives of my heart.

With a deep breath, I opened a new document, the cursor blinking back at me like a beacon in the evening haze. It was both a challenge and a promise, a call to spill my ink-dipped thoughts onto the digital canvas. My heart was a wild symphony of emotions, a cascade of feelings that yearned for release. "This is why you're here," I whispered to myself, a mantra echoing in the quiet corners of my mind.

I was in Paris, a city that had cradled literary icons in its arms, a city whose beauty had sparked a thousand tales. Each cobblestone street, each winding alleyway, each whispering breeze held stories waiting to be told. I felt a kinship with those authors who had walked these streets before me, their souls intertwined with mine through the shared love of this city.

Inhaling deeply, I let the scent of Paris fill my senses — the lingering aroma of fresh bread, the faint perfume of blooming flowers, the earthy undertones of rain-kissed cobblestones — and let them stir poetry within me. My fingers found their rhythm on the keyboard, dancing gracefully across the keys. Each word was a piece of my soul, a fragment of my essence woven into the narrative. Every line painted a vivid picture of the world I saw, every stanza a heartfelt homage to the city that had seeped into my being.

As the song continued playing on a loop, its melancholic melody became the soundtrack of my introspection. The emotions within me spilled onto the page like watercolors bleeding into paper. I wrote of random thoughts, fleeting moments, and ephemeral snapshots of life in this city.

I penned down the lovers, their stolen kiss a testament to the fervor of Parisian love. I wrote about the old man feeding the birds, a symbol of enduring kindness amidst the whirlwind of life. I painted a picture of the child chasing her wayward balloon, a tender reminder of innocence and wonder. The cyclists —— so free, so alive, their spirit echoing the city's own pulse. And of course, the pigeon and the poodle.

Each word I wrote resonated with the rhythm of the city, mirroring the anticipation of love and the thrill of adventure that Paris embodied. As the night deepened, my words became a living, breathing entity, a love letter to the city that had captured my heart.

In a Parisian cafe,
pen scribbles with delight,
Sipping coffee
under the city's soft twilight.

Brinner on the table,
a charming sight,
Where day meets night
in a writer's flight.

As twilight unfurled its vibrant canvas across the sky, painting the world in hues of orange and purple, my words flowed like a river. The poem I was crafting wasn't merely a collection of words; it was an outpouring of my soul, a tribute to the city that had stolen my heart. It was a silent prayer, whispered into the ether, for the world I yearned to explore.

Suddenly, my words halted, my thoughts drifting towards Heck. A soft sigh escaped my lips as I murmured into the cool evening air, "How's married life?" This habit of mine, talking to Heck as if the wind could carry my words to him, had become a part of my ritual.

I closed my eyes, letting the silence envelop me, waiting for answers that never came. My heart ached with a sweet, melancholic longing. "I hope you're happy," I whispered, each word heavy with unspoken emotions, "and I wish I could be, too. 'Night, Heck."

My fingers hovered over the keyboard, the melody of the song wrapping around my thoughts. The silence that followed was not just an absence of sound but a pause, a breath, a space for lost words and unvoiced feelings. It was a moment of introspection, a quiet acceptance of the path I had chosen, and the paths left unexplored.

And as the night unfurled its dark velvet cloak over the city, I knew that I had captured a piece of Paris within my lines. My words, a witness to my journey, were now forever etched in my own chronicles. Each phrase, each sentiment, each unspoken longing, immortalized under the watchful gaze of the stars. The city of love had become a part of me, its essence interwoven with my own, shaping my narrative, one word at a time.

23

JUST ANOTHER NIGHT IN CAFE

(Heck)

It was kinda cold tonight. Summer was paving the way to autumn. I could see my breath, like little ghosts escaping my lips, disappearing into the night. My hands were shoved deep into the pockets of my tattered jeans, the denim fraying at the edges, threads hanging loose. The cigarette, a glowing ember in the darkness, hung limply from the corner of my mouth.

There was something comforting about the burn, the smoke curling upwards, getting lost in the night. The taste of nicotine, bitter and addictive. It was a familiar sting, a constant in my life of variables.

Tribeca Trickle. Our café. A lighthouse of warm light in the cold, stark night. It felt strange, walking in there without her. The bell above the door jingled as I stepped inside, announcing my presence to no one in particular. The smell of coffee, fresh pastries, and her...

No, she wasn't here.

"Hey," Lily with her freckles and new red hair, greeted me. She was disappointed the last time she saw me with Sophie. But today, she was back to her typical cheer. "The usual?"

I nodded, not trusting myself to speak. Her eyes, understanding and pitying, met mine as she led me to our spot. The corner booth, secluded, intimate. The seat opposite mine was empty. It felt wrong.

I sat, fingers drumming on the wooden table, the rhythm of my anxiety. God, I missed her. Missed her laugh, her touch, her smell. The way she'd roll her eyes when I said something stupid, the way she'd lean into me, her body fitting perfectly against mine.

I wondered if she was thinking about me. In Paris, surrounded by beauty and culture and all things new. Did she miss me? Or had she moved on, leaving me behind in this crowded city, chained to old memories and a love that refused to fade?

"Here's your coffee," Lily placed the steaming cup in front of me. "She... um, she'd want you to move on, you know?"

I looked up at Lily, her words hanging in the air between us. She was right. Sara would want that. But what I wanted, what I needed, was her. And she was a thousand miles away, living a life that no longer included me.

"I know, Lily," I murmured, staring into the swirling black liquid. I could see my reflection, distorted and broken. "I just... I can't."

And with that, I sunk back into my thoughts, the café fading into the background, the taste of the coffee bitter on my tongue. Just like the taste of loneliness. Just like the taste of loss. Just like the taste of her absence.

My thoughts began to wander, aimlessly drifting back to the remnants of my marriage — what it had become. Reflecting on it, I realized it should have never transpired. Marriage altered me; it transformed her. We found ourselves unable to meet eye to eye, our perspectives diverging more with each passing day.

There were nights when our bed remained half-empty. Sometimes, I was the one who wasn't home; other times, it was she who was conspicuously absent. Neither of us sought explanations. Silence became our unspoken agreement. On the rare occasions we found

189

ourselves under the same roof, our interactions often escalated into quarrels, sometimes even violently so.

The trajectory of our relationship wasn't merely leading us nowhere; it had veered dramatically off course, hurling us into a desolate terrain of broken vows and fragmented dreams.

Sophie... she'd changed. And not for the better. Maybe I had played a part in her transformation, but it was never what I wanted. Who would want this? No one. Sure, guys might fantasize about having a woman like that, but that's all it should be — a fantasy.

"Tell me, could even the most understanding man stomach the thought of another man's presence inside his wife? What the fuck is that? What kind of twisted reality is that?" I muttered to myself Could be a sick dude's kink. Some sick perversion of normality. Maybe for some, but not for me.

Sophie had suggested things... messed up things. She wanted another man while I was with her. Fucked up shit! Another man's dick in her ass while I fuck her! Could you endure that? Could anyone? There was no indication of where that road ends. Was it just a game to her? A test to see just how much mental torment I could withstand?

How could you love someone like that? I mean, sure, it was probably possible. Yes, it's conceivable, but it's akin to dissecting a film character layer by layer, delving into their past. Take Julia Roberts' portrayal of a prostitute in *Pretty Woman* as an example. It was understood that she had a backstory. However, if you were to truly dive into it, taking stock of all her experiences, the movie would undoubtedly take on a different tone.

Scenarios like a ménage à trois and gangbangs weren't merely exciting scenes from adult films. They represented a harsh reality for some. When this reality infiltrated your marital life, it introduced an entirely new set of rules. It was a game I staunchly refused to participate in. I knew I was simply looking for excuses to get out of that life, like that wasn't how I rolled, or at least wanted to. I was lying to myself. I was amoral and indifferent enough, but the real truth was, I needed to be somewhere else.

So, I made my decision. It was time to cut the cord, to free myself from the chaos and confusion that had become my life with Sophie. It was what I needed. For both of us.

A kid fresh off the block would probably sell his soul to be in my shoes, but would he still want that once she told him he's gotta put a ring on it? Love her, despite her being... well, her. Try kissing her after she had some other guy's taste lingering in her mouth. Messed up, right?

I know I might sound like some self-righteous prick, but come on. You were supposed to be hitched to the love of your life. Sure, it was a jackpot if the love of your life also happened to be your wildest fantasy in bed, but being the shared fantasy of a whole bunch of guys? That was a different story.

Or perhaps I was just fooling myself. Maybe I was just trying to justify why my life with her was over. It was all about rationalizing my own choices. If I still craved her, I could easily shrug it off, thinking, "a fuck is just a fuck, nothing more." But I chose the other path.

There shouldn't be any love lost. Truth was, love was lost way before then, if I was being brutally honest. There was a time when I thought she was the love of my life, until she wasn't. She no longer stirred anything in me. My happiness had faded. Lust was there, but eventually that was all there is, and when it runs out, there was nothing. Marrying her was a mistake. It was a confusing time. Too much negativity. I was too much of a coward to admit it, even to myself.

I found myself torn between staying or leaving, which was bizarre in itself. Why even question it? If it felt like that, then maybe it was the right time to leave. Was this how cheaters justify their actions? I wasn't one. I've always been a one-woman man.

Well, not always. But I don't think I've ever strayed like this. We were finished even before we put it into words. Or at least, I was. There was no excuse, but there was a reason, and that reason was Sara. She was the game-changer. The one who shook me awake from my zombie-like existence. I didn't realize it then, but I was simply going through the motions, drifting wherever the current took me, until she came along.

Suddenly, I had a new purpose, a new reason for being. Now I actually wanted to be somewhere, with someone. It seemed so basic, so elemental, but the feeling was utterly new, utterly transformative.

As much as it pained me, I had already made up my mind — my life with Sophie was over. So, I packed my bags and left. Seeking some semblance of a fresh start, I found myself leasing a modest apartment in Midtown, conveniently close to my gallery. This new place was meant to be a temporary safe place, a refuge while I navigated through the complexities of my life and the impending divorce.

Sophie's reaction to my departure was tumultuous, to say the least. She vehemently opposed the idea of a divorce, primarily concerned about the significant changes it would bring to her lifestyle. Meanwhile, my lawyer, Jeremy, was diligently laying the groundwork for the divorce proceedings. At this point, there seemed to be no turning back.

Peter, in a bid to salvage what was left of our relationship, attempted to reach out to me, hoping to dissuade me from my decision. However, I found myself deliberately ignoring his calls, too entrenched in my resolve to reconsider. Amidst all this, my parents remained blissfully unaware of the turmoil unraveling in my life. I couldn't bear the thought of them witnessing the chaotic mess my life had become.

Inhaling deeply, I sparked up another cigarette. The taste was bitter and familiar, filled my mouth as I exhaled slowly, watching the smoke curl and twist in front of me. An empty seat stared back, its vacancy a stark reminder of her absence.

Suddenly, it hit me — I wasn't hidden away in the café's back alley. I quickly stubbed out my cigarette, trying to sidestep any hassle. But really, the idea of trouble? It hardly made me flinch. Makes you think, right? Who decided we shouldn't smoke in bars and restaurants? Here we are, in New York City, a place swimming with every kind of chaos you could imagine. Yet, they zero in on us, just folks looking to savor a smoke.

I could almost see her there... Sara. Her eyes would narrow every time I lit up, a silent disapproval etched on her pretty face. She never said a word, though. Never told me to quit. Oh, there were times she hinted that I should quit, but she ain't forcing me. That wasn't her style. "You are not here, Sara. I'm gonna fuck smoke a pack," I grumbled.

Sara was all about boundaries. Respect. She had this thing about personal space, about letting people make their own choices. But I knew she cared. It was in the way she looked at me, her eyes filled with quiet concern.

"I need you, Sara," I found myself whispering into the cool air. The words hung there, suspended for a moment before being carried away by the breeze.

The café around me hummed with life, but it all seemed distant, blurry. I was lost in my thoughts, in memories of Sara. Of us.

Her laugh echoed in my ears, a soft melody that used to be the soundtrack of my days. Now, it was just a ghost of a sound, a haunting memory that made my heart ache.

I ran my fingers over the table, tracing the patterns on the wood, the little dents and scratches. Each marked a story, a shared memory. Our memory.

"She'd want you to move on, you know?"

The voice startled me out of my thoughts. It was Lily, a soft sadness in her gaze.

"Yeah," I murmured, taking another drag of my cigarette. "I know."

But knowing and doing are two different things. And right now, moving on felt like trying to climb a mountain without a rope. Impossible.

So I sat there, lost in my thoughts, the taste of the cigarette bitter on my tongue. A poor substitute for her. But it was all I had. For now... or I gotta find her ... in Paris.

I was still sinking into the worn-out cushions of a café chair, my mind tangled up with thoughts of Sara, when my phone decided to join the conversation with a buzz. It was Tess, my globe-trotting friend who had a penchant for meeting people during her travels and, similar to picking up stray kittens from the streets, bringing them back to America. Her latest find was Zaldy, now my apprentice at the gallery.

"Hey, you anywhere near our old haunt?" she asked, her voice dancing over the line. Andrew, my best man and her favorite travel companion, was with her, she explained.

"I thought you guys were in Europe?" I asked.

"We got back last night," she replied. I could almost hear the music in the background.

"So, are you in?"

Not exactly in the mood, but hell, the way I saw it, I had two options: go home to the empty apartment or head to The Broken Shaker for a night out with friends. Not really a tough choice. "Okay, see you!" I threw some bills on the table, left the quiet sanctuary of the café, and marched towards the promise of noise and distraction.

The Broken Shaker wasn't your average bar. Burrowed in the heart of the Flatiron District, it was a rooftop haven that boasted a panoramic view of the city. But it wasn't just the view that made this place special. The Shaker was a clash of cultures — a space that felt as cozy and familiar as your grandmother's living room, yet vibrant and edgy with its neon signs and vintage rock posters.

I spotted Tess and Andrew easily enough. They were huddled over their drinks, their heads bowed together in a manner that reminded me of monks deep in prayer.

"Hey, barkeep," I drawled. I slid onto a stool next to them, ordered my usual, and let the humdrum of the bar wash over me. The worn-out leather felt like an old friend. "Hit me with the usual."

Andrew looked up from his drink, his pink shirt a stark contrast to my monochrome ensemble and Tess's bohemian riot of colors. "So, how's the old ball and chain?" he teased.

I laughed, taking a long swig of my freshly poured, ice-cold beer. "Man, I miss the bachelor days."

"Marital bliss got you down already?" Tess clinked her bottle against mine, a mischievous sparkle in her eyes.

Like an albatross, I thought to myself. "Nah, just the usual jitters," I reassured them and quickly changed the subject. "So, how was Europe? Tess, did you pick up another lost soul like Z?"

Andrew chuckled, "She couldn't. I kept her on a short leash this time."

We bantered back and forth, just a bunch of twenty-somethings shooting the breeze. But then, the conversation veered towards their trip to Paris.

"You remember that American barista we met?" Tess asked, her eyes glowing with the memory. "In that quaint little café?"

Andrew grinned, "Yeah, she was a looker."

"I know," Tess chimed in, looking at me with a knowing smirk. "Andrew here was totally smitten."

His face flushed slightly as he added, "Her name was Sara, wasn't it?"

"Sara?" I echoed, playing it cool. "What'd she look like, this Sara?"

"Doe-eyes," Andrew replied, his words hanging in the air. "Hazel doe-eyes."

My heart did a somersault. Was it possible? Could it be the same Sara? The one who's been playing hide and seek in my thoughts? But hey, life's a twisted game sometimes, and all we can do is play along.

"Where'd you run into her?" I found myself asking.

Tess raised an eyebrow, her senses for juicy gossip tingling. "Why the sudden interest, Heck?"

"In some artsy café," Andrew shrugged. "Can't remember the name, but I can look it up if you want. What's got you all curious?"

"Not sure yet," I mumbled, my mind already racing with possibilities. I had to find her. See her. If that wasn't a sign, I wouldn't be sure of any much anymore. The bar suddenly seemed too noisy, its neon lights too harsh. But hey, life's a wild ride, ain't it? And sometimes, all you can do is buckle up and go along for the ride.

The insistent ring of the phone yanked me from the depths of sleep. "Oh, for the love of..." I groaned, squinting against the intrusion of the morning light. At least, there's no more Sophie, not that it mattered much to me anymore. The thought of her being the first sight of my day no longer appealed to me.

Rubbing my eyes, I checked my wristwatch — it was 10 a.m. sharp. A string of colorful expletives filled the room. I was late, disastrously late. The gallery wasn't going to open itself, and Zaldy was probably bombarding my phone with frantic messages by now. But then again, what was the benefit of being the boss if I didn't have the liberty to arrive at work at my convenience?

Reluctantly, I reached for the phone. It was Mom. Don't get me wrong, I love my mom, but her calls weren't exactly my favorite. Was it a 'mom-and-son thing'? Taking her calls always seemed like a task. Or perhaps there was this anticipation of hearing something unpleasant or expectations. Could my post-traumatic stress stem from a childhood where all the attention was focused on me as an only child? I'm not sure. What I did know was that I didn't expect any 'mom-isms'.

"Ma, you know full well I'm no good in the mornings," I grumbled into the receiver. "But for you, I'll make an exception."

"Hector," she replied, her tone stern. The use of my birth name was a clear sign — she meant business. Here we go! "Aren't you supposed to be at the gallery by now?" She questioned.

"I know, Ma. Zaldy must be blowing his man-bun right now." I tried to deflect, hoping to sidestep whatever plans my mother had brewing.

"Never mind that. When he couldn't reach you, he came to me for the spare key," she informed me. Great, just great! That wasn't the main message though... not the punch line. Now she knew I had the day free, leaving me effectively cornered. Zaldy knew the drill — in case of an emergency, he could always get the spare key from her. I suppose I could have given him one, but the paintings in the gallery were worth a fortune. It wasn't a question of trust, but security.

"I miss you, my darling boy. Why don't you make your mother happy and join me for brunch? I'm sure Maria can whip up your favorite eggs Benedict," she coaxed. Now, the bribe. How could anyone resist that? A proper brunch at her swanky Fifth Avenue apartment was always a treat. It was just around the corner from my place, yet it felt like a different world entirely.

"Of course, Ma," I capitulated, summoning all my charm to sound as sweet as summer cherries. "Could you ask Maria to get started on my espresso?"

"She's already working on it, waiting for you," came her prompt reply, followed by the abrupt silence of a disconnected call.

With a sigh, I tossed the phone aside and hastily pulled on my usual attire: a pair of well-worn jeans and a black T-shirt that had seen better days. Deciding to walk, I relished the opportunity for fresh air and a chance to clear my cobwebbed mind. I needed a moment to gather my thoughts and ponder why such an early summons was necessary. Despite my occasional annoyance with my overbearing mother, I've always harbored a soft spot for her — a proud Momma's boy, indeed.

As I approached the place I used to live, I felt like I was crossing into another dimension. A bubble of privilege harking back to an era untouched by recession and scarcity. The grandeur of the marble floors, the priceless art adorning the walls — it all served as a stark reminder of the wealth that surrounded me. There were times when I missed this place.

Eugene, our ever-dutiful butler, stood waiting as always. "Eugene, still standing tall, I see," I greeted him, managing a wry grin.

"But you're taller than me now, Master Hector," he retorted, an affectionate chuckle in his voice. Despite the passing years, he never stopped addressing me with the title he'd used since I was seven.

Mom made her entrance into the living room, looking radiant as always in her sleek, tailored black dress and extravagant pearls. As I leaned in to kiss her on the cheek, I couldn't help but admire how well she carried herself. "You look stunning, Ma. You didn't need to dress up just for me. To me, you're the most beautiful woman there is. This dress really suits you." I complimented her, planting a kiss on both her cheeks. I knew she liked that.

"It's from Carolina Herrera," she casually mentioned, as if it weren't obvious to anyone who knew her love for the designer's work.

Settling into my usual spot at the dining table, I faced Mom who was seated elegantly at the right of the head of the table. The spread for brunch was a feast for the senses, prepared meticulously by their talented in-house chef. Eggs Benedict, smoked salmon, and a selection of pastries, still warm and fragrant from the oven, graced the table. We ate, we chatted, we relished the moment. It was just another typical

Monday in the Archibald residence. Just another breakfast. No biggie.

At her subtle signal, Eugene approached Mom with a mysterious brown envelope. She slid it across the table towards me with a grave look on her face. "Hector, a member of the press sold me this. Just one in a long line of photos I've had to buy over recent months. Otherwise, they'd be splashed all over every tabloid in the city." Her voice bore an uncharacteristic edge of seriousness. I've heard this before. Page 6 bullshit. I just hope I wasn't being Me Too'd maliciously. But this time felt like I was in for it.

Cautiously, I took the envelope and opened it. Inside, as I had suspected, were candid shots of Sophie in a bar, clearly intoxicated and in compromising positions. I didn't need to pore over them; I was already familiar with their content. Silently, I slid them back into the envelope. It was an amusing thought, considering this was how I'd always pictured her college days spent at sorority soirees. But I got where Mom was coming from… Sophie was married now to this family. My mom still had no idea that Sophie and I no longer live on the same roof. I gotta tell her soon. But not today.

"Heck, what's happening? I thought you two were preparing to start a family together. Why is she behaving like this, risking our family's reputation?" Disapproval laced her words.

"I'm sorry, Ma. We're having problems, and I don't think they're fixable," I admitted, taking a slow sip of my second cup of coffee, letting the bitter taste linger on my tongue. Now, I wished this cup was of an old fashioned instead of coffee.

"Do you really want a divorce, my darling?" She asked gently, reaching across the table to clasp my hand. The moment she broached the topic of divorce, I knew which path she hoped I'd tread.

"I don't see any other option," I confessed, leaving my statement hanging in the air. But Mom knew me better than anyone; she could sense there was more to my story. I felt her silent agreement. There was no need for her to say more.

"Is there someone else, Hector?" She asked, her eyes searching mine.

199

I simply nodded, confirming her suspicions. She didn't press for more details. She understood. Just like that. She could read me. She knew perfectly well what was in my head.

"Your father can handle the divorce proceedings. He'll make it swift and hassle-free," she assured me. Sensing my reluctance, she tightened her grip on my hand and offered me a comforting smile. "He loves you, Hector. It's just... well, you know... he's not good at showing it."

"But why is it so hard for him, Ma?" I queried, my eyes searching hers.

"You and your father come from different generations, Hector. When you were born, I made it a point to shower you with all the love and attention, which was how I was raised. Your father, however, wasn't as fortunate. His upbringing was steeped in discipline, with little room for affection. That's just who he is, it's how he operates. Any hint of emotion would trigger an internal crisis. You know that, my darling" she reminisced, a nostalgic smile playing on her lips. "But he was a devoted husband to me. His problem is that he doesn't know how to express his feelings. And you never really gave him a chance to."

I wasn't prepared for this level of emotional conversation. Too early for me. So I quickly changed the subject, much to my mother's disappointment. "Ma, I need to go. Thanks for the wonderful brunch, I really enjoyed it," I said, gently pulling my hand from her grasp and standing up. I placed the white linen napkin neatly on the table.

Eugene stepped forward to assist Mom as she rose from her chair. She moved toward me and enveloped me in one of her signature warm embraces. "I love you, Hector," she whispered, her smile reminiscent of happier times. She then tenderly patted my cheek.

"Love you, too, Ma," I responded. I began to walk towards the living room, but paused and turned back towards her. "Ma, I'm going to Paris."

A look of understanding crossed her face. "Go, find her," she encouraged, blowing me a gentle kiss.

24

SHAKESPEARE & COMPANY

———

(Sara)

Thursday, my day of freedom. A day when the world of work and responsibility took a backseat, allowing me to explore the city that had become my home. I decided to venture to the Latin Quarter, a district steeped in history, culture, and the allure of the unknown.

As I meandered through the narrow, cobbled streets, quaint shops and cafés flanked either side. The smell of freshly brewed coffee and warm croissants wafted through the air, mingling with the scent of old books and the faint aroma of spices from a distant boulangerie. It was the sort of place that felt frozen in time, a cinematic tableau preserved in amber.

A memory, as delicate as gossamer and as potent as a well-aged wine, found its way to me. *Midnight in Paris*, the movie Heck and I had huddled together to watch on his mobile phone, our laughter and dreams spilling into the quiet night. His words echoed in my mind, urging me to find my own rhythm in this city, to pen my thoughts, dance under the rain-soaked skies just as Gil Pender did, and perhaps, stumble upon my own version of Gertrude Stein.

As the River Seine hummed in the distance, I found myself drawn to the familiar warmth of Shakespeare and Company. An iconic bookstore, it was a treasure trove of stories, its walls exuding an old-world charm that was as comforting as it was inspiring. The shelves were adorned with books, each promising a voyage into another realm, another existence.

My fingers traced the spine of a worn copy of *A Moveable Feast*, Hemingway's intimate letter to this very city. The scent of the pages was a heady mix of musty ink and the echoes of countless hands that had held it over the decades. A wave of gratitude washed over me, painting my heart with tones of contentment. Today, the usual throngs of tourists were absent, replaced by hushed bibliophiles lost in their literary worlds. I picked up a copy of another Hemingway — *The Sun Also Rises*. His narrative chronicles the journey of American and British expatriates who traveled from Paris along the Camino de Santiago to participate in the Festival of San Fermín in Pamplona, where they witnessed the exhilarating running of the bulls and traditional bullfights.

With my newfound treasure cradled under my arm, I stepped back into the crisp air, ready to savor a café au lait at the coffee shop that sat like a cozy secret next door. As I nudged open the door, I was greeted by the warm, inviting aroma of coffee, wrapped in the soft symphony of hushed conversations.

The hum of conversation and the clink of cutlery on porcelain filled the café. As I weaved my way through the patrons, a vacant spot by the window beckoned to me. I was about to claim it when my heart stuttered in my chest. There, settled in the shadowy corner, was a face that belonged to a chapter I thought was closed.

He wore his familiar attire — a pair of jeans that had seen better days, worn thin from countless adventures, and a faded grey T-shirt that clung to him like a second skin. The day-old stubble on his face, his nonchalant charm, framed his lips as he casually drew on a cigarette. His smoking habit remained unchanged. Even in New York, I casually reminded him of its impact on his health, careful not to sound too intrusive. He was a regular in the smoking area, placed in an outdoor corner of the café.

Our eyes locked, and for a heartbeat, the world around us ceased to exist.

"Heck?" My voice wavered, caught between shock and a rush of emotions that threatened to spill over.

"Sara," he responded, extinguishing the glowing ember of his cigarette in an empty paper coffee cup. His voice carried a note of surprise, underpinned with something deeper — could it be relief?

My name hung in the air, a ghost from our shared past. For a moment, we were no longer in the bustling café but back in our old haunt, where laughter and dreams were as plentiful as the stars above.

"What are you doing here?" I managed to ask, fighting to keep my voice steady against the tide of memories washing over me.

"I rolled the dice on fate," he replied, his eyes never leaving mine. "Hoping I might find you."

His words hung in the air, a confession that sent a shiver down my spine. He paused, his gaze softening as he studied my face, drinking in the changes time had etched upon my features.

"You look well, Sara," he finally said, his voice a tender whisper against the noise of the café. His words weren't just an observation; they were a bridge, reaching out across the distance that had grown between us.

I nodded, not trusting myself to speak. The moment stretched out, a thin line between reality and the surreal. Heck's gaze held mine, a silent conversation passing between us. Then, he was moving toward me, the distance closing like the final pages of a well-loved book.

The world around us seemed to blur, the hum of the coffee shop fading into an indistinct murmur. My heart pounded in my chest, a wild drum echoing the rhythm of anticipation.

Heck stopped before me, close enough for me to see the flecks of gold in his blue eyes. He reached out, his fingers gently brushing a strand of hair from my face. His touch sent a shiver of excitement down my spine, a spark jumping the gap between us.

"Oh, Heck!" I cried and threw myself on him. He chuckled and wrapped his arms around me.

"I knew I would find you in one of the places Gil Pender went to," he whispered in my ear. I could feel his warm breath and his lips lingered softly on my cheek. Then he stepped backward and held my face to see me clearly. "You've no idea how I missed you," he said, his voice a whisper against the backdrop of clinking cups and hushed conversations.

I nodded, unable to form words. The air around us seemed to grow thick with tension, an electricity that buzzed along my skin. And then, his lips were on mine. It was a kiss born of longing and surprise, passion and tenderness. His taste was familiar, a blend of coffee, cigarette, and the faintest hint of mint, a sensory memory that flooded back with startling clarity.

Heck kissed me with the passion of a man starved, each motion imbued with a raw intensity that left me breathless. Yet, within this burning feeling, there existed a thread of gentleness, almost like an act of worship. This experience stood in stark contrast to the first and last kiss we shared outside our café. However, as he poured his soul into the embrace, it was evident that he was investing everything into this moment. The kiss resonated with a deep sense of not wanting to part, evoking the heartbreaking sentiment that this might once again be our final farewell.

In that moment, our surroundings disappeared. There was only Heck and me, two bodies entwined in a dance as old as time. As he pulled away, my heart ached with a sweet kind of sorrow, a longing for more. But as I looked into his eyes, I saw a promise — this wasn't the end, but rather, a new start. For both of us.

25

MIDNIGHT IN PARIS

(Heck)

Sitting in that cozy café, it was just me and Sara, lost in our world. It felt like a déjà vu of those endless nights in our New York café, sipping on lukewarm coffee and trading stories. Same time as last year, the tail-end of summer. The city, oh man, Paris was about to hand over the reins to autumn.

We decided to stroll down by the River Seine, the setting sun casting an orange glow on the water. I couldn't tear my eyes away from her. She was the beat pulsing through my veins. As we passed under a lamp post, the light hit her face just so, making her look ethereal. There she was, my Sara, but with subtle changes. A little more slender, her river-like brown hair now cut short, brushing her shoulders. But those eyes, they were still the same, still captivating hazel brown.

And then, out of the blue, it started to rain. The kind of rain that only Paris knew how to serve. The timing suggested the universe itself was giving its approval.

"Heck! The rain!" she squealed, her eyes lighting up like fireworks. She twirled around, arms stretched out, soaking in every drop. This... this was her dream, to walk under the romantic Parisian rain. I was glad it was with me. My heart was flipping cartwheels inside my chest.

At that moment, I couldn't help myself. I grabbed her, pulled her close, and kissed her right there under the rain-soaked skies of Paris. The kiss was like tasting the first snowflake of winter, a burst of cold followed by warmth spreading through you. The rain was coming down harder now, drenching us, but we didn't care. We were lost in each other, the world around us blurring into insignificance.

That kiss, man, it was like biting into a ripe peach on a blistering summer day. The rain, it was coming down like it had a vendetta against the ground, but us? We didn't give a damn. Every cell in my body was chanting her name like a mantra. My hands, they were explorers, tracing the map of her body… every curve, every dip. Craved her. Yearned for her. The air, it was crackling, like the city was holding its breath, waiting.

City lights danced on the wet cobblestones, playfully teasing the puddles. Rain was falling all around us, soft whispers against the skin. The Seine, she was murmuring sweet nothings, serenading us. Just us, Sara and me, lost in our own world. A moment, frozen. An emotion, I'd chase it till my last breath.

"God, I want you." It slipped out of my lips, raw with longing.

"Let's get out of here, Heck," she whispered back, her eyes pleading.

Didn't even think twice, just flagged down the next taxi approaching us. Handed the cabbie two crisp fifty euro notes. His eyes nearly popped out of his head. But looking at us, soaked to the skin, he must've figured the dough was worth the possible water damage to his back seats.

We hit Sara's flat, and, man, I was a goner. Couldn't wait, not a second more. With an urgency driven by my overwhelming emotions, I pulled her in, kissed her with the intensity of someone possessed. Her arms, they found their way around my neck. Her mouth tasted like heaven, couldn't get enough. My lips, they went on a joyride, tracing a path from her jaw, behind her ears, down her neck to her collarbone. A journey through a landscape of sensation that I never wanted to end.

"Heck... please..." she breathed out, her breath hitching.

Her dress soaked and sticking to her like a second skin, wasn't doing a very good job of hiding her curves. My hands, naughty little devils, they found their way under her clothes, seeking those twin peaks that had been taunting me ever since I caught a glimpse of her white lace bra back at the café so long ago. When I unclasped her bra and touched her, she let out a moan and tangled her fingers in my hair.

I yanked up her dress, pulling it over her head and letting it drop to the floor, leaving her as bare as the day she was born. She stood there, all naked and beautiful. And me? I was just standing there, feasting my eyes on her. Her chest was heaving, shallow breaths coming out in quick succession. There she was, in front of me, in her black lace panties and bra.

She was a sight for sore eyes, man. A damn vision.

I stood there, drinking in the sight of her. This is the moment when I knew I had a good life. Sara's hand, it started creeping down my stomach, her fingers burning a trail through my rain-soaked tee. She toyed with my belt, dipped lower, and I clenched my jaw as she wrapped her hand around me, already hard as a rock inside my pants.

"Heck," she breathed out, her lips barely an inch away from mine.

Words, they were stuck in my throat like stubborn hiccups. I looked at her, really looked at her, and when I cradled her face in my hand, she leaned into the touch. Before the moment could slip away, I closed the gap between us. Our bodies smashed into each other, and when my hands left her face and cupped her breasts again and kissed her... I slipped off her bra and tweaked her nipples.

She let out a moan, hot and heavy, her hand rubbing against the bulge in my pants. That's it. I lost it. I wanted her all, and I wanted her now. "God, Sara, I want you badly!"

My hands, they found her ass, cupping it, giving it a good squeeze before hoisting her up. Her legs, they went around me like a vise, arms slung around my neck.

"You keep holding on like that, we ain't gonna make it to the bedroom," I teased, my hands roaming down her thighs, gripping her tight.

Our kisses, they slid into each other, one after another, tongues dancing a passionate tango. When she moaned again, well, let's just say she wasn't the only one excited. She tasted like a dream, and, man, I wanted to devour her whole.

I didn't think we'd make it to the bedroom. Didn't even break our kiss. Just carried her over to the small dining table and sat her down real gentle-like. Her hands, they found the hem of my shirt, yanked it off in no time flat.

A shiver shot down my spine as her fingers spread out across my abs, tracing the hard lines, exploring my skin. It felt amazing.

I slipped a finger over the top of her panties, sliding them down her thighs and leaving her naked in front of me. Then, I dropped on one knee, bringing my face to her core, and she whimpered.

One of her hands gripped my shoulder, the other one running through my hair as our eyes locked. She watched me as I closed my lips over her, flickering my tongue over her pleasure nub.

After a few moments, her eyes closed, back arching as she gasped with pleasure, and I licked her and sucked her, my hardness getting harder just from seeing her writhe with pleasure.

The pleasure I was giving her.

When her hips started thrusting towards me, the grip on my hair tightening, I knew she was getting closer, desperately chasing her orgasm. I slipped a finger inside her, massaging her from the inside, and then I slipped another.

"Oh, yes," she gasped, rolling her hips. "Oh, please."

I smiled to myself, watching her body arch and move and beg for a release. I could do this to her all night and never get tired of it.

She cried out one last time, her muscles tensing, and I felt her squeezing around my fingers inside as her orgasm washed over her body. I planted a soft kiss over her wetness and rose to my feet.

Breathing hard, she fluttered her eyes open, dreamy and aflame with desire. Sweat glistening on her skin like morning dew. I fumbled with my belt, letting myself free. Her eyes darted down, a lick of her lower lips that sent a jolt through me.

"God, Heck," she breathed out, her voice barely above a whisper. She inched closer to the edge of the table, her thighs closing around me like a vice.

I positioned myself at her entrance, holding back the primal urge to claim her then and there. Our lips found each other, a slow dance of passion and need. I nipped at her lower lip, a teasing promise of what was to come. And then, with one swift motion, I was inside her, filling her completely.

She cried out, breathing harder now as her nails dug into my back. My insides were burning. My skin was burning. I slid out all the way before thrusting in again, and with each movement, her breasts swayed. Her back arched as she tried to pull me closer to her.

Soon, I couldn't control the hunger inside me, and slow teasing thrusts turned into faster, more demanding ones as our bodies collided, the sound of skin on skin echoing.

Someone might hear us from behind the door. I didn't care about that, though, buried deep inside her, feeling the warmth around my hardness and her sweet breath over my lips.

"Harder," she demanded, breathless.

I gripped her hips tighter, keeping her in place as I dove harder inside her, feeling the fire pool to my stomach. God, I wasn't going to last much longer.

Reaching between us with one hand, I let my thumb slide over her wet nub, taunting it in circles as I continued pounding inside her, and soon, her body tensed, her legs wrapping tighter around me as she came once more.

Her heat enveloped me. I grunted, picking up speed, chasing my own orgasm. Three more thrusts, and I was trembling as I spilled inside her.

Damn, this... this was something else.

We lingered there for a few more moments, my body towering over hers now splayed out on the table. Just breathing. In sync. Riding out the aftershocks together.

Then, in one fluid move, I scooped her up in my arms and headed for the bed. Soft sheets, softer woman. Yeah, this was just right.

We spent the subsequent days just like that. We explored each other's bodies and minds. Ran through almost everything that happened since we last saw each other. We kept no secrets, no judgment. We had a lot of catching up to do. Outside of our strong feelings, we were practically strangers to one another. Very different lives but now finally merging. She was the one who had slipped away but fate refused to keep it that way. We knew goodbyes were difficult, at this point, I couldn't say what we would give up or sacrifice to avoid experiencing such pain again. I told her how I found out where she was, and it didn't take much thought to decide to follow. It was what I needed to do. I knew it. It was the natural thing to do. Maybe not the right one at least for everyone else, but exactly right for me. Just two humans sharing a connection, making it deeper and more meaningful with every passing second.

26

JUST US

―――――

(Sara)

In the cocoon of warmth and water, Heck and I found ourselves entwined, our laughter ricocheting off the tiled walls, creating an echo that danced around us. We were adrift in a world that belonged solely to us, a world where the hands of the clock seemed to be still, and we were the only souls breathing life into it. Giggling like love-struck teenagers, we reveled in the intoxicating presence of each other. These moments mirrored the first month of our meetings at our usual café spot in New York a time when everything felt like it could or should go on forever. But, this time, it truly felt as though it would.

"Heck! No!" I playfully objected as his day-old stubble grazed the sensitive skin my nape, eliciting a shudder that rippled through my frame.

"Hmm… make me," he teased, his voice a tantalizing whisper against my skin. His tongue traced a scorching path across my collarbone, while his hand ventured to tease my nipples, igniting a firestorm of pleasure within me.

The wave of pleasure was so overwhelming that I found myself squirming out of his arms. But Heck was swift, his strong arms folding me back into his warm embrace. "Did I tell you I love you?" he asked, his voice low and husky.

I was taken aback. Those three words had been unspoken between us. They had hung around in the air, in our shared glances, in our lingering touches, but never had they been uttered. We didn't need to say them; we felt them, in every heartbeat, in every breath. Yet, hearing them from Heck, feeling the weight of his confession, was a revelation. It was a seismic shift, a turning point in our entwined journey that promised more adventures, more shared laughter, more of us.

Rising on my tippy toes, I reached up to entwine my arms around Heck's neck, drawing him closer. "No," I whispered, my words a breath against his skin, "But I know, Heck." Our lips met in a passionate kiss, unchanging as the cosmos yet as new and vibrant as the blossoming dawn. His hands traced a path over my body, each touch an echo of familiarity that sparked shivers, cascading down my spine like a waterfall.

The rhythm of our bodies swayed to the symphony of our love under the soothing spray of the shower. It was a melody composed of longing looks, shared secrets, and whispered promises, now finding expression in the intimate dance of our bodies.

"I can't get enough of you, Sara," he murmured, his voice a silk thread weaving through the steamy water. He turned me to face the cool tiled wall, his lips embarking on an expedition, wandering from my nape to the landscape of my back, then venturing lower, igniting a trail of fire that set my senses ablaze. His hands were a delicious blend of strength and gentleness, now on my breasts, each touch sending ripples of pleasure surging through me, like waves crashing against a solitary shore.

"Oh, Heck!" I gasped. He knew the desperation laced in my voice. He parted my legs, his hand venturing lower, to my wetness, testing the waters of my readiness. Then, his hardness filled me. His movements were gentle at first, but as I matched his rhythm, he gripped my hips, setting a faster tempo. In these moments with Heck, I was no longer the girl who stared at the ceiling waiting. With him, my moment was frozen in time. All I could see was a snapshot of our shared desire and love. Our hearts drummed a synchronized rhythm, our breaths intermingled in the steam-laden air, and our bodies moved in harmony, as though guided by an unseen maestro.

Every touch, every whispered word, every shared glance was charged with an electric current of desire and intimacy. It was as if we were two celestial bodies pulled into each other's orbit, revolving around a shared axis of love and longing. This was more than mere physicality; it was a spiritual connection, a blending of souls that transcended the boundaries of the physical world.

———

In the gentle afterglow of our shared intimacy, I was bundled in bed with Heck's arms around me. I felt an irresistible urge for adventure. "Let's follow Gil Pender's journey in *Midnight in Paris*," I suggested, my eyes dancing with eagerness. Heck's face spread into a grin that mirrored my own excitement.

It took us just a few minutes and our journey commenced at the majestic steps of Saint-Etienne du Mont, the very spot where Gil was first spirited away into the enchanting world of the past. The ancient church, with its labyrinthine carvings and lofty spires, exuded a mystique that transported us back in time, a sensation as thrilling as it was disorienting.

Our next stop was Quai de Bourbon, on the picturesque Ile St Louis. This was where Gil had been swept off to a party buzzing with the likes of Cole Porter, Scott, and Zelda Fitzgerald. As we stood there, the echoes of past revelries seemed to resonate around us.

"I love how Gil senses the oddity of his surroundings," I mused, my arms snaking around Heck's waist as we admired the age-old architecture. "It's so surreal that we're standing right here, where it all happened."

"Me, too," Heck responded, his smile lighting up his face as he planted a tender kiss on my forehead. "Did you know that Bricktop, the singer and dancer, ran the famous nightclub Le Grand Duc at 52 rue Pigalle? And the real-life Bricktop, Ada Smith, made a cameo appearance in Woody Allen's 1983 film *Zelig*, visiting her actual nightclub."

"Heck, you never cease to amaze me! How do you know all this?" I asked, genuinely surprised by his knowledge.

"Well, your man isn't just a pretty face," he teased, his eyes twinkling with mischief.

Unable to resist, I leaned in and kissed him. It felt as natural as breathing, this public display of affection mirroring the private moments we shared. It was a testament to our growing bond, a love that seemed to deepen with every shared experience, every stolen kiss.

Our journey through time and space continued as we meandered towards Le Polidor, located at 41 rue Monsieur le Prince. This was the spot where Gil eagerly sought Ernest Hemingway's critique of his novel.

"What's your trivia about this place?" I playfully challenged Heck, my eyes sparkling with anticipation.

"Hmm... Le Polidor dates back to 1845," Heck began, a hint of pride in his voice. "It was a literary hotspot, frequented by Hemingway, Paul Verlaine, André Gide, James Joyce, Antonin Artaud, and even beat poet Jack Kerouac." His words painted an image of a bustling café filled with the chatter of literary geniuses, their ideas seeping into the very walls of the establishment.

"And the launderette?" I probed, eager to continue our adventure.

"That is a tale for another tour," Heck responded with a mysterious smile, sparking a flame of curiosity that promised future escapades.

Our next stop was the Rodin Museum, a tranquil sanctuary brimming with Rodin's masterpieces. Each statue narrated its own tale, their silent stories resonating within the verdant garden. We stood in awe, allowing the beauty of the place to seep into the very marrow of our being.

As we traced the footsteps of Gil's fantastical adventure, I felt a profound connection not only with the city but also with Heck, and more importantly, with myself. This was more than just a tour; it was a tangible representation of our shared bond, our mutual love for this film and this city, and our joint endeavor to embrace the present moment. It was our love story, delicately etched within the heart of Paris, like a secret whispered into the wind, carried away to be savored only by those who dared to listen.

"Sara, how about visiting Guernsey?" Heck's question broke the silence.

"Are we...?" My words trailed off as I covered my mouth with my hand, eyes sparkling with anticipation. Guernsey had always been on my bucket list, and Heck knew that — it was one of my favorite books and films.

He pulled me into his embrace, and I melted against him. "Let's trace my great grandpa's long lost love and your dreams, Sara," he murmured into my ear. I looked up into his eyes and planted a kiss on his lips, right under the watchful gaze of a Rodin statue.

27

―――――

(Heck)

Finally, there we were. Me and Sara, on a plane, jetting off to Guernsey. My treasured painting's history. Her dream. It was like two worlds colliding in the best possible way.

"Heck, I feel like Juliet Ashton!" She was buzzing, her eyes wide and bright, clutching her book, *The Guernsey Literary and Potato Peel Pie Society*. It was about Juliet's adventure in the place called Guernsey. Sara couldn't get enough of it. And me? Well, I was just happy to be on this ride with her.

I held her face with both hands and kissed her lips. "I know," I said as I traced my thumb over those kissable lips. Damn, my girl was beautiful!

"And why are looking at me like that?" she teased.

"I can't get enough of you."

"I'm yours," she said, smiling confidently.

If she was food, I'd be a glutton. Finding the right words? Man, that was a tough one. It was like trying to catch smoke with your bare hands or paint a picture with a melody. But love, love has a way of untangling even the trickiest of knots.

So, there I was, lost in her eyes, drowning in the silence. Words? Nah, they had taken a backseat. Because sometimes, words just don't cut it. They're too neat, too tidy. Love is messy, raw, and beautifully chaotic. I did not want to spoil a perfect moment with my reckless words.

Instead, I leaned in, closer, closer still, until there was no space left for words. Our lips met, a silent conversation, a secret shared. It was a whisper in the dark, a promise etched on the canvas of time. It was everything that needed to be said, and nothing at all.

Our lips met again, a magnetic pull drawing us together. It was a soft collision, a tender meeting of mouths that sent a shiver down my spine. Her lips were warm and inviting, a sweet haven that felt like home. I cradled her face in my hands, my fingers tracing the delicate contours of her cheekbones as I deepened the kiss.

Her breath hitched, a tiny gasp swallowed by the intensity of our connection. My thumb traced the curve of her lower lip, the softness sending sparks of desire coursing through me. I could taste the faint hint of her strawberry lip balm, a sweetness that made me crave more.

The world faded away, replaced by the rhythm of our shared breaths, the intoxicating scent of her perfume, and the overwhelming sense of rightness that filled me. This was more than just a physical act; it was an intimate dance, a silent conversation spoken through the language of touch and sensation.

So, yeah, I kissed her again. Because sometimes, love doesn't need words, it just needs... to be.

The moment the wheels of our plane kissed the tarmac, I could feel it. The excitement, the thrill of the unknown. Sara squeezed my hand, her eyes wide and sparkling, a mirror to my own anticipation.

We stepped out into the chilly Guernsey air, a sharp contrast to the controlled cabin temperature we'd just left. It was almost winter, and the air was crisp and clean, carrying the faint scent of sea salt mixed with the earthy aroma of fallen leaves. I took a deep breath and filled my lungs with air. I looked at Sara, her hair was ruffled by the wind. Her face was full of wonder, taking everything in.

There was this neat little ride waiting for us, a vintage Mini Cooper, decked out in blue with white stripes. The ideal sidekick for our big adventure.

"Good Lord, Heck! Where'd you find this beauty? Can we even foot the bill?" She asked, her excitement quickly turning into concern.

I kissed her forehead, gently lifting her chin. "Don't you fret about that," I said.

"You loaded or something, Heck?" She asked, eyes wide. "Those first-class plane tickets... I've never flown like that before."

"Nah, not me. But my folks, they're loaded," I said, giving her a sly wink.

"That's exactly what rich kids say when they're actually rolling in it." Now she was grinning.

I let out a soft laugh. "Alright, enough chit-chat. Help me with the bags, will ya?"

We loaded our bags and set off, leaving the airport behind. The roads were narrow and winding, meandering through lush green hills dotted with grazing cows and sheep. It was like stepping into a painting, a beautiful canvas brought to life.

As we drove, we passed through a small village. Children, bundled up in colorful winter coats, ran around playing, their laughter ringing through the air. The locals, wrapped in warm sweaters, waved at us as we drove by, their smiles as welcoming as a warm hearth on a cold day.

Fields of faded gold gave way to clusters of stone houses, their roofs dusted with the first hint of winter's frost. And then, we saw it. Our place. A charming old stone cottage nestled amongst tall trees, its windows glowing warmly against the encroaching dusk.

And at that moment, as we pulled into the driveway, the last rays of the setting sun painting the sky in hues of pink and orange, I knew we were exactly where we were meant to be. It wasn't just about tracing my roots or Sara's love for her book. It was about us, creating our own story on this beautiful island.

We found the keys under one of the flower pots as instructed. When I unlocked the door, Sara was mesmerized once again. Who wouldn't? The inside of the house was warm, filled with rustic charm. Old wooden beams crisscrossed the ceilings, and a fireplace sat waiting for a roaring fire. There was a sense of timelessness about the place, like we'd stepped into a sepia-tinted photograph.

It looked like it had been pulled straight out of a storybook, its stone walls whispering tales of the past. It had belonged to an old family, perhaps, someone can help me trace the woman in my painting that came from the first Hector Archibald, a German soldier who'd once made this island his home.

I checked the kitchen. A charming blend of old-world charm and modern convenience. The stone walls were lined with wooden cabinets, their dark tones contrasting beautifully with the white marble countertop. An old cast iron stove sat proudly in one corner, its black surface gleaming under the soft glow of the overhead lights.

There was a small dining area next to the kitchen, a rustic wooden table surrounded by four chairs. A vase of fresh flowers sat in the center, their sweet scent filling the air. It was perfect for intimate meals, a place where we could share stories over home-cooked dinners.

Adjacent to the dining area was the cozy living room. A plush sofa sat facing a stone fireplace, its hearth filled with logs ready to crackle into life. A thick rug covered the floor, its soft texture inviting bare feet. A bookshelf filled with books lined one wall. Sara was already there checking the books and the tales that had been shared in this room.

As for the food and supplies, the owner had outdone himself. The refrigerator was stocked with local produce — fresh milk, butter, and cheese, a variety of fruits and vegetables, and even some homemade jam. The pantry held an array of spices, flour, sugar, tea, and coffee — everything we would need to whip up hearty meals.

In one of the cabinets, I found a basket filled with local treats — freshly baked bread, a bottle of local cider, and a box of Guernsey gâche, a traditional fruit loaf. It was like the host had left us a culinary map of the island, inviting us to explore its flavors.

It was clear that our host had put a lot of thought into making our stay comfortable. From the cozy furnishings to the well-stocked kitchen, every detail spoke volumes about the warm hospitality we were about to experience during our stay in this charming cottage.

Sara strolled in, a dog-eared book splayed wide in her hands. "Heck," she breathed, her voice a gentle whisper in the quiet of the room. "This place... it's like some kind of paradise, isn't it?" Her eyes were all lit up, shining like a kid who'd just walked into a candy store, only the candies were replaced with old stone walls and worn-out rugs and the sweet scent of age.

I moved closer, pressing my lips to hers. Man, this was something I could never get enough of — the taste of her, the feel of her. "So," I murmured against her lips, pulling back just a bit. "What's on the menu for tonight?" I gestured towards the kitchen, stocked with food, courtesy of the generous owner.

She looked at me, her eyes dancing with mischief. With a tug on my hand, she declared, "I'm not hungry, Heck. Not for food, anyway." Her voice dropped to a sultry whisper as she added, "I want you. Right here, right now."

Who was I to refuse a request like that? We didn't need a bed or fancy silk sheets. Just us, the cold stone floor beneath us, softened by an old rug. And in that moment, as we lost ourselves in each other, it felt like everything else just faded away. It was just Sara and me, making love in our own little slice of paradise.

————

Next day, we were out and about. St. Peter Port, it was like stepping into a postcard, y'know? All cobblestone streets and pastel houses, like some artist got happy with his palette. There was a castle, straight out of a fairy tale, standing tall and proud. And the harbor, man, it was something else. Boats bobbing, seagulls squawking, that salty sea air filling your lungs.

People here, they got this easy-going rhythm, like life's a jam session and they're just playing along. Young 'uns darting around, their giggles bouncing off the ancient stones. Elderly folks, bundled up against the chill, parked on benches, soaking in the last rays of the setting sun. Faces like maps, each wrinkle a tale waiting to be told. Shopkeepers hollering from every nook and cranny, their voices a harmony in the symphony of the port.

Suddenly, Sara's tugging my arm, her voice a firecracker of excitement. "Look, Heck, the Little Chapel! Ever seen anything like it?" She pointed at this tiny chapel, all decked out in shards of china and pebbles. Like someone scooped up a chunk of night sky, dusted it with stardust, and plonked it right there. Her eyes were as wide as saucers, drinking in the sight like she couldn't quite believe it was real. Like she'd stepped into the pages of her favorite book.

I pulled her close, pressing a kiss to the palm of her hand. "So, what's it gonna be? Paris or Guernsey?"

She laughed, her eyes sparkling. "Love them both," she said. "But they're even better with you in them."

———————

The best about Guernsey? Place like no other, y'know? Got the ocean on one side, mountains on the other. Like nature couldn't make up its mind or something. The ocean, man, it was a whole different world. Waves crashing, tossing around like they've got someplace to be. That salty tang in the air, got right into your lungs, made you feel alive. And the color, this deep, dark blue, like someone spilled ink all over. Goes on forever, like it's trying to touch the sky.

Then you got the mountains. All rugged and wild, reaching up towards the clouds. Green, so much green, like the earth was wearing its best outfit. Peaks dusted with white, like a baker got happy with powdered sugar. Makes you feel small, y'know, standing there, looking at all that majesty.

And then there's Sara. She's found her sweet spot. Wrapped up in blankets, not giving two hoots about the morning chill. There she is, every day, just her and her pen, scribbling away. It's like she's trying to bottle up the whole world — the ocean, the mountains, everything, on paper. Her eyes, man, they're sparkling, lips moving but no sound coming out, like she's whispering secrets to the universe or something.

She must've felt my gaze, 'cause next thing I know, she's waving at me. Then she's blowing me a kiss. Her hair's all tangled, dancing in the wind. And that smile of hers, it was a killer. Wide and bright, could knock you off your feet. Best part? Seeing Sara this happy. She was practically glowing, full to the brim with joy and excitement. And me? I was just drinking it all in. Every grin, every giggle, every little gasp of surprise. Felt like I was falling head over heels for her, all over again.

Moments like these, man, they made you hit pause. You started thinking about life, love, the whole shebang. About how we were all just characters, navigating our way through the chapters of our own stories. Just trying to figure it all out, one day at a time.

This trip, it wasn't only about tracking down the lady my great-great-granddaddy got all starry-eyed over, or making Sara's dream come true. Nah, it was about us. About digging deep and finding ourselves, and each other, in this stunning, far-flung corner of the world. And man, I gotta tell ya, never have I felt so alive, so plugged in. It was like we were front and center in our own private fairy tale, right there on that unassuming island.

So yeah, Guernsey? It wasn't just a spot on the map. It was a vibe, an adventure. And it was all ours.

28

HOME

___

(Sara)

In the quiet of the night, with only the soft hum of Parisian life as my soundtrack, I found myself wide awake. Heck was sleeping soundly beside me, his chest rising and falling in a rhythm that was as comforting as it was hypnotic. I studied his face in the dim light filtering through the curtains, the sharp angles of his cheekbones softened by sleep, the dark stubble on his chin.

His eyelashes were long and thick, casting shadows on his cheeks. His lips were slightly parted, and I could feel the warm puffs of his breath against my skin. I traced my fingers gently over his face, careful not to wake him. He stirred slightly, a smile playing on his lips even in sleep. It was a sight that tugged at my heartstrings.

I quietly slipped out of bed, picking up Heck's discarded shirt from the floor and pulling it over my bare form. The fabric was still warm from his body heat and smelled faintly of his cologne and cigarette, a scent that had become as familiar and comforting as home. I padded over to the window, staring out at the Parisian night. The city was bathed in the golden glow of streetlights, their reflection dancing on the river Seine.

Paris is indeed beautiful — a city that even in the throes of night, pulsates with an undeniable beauty. It was a treasure trove of everything my heart yearned for: the arts, literature, enticing cuisine, awe-inspiring architecture, and a vibrant culture that was as intoxicating as the finest French wine.

More than just the city's offerings, it was the unhurried rhythm of life that had begun to grow on me. The frenzied pace of New York, where every second was a sprint against time, seemed like a distant memory. Back there, life was a blur, a high-speed chase where breakfast was a hastily grabbed coffee and bagel, consumed in quick bites while dashing to work. But here in Paris, mornings unfurled at a leisurely tempo, allowing one to truly savor their breakfast, to appreciate the delicate crunch of a croissant or the rich aroma of freshly brewed coffee.

And then there was the idyllic tranquility that descended on the city at three in the afternoon. The once bustling streets would hush into a peaceful quietude, as if the entire city had pressed pause on work, choosing instead to indulge in a brief respite.

I recalled a phrase I'd heard somewhere, perhaps from *Emily in Paris*, that seemed to aptly encapsulate this contrast: Americans work to live, while Parisians live to work. It was a statement that rang with truth, capturing the essence of the two distinct cultures. I swore I could hear *'Que reste-t-il de nos amours?'* in the distance.

No wonder then that Paris has been a beacon for writers over the centuries, a city that lured them with its promise of inspiration and creative fulfillment. The same allure had drawn me here, beckoning me to its cobblestone streets and charming cafés, inviting me to write.

I studied Heck's sleeping form, his features softened by the gentle embrace of slumber. He looked so serene, so at peace, lost in a world of dreams. I knew that if I chose to make Paris my permanent home, he would willingly uproot his life in New York to join me. But was that what I truly wanted? Could I bear the knowledge that he was leaving behind the gallery he loved, his family who meant the world to him? I think I may have already found what I was looking for here. Meaning, my time here may be over.

It wasn't as if I didn't harbor my own share of homesickness. I missed my mother and my two sisters fiercely. Yet, Heck was an only child, and the thought of pulling him away from his doting mother gnawed at my conscience. My mother, on the other hand, still had Greta and Jill to keep her company.

Greta, the eldest, had married a local and decided to settle down in Madison County, the same neighborhood where our mother resided. Mom was always on hand to babysit my adorable nephews whenever the need arose. Jill, on the other hand, had relocated to DC, seeking new opportunities. Despite the distances that separated us, we made it a point to stay connected with our mother, ensuring she never felt alone.

This line of reasoning was convincing me that it was time to go. I didn't have to really. All I needed to do was to take a look at Heck. A sigh escaped my lips, a soft whisper in the tranquility of the room. "Should I give up all this, Heck?" I asked the silent figure beside me. The words hung heavy in the air, an unspoken confession of the turmoil within me. But deep down, I knew the answer. Damn it, I knew I would sacrifice it all for him.

I was acutely aware of Heck's love for Paris, yet I also sensed the longing tug that New York held over him. The life he had left behind was a stark contrast to the one we were leading here, amidst the art and the culture of the French capital.

He had opened up to me about his family's staggering wealth, about coming into his trust fund at the age of 21. He spoke of the freedom it afforded him, how we had the luxury to choose any corner of the globe as our home without a backward glance. His words painted a picture of limitless possibilities, yet they also hinted at the weight of his legacy. He was the lone heir to a banking dynasty, a mantle he had no desire to don.

His reluctance to follow in his father's footsteps to pursue his passion was something I deeply admired. His desire to carve his own path rather than tread the one laid out for him was a proof of his strength and individuality.

Heck's money held little significance for me. My love for him wasn't tethered to his bank balance but to the man he was — kind, passionate, fiercely independent. Yet, I couldn't ignore the fact that he had obligations to his family, a future that he would eventually have to confront. The last thing I wanted was to be an anchor, holding him back from his responsibilities. My love for him was too deep, too selfless, to ever stand in the way of his path.

As the first light of dawn started to seep into the sky, I made up my mind. I would tell Heck in the morning. We could go back to New York, back to his life, back to mine. Because no matter where we were, as long as we were together, it would be home.

My heart ached at the thought of leaving Paris, but it also fluttered with excitement at the thought of our next adventure. With Heck by my side, I was ready for whatever came our way. And as I climbed back into bed, pulling his warm body close to mine, I whispered into the night, "It's time to go…"

29

SOPHIE AND THE BAD NEWS

(Heck)

There it was again, that damn cigarette between my fingers. I'd been trying to kick the habit — swear I'd been trying… but right now, it felt like an old friend. There was something comforting about the way it hung lazily from my lips, a toxic lullaby that tasted of rebellion and nostalgia.

I stood by the window, looking down at the world below. The Parisian streets were coming to life, cobblestones echoing with the rhythm of the city as people hurried to work. Each footfall was a note in the symphony of the morning, each face a story waiting to be told. I could've stayed there forever, just watching, with Sara by my side.

Sara… just thinking about her made something inside me glow. She was still sleeping, a picture of serenity nestled among the white sheets. No makeup, no pretense, just Sara. Her long brown hair spread out on the pillow, a cascade of chestnut waves glowing in the morning light. Her eyes, those doe-like wonders, were closed now, her thick lashes casting delicate shadows on her cheeks. A white sheet draped over her, revealing just enough to tease the imagination. She was beautiful, effortlessly so.

So, there she was. Just like that. Lost and found in the city of lights.

She'd darted away from New York, leaving a trail of broken pieces. My pieces. Not on purpose, though. She didn't mean to. But damn, it hurt.

But here? Here, it was just us. No complications. No mess. Just her and me. And Paris.

She told me everything. How she got here, what she did. Trying to forget that fucking frog, Matt. Trying to forget me. She managed to wipe the slate clean, all but one corner. That corner with my name etched on it. She couldn't scrub that away. Just like I couldn't shake her off me. The connection. It was there, pulsing, alive. It wasn't just a feeling. It was... kismet? Destiny? Imprinting? Call it what you want. All I know is, it was real. We both felt it.

And now, here we are. Together in Paris. Like we'd drawn it into existence. Love, tangible and present. She said she thought she was dreaming when she saw me. Imagine that. Your dream girl telling you that you're the guy in her dreams. And not the Freddy Krueger kind. If every day was like this, it'd be heaven. Pure, unadulterated bliss.

Marriage? Who needs it? I just want her. By my side. Let the world chatter. Label me a womanizer, call her a home-wrecker. Everyone else's opinion or standards were non factors at this point. Our happiness wasn't up for public debate. It was ours. Their judgment? Screw it. If they couldn't handle it, they're out. Cut off. I've got all I need right here, right now. And it was more than enough.

A smile found its way to my face. Life, it seemed, was pulling out all the stops to make up for lost time. Just when I thought things couldn't get any better, they did. Each moment with Sara was like a brush stroke on the canvas of my existence, each memory a splash of vibrant color that breathed life into my world.

Sara. She'd flipped my world on its axis, you know? Like she'd walked into my life and turned on the lights. She changed the game for me. Change of perspective. Change of the end goal. Everything's different now. The way I see things. What I want. Who I want. I probably was a different person.

Sophie? She was a memory now. Just another sorry chapter in a turbulent life. A cautionary tale. A ghost in the back of my mind. Sara, she speaks my language. Gets me. Really gets me. No secrets with her. No holding back. No second-guessing. The difference was vast. There was no need to pretend or settle. This was most likely what the luckiest ones felt.

We were finally free, weren't we? Free to be us. To be together. Free to move on from our previously complicated lives. Uncomplicated at last. At least, that was what I thought.

But then, reality decided to drop by. Literally. My phone buzzed on the bedside table. Heisenberg Sophie's name lit up the screen. My heart did a double-take. Sophie... The past has this nasty habit of sneaking up on you when you least expect it.

A rush of emotions hit me like a freight train. There was a time when Sophie's name would have had my heart doing somersaults. But now... Now it was different. I was different. Sara lit a fire in me that just wouldn't go out.

I looked at her, sleeping all peacefully, with no clue about the tempest stirring up in me. I feel this fierce need to shield her, keep this moment untouched, perfect. So, I decided to give that message a pass. For now. I wanted to soak up the calm of this morning, with her, the woman who changed my whole understanding of love and happiness.

But my phone, it wouldn't let up. Insistent little bugger. I took one last drag of my ciggie, reached for the phone, and planted a soft kiss on Sara's forehead. Didn't want to disturb her sweet slumber.

It was Sophie again. Missed calls and multiple messages. Wanted me to call her, it was urgent. I hated those kinds of SOS calls. They were never good news. And coming from Sophie at this point, I knew it was going to be bad. I dialed her number, she picked up on the first ring. No chit-chat, straight to the point.

"Are you sitting down?" She asked.

"None of your business, why?"

"You should take a seat, Heck."

"Just spit it out, Sophie," I snapped. My voice was sharp, but I didn't care.

She took a deep breath. "I'm pregnant."

"How do you know?" I shoot back.

"Did three tests this morning. Pretty sure." She sounded annoyed.

"Seen a doctor yet?"

"Didn't I just say I found out this morning?"

"Is it mine?"

"I… don't know."

"How the hell don't you know that!" I barked.

"Do you really want an answer to that?" She threw back at me.

"For fuck's sake, Sophie! How many guys are we talking about here?" My hand shot to my temple, pulling at my hair.

"I don't know! I didn't know I was supposed to be counting. I haven't been keeping score."

"You not knowing how many is a sign you should have been counting. So, what's next? You keeping it?" I asked.

"I don't know. Just found out, remember? Haven't processed it yet. Just thought you should know."

The call ended, and I was left with a head full of more questions than answers. That was a new one. Heard before she was late, but never pregnant. That was a game-changer. Whole life's trajectory shifting. No matter who the kid's dad will be, that child's in for a tough ride. Divorce kid and all. What if it's mine? Could well be. How can I let my own flesh and blood be raised by Sophie? Starting off on the wrong foot, that's what we'd be doing. And leaving that kid with Sophie, mine or not, that's exactly where we'd land. Sophie ain't cut out for motherhood. She's barely more than a kid herself. And me? Well, I ain't exactly ready to be called 'Dad.'

Now, don't get me wrong. I ain't here to preach or hand out life lessons. But that kid don't deserve a raw deal. Not if I can help it. No kid of mine, or potential kid of mine, is gonna grow up wanting. Might not be the most put-together guy, but I handled my shit. I didn't always come through on my promises, but I do what I can. I'll raise that kid, Sophie or no Sophie. We'll figure that out when we get there. Right now, it's just me. No me-and-Sophie. But that's okay. Parenting, co-parenting, whatever. I'll work something out. Don't know how I'm gonna pull it off yet, but I will. I ain't no deadbeat. I ain't a kid. I'm a man. This is part of the deal.

I looked over at Sara, still lost in dreamland. I traced her lips with my fingers, she smiled like she was dreaming of us. How do I break it to her? *Not now, Heck,* I told myself. Today, I just want to enjoy the day. Just us. I slid back in next to her, cradled her head in the crook of my arm, shielding her from any unpleasantness. For now, at least. I was such a pussy.

30

MISSING THE SKYLINE

———

(Sara)

Café Boheme was a bubbling cauldron of adventure, the air thick with the heady aroma of roasted coffee beans and frothy milk, an aroma that promised comfort and familiarity. My fingers danced over the espresso machine, coaxing a latte into existence for the waiting customers. Colette, my boss, nudged me with a knowing smile and pointed towards the café's outdoor seating area.

"Look at Heck," she said.

My gaze followed her subtle cue, landing on Heck. He was hunched over his worn, leather-bound notebook, its pages brimming with the chaotic beauty of his thoughts, each scribble a testament to his restless mind. His fingers moved purposefully, etching words onto the paper with the same fervor a painter might apply to a blank canvas. He was an enigma shrouded in mystery, a captivating tale waiting to be unraveled.

"Sara," Colette urged, her eyes twinkling with mischief and unspoken stories. "Why don't you take him his coffee?"

With a sigh, I wiped my hands on my apron, the fabric rough against my skin. The latte was ready, warm in a ceramic cup. As I approached

233

Heck, the café noises faded into a gentle hum, and all I could hear was the rhythmic tapping of his pen against the notebook.

"You should see more of this city, Heck," I said, setting his coffee down with a soft clink.

He looked up, his eyes mirroring the blue of the Parisian sky. Today, the gold specks were visible. "I've seen the city, Sara. But it's not the same without you."

In my periphery, I caught sight of Heck's notebook. This time, he had traded words for sketches. His pen was weaving an intricate tapestry of ducks in a pond, surrounded by lush trees and joggers in motion. It was unmistakably Central Park in New York City – our city.

The afternoon was lazily stretching out its limbs, most Parisians surrendering to their customary siestas. Only two lovers, lost in their own world, remained from the earlier rush, cradling the lattes I had served them. I seized the opportunity, sliding into the chair beside Heck.

"That's beautiful, Heck," I found myself saying, resting my chin on his shoulder. He turned his head, planting a soft kiss on my lips that tasted like longing and promise.

"Despite the beauty of Paris, New York has its own charm that I find comforting." His words lingered in the air, a poignant confession wrapped in a cocoon of longing. His sentiment stirred something within me, a familiar ache for the concrete jungle we had left behind. New York.

"Do you miss it?" I asked, my voice barely a whisper, as if afraid to shatter the moment.

Heck paused, his gaze distant, lost in the labyrinth of his thoughts. "Every day," he admitted, his voice echoing with homesickness. "But it's not just the city I miss. I miss my work, too."

He took a sip from his latte, the foam leaving a playful mustache on his upper lip. I reached out, wiping it away with my fingers, and found myself smiling at the intimate moment. Even in silence, there was a kind of comfort. No need for words, really. His eyes met mine, a silent conversation passed between us.

His voice softened as he continued, "There's also my father," he murmured, a hint of reluctance in his tone. "He wants me to delve into the banking world. Perhaps it's time for me to look into it. Time to get serious, and embrace who I am." His seriousness? You could practically touch it. His gaze lingered on me, his fingers tracing the contour of my jaw, a habit he often indulged when seeking comfort in my presence. I caught his hand mid-air, bringing it gently to my lips.

"You have your choices. Do what makes you happy. You can always discover yourself without losing who you are in the process. Your passion for arts and writing defines the Heck I know. But I also know and acknowledge your sense of responsibility. Learning the ins and outs of the business and eventually taking the reins isn't a bad idea. It's in your blood, as inherent as the blue in your eyes. When push comes to shove, you can still do you, but in a dashing suit," I reassured him, all the while lost in the captivating blues staring back at me.

"To be honest, I would like to see myself in that chair and suit someday…" His words hung in the air, like a new chapter of in the story waiting to be written.

"Of course you would. You're an Archibald. That chair is your destiny, whether you like it or not. It's right there for the taking, right? But it's also yours to lose, you know? But I know, too, that your love for arts and writing will never fade away. You just need to find a way for them to coexist. And remember, you'll always be my Pender," I responded, my smile softening my words.

"How lucky am I to have you?" He teased, his eyes twinkling with mischief.

"You've no idea!" I laughed, the sound echoing around us. Swiftly, I leaned in, pressing a quick kiss to his lips.

But a knot of unease twisted in my stomach, a silent alarm bell ringing in the depths of my being. Heck didn't need to voice his thoughts. His eyes, those mirrors of his soul, spoke volumes. We were both strangers in this foreign land, our hearts echoing with the familiar cacophony of New York. I was well aware that Heck's stay in Paris was temporary, yet there was a part of me that clung to the hope that he wouldn't leave me behind.

I found myself studying Heck, his face a canvas of emotions. There was something more, an unspoken worry that seemed to weigh heavily on him, more than just the longing for the familiar skyline. I sensed his unease but chose not to press him. Heck was a man who valued his space and I trusted him enough to know he would share his worries when he was ready.

"Maybe we should go back," I found myself suggesting, my heart pounding against my rib cage like a desperate plea.

Surprise flickered across Heck's face, swiftly replaced by a happiness that he couldn't quite hide. "What about your dream of writing?" he asked, concern edging his words.

"Of course, I will write," I responded, my tone resolute. "I found my Pender and he's right here with me."

Heck's smile was my reward, a silent acknowledgment of our shared dreams and hopes. His pen, once again, sought refuge in the pages of his notebook. "Maybe we should, Sara. Maybe we should," he echoed my thoughts, painting a picture of a shared future that was both exciting and terrifying in its uncertainty.

———

That night, in my modest living room, Heck and I planned our move back to New York. A bottle of rich, red wine was our only companion, its warmth lending courage to our dreams.

"I can secure us a new apartment in SoHo if you're not keen on the Upper East Side," Heck proposed, his fingers tracing hypnotic circles around the stem of his wine glass. I found myself nestled against him on the worn-out couch, swathed in one of Heck's oversized T-shirts and my underwear.

"Hmm… I don't want to make plans tonight. I want to make love," he whispered into my ear, his breath tickling my neck. He knew this intimate game of ours, how to tip the scales in his favor.

A giggle escaped my lips. "Heck! Stop that, let's finish this first," I protested, playfully extricating myself from his hold. I set down my wine glass, its contents left untouched. "I want to go back to my familiar place, the one on 89th," I confessed.

Surprise etched itself onto Heck's features. "The one you shared with Matt?"

"No. Of course not!" I rushed to clarify. "Veronica mentioned that Matt moved out. Hope, our friend, bought the building and gave it a new lease of life. There's a vacant unit on the 5th floor."

"Do you really want it?" He asked, carefully studying my expression. Then, as if reading my hesitation, he probed, "What's stopping you?"

"I hate to ask… no… beg Hope if she could loan me to cover the initial rental deposit and advance payments," I admitted, my pride getting the better of me. She played a key role in my relocation to Paris; without her invaluable assistance, I simply wouldn't be here. Her support was not merely financial and logistical but emotional as well, providing me with the encouragement and confidence needed to embark on this new chapter of my life.

"Hey, that's going to be our place, let me handle it," Heck offered, his tone laced with sincerity.

"No, Heck. I know you're well-off, but I don't want your money," I countered, my voice firm.

"You're not getting my money, that is my place, too. Where do you think I will stay when we reach New York?" He retorted, his words as much a question as they were a promise.

"You're moving in with me?" The prospect sent a surge of excitement coursing through my veins. What was once a dream was now within touching distance, and the thrill of it all was intoxicating.

"No, we're moving in together," he clarified, the words hanging in the air like a promise. With that declaration, he claimed my lips with a passionate kiss, his hands exploring the contours of my body with a familiarity that sent shivers down my spine. His touch was a language only we understood, a silent conversation that stoked the embers of our shared desire.

"Oh, Heck!" I gasped. That sound was a white flag, a surrender to the intoxicating dance of passion we were entwined in. He gently laid me back on the couch, standing up to divest himself of his jeans. His clothes pooled at his feet, revealing him in all his raw masculinity. My heart pounded in my chest, matching the rhythm of our anticipation.

He slid off my underwear with practiced ease, leaving me in nothing but his oversized T-shirt. His hand traced a tantalizing path down my body, causing me to arch my back in response. His fingers found their way to the moist apex between my legs and when he inserted a finger inside me, I was lost in a sea of pleasure. "Please don't stop..." I begged, my voice barely a whisper against the symphony of our shared desire.

The rhythm of Heck's fingers inside me coupled with the sensual assault of his tongue on my nipples was a sensory overload, enough to tip me over the edge into a world of ecstasy. As the waves of my climax began to ebb, he filled me completely, causing his name to spill from my lips in a fervent cry.

"My God, you're beautiful," he whispered, his gaze locked onto mine, a mirror reflecting the raw desire and love that pulsated between us. He took me to heights I had only dreamed of, our bodies moving in a rhythm as old as time itself, until he too reached his peak, crying out my name in a fervent release.

31

LOVE OR RESPONSIBILITY?

(Heck)

I hadn't broken the news to Sara yet. I was at a loss on how to do so. It was killing me... keeping, hiding anything from her, let alone as critical as Sophie's pregnancy. I was a coward, was I? I knew this revelation would hurt her deeply, and I wasn't ready to face that. We were only getting started, and I was already fucking it up. God, I hoped this wasn't a bad omen... my own brand of unfortunate fuck-ups! The thought of losing her again was unbearable. After all, I had only just found her.

Phone pressed to my ear, I was pacing the floor of Sara's flat. Jeremy Thomas, my lawyer, fixer and troubleshooter. The one my Dad assigned to tail my unfortunate events, a slick guy with a silver tongue on the other end.

"This seems straightforward enough," Jeremy began, "we could cite irreconcilable differences. She signed the prenup, so by default, she'll only get what was stipulated in that agreement. Her lawyer might bring up the issue of child support, but we can hold off until the paternity test results come through. I know this isn't the route you'd prefer, but given Sophie's current lifestyle, she's going to run out of resources soon. She's not going to have much after the divorce. The best course of action is to sweeten the deal, if you know what I mean."

"Look, just do whatever needs to be done. If it's money, should be simple enough," I responded, my words bouncing off the bare wall of the empty room. "I want this marriage to be over."

His response was a murmur of legal jargon and reassurances. I wasn't really listening; my mind was elsewhere. The silence of the flat felt heavy, a stark contrast to the usual warmth when Sara was around.

"I want a divorce, no matter what it costs me," I said firmly.

After hanging up, I found myself sinking into the worn-out fabric of the couch, my mind spiraling into a whirlpool of thoughts. Sophie's pregnancy, an unexpected revelation, loomed over my conscience like an ominous storm cloud threatening to burst any moment. What if the child was mine? The possibility of the child being mine tugged at the corners of my mind, adding another layer of complexity to an already convoluted situation.

I still harbored the intention to divorce Sophie. That much was clear. My heart yearned for Sara, her laughter resonating in my ears even in her absence… I am still going to marry her. But the question remained: how would everything play out with this newfound complication? I… no, we were just in the process of untangling our mess… trying to uncomplicate our lives, right? And then — bam! This happens. Ridiculous irony, isn't it?

These circumstances weren't unheard of, were they? It happened all the time in the real world right? I mean, look around, every second, marriage seemed to be teetering on the brink of divorce. A staggering fifty percent of all marriages ended up in the cold, impersonal offices of divorce attorneys. People changed… changed their minds, they evolved, and so did their feelings. People fell out of love for so much less all the time. Even for nothing. It was not actually impossible to wake up one morning and not love the other person anymore. Shit happened. Sophie and I weren't exceptions. It wasn't uncommon for people to realize that they had pledged their lives to the wrong person.

Just looking at how things were going before I ran into Sara again, it was pretty much inevitable. I'd already moved on from Sophie, even before I decided to head off to Paris. Maybe even before that, really. Sara was… well, she was closer to what I needed.

And soulmates? Well, I discovered this late in the game. Or is it too soon? I've consistently guarded my emotions, concealing them beneath the accumulated layers of life's pains and sufferings. Yet, in Sara, I found a resonance, a harmony previously unknown to me.

My situation was not unique, just another tale in the myriad stories of love, deceit, and self-discovery. Yet, it felt overwhelmingly personal, a labyrinth I was navigating alone. The path ahead was shrouded in uncertainty, but I knew I had to press on, confronting the reality of my situation and the consequences of my choices.

I didn't want to burden Sara with the responsibilities of parenting. She didn't need that kind of baggage. She deserved better. But I knew her, knew her heart. She'd support me, stand by me. Maybe we could get a full-time nanny, set up a home for the kid near ours. Yeah, that sounded like a plan that could actually work. There were always ways.

In the quiet, I had the solitude to mull over everything before we moved back to New York. I was due to meet my old man, and tell him I was ready to learn the banking business. Sara had made me realize my potential, made me see the future I could have.

The girl who made me accept that I'm an Archibald. Dad would love her, I was sure of it.

As I sat there, staring at the faint golden sunlight that filtered through the window, I felt something stir in me. Fear? No. Anticipation? Maybe. But more than anything, I felt ready. Ready to face whatever was coming, ready to be the man I needed to be. For Sara, for me, and maybe even for a little one who might share my name.

———

It took a whole lotta nerve, y'know, before I could punch in my old man's digits. My heart was slammin' against my ribcage, like it was trying to break free or somethin'. My heartbeat felt like Flea's bass thumping, slapping, getting quicker as it went on, building up the suspense, but this one's climax was fatal instead of pure euphoria. This wasn't just some random chitchat, this was one of those big, life-altering, choose-your-path kinda moments.

On the third ring, he picked up. "Son, where are you?" No beating around the bush with Archibald. We don't do small talk, we get straight to the point.

"Dad," I stammered out, voice all shaky like a leaf in the wind. There was a long pause, filled with nothing but the crackle of the line and the distant hum of New York. "I'm in Paris."

His disappointment came through clear as day, even over thousands of miles. "And what exactly are you doing there?"

How do you tell a man who's about as emotional as a brick wall that you've gone halfway 'round the world to chase after a woman who makes your heart race like a damn derby horse? That ain't our style, no sir. So instead, I said, "Needed a change of scenery, Dad. Also... I'm getting a divorce."

There was a pause on the other end of the line, the sort of silence that was louder than any words could be. Like a grenade just went off, only you can't hear a thing.

"How much is this gonna cost us?" he finally asked. Typical Hector Archibald III, always worried about the bottom line.

"I got Jeremy on it," I reassured him. "Sophie signed the prenup. A decent settlement, she can have the apartment."

"Let the suits handle that," he said, surprisingly chill about it all.

"But there's something else, Dad," I blurted out, words tripping over themselves to get out.

"What now?"

"I didn't just come to Paris for the hell of it. There's a girl , from New York, too. She moved to Paris right before I tied the knot with Sophie," I confessed.

"Go on," he said, and I could almost see the eyebrow raise.

"Her name's Sara. And she's… she's something else, Dad."

Told him how she made me feel like a man come alive, how her laughter was the best sound in the world, how being with her felt like finally finding my way home after getting lost for so damn long. Told him I was crazy about her, no two ways about it. It's kind of odd, you know, opening up to my old man like that. I mean, it's something that just never happened before — pretty much unthinkable. But there I was, somehow finding the words, telling him all about my girl. It felt like stepping into uncharted territory, breaking down walls that had always been there, silent and solid. Yet, in that moment, it just felt right, almost necessary. Like sharing a part of my life that was too significant to keep to myself.

"And we're coming back to New York," I added. "I'm ready to step up. Learn the ropes of the family biz."

It was so quiet on the other end, you could've heard a pin drop. Then, outta nowhere, laughter. The real kind, warm and genuine. Like uncorking a bottle of champagne.

"Guess it took the right woman to make you see the light, huh? Why couldn't you figure that out before marrying Sophie?"

"It's complicated, Dad," was all I could say.

"So when should I expect you back?" His tone was all business again, more boss than father.

"Few weeks, tops." I promised.

Then I hung up, feeling lighter than I had in what felt like forever. Like I'd been carrying around a hundred-pound weight and just let it go. The room was quiet, except for the distant hum of Paris outside the window. But inside, everything was calm. Peaceful. Like I'd finally crossed some invisible finish line. And you know what? Despite the awkward starts and stops, it turned out to be one of those conversations that changes things, subtly shifting the dynamics in ways I hadn't anticipated.

Sure, I was scared. Terrified, even. But also... excited. Like, really excited. For the first time in a long while, I was looking forward to whatever came next. And I knew, deep down, that no matter what happened, I had Sara by my side. And that made everything okay. Better than okay, actually. It made everything... perfect.

32

HELLO, NEW YORK!

(Sara)

As the daybreak unfurled its golden tendrils of light, I awoke to the gentle caress of the sun on my skin. Its rays snuck in through the cracks of the vertical blinds, painting a kaleidoscope of shadows on the bare walls of our new apartment. Heck and I had returned from Paris last night, our bodies weary yet hearts brimming with anticipation. Our new home was stark, save for the bed, stove, and fridge — a blank canvas awaiting the brush strokes of our shared dreams.

Veronica, ever the gracious friend, had loaned us some bedding. The soft sheets still held the warmth of our passionate embrace from the hours past. Fatigue and jet lag had been no match for the magnetic pull between us, our bodies entwining on this very bed, christening our nest.

I slid from the sheets, the cool morning air brushing against my naked skin. My eyes scanned the room for my scattered clothes, pieces of fabric strewn around like remnants of our passion. Our luggage sat in a corner, untouched, promising the thrill of unpacking and setting up our new life.

Before I could reach my clothes, a pair of strong arms snaked around me from behind. Heck, his body a warm haven against the chill of the morning, drew me into his embrace. "Where do you think you're going?" he murmured, his voice roughened by sleep, the sound sending delicious shivers down my spine.

"I need to get dressed," I replied, though my words lacked conviction. "We have a home to furnish."

His laughter, rich and resonant, echoed around the empty room. "And we have all the time in the world, Sara." His words hung in the air, an indication to the new chapter we were about to embark on, together.

"Come on," I protested.

Heck chuckled, his breath tickling my ear. "Let's stay in bed a little longer, Sara." He stretched an arm towards the bedside table, retrieving his credit card and extending it towards me.

I recoiled instinctively, my hand pushing the card away as if it were aflame. "Heck, no!" I protested, my voice echoing my surprise. "I'm not spending your money."

His face softened, his eyes crinkling at the corners as he looked at me. "Sara," he began, his voice steady yet tender, like a lighthouse guiding me through a storm.

His words hung in the morning air, heavy with sincerity. I turned to face him, my gaze locking with his. His eyes were a tranquil sea, filled with a genuine willingness that was difficult to resist. A sigh escaped my lips as I gingerly accepted the card from his outstretched hand. "Alright," I conceded, "but I'm not splurging."

A slow, satisfied smile spread across Heck's face as he drew me back into his embrace. "I wouldn't expect anything less," he murmured, his voice a soothing balm in the early morning's stillness.

I pivoted, my gaze drawn to Heck's face like a moth to a flame. His features, etched with the softness of sleep, evoked an intimacy that tugged at the corners of my heart. "Time to rise, you drowsy dreamer," I teased, my voice a whisper in the stillness of our morning sanctuary. "We need to scout out a local café for breakfast until I can breathe life into our kitchen." A playful peck on his nose sealed my words, a silent promise of the adventures that awaited us.

His response was a contented hum, his arms tightening around me in a gentle protest against the real world. "Let's linger here awhile longer," he murmured, his words weaving a warm cocoon around us. Nestled within the cradle of his arms, my head found its favorite spot — the comforting hollow between his head and shoulder. "I could wake up to this every morning and never tire of it," he confessed, his voice barely above a whisper, adding another thread to the tapestry of our shared dreams.

"Me, too," I echoed, my words a soft sigh, as I traced the contours of his face with my gaze. Our eyes locked, creating a silent conversation that only we could comprehend.

A sudden shift in his expression caught my attention. "Could you spare a few hours without me after lunch?" he asked, his question hanging in the air like an unfinished melody.

"Absolutely," I responded, my voice steady despite the flurry of unspoken thoughts. I refrained from probing further, knowing that his past was a labyrinth he was still navigating.

As if sensing my silent introspection, he broke the silence. "I'm meeting with my lawyers for the divorce proceedings and I have something significant to discuss with Sophie," he confessed, his voice holding a note of trepidation.

"Of course," I responded, nestling my chin on his chest, seeking the comfort of his steady heartbeat. My gaze traced the contours of his face, drinking in every detail. "Heck, take your time. There's no need to rush through this maze. I'm content just being here, sharing these moments with you. Whatever it is can wait."

His thumb swept across my chin in a gentle caress, a simple gesture that held a world of comfort. "I want to see a ring on your finger, Sara," he whispered, his words laden with promise.

His declaration caught me off guard, rendering me speechless. My heart pounded like a drum in my chest, the rhythm echoing my surprise. "Oh, Heck..." I managed to whisper, my voice shaky with emotion. Overwhelmed, I leaned in to capture his lips with mine, sealing our promises in the sanctity of our shared moment. He drew me closer, his arms a protective shield against the world. We remained entwined, lost in each other, until reality beckoned us to rise and greet the day.

33

(Heck)

"Welcome to my world, Sara," I said, arm sweeping wide across the gallery. Her eyes? They lit up, soaking in all the cool stuff around us. Helped her ditch that winter coat, revealing a snug white turtleneck and those jeans, oh man, fitting just right, tucked into her leather boots. She was a knockout.

"This place? It's kinda my hideout," I let slip, "a spot where I just get lost in all this art." Couldn't wait to show her this slice of me for the first time.

"I get it," she shot back. Up on her tiptoes, arms finding their way around my neck, and bam — a quick peck on the lips. "This is wild, Heck! Way beyond what I imagined!"

Laughed a bit, you know, that nervous kind. Felt this warmth kinda bubbling up 'cause she was all excited. Hadn't brought anyone here before, not even Sophie. We just kinda wandered through the gallery, our steps echoing around, bouncing off those shiny concrete floors. The place? Packed with all sorts of cool, vibrant art pieces, each with its own story. Stories I was itching to spill to her someday.

"And this guy," I nodded towards this dude, rocking those lived-in jeans and a black hoodie, hair all tied up in a neat man bun. He was deep into setting up paintings. "Meet Zaldy, my go-to guy."

Zaldy stopped what he was doing, looked up, and boom, his face broke into this warm grin. "Pleasure's all mine, Sara. Heck's been chatting you up quite a bit."

"Hello, Zaldy," Sara shot back, cheeks going a bit pink. She reached out, and they shook hands, all friendly-like.

Shot Zaldy a knowing wink as we kept moving, taking Sara deeper into my personal sanctuary within the bustling gallery. Swung open a door. "Check this out," I said, stepping into what's pretty much my brain made room. The place was soaked in sunlight, streaming through those big windows. My desk? Right smack in the middle — a wild mess of sketches, scribbles, and ideas half-baked. Pure chaos. Pure me.

"This? So you, Heck. Like, if you were a room, this would be it," she said. But then, her gaze snagged on this portrait. *The Girl in Guernsey*. Used to hang in my bedroom, but I moved it here right before jetting off to Paris. Why? Beats me. But glad I did, or it'd still be in my old spot, now Sophie's turf. Watching Sara take in the painting, her eyes all wide, felt kinda special.

"Got to deal with some client stuff real quick," I told her.

"All good, Heck. No rush," she said, throwing me one of those smiles that just does things to me. "Seriously, I could hang here all day."

Wrapped her up from behind, just like that, pulling her close. She just leaned back against me, her head finding that spot on my chest. Dropped a kiss on her hair, soaking up the moment. It was how we say "us" when words just kinda stumble.

Then, bam, the quiet's shattered. Sounds like my client's making an entrance. "Guess it's showtime," I said, half-turning towards the commotion.

Sara spun around to face me, pressing a quick, sweet kiss. "Go on,

Pender. You got this," she said, all encouragement.

But leaving her? Nah. Grabbed her hand, our fingers tangling up. Off we went, together, into the heart of the noise.

"Hey, Hecky!" Eleven year old Samantha Collins' high-pitched voice rang out. She owned the room like nobody's business. Her "hello" bounced off the walls, making sure everyone tuned in.

"Oh, Heck!" A voice echoed with surprise as she spotted me in the crowd. It was Hope Collins, married to one of the hottest Hollywood stars Richard Collins. Samantha's mother. "I've been on a hunt for some contemporary art pieces to enhance our home decor. Additionally, I've been contemplating private art lessons for Samantha. She seems to have developed quite a passion for the arts."

Before I could even do the whole "this is Sara" bit, Sara's already on it. "Hope! And Sam! You're the VIPs today!"

Hope and Sam whip around, eyebrows up. "Sara? What brings you here?" they shoot back, totally didn't see that coming. And Sam, still clutching my hand, looks up all puzzled, trying to piece together this grown-up puzzle.

"I'm here as Heck's guest," Sara responded, kinda playing it down.

So, guess it's on me to clear things up. "Looks like you guys have already hit it off," I start. "But, gotta set one thing straight. Hope, Sara's not just hanging out. She's, uh, my girlfriend."

Hope's face? All lit up. "Oh my God! You gotta spill. I absolutely adore love stories!" She was practically bouncing.

Then Sam, all wide-eyed innocence with a dash of sass, "So, you're saying you couldn't wait for me to grow up to marry me?"

Couldn't help but laugh. "C'mon, Sam! By the time you're ready, I'll be this old dude. Grey hair, wrinkles, the works," I say, nudging her into a giggle.

"I suppose..." she trailed off, rolling her eyes in mock disappointment before making a beeline towards Zaldy.

"She certainly knows how to keep everyone on their toes," Hope commented, her smile warm as she watched her daughter disappear into the crowd. Hope Ortega-Collins was the only heir of Oliver Ortega, a Filipino tycoon known for his mall chains and global retail empire. He had been my father's top client. Hope herself was a striking beauty, with a captivating blend of Asian and American features... she's like this perfect mix, kinda stunning. There was a minute when my dad thought me and her, maybe? But nah, it was way too late. She went and fell hard for Richard Collins, that British actor even before our paths crossed. They did the whole whirlwind thing and tied the knot within a year. Different journeys, but somehow, here we are, still in the same orbit.

"So, how'd you guys bump into each other?" I was bouncing looks between them, couldn't help it.

Sara was holding onto me a bit tighter, then spilled, "We were neighbors before Hope turned our building into something out of a magazine. Suddenly, she's our landlady." She stepped closer, grabbed Hope's hands. "Been meaning to catch up, just got swept up in moving and getting my bearings in Heck's world."

"Let's make time for brunch this week, no excuses!"

Then it clicked for me, and I let out a laugh. "You're the 'Hope' Sara's been mentioning all this time. How did I miss that?"

Hope just laughed it off, graceful as ever. "Well, Heck, that was all Yumi, Dad's right hand. She's the one keeping the plates spinning. Me? I'm over here trying to not drop the ball with my books and films. Couldn't do it without her."

The chat just rolled on, easy. Slipping from art to why schools should jazz up their creativity game. Threw in the idea of hooking Samantha up with a new art guru — Hope and Sam? They were all ears. Slid away then, letting the three of them catch up, while I dove into a sea of unread emails and scribbles left from my Paris skip-out.

Then Hope and Sam waved off, and there Sara and I were, cruising towards the Upper East Side. Felt this vibe from her, all curious, as we pulled up outside the Museum of Modern Art. Her eyes? Lit up like a Christmas tree. We drifted towards Tribeca Trickle, our spot, and bam —flashbacks of those wild, spur-of-the-moment nights hit me.

Lily, our go-to barista with her vibe that could light up Times Square, was all smiles. "Hey, you two! Back together, huh? The usual brinner?" she chirped, handing over the menu.

"Absolutely, and it's wonderful to see you too, Lily! Wouldn't miss it for the world," Sara shot back, all grins.

We snagged our usual booth, cozy and crammed with all those moments we've stacked up. And Sara, looking at me with those eyes sparkling, made everything else fade out. "Here we are," I whispered, fingers dancing over her face. "No more strangers." This place, with her by my side, those hazel eyes pulling me in — it's like my personal brand of insomnia.

"Why are you staring at me as though I'm about to disappear?" She teased, voice all soft.

"I'm just in awe," I confessed. "We're here, where it all began."

She leaned in, pressing a soft kiss to my fingers that cradled her chin. "If this is a dream, Heck, please don't wake me up," she breathed.

Couldn't help it — I leaned in for a kiss. Eyes shut, I threw a wish out there — if this is a dream, let me stay asleep just a bit longer.

34

THE ARCHIBALDS

(Sara)

As I slid into Heck's prized blue 1976 Datsun 280Z, I felt a strange sense of awe. Sitting in the passenger seat, I was immediately struck by the breathtaking work Heck had done. He had painstakingly rebuilt this car from the ground up, drawing inspiration from the one Tom Cruise drove in *Vanilla Sky*. The interior was a harmonious blend of tradition and passion, a witness to the car's storied past and Heck's unwavering dedication.

The seats, upholstered in the richest, deep blue leather, embraced me, offering comfort and security simultaneously. It felt as though the seats were whispering secrets of high-speed chases and heart-stopping moments from the car's cinematic counterpart, promising an adventure of our own.

The dashboard, a masterpiece in itself, boasted polished chrome accents that caught the streetlights, casting playful reflections around us. Each meticulously restored gauge seemed to wink at me, inviting my imagination to roar with the engine and thrill at the ride. The steering wheel, with its simple yet elegant design, was wrapped in matching deep blue leather, almost as dark as the sleek, black dashboard.

Running my fingers over the smooth leather and cool chrome, I couldn't help but feel a deep connection to the car. Heck had not only rebuilt a replica of David Aames' Ferrari 250 GTO, but he had also infused it with life, personality, and soul. This car was a bridge between the past and the present, a tangible manifestation of Heck's aspirations and his love for restoring beauty.

Upon opening the dashboard, I expected to find a 25-year-old mobile phone but was instead greeted by a collection of CD albums. Pulling out two, I held each CD in one hand, attempting my best Penelope Cruz impression. "Jeff Buckley or Vikki Carr?" I asked.

"I would like to say, Jeff Buckley or Vikki Carr, both simultaneously, but could you pull out Todd Rundgren for me?" Heck responded with a wink.

As the song "Can We Still Be Friends" filled the car, I closed my eyes, enveloped in the luxurious interior and the music. A surge of excitement mixed with a hint of nostalgia washed over me. It was as though I was stepping into a scene from *Vanilla Sky*, about to embark on an adventure with the man of my dreams.

The night was a swirling blend of nervousness and excitement. The distraction of the car was welcome as we drove through the city. The more I thought about this dinner, the more rattled I became. The air was thick with unspoken expectations — would they approve of me?

I let the powerful hum of the engine reverberate through my body, mirroring the thrumming beat of my heart. I found myself stealing glances at Heck, his features bathed in the soft luminescence of the dashboard. His calm demeanor was a stark contrast to the tempest of emotions brewing within me.

Tonight, I had carefully selected my best navy blue dress, a sleeveless fitted top cinched at the waist before cascading into a flowing skirt that playfully danced around my knees. I couldn't help but hope it was an appropriate choice for our undisclosed destination.

Occasionally, Heck's gaze would wander my way, his eyes softening at each meeting, igniting a warmth that radiated throughout me, as if checking how I was taking all this.

Breaking the comfortable silence, Heck turned to me, "You're exceptionally beautiful tonight, Pender," he declared, pressing a tender kiss to my hand. Our playful pet name for each other, 'Pender', always brought a smile to my face. The surprise in his voice as he complimented my transformation was intense. My usually untamed hair now rested in a messy bun, accentuating the gentle curve of my neck.

"Do you think they'll like me?" I asked, my voice barely more than a whisper.

"What's not to love?" he countered. His gaze then dropped to my neck. "Something's missing," he observed.

"Should we turn back?" I asked, my heart skipping a beat.

"No need," he assured, "I have a gift for you in the backseat. Could you get it?"

Twisting around, I spotted a rectangular box swathed in blue wrapping paper and bound with a white ribbon. Was that a Tiffany's box? As I handed it to Heck, he urged, "It's for you, Pender. Open it."

"Heck, you're absolutely spoiling me. What happens if I get too accustomed to this?" I asked, my words laced with playful teasing.

"That's precisely the plan!" he retorted with a grin.

With trembling fingers, I unwrapped the box. A diamond necklace nestled within — an unexpected gift from Heck. "Heck, it's gorgeous!" I exclaimed, momentarily forgetting my rule against accepting pricey gifts.

"I know your rule, but just for tonight, can we make an exception?" His pleading eyes melted any resistance I had. Grinning, I kissed his cheek and thanked him, attempting to clasp the necklace myself.

As Heck tried to help, I playfully chided, "Eyes on the road, Pender.

I've got this." No sooner had I fastened the necklace, I announced with pride, "See? Your girl is a true Girl Scout."

"It suits you beautifully," he murmured, pressing another kiss to my hand.

As we arrived at a grand apartment complex, Heck tossed the keys to a waiting figure, likely the doorman. He then came around to open my door, a gesture that stirred a wave of affection within me.

"Ready?" he asked, extending his arm. I nodded, slipping my hand into his, my heartbeat echoing the rhythmic click-clack of my heels on the cobblestone path leading to the entrance.

As we neared the living room, two striking figures — tall, trim and fit — their ages elegantly worn in their early sixties, extended a warm welcome. They were immaculately dressed, exuding an air of affluence even within the comfort of their own home — a concept I was still acclimating to.

Their demeanor was relaxed, their expressions light and welcoming. It was clear that they carried their wealth with an effortless grace, making everyone around them feel at ease.

"Dad, Mom, this is Sara," Heck introduced me, his voice reverberating through the grandeur of the expansive foyer. His parents, embodying the essence of elegance and decorum, welcomed us with warm smiles that reflected their inherent kindness. Their handshakes were firm, yet exuded a sense of warmth and welcome. It was clear to see these were the individuals who had shaped Heck into the man he was.

His mother stepped forward, her movements graceful as she planted tender kisses on both my cheeks. "Welcome, dear. Please, call me Helen," she said, her smile radiating sincere affection. I couldn't help but feel acutely conscious of my modest attire in comparison to the sophisticated woman standing before me. She was clad in an impeccably tailored beige pencil-cut dress, and her ears were adorned by pearls that shone with a luster rivaling that of the moon.

"You look stunning," she complimented me, her words flowing with such ease that I almost believed them. Standing next to her, however, I couldn't shake off the feeling of being rather less than stunning. She was a vision of beauty, her presence alone commanding the room.

"Thank you," I stammered, my throat constricting with nervousness. "You look... you look just as lovely. So regal. Those pearls are exquisite," I blurted out, instantly regretting my hasty words.

To my surprise, Helen simply laughed, her eyes sparkling with mirth. "They were a gift from Hector." With this, she subtly shifted my attention towards her husband.

"Hector, Sara," he announced. His voice struck a familiar chord, his face mirroring the sentiment. I had met him before, but the where and when seemed to elude me. Noticing my confusion, he smiled. "I've been blessed with a photographic memory, one of my many talents. To alleviate your confusion, I believe our paths have crossed before. Were you by any chance at my meeting with Millifords?" He casually asked, gently clasping my extended hand.

Recognition flashed in my eyes, and I gasped, placing my hands over my face the moment he released mine. "Oh, my God!" I exclaimed.

"Hold on! Were you the girl I bumped into in the hallway?" Heck interjected.

Disbelief washed over me. Our paths had intertwined long before the café meet. "You were that grumpy guy!" I blurted out, the room erupting into chuckles at the unexpected revelation. What an extraordinary way to break the ice!

As laughter filled the room, a butler handed us our drinks, and I stood there, still reeling from the surreal turn of events. This made me totally weird out.

I was still flabbergasted about my first encounter with Heck. It wasn't exactly as I remembered it — he was brusque and seemed rude, or at least that's how I perceived it. Had I recognized him as the guy who rudely bumped into me earlier, I probably wouldn't have engaged in conversation with him at the café. Interestingly, he didn't recall our clumsy collision either. Quite a twist of fate, wouldn't you say?

With a cocktail glass cradled delicately in one hand, Helen, in her full Elspen Catton mode, looped her arm through mine, guiding me on a visual journey through Heck's past — a photographic tapestry that adorned the walls of the room. Images of Heck from infancy to adolescence, from his first steps to his boarding school days, were captured in frozen moments. A particular photo of Heck engaging in a polo match caught my attention, my fingers lingering on the frame.

"He excelled in polo," Helen shared, her gaze locked onto the same photograph. "But after a knee injury, he traded his mallet for a paintbrush."

"I wasn't aware," I admitted, my voice barely rising above a whisper.

"It's not a chapter of his life he often revisits, but art has always been his first love, even more than sports. Polo was an expectation, not a passion. It was something he needed to do because he is an Archibald," she explained. I get it, the sport of kings.

My eyes found Heck across the room, deep in conversation with his father. Helen followed my gaze, her eyes reflecting a mother's pride.

"He's found his peace now, he doesn't usually tell me things but I can tell. Especially after the heart-to-heart talk with his father when you two were still in Paris and he wanted to bring you back home." Helen's gentle words interrupted my thoughts.

"He seems more content... more comfortable," I agreed, a wave of relief washing over me. Or at least I hoped.

"Here, look at this one." Helen drew my attention towards a photo of an 11-year-old Heck, clad in a black tie suit, positioned in front of a piano. "He despised those lessons, but I insisted, even bribing the music organizer for a solo performance. He was quite cross with me back then," she reminisced, setting off a round of laughter between us, envisioning a young, disgruntled Heck. The idea that Heck played classical music was mind-boggling to me. I amused myself by picturing him sneaking a Jeff Buckley number into the middle of a

Mozart recital.

My gaze was suddenly drawn to a snapshot of a young Heck, barely out of his teens, grinning behind the wheel of a sleek sports car. Helen's smile, warm yet subtly guarded, did not go unnoticed. Tentatively, I asked, "You weren't in favor of this?"

"Those were turbulent years, filled with heartache," Helen confessed, her voice imbued with traces of old anxieties. "He was going through a rebellious phase, developing an unhealthy obsession with street racing. Many nights were spent in wakeful worry, praying for his safety. He had erected walls around himself, becoming distant and resenting any attempts at meaningful conversation. The more I implored him to reconsider his choices, the deeper he seemed to plunge into his rebellion." She paused, taking a deep breath before continuing with a smile, "Eventually, we realized that the key was not to restrain him, but to indulge his passion. Those machines brought him a joy that even the polo ponies could never match."

"I'm sorry, Helen," was the only response I could manage, my hand instinctively reaching out to clasp hers in a gesture of shared understanding.

She shook her head, her smile resurfacing. "That's all water under the bridge now. It was just a phase of youthful rebellion. He needed to experience it, to get those wild impulses out of his system. He's found his peace, his happiness, and that's all that truly matters," she reassured me, her words serving as a balm to my lingering concerns.

Just then, the butler announced that dinner was served. Heck made his way over to us, planting a soft kiss on my lips before affectionately kissing his mother's forehead.

The dining room was a symphony of crystal and silver, the table laden with mouthwatering dishes and fine wine. We settled into a rhythm of casual conversation, punctuated by laughter and the clink of glasses. Despite the grandeur that could have lent an air of intimidation, there was an underlying warmth that permeated the room. The food was exquisite, but what struck me more was how the Archibalds effortlessly made me feel at home. They had welcomed me into their world with open arms, making this luxurious setting feel as comforting as my own humble home.

Hector cleared his throat, drawing our attention. He raised his glass, the crystal catching the light, casting a prism of colors around the room. "Here's to Heck, finally joining me in our family legacy. And to Sara, a welcome!"

I lifted my glass in response, its rim meeting Heck's with a delicate chime. "Thank you," I murmured, my voice barely audible over the hum of contentment resonating in the room.

"Welcome to the family, Sara," Helen chimed in, her glass raised in a toast, her smile warm and inviting.

"So, Sara, now that you're back in New York, what plans do you have?" Hector queried, his tone casual yet curious. "You could always join us in the banking sector."

"Oh, I'm afraid finance and I are not the best of friends," I laughed, the sound ringing out pure and clear. "But on a more serious note, I will be rejoining Millifords in a fortnight. Given your business dealings with them, it seems our paths might cross more often," I added, my gaze drifting towards Heck. A fleeting thought crossed my mind — was I truly using the term 'fortnight' as though I was residing in Guernsey, clad in a Victorian-era dress?

"We'll see how well you negotiate when you're on the opposing side of the boardroom," Heck quipped, his eyes twinkling with playful mischief.

"Ah, but I have my charm to rely on," I countered, a mischievous smile playing on my lips. My remark elicited a round of laughter, adding another layer to the evening's joyful symphony.

Helen then turned her attention to Heck, "And what of your art gallery?" Her question hung in the air, an unspoken challenge wrapped in maternal concern.

"Zaldy will captain that ship," Heck responded, his voice steady. "We're mulling over the idea of recruiting another curator and restorer. It is pretty much self-sufficient at this point. But my weekends will still be devoted to the gallery. It's like Sara, who plans to write her novels in between her corporate commitments. We won't forsake our passions," he explained, his eyes locked with his father's in a silent conversation of understanding and respect.

A spark of excitement ignited in Helen's eyes, her voice laced with pride and eagerness. "My darling boy, I could lend a hand to Zaldy if you wish. The artistic streak you bear was inherited from me. I fear I would lose myself, be adrift without an anchor, if I were ever torn away from all that is beautiful and meaningful in this world. The realm of art and I have been inseparable companions for as long as I can remember. To me, these things were not merely outlets or indulgence. They were expressions and feelings of someone. "

Her voice swelled with conviction as she offered her assistance, "I could be a valuable asset to your team," she volunteered, her voice rising like a symphony reaching its crescendo.

Heck's laughter, rich and warm, echoed around the room. "Mom, are your philanthropic activities not keeping you sufficiently entertained?"

"It's not about boredom, my dear," she retorted, her eyebrows arching towards Hector in a silent plea. "When everyone else is chasing their dreams, why should I not pursue mine?"

In response, Hector reached for Helen's hand, bringing it to his lips in a tender kiss. A silent agreement was sealed in that gesture, an understanding that passion should never be stifled.

"Just promise me one thing, Mom," Heck interjected, his tone half serious, half teasing. "Don't turn my gallery into a battlefield, and spare poor Zaldy the torment."

"Of course!" she retorted, her laughter ringing out like a bell, infectious and joyous. It spread across the table, wrapping us all in amusement.

The elephant in the room — Heck's divorce — remained unaddressed, a fact I appreciated. I didn't want anything to ruin this beautiful night where I found myself drawn into their world, captivated by their stories and shared history. I felt less a stranger and more a welcomed guest. As the evening waned, I realized this wasn't merely a dinner; it was a window into Heck's life, his past, and perhaps, our shared future.

35

NAME YOUR PRICE

(Heck)

The conference room felt like a scene straight out of a sci-fi flick, all cold, sterile vibes with its glass and steel stretching out everywhere. Kinda felt like it echoed the tension, too, you know? Like walking into a fog you can't see but sure as hell can feel. There was Sophie, sitting across the table, her lawyer playing shadow. Mine was on my left, silent as a grave. This whole setup was supposed to be the final curtain call, the big dramatic ending to our divorce saga. But Sophie, oh she definitely missed the memo.

"No more divorce, Heck," she kinda stumbled over her words, her voice shaking like she was about to deliver a big speech. "I want us to raise our child together, you know, like a proper family should." It was almost like she was trying to convince herself as much as me, her words teetering between a plea and a declaration that this was somehow the right move.

Her words landed like a punch to the gut, robbing me of my breath. Anger, hot and wild, began to bubble up. "That's not up to you. You can't be serious, Sophie!" I shot back, louder than I meant to. "We're done. This... this is just us tying up loose ends."

And then, the kicker. "No, Heck! I am dragging the Archibald name

264

through the mud!" She just tossed it out there, like tossing a match into a pile of dry leaves. Suddenly, she shifted gears. What started off kinda soft and sincere flipped into this full-blown fury, like a storm brewing on the horizon, all dark and threatening. You couldn't tell what she'd pull next. It was like meeting her for the first time, discovering this whole other side to her.

Talk about hitting below the belt. The Archibald name, the pride of my family, was now a weapon in our dirty little war. Sophie knew exactly where to hit for maximum damage. And, damn, it did. She knew she couldn't hurt me, so she went for the jugular instead. Gotta say, as much as it irked me, she was making headway.

Then, with that look of innocence plastered all over her face, as if she was the picture of purity, she dropped another bomb. "Remember our little adventure with Zadie?" Her tone, oh-so-sweet, dripping with honey. "Caught the whole show on video. Thinking it might be time to give the press something juicy. Let's show the world who's really fit to run this banking show." Inside, I had to laugh. A sex tape? Really? What is this, the 90s? Like, who doesn't have one of those lurking around?

I was standing there, kinda floored. "Just imagine the look on your mom's face, seeing her golden boy in all his glory," she sneered, this wicked laugh just slipping out. Part of me gets it, you know? A video of me floating around wouldn't be the end of the world. 'Might not even be a premiere. But Sophie? With her connections? She could turn it into her personal nuke.

"I've already got a publicist on retainer, ready to spin me as the innocent victim of the Archibald family's debauchery and perversion," she boasted, talking like she wasn't right there with me in that video.

"So, what's the deal, Sophie? What do you want?" I spat out the words, each one tasting bitter on my tongue. "Just spit it out. How much to make this whole thing go away? Just tell me the magic number to get you sign that godforsaken paper!"

She leaned back, a smug grin plastered across her face like she was a cat that had finally cornered her prey. "Oh, Heck," she purred. "I know my worth. Believe me, you don't have deep enough pockets. Our kid's gonna sit pretty on top of your family empire. That's my end game."

I could barely wrap my head around what I was hearing. "You've lost it, Sophie! You're nothing but delusional. You and me? We're done. I'm going to marry the woman I love," my voice softened at the thought of Sara, "and you should find someone who makes you happy. I found mine. If that child is mine, he won't want for anything, he will be well provided. I will make sure of that."

The room? Felt like it was shrinking around us... the walls inching closer. And her eyes, man. Used to be all warm and fuzzy, now they're shooting daggers, icy with this resolve that kinda alarmed me. "Why settle for just baby mama status when I could have you, plus the whole Archibald treasure chest, huh?" she hissed, like venom dripping from each word. "Don't even dream about marrying her. I'll destroy her, Heck. If you leave me, I swear I'll bring Sara down with us. Do you think, I don't know about her?"

Boom. Her words hit me like a sucker punch. "You fucking bitch!" I could feel my blood run cold. The thought of Sophie hurting Sara... tarnishing her life. It filled me with a kind of rage I'd never known. I shot up from my seat, my fists clenched so tight they hurt. I was this close to losing it, to doing something I'd regret. But no, I gotta cool it, gotta get out before I do something stupid.

But then, she crumbled. Tears started flowing, and she was all, "I love you, Heck. Can't we hit the reset button, do it right for our baby?"

She knew how to play me. That child, that tiny, not-even-here-yet person. She knew it was my Achilles' heel, that I'd walk through fire for that, happiness be damned.

"That ship, Sophie? It's long since sailed," I said, the words felt like weights. "Us? Nah, that's a hard pass. Loved you, though. Really did. You were my world, once." Took a moment, you know, to just breathe before dropping the hammer. "But that's history now."

So, there I was, staring across at what used to be my everything. Inside, it's like a hurricane. Anger, frustration, a bit of *what the fuck*?

And somewhere in there, a whisper of fear. Like I'm caught in some bad dream, scrambling for the exit.

Jeremy, my lawyer, decides it's time to play fucking peacemaker and cleared his throat. "Maybe we should take a break, come back when heads are cooler," he suggested, fiddling with his shiny gold tie.

That set me off. My anger turned on him. "You're supposed to handle this, Jeremy! That's what I'm paying you for!" I snapped. I needed out.

And with that, I was out of there and hit the elevator button. Down to the street. Outside, I gasped for air. Lit up a cigarette, inhaled half in one drag like it was oxygen. Anger's bubbling, about to spill over. All I could think about was getting back to Sara. She's got this way of smoothing out the edges.

36

BYE, SARA.

(Heck)

Shaking off the winter's bite that clung to my coat, I stepped into our warm and cozy apartment. The day's events had twisted everything, flipping my universe on its head. There she was, Sara, lounging in our living room, her eyes twinkling like a fresh winter snowfall when they landed on me. A grin spread over her pretty face, casting a glow that outshone any artificial light in our intimate space.

I tried, man, did I ever try, to match her cheer, but my heart was a lead weight, sinking with a secret I never wished to harbor. The day's encounter with Sophie had left a bitter taste in my mouth, a grim reminder of a past I'd rather forget. But here, in the warmth of our home, with Sara's radiant smile lighting up the room, I found a sliver of hope. Maybe, just maybe, things would turn out alright.

"Finally, you're back," she chirped, springing up from the couch and bounding towards me. She planted a kiss on my lips, sweet and welcoming.

I wrapped my arms around her petite waist, returning the kiss with passion, not wanting to release her. But I had to. I cradled her face with both hands, peering into her hazel eyes... those same eyes that roped me in and made me fall hard. "You've got the most beautiful mug I've ever seen," I murmured.

"Yeah, yeah," she replied nonchalantly, her eyes studying my face. "Hey, what's eating at you?"

"Nothing. Just wanted you to know I could say that to you every day, and it'd never get old," I managed to say, trying to keep my voice steady.

"Hmmmm... what's the plan? You up for takeout or should I try my hand at cooking? Can't guarantee it'll be edible though, and no complaints allowed," she said. Her words were playful, her lips peppering my cheeks with quick, affectionate pecks.

You didn't really know where you stood with fate. At times, it felt as though the stars had aligned perfectly in your favor, and at other times, it seemed to treat you harshly without mercy. This was one of those harsh times. It was as if fate was fucking with me, had cruelly shown me a glimpse of a happy, idyllic alternate universe, only to ruthlessly snatch it away just as Sara and I were preparing to dive in. It felt like a cruel joke. Just like being Punk'd, but with God almighty sitting on Ashton's chair, and the world itself playing the role of accomplice. Such moments were the reason I found it hard to believe in God. Omniscient and omnipresent, my ass!

Man, how was I supposed to drop this bombshell on her world? She was my anchor. My ray of sunshine piercing through the darkest clouds. She was the only one who had a knack for making me laugh until I could no longer stop. She taught me what it really meant to love and in return, to be loved. She was here now, in this situation, all because of me. I took her away from a life she'd painstakingly built for herself, and here I was making a royal mess of it all over again.

What a bloody idiot! I felt like such a dumbass. Maybe it was high time I got my head checked, to see if there was any smidgen of sense left in it. And while I was at it, maybe I should have her head examined, too. Just to figure out what the hell she saw in a disaster like me. Why she'd willingly dive headfirst into this calamity I called life? Love's a real trip, ain't it? Makes you do all sorts of crazy things. Things like believing in a screw-up like me.

Her laughter, it was like music, filling up the room and making everything else seem insignificant. As I stared in to these hazel eyes, they held the kind of warmth that could thaw the coldest hearts. And her smile, don't get me started on that. It all came so naturally. Effortless. There was no need to try. It just happened. As I said, it could light up a room, hell, probably even a whole city.

And yet, here I was, poised on the brink of raining on her perfect parade, all set to suck the joy right out of it. A quick switch from bliss to misery — it was as if there wasn't even enough room for a dull, normal moment in between. The whole thing felt so damn arbitrary, like a cruel twist of fate. The thought alone felt like a punch in the gut. It just didn't sit right. It wasn't right. It wasn't fair. How does one bring themselves to hurt a beautiful angel right in front of them? To cast a shadow over their sunshine? The mere thought was enough to shatter my heart into a million pieces. But then again, life's funny that way, ain't it? One minute you're on cloud nine, the next you're free falling with no parachute.

As I looked at her, my heart heavy with the weight of the impending storm, I couldn't help but wonder — how did I end up here? How did I get to a point where I was about to hurt the one person who had shown me what it meant to truly live? Every single one of my screw-ups had led to this moment. A grand compilation of nonsense, layered with pure, unadulterated fuckery. What once seemed inconsequential had morphed into life-altering crap. And the worst part? It wasn't even me bearing the brunt of it all. If only I'd known.

But life doesn't come with an instruction manual, does it? I'm a writer. Why not pen down some 'Living for Dummies' handbook? You've gotta roll with the punches, and take it on the chin. Pay your dues. And right now, this was one hell of a punch.

"Sara," I started, my voice barely louder than a whisper. The words felt like shards of ice lodged in my throat. "We need to talk."

Her smile faded instantly, replaced by a flicker of worry. The room was hushed, save for the gentle patter of snowflakes kissing the windowpane. It was as if Mother Nature herself was mourning alongside us, the season's last snowfall gracing the world outside.

"Something wrong, Heck?" she asked, her voice shaky.

"I... I don't know how to say this, Sara," I confessed, the weight of my secret pressing down on me. "I fucked up. Sophie... Sophie's pregnant."

The room seemed to spin as the words spilled out. It felt as if someone had sucked all the air out, leaving us in a stifling vacuum of silence. Sara simply stared at me, her eyes wide with shock and disbelief.

"But... but you were separated... before you went to Paris to find me?" she stammered, her voice barely audible.

"Yes. I don't know how far along she is or if that happened after I left," I mumbled, running a hand through my hair. I was scrambling for an honest answer, but all I found was a painful truth.

"I thought we had something good, Heck. I thought our future is right out there," Sara's voice wavered, the words barely a whisper.

"We are, Sara. We damn well are. Don't let a moment of doubt convince you that what we have is over or that we don't have a future together," I responded, my voice shaking as much as my resolve. "The day I found you, whatever I had with Sophie ended. It was like a chapter closing." My voice cracked, the words slicing through me like a hot knife.

Life sure knew how to throw curveballs, didn't it? Just when you think you've got the hang of it, it tosses you a slider. And man, this one was one hell of a slider.

Tears welled up in Sara's eyes, spilling over tracing rivulets down her cheeks. I reached out to wipe 'em away, but she pulled back, creating this splitting gap between us.

"I... I can't, Heck," she whispered, her voice barely audible over the deafening silence. "I can play second fiddle... but I won't rob a kid of his dad."

"Sara, I don't even know if that kid is mine…" I began, but she cut me off.

"Heck, that doesn't matter, you're still married to her. To the world, that's your baby." Her tears kept falling, like a dam had broken. God, it was tearing me apart to see her like this.

"I love you, Sara. I've never loved anyone else like I love you," I managed to choke out.

"Heck, I feel like I've been gutted. I can't…"

Before she could finish, I pulled her into my arms, hating myself for every tear she shed because of me… for hurting her. I hated myself for bringing her back to this. I promised a new life. This wasn't what I had in mind. I was supposed to be her source of comfort, security, and bliss. We were supposed to be together.

We stayed like that, lost in our little world. No idea how much time slipped by; it was just us, holding onto each other like a lifeline. It felt like the last time we were going to be together just like this. It was never going to be the same. When her tears finally stopped cascading down her face, she swiped at the remnants with the back of her hand. I brushed my thumb against her damp cheeks, staring into her eyes. Those bright, lively eyes that greeted me with so much love, now clouded with nothing but pain.

She took a step back, attempting to force a smile on her tear-stained face. She inhaled deeply, a shaky breath filled with emotions. "Heck," she whispered, voice thin as a spider's web. "I love you. More than anything else in this messed-up world. But I know, as long as I'm around, as long as we're… this, you'll never be able to see or think straight. You'll never be able to make a fair call. Because I know you'd always pick me."

"And I would, Sara. Every damn time," I told her, my words raw and honest, straight from the gut.

"I know, Heck. And that's why I'm going to give you some space." Her words hung heavy, like a black cloud ready to burst.

"No, Sara, don't do this. Not to us. I can't let you walk away again," I pleaded, desperate. I reached out, grabbing her arm, not wanting to let her slip away.

"Heck, why can't I have you?" She choked out, tears streaming down her cheeks again like tiny rivers of pain, each a dagger stabbing straight into my heart.

"You do have me, Sara. In every way that matters. I let you go once, and it nearly killed me. I won't make that mistake again."

She slid out from my hold, like water slipping through fingers. She looked at me, eyes all red and puffy, but still the most beautiful thing I'd ever seen. Tried to smile, but it was more of a wince. She traced her fingers along my face, wiping away tears that hadn't even fallen yet.

"You're the best damn thing that's ever happened to me," she said, voice all choked up. "I've never been this happy, Heck. Never felt this kind of love. You are not just the love of my life. You are my life."

She paused, like she was trying to find the right words. Or maybe just the courage to say 'em.

"I love you so much it hurts sometimes. And I can't stand the thought of you hurting. Of you having to choose."

I put a finger to her lips, stopping her mid-sentence. "No, Sara. There's no choice to make. It's always been you. Just you."

"I know, Heck," she said, her voice barely a whisper. "And that's why we have to do this. I need to step back, give you some space to think, to plan. You can't do that with me around."

"No, Sara. Listen to me," I said, grabbing her hands. "Jeremy's working on the divorce. I'm gonna marry you. I can't let you go again. Not even for a second."

It felt like the room spun around us, like we were in the eye of a hurricane, everything else just a blur. But in that moment, it was just us. Just me and Sara. And that's all I needed. That's all I wanted.

"Heck, if I don't give you this space, you'll make a mistake. A big one. And you'll regret it, and then you'll resent me for it. No, Heck. I love you too damn much for that. You got to sort things out with Sophie. You lost me once, stumbled upon me again. I'm sure as hell you can find me one more time."

"No..." My voice was barely a whisper. But I knew she heard it. Felt it.

"I'm going to leave, Heck. When I close the door, I need you to pack up, go to your folks or somewhere far from here. I want you to think about you. Not Sophie. Not me. Not your kid. I'll come back tonight, and I expect you gone. I can't bear to watch you walk away."

"But we don't have to do this. Don't go," I begged her.

"But we do, Heck. For me. For us. I don't want you to screw this up."

She closed the gap between us, her lips finding mine in a kiss that was all kinds of wrong and right. Her lips, they were soft, like rose petals after a morning dew. And her mouth, it was wet and inviting. You'd think a painful goodbye kiss would be the opposite of desire, but darn, it felt more like a prelude to making love. I could feel my heart hammering away in my chest, like a drummer gone wild at a rock concert. I just couldn't get enough of her. So, I cradled her face in my hands, taking the reins of the kiss. It started off soft and gentle, like two feathers caught in a playful breeze. But then, things began to sizzle.

She parted her lips just a smidge, a silent invitation I couldn't say no to. I accepted, and our tongues met halfway. It was an odd sensation, like some kind of intricate dance. Our tongues, they were twirling and twisting, mapping out the contours of each other's mouths. There was no resistance, only submission to own longing.

The taste of her was intoxicating, a mix of her lip balm and something uniquely her. It was a flavor that I could never get enough of. And then, there was the feeling. The feeling of her tongue against mine, the warmth of her mouth, the way her breath hitched when I pulled her closer. It was a whirlwind of sensations that left me dizzy and wanting more.

I kissed her with all the passionate intensity I could muster up with. Everything I had left. We were lovers in every sense. Her lips were soft, tightened only by her face being pressed on mine. Our future was clouded for now. We only had these repeated kisses to hang on to. I refused to lighten my grip on her. So did she, at least for now. Shaken that this suddenly was the last.

It was a kiss with certainty that it would never happen again. Not like this. I knew it was never going to be this good again. No love was lost, but innocence, warmth, and physical longing. Like the kiss of the dying. A dying and forsaken union, that is. Memorable enough to take with you where there is only nothingness. Your life did not depend on it. Her memory of you will. There were no inhibitions. Just pure unadulterated unconditional love. This love was not intangible. You could see it, feel it, touch it. It was the only acceptable thing to be overwhelmed by. As if the longing has already started. As if this affection was trying to convince the gods to change their minds. Make it not the last.

But just like that, it was over. We pulled away, both of us breathless. Her eyes were glossy, swollen. Trying to hold the tears back, and so was I. The slightest touch could have caused me to shatter, such was my volatile and delicate state. When that kiss ended, it felt like my heart was being ripped out of my chest. It was a pain that was both physical and emotional, a pain that reminded me of what I was losing. Suddenly, the pain from everything that had happened washed over me as if it were brand new. And in a way, it was. This was the first time I had been hurt so deeply, a direct result of loving just as intensely.

It tasted like the end, bittersweet and full of regret, a goodbye wrapped in a promise of a second chance. I held her tight, held her in place, like I was trying to freeze this moment before everything went belly-up... trying to memorize the feel of her in my arms, knowing every second counted.

I knew both of us wanted to hold on, one more time. But knowing

Sara, she'll always do what is necessary. As she pulled back, there was this look in her eyes. A look of finality, like she'd just closed the book on us. She turned on her heel, leaving me alone in the silence. It was deafening, the quiet, like the world had stopped spinning. The snow kept falling outside, painting the world white, like even the heavens were weeping with me. All I could do was stand there, watching the only woman I ever truly loved walk out of my life, again. It was all on me. All my fault. My heart breaking into a million tiny pieces. Finally, I got a taste of what real suffering felt like.

———

I couldn't remember how long I stayed there, hoping she'd come back. I was paralyzed mentally. As if I banished and exiled my own capacity for reasoning. Time seemed to stretch out in front of me, each tick of the clock echoing the emptiness she'd left behind. Was it minutes? Hours? I couldn't tell. It seemed irrelevant. All I knew was that she was gone. I'd lost her once before, but I was hellbent on not letting history repeat itself. Just how many times does a guy gotta screw up before he knows what to do or how to play his cards right?

Sure, this mess was my doing. I was the architect of my own downfall. These are the fallout of letting my lower head do the thinkin', right? The aftermath of believin' things just sort themselves out. But at that moment, I felt like a scared kid again, ready to run back to his father for one last lifeline. If there was someone who knew how to get things done, it was my dad. There was no shitstorm that this man hasn't survived. If it was a war, he was the general calling the shots, no opponent could touch him or outsmart him. And, right now, it's wartime. I needed his legal know-how and his network of influential friends. Anything and everything that could help me cut ties with Sophie for good. Actually, anything that resolves this mess.

It was a childish move, maybe even a little immature. But if swallowing my pride meant getting Sara back, then so be it. I didn't know how long it would take, or how many bridges I'd have to cross—or burn—to get there. I was indifferent to the idea of humbling myself before the man for whom I had previously expressed disdain. But I was determined to figure it out. and get it done. No more fucking around, Heck!

I was going to clean up this mess, find Sara again, and make things right. No more screw-ups. No more detours. This time, it was about our happy ending. And I would fight tooth and nail to make that happen.

37

HOMECOMING

(Heck)

As I stepped through the familiar, polished hallway of my folks' place. I locked eyes with mom. Didn't want to be here, really. Felt like defeat, like I was waving the white flag. Like I'd screwed up big time. Yeah, in so many ways, it screamed "disappointing failure at life."

Then, bam — her face did this thing. Surprise sparking, only to get swallowed up by a tidal wave of worry as she took in the whole picture: me, looking like a hot mess, luggage in a death grip. It's like you could almost taste the concern hanging thick in the air. Without uttering a word, she hurried towards me, wrapping me up in one of her hugs that felt like home. Pride? Ego? Gone. Just like that.

"Eugene," she softly called out, her voice slightly muffled against my shoulder. "Please take Heck's bags to his old room."

Her instruction reverberated through the quiet expanse of the house, stirring the silence that hung heavily in the air. Felt like I was crashing the party, bringing my gloom and doom into the cheerful vibes of my childhood home. This memory, with my pain and anguish, will stain this place forever…just like in the past with all those troubles I put her into.

"Ma, I'm sorry. Didn't know where else to go..." Words barely made it out as I buried my face deeper into her shoulder, trying to rub off the sting of that last blow-up with Sara. The shame, the grief, it's heavy, you know? All that sharp-edged bitterness and angst I cart around? Gone. Just like that. Felt small again, like a lost kid.

"Oh, my darling," she said, voice all gentle-like, hand moving in those familiar comforting circles on my back, just like when I was little. "This is your home. You're right where you need to be."

Home. Funny, hasn't really felt like it for a while, not since I took off. But now? Yeah, it felt like I'm home..

As always, she didn't press me for more details. Didn't cross the line. . . no overstepping. She understood my need for silence, knew that words would come when they were ready. She steered me to the living room, fixed me a drink, and settled next to me. Her presence, a comforting constant in the storm of emotions raging within me. A silent reassurance that I had made the right decision by coming here. I was ready to admit my defeat. Own up to my screw-ups. I was ready to confide, to unload. At last.

I looked at the amber liquid swirling in the crystal glass before taking a deep one. The liquor about to unlock all sorts of stuff. Pride, sure. But guilt? That's the real kicker here. Took another one of those deep breaths — you know, the kind that's supposed to steady you but never really does — and broke the silence.

"Sara... she asked for some space," I slipped out in a whisper so quiet, you'd think the words were heavy. And man, they were — packed with regret and a kind of disappointment that just sticks to you. Once those words hit the air, they just stayed there, hanging, like they were proof of how messed up things got.

My mother, she just nodded, like she got it without needing the whole story. Her hand found mine, a silent kinda comfort. "Your father will be home any minute now," she said, eyes locked on mine, and I swear, it was like she was mirroring every bit of that ache. "We're supposed to attend a cocktail party with one of his banking associates."

Felt embarrassed as I realized the inconvenience my sudden arrival might have caused. "I'm sorry, Ma," I apologized quickly. "You should go ahead without me. I just... I need some a place to think."

However, my mother was quick to dismiss my concerns. Shaking her head, she tightened her grip on my hand. "Nonsense! Heck, you are our priority, not some social gathering. Your father will know what to do. We don't get to help you out as much as we like because you won't let us. Let us help you handle this one." I knew she was right.

Just as her words trailed off, bam — the front door swung open. It was my father. My old man didn't drop a single question as he took in the whole scene. His eyes did this little dance from Mom to me, and he got the whole picture without anyone saying a word. Smooth as anything, he strolled over to the bar, fixed himself a drink, and then he was right there with us, not needing to say it out loud but making it crystal clear: family first, no matter what.

This? Gotta say, it's a first for us. Can't remember ever hitting this kind of crisis mode before. Felt like we're all suddenly in the war room, strategy session in full swing.

This unusual scene of me sitting with my parents on either side was far from typical in our family dynamics. In fact, it had never happened before... yeah, not our usual setup. I mean, the last time we were all huddled like this was when I totaled the car. Almost gave Mom a heart attack. I've never been big on the whole 'let's sit down and have a serious chat' vibe. But at this moment, man, it felt right, almost necessary.

I've always had this thing about asking for help — like, no thanks, I got it. But here I am, doing just that. And you know what? Damn glad I did. I was determined to fight for the woman I loved, and I knew these two people would help me navigate through this shit storm.

"Sophie... ain't signing the divorce papers," I started, voice all choked up.

Then, the dam broke. Told 'em about the lawyers' meet, how the air was so thick you could cut it. I recounted Sophie's threats. Nah, I'm not one to get rattled easy — it takes a lot to shake me up. But this? This whole dragging out of what should've been a straightforward split? That grinds my gears. And yeah, being away from Sara through all this mess didn't make things any easier.

Apart from Sophie's threats, I shared Sara's selfless decision to step back so I could make an unbiased decision. And then, I dropped another bomb: the whole fear about maybe having a kid with Sophie on the way. Talk about complicating the plot.

"Heck," my mother started, her voice soft yet firm, "Sara didn't say it was over. She simply wants you to have your own space so you can make a fair decision without her influence. She wanted to give you clarity to get through this." She paused, her gaze thoughtful. "She knows, as do I, that if she were around, you'd always choose her, regardless of the circumstances."

My mom was right. Sara, she'd put her own shot at happiness... a real chance, finally... on the back burner. For me.

Could hear it, the respect in her voice. "That's why I think of her more highly now. I like her more," she let slip. Her words, they were like an echo of my own thoughts, put a stamp on my feelings for Sara. Even managed to toss a sliver of hope into the gloomy pit I was in.

"The issue at hand is both simple and complex. That's what we're dealing with," my father began, his voice firm yet carrying an undertone of controlled anger. "But no mountain is high enough. Nothing is, not to us. We won't let anyone threaten our family. Especially not them!"

By his use of "them," I knew what my dad was thinking. Brought to mind Isidor Rabi's 'You drop a bomb, and it falls on the just and the unjust.' Sophie ain't gonna be the only one in the blast radius, I swear. There'll be collateral damage.

"They didn't know who they were fucking with," his words, they kinda filled up the room, like he'd drawn a line in the sand. Yeah, the man had his flaws, but when it came to getting what he wanted? He was a maestro. Think wartime general, but swap the battlefield for the living room. Pure class. "And what advice did your lawyer offer?" he asked, shifting his gaze to me.

"I... I left Jeremy behind in the meeting, Dad. I haven't had a chance to talk to him yet. My primary concern was Sara," I admitted, guilt subtly lacing my words.

"Fuck him! He's done. Consider him fired. We wouldn't be having this conversation if he could do his job. Let my legal team handle this situation," Dad declared, his tone deadly serious. "It's better if you're kept out of the loop."

When he spoke like that, you didn't argue. Smartest thing to do was shut up and let him call the shots. Let the maestro work his magic. Besides, I had no desire to deal with Sophie. I will let him deal with her and her family. I'm no coward or trying to dump my responsibilities or my mess to my folks, but at this point...there's no one else in my priority but Sara.

Sophie could make all the threats she wanted, but me going back to her? Not happening. Not in this lifetime. As far as I'm concerned, we're history. Closed book. For good. If this means letting my old man do his damage to make this happen, who the fuck cares?

Without missing a beat, my father rose from his chair, placing his whiskey glass down on the table with a resounding clink. He strode purposefully toward his office, adjacent to the living room. I knew without a doubt that he was about to make some calls he didn't want me privy to. His "team" or whatever sanitized term he used for his hired guns could take down whole corporations or tiny countries if they felt like it. Those Sullivans? They were about to get a rude awakening, and they didn't even know what hit 'em.

"Heck," my mother began in her gentle voice, "let your Dad be your father this time. Allow him to shoulder some of your burdens. Your focus right now should be on sorting out your feelings and figuring things out with Sara." Felt like a load off, her words did, like giving in to some higher power. They were stepping up, tackling this beast that was bigger than me. Felt a pang right there, regretting my earlier childish tantrums and petty snipes at them. How'd I still rate this kindness from them.

Feeling vulnerable, I turned to look at my mother. My voice wavered slightly as I confessed, "I just found her, Ma. She's the woman who brought color into my otherwise monochrome world." No lies there. She was, and she still is. She's knocked me off my feet. A helluva lot more than Sophie ever did.

"I know," she replied, her eyes soft with understanding. "I've seen you two together. I've never seen you as happy as you are when you're with her, Heck. We've never seen you this way before. She's brought out of you a tenderness no one's ever had." Her words rang true, further cementing my resolve to fight for Sara. . . with or without them.

My father returned to the room, settling on the couch next to my mother. His voice was steady, resolute as he began, "Listen well, son. When you made the decision to marry Sophie, I didn't voice any objections because I knew you loved her," he paused and took a swig of his drink. "That's what you said. However, I did have someone compile a comprehensive dossier on each member of her family. I kept those files for times like these. Peter Sullivan was teetering on the brink of bankruptcy. His hedge fund dealings were suspect at best. He'd been accepting money from dubious sources. Funds linked to the Indonesian junta, arms trafficking. I won't bore you with the details. I also don't want you fucking up the game plan, so stay out of it. Peter was also skimming off the top, and from the wrong people. Either I get to him first, or some government suits will. I hope for the love of God, you haven't gotten into bed with him."

Yeah, I knew where this was headed. The fallout hits saints and sinners alike, but looked like there'd be more sinners than saints this time.

Under normal circumstances, I would have bristled at this revelation. I didn't want him to fix things for me. But today, I found myself grateful he was fighting in my corner. "I'm sorry, Dad. " was all I could muster.

"You are my son. This is my job," he replied. "Focus on transitioning and your training. Sara isn't going anywhere. Give both her and yourself some space. My legal team is already on the case. So do nothing. They'll handle Peter Sullivan. He wouldn't stand a chance. If his daughter doesn't back down, I'll make sure that the Justice Department, the IRS, the SEC, even the central bank, are all breathing down his neck. Every conceivable nightmare he can imagine. Every transaction he ever did will be scrutinized, every bank account all over the world, be it be under his name or any of the dummy names he can think of will be frozen or otherwise unreachable to him. All his connections will shun him like a pariah. Once the full weight of the government comes bearing down on him, he'll ensure his daughter signs those divorce papers. He will make her do it himself, believe me, son. Also, Sophie won't get a dime from you. If she decides to continue with her supposed pregnancy, which I highly doubt she will after this, she'll have to provide a paternity test proving the child is yours. If that turns out to be the case, the child will be fully supported," he laid out his plan in a straightforward manner.

I simply nodded, feeling like a child once again. The thought of his strategy loomed like a shadow, yet I had no desire to dwell on it. I trusted him to handle it. I knew clearly it was already handled. For the first time, I truly appreciated the power that came with being an Archibald. For years, I had harbored a deep-seated dislike for my heritage, distancing myself from it as much as possible. Now, however, I was beginning to understand why my father behaved the way he did all these years. The realization dawned on me that money and power were, indeed, capable of solving everything.

Together, we sat in contemplative silence—a family... at long last. Observing my father, I recognized that beneath his imperfections and authoritarian behavior, there lay a tenderness he perpetually sought to shield from the world. Clasping my mother's hand, his gesture seemed to convey a silent assurance that 'Things will be alright.'

This homecoming, while vastly different from what I had anticipated, was precisely what I needed at this moment.

The resolve to win back Sara stirred within me. What's more, I decided to fully embrace my role as an Archibald. This choice stemmed not from a desire to fulfill my father's expectations but from a deeper, more personal conviction. It was time to claim what was rightfully mine, to step into my legacy.

Epilogue

SUNDAY SUNSET

———

(Sara)

"Here's your latte, Sara. Decaf, as you requested," Lily announced, placing the steaming mug before me along with two chocolate chip cookies. She glanced at my laptop screen. *"Sunday Sunset,* huh?" she read aloud.

"Thank you," I responded with a smile. "Yes, I'm putting the final touches on my work in progress. I've finally found the perfect title for this manuscript."

"That sounds wonderful! I'll leave you to it then. Just buzz me when you need anything," she said with a wink before turning away to attend to other customers.

I watched her go, gratitude warming my heart. She was woven into the fabric of our story — the story of Heck and me. This place, our cherished haunt, brimmed with memories. At times, the recollection was painful, yet it also offered an odd comfort. It was the nearest I could get to feeling Heck's presence. It's been a month since I returned that night to the empty shell that used to be our home. Heck was gone, just as I asked him to. That first night, I cried until my eyes were dry and raw, until all that was left was an aching hollowness where my heart used to be.

Every room echoed with his absence, every corner a cruel reminder of the man I'd lost. I could still smell his aftershave in the bathroom, see his fingerprint smudges on the mirror. I missed him so much it hurt, like a phantom limb, an ache that never really went away.

In the days that followed, I tried to pick up the pieces, to put my life back together. I went back to work at Milliford & Associates. Kelly, my boss, was glad to have me back, though she wore her usual poker face. Both Andi and Alexi expressed their delight at my return. We attempted to resurrect our morning coffee ritual, but those initial few days, I found myself disinterested. Paris had altered me. Heck had transformed me. I was no longer the perpetually disgruntled Sara, bemoaning the world's injustices. I had come to realize the world didn't revolve around us; it had more urgent crises to attend to.

Now, I found myself relating more than ever to Kelly's approach — prioritizing tasks, ensuring they were completed by day's end. The world wasn't idly waiting for us; we needed to keep pace or risk being left behind. Thus, I poured my heart and soul into my nine-to-five job. Then, I would spend my evenings writing. Occasionally, I would write at Tribeca Trickle, particularly when the memories of Heck within our home became too overwhelming.

I made a point to abstain from attending meetings with Gold Standard Bank. Heck and I had made a pact to meet once he had sorted out his complications. There were moments when I was tempted to call him, to ask him to return. But I knew Heck would abandon everything to rush back to me, compromising his ability to make an unbiased decision. Yet, every single day, every minute, every second, my thoughts invariably drifted back to him.

However, this morning was different. There was an unusual sensation, a nagging discomfort nibbling at the periphery of my consciousness. This wasn't about missing Heck. I felt out of balance, out of tune with myself.

I opened my vanity drawer. My eyes caught something. . . and then it dawned on me. My Tampax box had remained untouched for weeks.

My period was late.

Two weeks late.

A chilling wave of anxiety surged through me, stirring a nauseous sensation in my stomach. I sprinted to the bathroom, frantically sifting through the cabinet until my fingers closed around the pregnancy test I'd stashed away. My hands trembled as I unboxed the test, the plastic stick feeling cold and alien in my grasp.

I meticulously followed the instructions, setting the test down on the sink afterward. The wait for the result was torturous, each second ticking by at a maddeningly sluggish pace. I paced the confined space, a tempest of emotions raging within me — fear, hope, desperation.

Then, finally, I dared to glance at the test. Two red lines stared back at me. Positive. I was pregnant.

The revelation rooted me to the spot, shock freezing me in place. Then, a tidal wave of emotions swept over me — joy, anxiety, confusion, relief. I was going to have a baby. Heck's baby. A piece of him would always be with me. Should I tell him? Or should I withhold the news until his return — if he ever returned? The prospect of single-handedly raising our child seemed dauntingly immense.

I collapsed onto the floor, the positive test clutched tightly in my hand, a jumble of tears and laughter spilling from me. My life had just veered onto an unexpected path, one that simultaneously terrified, exhilarated, and challenged me. But one thing was certain: I was not alone. I carried a piece of Heck within me, and that made everything seem a tad less terrifying.

"You can do this, Sara," I whispered to my mirrored image before rushing out of the bathroom and going to the place where it all started… Tribeca Trickle..

And so, here I am, doing the only thing I know best — writing. "Sunday Sunset" was a poem by Heck that I had the honor of helping to publish in *The New York Times*, a parting gift before my departure to Paris. But now, I've adopted both its title and concept for my novel, a personal tribute to myself and to Heck. For months, I labored over this untitled work, then halted abruptly when Heck departed from my life.

Today, however, marked a change. I reopened my manuscript with the intention to pick up where I left off. Yet, words proved elusive; forming even a single coherent sentence felt like an insurmountable task. I recalled how Heck once curated a playlist to inspire my writing sessions. Fishing my AirPods from my bag, I inserted them and scrolled through our collection of songs. The opening chords of Remy Zero's "Fair" filled my ears as I closed my eyes, resting a hand on my flat stomach, feeling the new life stirring within. "We're going to be fine, sweetheart," I whispered, and with that, I began to write anew.

Recently, the pain was a constant companion whenever I thought of Heck, but so was the joy of our memories, blending bittersweetly with each sip of my latte. In this favorite nook of ours, amidst the ghosts of laughter and whispered dreams, I found a semblance of peace. With every word I typed, every sentence I perfected, I was not just crafting a novel — I was preserving a piece of us, a tribute to the love and loss that had shaped my very being.

Suddenly, a shadow cast over my workspace. I lifted my gaze. There, standing before me, was an unforgettable face. His hair was a tousled mess of waves, as though he'd just rolled out of bed. His stubble was so pronounced it suggested a shave was long overdue. His worn-out jeans and snug grey T-shirt were replaced by a charcoal grey suit and crisply pressed white shirt that hugged his frame in all the right places, highlighting his physique. Then, he smiled at me — that heart-stopping smile capable of lighting up my darkest days — the kind that could illuminate my entire world.

"Hello, Pender, is this seat taken?"

END

DEDICATION

To the maestros of music, the magicians of film, who have plucked strings, hammered drums, and woven soulful lyrics, the ones who put motion on pictures, and to those who have colored our world with their imagination, filling our minds with stories begging to be shared — you have truly inspired us.

Throughout the journey of writing this novel, your creativity has been a symphony resonating within us, lending depth and meaning to our existence. You possess the power to shift our perspectives, ignite hope, and rekindle our spirits in moments of despair.

You are our constants, the friends we invite into our solitude, providing us with the companionship of your artistry when we choose to be alone. Your influence constantly stirs our imagination, prompting us to craft scenes that mirror your passion and dedication.

Thank you for sharing the rawness of your despair, the solitude of your loneliness, the vibrancy of your joy, and the courage of your vulnerability through your art. Your creations are not just expressions but extensions of your soul, and they have found a home within the pages of our work. We can only hope our words will resonate as deeply as your creations.

To our dear readers, from the short story to this novel, thank you for welcoming Sara and Heck into your lives.

Lastly, to our book editor, Frances Amper-Sales, thank you for your patience and for bearing with us throughout the editing process. This novel wouldn't have been possible without you in it.

This book is dedicated to all of you, our silent partners, in this creative odyssey.

With deepest gratitude and utmost admiration,

Justine & Mike

ABOUT THE AUTHORS:

Justine Castellon

A brand strategist and corporate spindoctor with an inherent talent for crafting captivating narratives. Her professional insights blend seamlessly with her passion for literature. She authored and published two novels about Hope Williams through the seasons: *Four Seasons* and *The Last Snowfall*.

Mike Dee

A finance and real estate maven has ventured into the world of literature as a debut author. A keen film and music enthusiast, he writes with a rhythmic quality, a nod to his love of music, which fuels his passion for storytelling and adds a unique edge to his literary style.

Fall in love with these 3 charming romance stories from Justine Castellon

🌿 FOUR SEASONS

A struggling New York writer's dreams come true when a chance encounter with a Hollywood star shoots her into a glittering world of romance and fame. But, as love and illusions shatter, she must rebuild her life and rediscover her own voice in the aftermath of heartbreak.

❄ THE LAST SNOWFALL

A writer-turned-heiress marries a British Hollywood star, only to be swept into a high-stakes world of love, betrayal, and buried secrets. As ghosts from the past threaten her marriage and power struggles consume her father's empire, she must confront the ultimate question: how far will she go to protect the life she's built, and at what cost?

🌙 GNIGHT SARA/'NIGHT HECK

In a bustling New York City café, amidst the noise and chaos, two souls, a young copywriter and a reluctant heir, find a unique sanctuary. This romantic drama delves deep into the complexities of friendship, self-discovery, and the choices that define our lives.

www.justcastellon.com